BEARTOWN

BEARTOWN

- A NOVEL -

FREDRIK BACKMAN

Translated by Neil Smith

ATRIA BOOKS

New York   London   Toronto   Sydney   New Delhi

ATRIA
BOOKS

An Imprint of Simon & Schuster, Inc.
1230 Avenue of the Americas
New York, NY 10020

First Atria Books hardcover edition April 2017

ATRIA B O O K S and colophon are trademarks of Simon & Schuster, Inc.

For information about special discounts for bulk purchases, please contact Simon & Schuster Special Sales at 1-866-506-1949 or business@simonandschuster.com.

The Simon & Schuster Speakers Bureau can bring authors to your live event. For more information or to book an event, contact the Simon & Schuster Speakers Bureau at 1-866-248-3049 or visit our website at www.simonspeakers.com.

Manufactured in the United States of America

10 9 8 7 6 5 4 3

Library of Congress Cataloging-in-Publication Data

Names: Backman, Fredrik, 1981- author. | Smith, Neil (Neil Andrew), translator.Title: Beartown : a novel / Fredrik Backman ; translated from the Swedish by Neil Smith.Other titles: Bjornstad. EnglishDescription: New York : Atria Books, 2017.Identifiers: LCCN 2017000377 (print) | LCCN 2017000383 (ebook) | ISBN 9781501160769 (hardback) | ISBN 9781501160783 (eBook)Subjects: LCSH: Hockey stories. | Scandals—Fiction. | Sweden—Fiction. | BISAC: FICTION / Literary. | FICTION / Humorous. | FICTION / General. Classification: LCC PT9877.12.A32 B5513 2017 (print) | LCC PT9877.12.A32 (ebook) | DDC 839.73/8—dc23LC record available at https://lccn.loc.gov/2017000377

ISBN 978-1-5011-6076-9
ISBN 978-1-5011-6078-3 (ebook)

For my grandmother, Saga Backman, who taught me to love sports. What a quiet life I would have lived without her. I hope that the big bar in heaven serves proper dry martinis, and that they always show Wimbledon on the big screen. I miss you.

And for Neda Shafti-Backman, my funniest, smartest, most argumentative best friend, who picks me up when I need it, and keeps my feet on the ground when I deserve it. Asheghetam.

BEARTOWN

1

Late one evening toward the end of March, a teenager picked up a double-barreled shotgun, walked into the forest, put the gun to someone else's forehead, and pulled the trigger.

This is the story of how we got there.

2

B ang-bang-bang-bang-bang.

It's a Friday in early March in Beartown and nothing has happened yet. Everyone is waiting. Tomorrow, the Beartown Ice Hockey Club's junior team is playing in the semifinal of the biggest youth tournament in the country. How important can something like that be? In most places, not so important, of course. But Beartown isn't most places.

Bang. Bang. Bang-bang-bang.

The town wakes early, like it does every day; small towns need a head start if they're going to have any chance in the world. The rows of cars in the parking lot outside the factory are already covered with snow; people are standing in silent lines with their eyes half-open and their minds half-closed, waiting for their electronic punch cards to verify their existence to the clocking-in machine. They stamp the slush off their boots with autopilot eyes and answering-machine voices while they wait for their drug of choice—caffeine or nicotine or sugar—to kick in and render their bodies at least tolerably functional until the first break.

Out on the road the commuters set off for bigger towns beyond the forest; their gloves slam against heating vents and their curses are the sort you only think of uttering when you're drunk, dying, or sitting in a far-too-cold Peugeot far too early in the morning.

If they keep quiet they can hear it in the distance: *Bang-bang-bang. Bang. Bang.*

Maya wakes up and stays in bed, playing her guitar. The walls of her room are covered in a mixture of pencil drawings and tickets she's saved from concerts she's been to in cities far from here. Nowhere near as many as she would have liked, but considerably more than her parents actually consented to. She loves everything about her guitar—its weight against her body, the way the wood responds when her fingertips tap it, the strings that cut hard against her skin. The simple notes, the gentle riffs—it's all a wonderful game to her. She's fifteen years old and has already fallen in love many times, but her guitar will always be her first love. It's helped her to put up with living in this town, to deal with being the daughter of the general manager of an ice hockey team in the forest.

She hates hockey but understands her father's love for it; the sport is just a different instrument from hers. Her mom sometimes whispers in her daughter's ear: "Never trust people who don't have something in their lives that they love beyond all reason." Her mom loves a man who loves a place that loves a game. This is a hockey town, and there are plenty of things you can say about those, but at least they're predictable. You know what to expect if you live here. Day after day after day.

Bang.

Beartown isn't close to anything. Even on a map the place looks unnatural. "As if a drunk giant tried to piss his name in the snow," some might say. "As if nature and man were fighting a tug-of-war for space," more high-minded souls might suggest. Either way, the town is losing. It has been a very long time since it won at anything. More jobs disappear each year, and with them the people, and the forest devours one or two more abandoned houses each season. Back in the days when there were still things to boast about, the city council erected a sign beside the road at the entrance to the town with the sort of slogan that was popular at the time: "Beartown—Leaves You Wanting More!" The wind and snow took a few years to wipe out the word "More." Sometimes the entire community feels like a philosophical experiment: If a town falls in the forest but no one hears it, does it matter at all?

To answer that question you need to walk a few hundred yards down toward the lake. The building you see there doesn't look like much, but it's an ice rink, built by factory workers four generations ago, men who worked six days a week and needed something to look forward to on the seventh. All the love this town could thaw out was passed down and still seems to end up devoted to the game: ice and boards, red and blue lines, sticks and pucks and every ounce of determination and power in young bodies hurtling at full speed into the corners in the hunt for those pucks. The stands are packed every weekend, year after year, even though the team's achievements have collapsed in line with the town's economy. And perhaps that's why—because everyone hopes that when the team's fortunes improve again, the rest of the town will get pulled up with it.

Which is why places like this always have to pin their hopes for the future on young people. They're the only ones who don't remember that things actually used to be better. That can be a blessing. So they've coached their junior team with the same values their forebears used to construct their community: work hard, take the knocks, don't complain, keep your mouth shut, and show the bastards in the big cities where we're from. There's not much worthy of note around here. But anyone who's been here knows that it's a hockey town.

Bang.

Amat will soon turn sixteen. His room is so tiny that if it had been in a larger apartment in a well-to-do neighborhood in a big city, it would barely have registered as a closet. The walls are completely covered with posters of NHL players, with two exceptions. One is a photograph of himself aged seven, wearing gloves that are too big for him and with his helmet halfway down his forehead, the smallest of all the boys on the ice. The other is a sheet of white paper on which his mother has written parts of a prayer. When Amat was born, she lay with him on her chest in a narrow bed in a little hospital on the other side of the planet, no one but them in the whole world. A nurse had whispered the prayer in his mother's ear back then—it is said to have been written on the wall above Mother Teresa's bed—and the nurse hoped it would give the solitary woman strength and hope. Almost sixteen years later, the scrap of paper is still hanging on her son's wall, the words mixed up, but she wrote them down as well as she could remember them:

If you are honest, people may deceive you. Be honest anyway.
If you are kind, people may accuse you of selfishness. Be kind
anyway.
All the good you do today will be forgotten by others tomorrow.
Do good anyway.

Amat sleeps with his skates by his bed every night. "Must have been one hell of a birth for your poor mother, you being born with those on," the caretaker at the rink often jokes. He's offered to let the boy keep them in a locker in the team's storeroom, but Amat likes carrying them there and back. Wants to keep them close.

Amat has never been as tall as the other players, has never been as muscular as them, has never shot as hard. But no one in the town can catch him. No one on any team he's encountered so far has been as fast as him. He can't explain it; he assumes it's a bit like when people look at a violin and some of them just see a load of wood and screws where others see music. Skates have never felt odd to him. On the contrary, when he sticks his feet in a pair of normal shoes he feels like a sailor stepping ashore.

The final lines his mother wrote on the sheet of paper on his wall read as follows:

What you create, others can destroy. Create anyway. Because in
the end, it is between you and God. It was never between you and
anyone else anyway.

Immediately below that, written in red crayon in the determined handwriting of a primary school student, it says:

They say Im to little to play. Become good player any way!

Bang.

Once upon a time, Beartown Ice Hockey's A-team—one step above the juniors—was second-best in the top division in the country. That was more than two decades and three divisions ago, but tomorrow Beartown will be playing against the best once more. So how important can a junior game be? How much can a town care about the semifinal a bunch of teenagers are playing in a minor-league tournament? Not so much, of course. If it weren't this particular dot on the map.

A couple of hundred yards south of the road sign lies "the Heights," a small cluster of expensive houses with views across the lake. The people who live in them own supermarkets, run factories, or commute to better jobs in bigger towns where their colleagues at staff parties wonder, wide-eyed: "Beartown? How can you possibly live that far out in the forest?" They reply something about hunting and fishing, proximity to nature, but these days almost everyone is asking themselves if it *is* actually possible. Living here any longer. Asking themselves if there's anything left, apart from property values that seem to fall as rapidly as the temperature.

Then they wake up to the sound of a *bang*. And they smile.

3

For more than ten years now the neighbors have grown accustomed to the noises from the Erdahl family's garden: *bang-bang-bang-bang-bang*. Then a brief pause while Kevin collects the pucks. Then *bang-bang-bang-bang-bang*. He was two and a half years old the first time he put a pair of skates on, three when he got his first stick. When he was four he was better than the five-year-olds, and when he was five he was better than the seven-year-olds. During the winter following his seventh birthday he got such a bad case of frostbite that if you stand close enough to him you can still see the tiny white marks on his cheekbones. He had played his first proper game that afternoon, and in the final seconds missed a shot on an open goal. The Beartown youngsters won 12–0, and Kevin scored all the goals, but he was inconsolable. Late that evening his parents discovered that he wasn't in his bed, and by midnight half the town was out searching for him in the forest. Hide-and-seek isn't a game in Beartown—a young child doesn't have to stray far to be swallowed up by the darkness, and a small body doesn't take long to freeze to death in thirty degrees below zero. It wasn't until dawn that someone realized the boy wasn't among the trees but down on the frozen lake. He had dragged a net and five pucks down there, as well as all the flashlights he could find, and had spent hour after hour firing shots from the same angle from which he had missed the final shot of the match. He sobbed uncontrollably as they carried him home. The white marks never faded. He was seven years old, and everyone already knew that he had the bear inside him. That sort of thing can't be ignored.

His parents paid to have a small rink of his own constructed in the garden. He shoveled it himself every morning, and each summer the neighbors would exhume puck-graveyards in their flowerbeds. Remnants of vulcanized rubber will be found in the soil around there for generations to come.

Year after year they have heard the boy's body grow—the banging becoming harder and harder, faster and faster. He's seventeen now, and the town hasn't seen a player with anything close to his talent since the team was in the top division, before he was born. He's got the build, the hands, the head, and the heart. But above all he's got the vision: what he sees on the ice seems to happen more slowly than what everyone else sees. You can teach a lot about hockey, but not that. You're either born with that way of seeing or you aren't.

"Kevin? He's the real deal," Peter Andersson, general manager of the club, always says, and he ought to know: the last person in Beartown who was as good as this was Peter himself, and he made it all the way to Canada and the NHL, matching up against the best in the world.

Kevin knows what it takes; everyone's been telling him ever since he first stood on a pair of skates. It's going to demand nothing less than his all. So every morning, while his classmates are still fast asleep under their warm comforters, he goes running in the forest, and then he stands here, *bang-bang-bang-bang-bang*. Collects the pucks. *Bang-bang-bang-bang-bang*. Collects the pucks. Practices with the junior team every afternoon, and with the A-team every evening, then the gym, then another run in the forest, and one final hour out here under the glare of the floodlights specially erected on the roof of the house.

This sport demands only one thing from you. Your all.

Kevin has had every sort of offer to move to the big teams, to attend hockey school in a bigger town, but he keeps turning them down. He's a Beartown man, his dad's a Beartown man, and that may not mean a thing anywhere else, but it means something here.

So how important can the semifinal of a junior tournament be? Being the best junior team around would remind the rest of the country of this place's existence again. And then the politicians might decide to spend the money to establish a hockey school here instead of over in Hed, so that the most talented kids in this part of the country would want to move to Beartown instead of the big cities. So that an A-team full of homegrown players could make it to the highest division again, attract the biggest sponsors once more, get the council to build a new rink and bigger roads leading to it, maybe even the conference center and shopping mall they've been talking about for years. So that new businesses could appear and create more jobs so that the townspeople might start thinking about renovating their homes instead of selling them. It would only be important to the town's economy. To its pride. To its survival.

It's only so important that a seventeen-year-old in a private garden has been standing here since he got frostbite on his cheeks one night ten years ago, firing puck after puck after puck with the weight of an entire community on his shoulders.

It means everything. That's all.

On the other side of Beartown from the Heights, north of the road signs, is the Hollow. In between, the center of Beartown consists of row houses and small homes in a gently declining scale of middle-classness, but here in the Hollow there are nothing but blocks of rental apartments, built as far away from the Heights as possible. At first the names of these neighborhoods were nothing but unimaginative geographic descriptions: the Hollow is lower than the rest of the town, where the ground slopes away toward an old gravel pit. The Heights are on the hillside overlooking the lake. But after the residents' finances divided along similar lines, the names came to signify differences in class as much as in districts. Even children can see that the farther away you live from the Hollow, the better things will be for you.

Fatima lives in a two-room apartment almost at the end of the Hollow. She drags her son out of bed with gentle force; he grabs his skates and soon they're alone on the bus, not speaking. Amat has perfected a system of moving his body without his head actually having to wake up. Fatima affectionately calls him "The Mummy." When they first reach the rink, she changes into her cleaner's uniform and he tries to help her pick up the garbage in the stands until she shouts at him and drives him off and he goes to find the caretaker. The boy is worried about his mom's back, and she worries that other children will see him with her and tease him. As long as Amat can remember, the two of them have been alone in the world. When he was little he used to collect empty beer cans from the stands at the end of the month to get the deposit back on them. Sometimes he still does.

He helps the caretaker every morning, unlocking doors and checking lights, sorting out the pucks and driving the zamboni, getting the rink ready for the day. First to show up will be the figure skaters, in the most antisocial time-slots. Then all the hockey teams, one after the other in order of rank. The best times are reserved for the juniors and the A-team. The junior team is now so good it's almost at the top of the hierarchy.

Amat isn't on the junior team yet, he's only fifteen, but maybe next season. If he does everything that's demanded of him. One day he'll take his mom away from here, he's sure of that. One day he'll stop adding and subtracting income and expenditures in his head all the time. There's an obvious difference between the children who live in homes where the money can run out and the ones who don't. How old you are when you realize that also makes a difference.

Amat knows his options are limited, so his plan is simple: from here to the junior team, then the A-team, then professional. When his first wages reach his account he'll grab that cleaning cart from his mother and never let her see it again. He'll allow her aching fingers to rest and give her aching back a break. He doesn't want possessions. He just wants to lie in bed one single night without having to count.

The caretaker taps Amat on the shoulder when his chores are done and passes him his skates. Amat puts them on, grabs his stick, and goes out onto the empty ice. That's the deal: the caretaker gets help with the heavy lifting and tricky swing-doors that his rheumatism makes difficult and—as long as Amat floods the ice again after he practices—he can have the rink to himself for an hour before the figure skaters arrive. Those are the best sixty minutes of his day, every day.

He puts in his earphones, cranks the volume as loud as it will go, then sets off with speed. Across the ice, so hard into the boards at the other end that his helmet smacks the glass. Full speed back again. Again. Again. Again.

Fatima looks up briefly from her cart, allows herself a few moments in which to watch her son out there. The caretaker catches her eye, and she mouths the word "Thanks." The caretaker merely nods and conceals a smile. Fatima remembers how odd she thought it when the club's coaches first told her that Amat had exceptional talent. She only understood snippets of the language back then, and the fact that Amat could skate when he could barely walk was a divine mystery to her. Many years have passed since then, and she still hasn't gotten used to the cold in Beartown, but she has learned to love the town for what it is. And she will never find anything in her life more unfathomable than the fact that the boy she gave birth to in a place that has never seen snow was born to play a sport on ice.

In one of the smaller houses in the center of town, Peter Andersson, general manager of Beartown Ice Hockey, gets out of the shower, red-eyed and breathless. He's hardly slept, and the water hasn't managed to rinse his nerves away. He's been sick twice. He hears Kira bustle past the bathroom out in the hall, on her way to wake the children, and he knows exactly what she's going to say: "For heaven's sake, Peter, you're over forty years old. When the GM is more nervous about a junior game than the players, maybe it's time to take a tranquilizer, have a drink, and just calm down a bit!" The Andersson family has lived here for more than a decade now, since they moved back home from Canada, but he still hasn't managed to get his wife to understand what hockey means in Beartown. "Seriously? You don't think all you grown men are getting a bit too excited?" Kira has been asking all season. "The juniors are seventeen years old, practically still children!"

He kept quiet at first. But late one night he told her the truth: "I know it's only a game, Kira. I know. But we're a town in the middle of the forest. We've got no tourism, no mine, no high-tech industry. We've got darkness, cold, and unemployment. If we can make this town excited again, about anything at all, that has to be a good thing. I know you're not from round here, love, and this isn't your town, but look around: the jobs are going, the council's cutting back. The people who live here are tough, we've got the bear in us, but we've taken blow after blow for a long time now. This town needs to win at something. We need to feel, just once, that we're best. I know it's a game. But that's not all it is. Not always."

Kira kissed his forehead hard when he said that, and held him tight, whispering softly in his ear: "You're an idiot." Which, of course, he knows.

He leaves the bathroom and knocks on his fifteen-year-old daughter's door until he hears her guitar answer. She loves her guitar, not sports. Some days that makes him feel sad, but on plenty more days he's happy for her.

Maya is still lying in bed, and plays louder when the knocking starts and she hears her parents outside the door. A mom with two university degrees who can quote the entire criminal code, but who could never say what icing or offside meant even if she was on trial. A dad who in return could explain every hockey strategy in great detail, but can't watch a television show with more than three characters without exclaiming every five minutes: "What's happening now? Who's that? What do you mean, be quiet? Now I missed what they said . . . can we rewind?"

Maya can't help both laughing and sighing when she thinks of that. You never want to get away from home as much as you do when you're fifteen years old. It's like her mom usually says when the cold and darkness have worn away at her patience and she's had three or four glasses of wine: "You can't live in this town, Maya, you can only survive it."

Neither of them has any idea just how true that is.

4

All the way from locker room to boardroom, the boys and men of Beartown Ice Hockey Club are brought together by a single motto: "High ceilings and thick walls." Hard words are as much a part of the game as hard checks, but the building is solid and spacious enough to keep any fights that take place inside from spilling outside. That applies both on the ice and off it, because everyone needs to realize that the good of the club comes before anything else.

It's early enough in the morning for the rest of the rink to be more or less empty, apart from the caretaker, the cleaner, and one solitary member of the boys' team who's skating up and down the ice. But from one of the offices on the upper floor, the loud voices of men in smart jackets echo out into the hallways. On the wall is a team photograph from about twenty years ago, from the year when Beartown Ice Hockey's A-team was second-best in the country. Some of the men in the room were there then, others weren't, but they've all made up their minds that they're going back. This is no longer going to be a town languishing forgotten in the lower leagues. They're going back to the elite again, to challenge the very biggest teams.

The club's president is sitting at his desk. He's the sweatiest man in the whole town, constantly worried, like a child who's stolen something, and he's sweating more than ever today. His shirt is littered with crumbs as he munches a sandwich so messily that you can't help wondering if he's actually misunderstood the whole concept of eating. He does that when he's nervous. This is his office, but he has less power than any of the other men there.

Seen from the outside, a club's hierarchy is simple: the board appoints a president, who is in charge of the day-to-day running of the club, and the president in turn appoints a general manager, who in turn recruits A-team players and employs coaches. The coaches pick the teams and no one pokes their oar into anyone else's job. But behind closed doors it's very different, and the club's president always has reason to sweat. The men around him are board members and sponsors, one of them is a local councilor, and collectively they represent the largest investors and biggest employers in the whole district. And of course they're all here "unofficially." That's how they describe it, when the men with all the influence and money just happen to gather to drink coffee together in the same place so early in the morning that not even the local reporters have woken up yet.

Beartown Ice Hockey's coffee machine is in even greater need of a serious cleaning than the club's president, so no one is here on account of the contents of their cups. Each man in the room has his own agenda, his own ambitions for a successful club, but they have one important thing in common: they agree on who ought to be fired.

Peter was born and raised in Beartown, and he has been a lot of different men here: a kid in skating classes, a promising junior, the youngest player on the A-team, the team captain who almost made them the best in the country, the big star who went professional in the NHL, and finally the hero who returned home to become GM.

And at this precise moment he is a man who is swaying sleepily back and forth in the hall of his small house, hitting his head on the hat rack roughly every third time and muttering, "For God's sake . . . has *anyone* seen the keys to the Volvo?"

He hunts through all the pockets of his jacket for the fourth time. His twelve-year-old son comes down the hall and skips nimbly around him without having to take his eyes off his cell phone.

"Have you seen the keys to the Volvo, Leo?"

"Ask Mom."

"Where's Mom, then?"

"Ask Maya."

Leo disappears into the bathroom. Peter takes a deep breath.

"Darling?"

No answer. He looks at his phone. He's already received four texts from the club's president telling him he needs to get to the office. In an average week Peter spends seventy to eighty hours at the rink, but even so, barely ever has time to watch his own son's training sessions. He's got a set of golf clubs in the car that he uses maybe twice each summer if he's lucky. His work as GM takes up all his time: he negotiates contracts with players, talks to agents on the phone, sits in a dark video-room studying potential recruits. But this is only a small club, so when he's done with his own work he helps the caretaker change fluorescent light bulbs and sharpen skates, reserves buses for away matches, orders equipment, and acts as a travel agent and building manager, spending as many hours maintaining the rink as he does building the team. That takes the rest of each day. Hockey is never satisfied being part of your life, it wants to be all of it.

When Peter accepted the post, he spent a whole night talking on the phone to Sune, the man who has been coach of Beartown's A-team since Peter was a boy. It was Sune who taught Peter to skate, who offered him a place to stay when the boy's own home was full of alcohol and bruises. He became far more of a mentor and father figure than a coach, and there have been times in Peter's life when the old man has been the only person he felt he could really trust. "You need to be the lynchpin now," Sune explained to the new GM. "Everyone's got their own axe to grind here: the sponsors, the politicians, the supporters, the coaches and players and parents, all trying to drag the club in their direction. You have to pull them all together."

When Kira woke up the following morning, Peter explained the job to her in even simpler terms: "Everyone in Beartown has this burning passion for hockey. My job is to make sure no one catches on fire." Kira kissed him on the forehead and told him he was an idiot.

"DARLING HAVE YOU SEEN THE KEYS TO THE VOLVO?" Peter yells to the house in general.

No answer.

———

The men in the office go through what has to be done, coldly and dispassionately, as if they were talking about replacing a piece of furniture. In the old team photograph, Peter Andersson is standing in the middle; he was team captain then, GM now. It's the perfect success story—the men in the room know the importance of building up that sort of mythology for the media as well as the fans. Next to Peter in the photograph stands Sune, the A-team coach, who persuaded Peter to move home from Canada with his family after his career as a professional player came to an end. The pair of them rebuilt the youth team with the ambition of one day having the best junior team in the country. Everyone laughed back then, but no one's laughing now. Tomorrow those juniors are playing a semifinal game, and next year Kevin Erdahl and a few of the others will be moving up to the A-team, the sponsors will pile millions into the club, and their challenge to get back to the elite will begin in earnest. And that wouldn't have happened without Peter, who has always been Sune's best pupil.

One of the sponsors looks at his watch irritably.

"Shouldn't he be here by now?"

The president's phone slips between his sweaty fingers.

"I'm sure he's on his way. He's probably dropping the kids off at school."

The sponsor gives him a condescending smile. "Has his lawyer wife got a more important meeting than him, as usual? Is this a job or a hobby for Peter?"

One of the board members clears his throat and says, partly in jest and partly not, "We need a GM with steel-toed boots. Not slippers."

The sponsor smiles and suggests, "Maybe we should employ his wife instead? A GM with sharp stilettos would work pretty well, wouldn't it?" The men in the room laugh. It echoes, all the way to the high ceilings.

Peter heads for the kitchen in search of his wife, but finds his daughter's best friend, Ana, instead. She's making a smoothie. Or at least he thinks she is, because the whole countertop is covered with an evil pink sludge that's oozing steadily toward the edge, preparing to attack, conquer, and annex the parquet floor. Ana takes her headphones off.

"Good morning! Your blender's super-complicated!"

Peter takes a deep breath.

"Hello, Ana. You're here . . . early."

"No, I slept over," she replies breezily.

"Again? That makes . . . four nights in a row now?"

"I haven't been keeping count."

"No. So I see. Thanks. But don't you think it might be time to go home one evening and . . . I don't know . . . get some fresh clothes from your own closet or something?"

"Don't have to worry about that. I've got pretty much all my clothes here anyway."

Peter massages the back of his neck and really does try to look as delighted at this as Ana does.

"That's . . . just great. But won't your dad be missing you?"

"No worries. We talk a lot on the phone and stuff."

"Yes, of course. But I suppose you'll have to go home one day and sleep in your own bed? Maybe?"

Ana forces rather too many unidentifiable frozen berries and pieces of fruit into the blender and stares at him in surprise.

"Okay. But that's going to be seriously complicated now that all my clothes are here, isn't it?"

Peter stands motionless for a long while, just looking at her. Then she switches on the blender without putting the lid on first. Peter turns and goes out into the hall, and yells with rapidly increasing desperation:

"DARLING!"

Maya is still lying on her bed, slowly picking at the strings of the guitar and letting the notes bounce off the walls and ceiling until they dissolve into nothingness. Tiny, desolate cries for company. She hears Ana on the rampage in the kitchen, she hears her frustrated parents push past each other in the hall, her dad barely awake and vaguely surprised, as if every morning he wakes up somewhere he's never been before, and her mom with the body language of a remote-controlled lawn mower whose obstacle-sensor has broken.

Her name is Kira, but she's never heard anyone in Beartown say that. In the end she just gave up and let them call her "Kia." People are so sparing with their words here that they don't even seem to want to waste consonants. Back at the start Kira used to entertain herself by saying "You mean Pete?" whenever anyone in town asked after her husband. But they all used to look at her so seriously and repeat, "No, Peter!" Like everything else, irony freezes here. So now Kira merely amuses herself by noting that her children have names that demonstrate an exemplary economy with consonants, Leo and Maya, to stop anyone's head exploding at the council registry office.

She moves through the little house with practiced movements, getting dressed and drinking coffee simultaneously as she progresses ever onward through the bathroom, hall, and kitchen. She picks up a sweater from her daughter's bedroom floor in passing and folds it in one fluid motion without for a moment interrupting her exhortations that it's time to put the guitar down and get up.

"Go and have a shower; you smell like you and Ana set the room on fire and tried to put it out with Red Bull. Dad's driving you to school in twenty minutes."

Maya rolls out from under the comforter, reluctant but wise from experience. Her mom isn't the sort you argue with; her mom is a lawyer, and she never quite stops being one.

"Dad said you were driving us to school."

"Dad has been misinformed. And will you please ask Ana to clean the kitchen when she's finished making her smoothie? I love her dearly, she's your best friend, I don't care if she sleeps here more often than she sleeps at home, but if she's going to make smoothies in our kitchen she's going to have to learn to put the lid on the blender, and you need to teach her at least the most basic functions of a damned dishcloth. Okay?"

Maya leans the guitar against the wall and heads toward the bathroom, and when her back is turned she rolls her eyes so far that an X-ray would have confused her pupils with kidneys.

"And don't you roll your eyes at me. I can see you doing it even if I can't see you doing it," her mom snarls.

"Speculation and hearsay," her daughter mutters.

"I've told you, people only say that on television," her mom retorts.

Her daughter responds by closing the bathroom door with unnecessary force. Peter is yelling *"Darling!!!"* from somewhere in the house. Kira picks up yet another sweater from the floor and hears Ana exclaim, "Oh, hell," just before she redecorates the kitchen ceiling with smoothie.

"I could have done something else with my life, you know," Kira says quietly to no one at all as she slips the keys to the Volvo into her jacket pocket.

The men in the office are still laughing at the joke about stilettos when the sound of a tentative throat clearing reaches the desk from the door. The club's manager beckons the cleaner in without looking at her. The cleaner apologizes to them all, but most of the men ignore her, even if one of them helpfully lifts his feet when the woman reaches to empty the wastepaper bin. The cleaner thanks him, but no one notices. It doesn't bother her; Fatima's greatest talent is not disturbing anyone. She waits until she's in the hallway before clutching her back and emitting a short groan of pain. She doesn't want anyone to see and tell Amat. Her beloved boy always worries too much.

Sweat is stinging Amat's eyes as he glides to a halt by the boards down on the rink. His stick is resting on the ice, the moisture in his gloves makes his fingers slip a bit, his breath catches in his throat as lactic acid fills his thighs. The stands are empty but he keeps glancing up at them every now and then. His mom always says they must be grateful, the pair of them, and he understands her. No one is more grateful than her, toward this country, this town, these people, and this club, toward the council, their neighbors, her employer. Grateful, grateful, grateful. That's the role of mothers. But the role of children is to dream. So her son dreams that his mother will one day be able to walk into a room without having to apologize.

He blinks the sweat from his eyes, adjusts his helmet, and pushes his skates into the ice. One more time. One more time. One more time.

Peter has now missed four calls from the club's president, and glances anxiously at the time as Kira enters the kitchen. With a smile she looks at the sticky disaster on the countertop and floor, and knows that Peter must be screaming hysterically inside. They have different ideas about cleanliness: Kira doesn't like clothes on the floor, but Peter really loathes anything sticky and messy. When they first met his entire apartment looked like he'd been burgled, apart from the kitchen and bathroom, which looked like operating rooms. Kira's apartment was the exact opposite. It would be safe to say they weren't an obvious match.

"There you are! I'm late for my meeting at the rink. Have you seen the keys to the Volvo?" he splutters.

He's tried to put on a jacket and tie, with mixed results, as usual. Kira's outfit is impeccable, as if the fabric were in thrall to her body. She's drinking coffee and pulling her coat on in the same fluid, one-handed gesture.

"Yep."

He stands there red-faced, his hair on end, his socks smeared with smoothie, and asks: "Do you feel like telling me where they are?"

"They're in my pocket."

"What? Why?"

Kira kisses his forehead.

"That's a very good question, sweetie. I suppose I thought they'd come in handy if I was going to drive the Volvo to work. Seeing as it might be thought a little inappropriate if my clients' lawyer turned up in a hot-wired car."

Peter scratches at his hair with both hands.

"But . . . what the . . . You can take the other car, can't you?"

"No, because you're taking the other car to the garage. After you've dropped the kids off at school. We talked about it."

"We *haven't* talked about it."

Instinctively, Peter wipes the bottom of her coffee cup with a piece of paper towel. She smiles.

"Darling, it's written on the calendar on the fridge."

"But you can't just put things on there without talking to me."

She carefully raises one of her eyebrows.

"We did talk. We're talking now. We do nothing but talk. Listening, on the other hand . . ."

"Please, Kira, I've got a meeting! If I'm late . . ."

"Absolutely, darling. Absolutely. If I get to work late an innocent person might end up in prison. Sorry, I interrupted you. Tell me more about what happens if *you're* late?"

He breathes through his nose, as calmly as he can. "It's the biggest game of the year tomorrow, darling."

"I know, darling. And tomorrow I'll pretend that it's important. But until then you'll have to make do with the rest of the town thinking it is."

She's hard to impress. That's simultaneously what he finds most attractive and most irritating about her. He tries to find a stronger argument, but Kira just lets out a theatrical sigh, puts the keys to the Volvo on the table, and clenches her fist in front of her husband.

"Okay. Rock-paper-scissors, then."

Peter shakes his head and tries to stop himself from laughing.

"What are you? Eight years old?"

Kira raises an eyebrow again.

"What are you? A coward?"

Peter's smile vanishes in an instant as he fixes his eyes on her and clenches his own fist. Kira counts to three out loud, Peter does paper, Kira very blatantly waits half a second longer and then quickly forms her fingers into scissors. Peter yells at her, but by then she's already snatched up the keys and is heading for the door.

"But you *cheated*!"

"Don't be a sore loser, darling. Bye, kids, be nice to Dad. Or at least reasonably nice."

Peter stands where he is in the kitchen, shouting:

"Don't you dare leave! Cheat!"

He turns to look at the calendar on the fridge.

"There's not even anything on here about taking the car . . ."

The front door closes behind Kira. The Volvo starts up outside. Ana is standing in the kitchen, grinning, with a thick smoothie-moustache on her upper lip.

"Have you ever got the better of her at anything, Peter?"

Peter massages his scalp.

"Would you mind fetching my son and daughter and telling them to put their clothes on and get in the car?"

Ana nods eagerly.

"Sure! I just need to clean up in here first!"

Peter shakes his head imploringly and takes out a fresh roll of paper towels.

"No . . . no, Ana . . . please don't. I can't help thinking that would only make things worse."

Once the laughter in the office has subsided, one of the sponsors looks grimly at the club's president, taps his knuckles on his desk and asks:

"So? Is there going to be any problem with Peter?"

The president mops his brow, shakes his head. "Peter does what's best for the club. Always. You know that."

The sponsor stands up, buttons his jacket, and empties his cup.

"Well, then. I've got another meeting to go to, but I trust you'll explain things to him. Remind him where the money for his wages comes from. We all know how he feels about Sune, but we can't allow any leaks to the media about internal conflict here."

The club's president doesn't have to answer. No one knows more about the thickness of the walls than Peter. He'll put the club first. Even today, when he's going to be ordered to eject Sune from it.

5

Why does anyone care about hockey?

Perhaps that depends on who you are. And where.

No one really knows how old Sune is. He's the sort of man who seems to have been seventy for at least twenty years, and not even he can remember exactly how many of those he's been the A-team coach. Age has made him shorter, stress and diet have made him wider. Nowadays he has the proportions of a snowman. He's at work earlier than usual today, but is standing hidden at the edge of the forest outside the rink when the group of men emerge from the door. He waits until they get in their cars and drive off. Not because he's embarrassed, but because he doesn't want them to feel embarrassed in front of him. He's known most of them all their lives, even coached many of them. The fact that they want to fire him and replace him with the coach of the junior team is the worst-kept secret in town. There's no need for anyone to tell Sune not to turn the matter into a public conflict; he'd never do that to the club, and he knows it's about more than just hockey now.

Beartown is in a poor part of a big forest, but there are still a few rich men here. They saved the club from bankruptcy, and now they want payback: the juniors are to lead the march back to elite level. Tomorrow they're going to win their semifinal in the youth tournament, and next weekend the final. When the regional council decides the location of the new hockey-focused high school, they won't be able to ignore the town with the best junior team in the country. The team will become the heart of the town's plans for the future, and the high school will bring with it a new rink, and then a conference center and shopping mall. Hockey is becoming more than hockey, it's becoming tourism, a trademark, capital. Survival.

So the club is more than a club, it's a kingdom over which the strongest men in the forest are fighting for power, and there's no place for Sune there. He looks at the rink. He's given his whole life to it. He has no family, no hobbies, not even a dog. Soon he'll be unemployed; he doesn't know what he's going to live off then. Or for. Even so, he can't blame anyone—not the president and not the junior coach, and definitely not Peter. Poor Peter probably doesn't even know about it yet, but they'll force him to carry out the firing, make him wield the axe and explain his actions in the local paper afterward. To make sure that the club stands united, and that the walls remain thick.

Sooner or later any sports team has to decide what it really wants to achieve, and Beartown is no longer content merely to play. They'll replace Sune with the coach of the junior team, for one simple reason: when Sune talks to his players before matches, he gives long speeches about them playing with their hearts. When the junior team coach stands in the locker room, he says just one word: "Win." And the juniors win. They've done nothing else for ten years.

It's just that Sune is no longer sure that's all a hockey team should consist of: boys who never lose.

The little car rolls along freshly plowed roads. Maya is leaning her head against the window like only a fifteen-year-old can. Farther south, spring has arrived, but Beartown only seems to have two seasons, and winter is such an obvious fact of life here that summer always seems to catch everyone by surprise. No one has time to get used to the two or three months of sunlight that are granted to them before it is snatched away again, and for the rest of the year it can sometimes feel as if they might as well be living underground.

Ana flicks Maya's ear hard with her finger.

"What the . . . ?" Maya exclaims, rubbing that whole side of her face.

"I'm bored! Let's play a game!" Ana pleads.

Maya sighs but doesn't protest. Because she loves the smoothie-slurping idiot, and because they're fifteen and her mom is always telling her, "You never have the sort of friends you have when you're fifteen ever again. Even if you keep them for the rest of your life, it's never the same as it was then."

"Okay, how about this one: blind and brilliant at fighting, or deaf and brilliant at—" Ana says.

"Blind," Maya says without hesitation.

This is Ana's favorite game; they've played it ever since they were little. There's a degree of reassurance in the fact that there are still some things they don't grow out of.

"You haven't even heard the alternative!" Ana protests.

"I don't give a shit about the alternative. I can't live without music, but I can live without seeing your stupid face every day."

"Idiot," Ana sighs.

"Moron," Maya grins.

"Okay, this one, then: always have boogers in your own nose, or go out with a guy who always has boogers in his nose."

"Always have boogers in my nose."

"The fact that you picked that answer says so much about you."

Ana tries to hit Maya on the thigh but Maya swings away and punches her friend's arm hard instead. Ana screams and they burst out laughing at each other. At themselves.

In the front seat of the car, with an ability that has been finely tuned over the years to shut out the wavelength of his big sister and her best friend and sit isolated in his own thoughts, Leo turns to his dad and asks:

"Are you coming to watch me train today?"

"Yes . . . I'll try . . . but Mom will be there!" Peter replies.

"Mom's always there," Leo says.

It's a statement from a twelve-year-old boy, not an accusation. But it still feels like one to Peter. He's checking his watch so frequently that he has to tap it to reassure himself it hasn't stopped.

"Are you stressing about something?" Ana says from the backseat in that tone that makes you want to start throwing things if you happen to be stressed.

"I've just got a meeting, Ana. Thank you for asking."

"Who with?" Ana asks.

"The club's president. We're going to talk about the junior team's match tomorrow . . ."

"God, everyone keeps going on about the junior team. You do know that it's just a stupid game, don't you? No one really cares!"

She's joking; she loves hockey. But Maya quickly hisses: "Don't say that to him today!"

"He'll go crazy!" Leo agrees.

"What do you mean, crazy? Who'll go crazy?" Peter asks. Maya leans forward.

"You don't have to drive us all the way to school, Dad. You can drop us off here."

"It's not a problem," Peter insists.

"Not a problem . . . not for you, maybe," Maya groans.

"What's that supposed to mean? Are you ashamed of me?"

Ana interjects helpfully, "Yes!"

Leo adds, "And she doesn't want anyone to see you because then everyone in her class will come over and want to talk hockey."

"And what's wrong with that? This is a hockey town!" Peter says, taken aback.

"Yeah, but life doesn't only have to be about stupid hockey because of that," Maya can't help retorting, and considers opening the door while the car is in motion and rolling out; the snow is still deep and she doesn't think she'd break anything. It feels like it might be worth the risk.

"Why do you say that? Why's she saying *that*, Leo?" her dad demands.

"Can you just stop the car? Or just slow down, you don't even have to stop," Maya pleads.

Ana taps Leo on the shoulder.

"Okay, Leo, try this one: Never play hockey again, or never play computer games again?"

Leo glances at his dad. Emits a rather shamefaced little cough. Starts to undo his seatbelt and fumbles for the door handle. Peter shakes his head in despair.

"Don't you dare answer that, Leo. Don't you dare."

Kira is sitting in the Volvo, heading away from Beartown. She heard Peter throwing up in the bathroom this morning. If that's what hockey does to grown men in this town, what on earth must it be doing to the seventeen-year-old juniors who are playing in the game tomorrow? There's an old joke among the women of Beartown: "I just wish my husband would look at me the way he watches hockey." It's never made Kira laugh, because she understands it all too well.

She knows what the men of the town say about her, knows she's a long way from the loyal GM's wife they were hoping for when they appointed Peter. They don't think of the club as an employer, but as an army: the soldiers need to fall in whenever they're summoned, their families standing proudly in the doorways, waving them off. The first time Kira met the club's president was at a golf tournament organized by the sponsors, and while they were milling about having drinks before dinner he handed her his empty glass. So few women existed in his hockey world that when he saw one he didn't recognize, he took it for granted that she must be a waitress.

When he realized his mistake he just laughed, as if Kira ought to find the situation funny too. When she didn't, he sighed and said: "You mustn't take things too seriously, eh?" When he heard that she was thinking of carrying on with her career in parallel with Peter's, he exclaimed in surprise: "But who's going to take care of the kids?" She really did try to keep quiet. Well, maybe not *really*, but in hindsight she thinks she did *try*, at least. Eventually she turned to the president and pointed at his greasy, sausagelike fingers, which were clutching a prawn sandwich, then at his stomach, which was straining against the buttons of his shirt, and said, "I thought maybe you could take care of them. You have got bigger breasts than me, after all."

The next time a golf tournament was organized, "plus one" had been removed from the invitations. The men's hockey world expanded, the women's shrank, and there has never been greater proof of Kira's love for Peter than the fact that she didn't go down to the rink that day and punch someone. She learned that you have to be thick-skinned in Beartown. That helps you deal with both the cold and the insults.

Ten years have passed since then, and she has come to realize that things feel a whole lot better if you have a really good stereo in the car. So she turns up the volume. Plays Maya and Leo's "louder-louder list," not because she likes the music but because it makes her feel close to them. When children are young you think it will pass, the guilty feeling you get in your stomach when you leave home each morning. But it never does, it just gets worse. So she has their music collections on her phone, lists of songs that have been selected because each is the sort that makes one of the children shout "LOUDER! LOUDER!" when it comes on the radio. She plays them so loud that the bass makes the door panels vibrate, because sometimes the silence of the forest drives her mad. The early-afternoon sky hovers just above the trees almost all year round in these parts, and that can be hard to get used to for someone who grew up in a big city where nature was something used primarily as a screensaver.

Naturally, everyone in Beartown hates the capital, and they've developed a permanent sense of resentment at the fact that the forest contains all the natural resources but all the money ends up somewhere else. Sometimes it feels as if the people of Beartown love the fact that the climate is so inhospitable, because not everyone can handle it: that reminds them of their own strength and resilience. The first local saying Peter taught Kira was: "Bears shit in the woods, but everyone else shits on Beartown, so forest people have learned to take care of themselves!"

She's gotten used to a lot, living here, but there are some things she'll never understand. Such as how a community where everyone fishes has precisely zero sushi restaurants. Or why people who are tough enough to live in a place with a climate wild animals can barely endure can never quite bring themselves to say what they mean. In Beartown silence always goes hand in hand with shame. Kira recalls how Peter explained it when she asked him why everyone seemed to hate people from the big cities so much: "People in the big cities don't feel enough shame." He's always been worried about what people think. Whenever they get asked out to dinner, he goes to pieces if Kira buys a bottle of wine that's too expensive. That's why he refuses to live in one of the expensive houses in the Heights, even though Kira's salary would allow them to. They carry on living in their little house in the middle of town out of sheer politeness. Peter wouldn't budge, even when Kira tried to entice him saying, "More space for your record collection."

Ten years, and Kira still hasn't learned to live with the town yet, only to coexist with it. And the silence still makes her want to buy a drum and march around the streets banging it. She turns the stereo up again. Drums the steering wheel. Sings along so animatedly to each song that she almost drives off the road when her hair gets caught on the rearview mirror.

Why does Kira care about hockey? She doesn't. She cares about a person who cares about hockey. And because she dreams of a summer—just one—when her husband can look his town in the eye without lowering his gaze.

Sune's chest rises and falls below slouched shoulders as he starts to walk toward the entrance to the rink. For the first time in his life he feels his age, his body moving with slithery movements, as if some-one's tried to put a tracksuit on a bag of jellyfish. But when he opens the door a great calm still settles over him, the way it does every day. This is the only place in the world that he really understands. So he tries to remember what it's given him rather than what they're planning to take away from him. A lifetime in the service of the sport, which is more than most people can say. He's been blessed with a few moments of magic, and has seen two immortal talents born.

The noisy buggers in the big cities will never be able to understand that. What it feels like to nurture a truly talented player on a really small hockey team. Like seeing a cherry tree in bloom in a frozen garden. You can wait years, a whole lifetime, maybe several, and it would still be a miracle if you experienced it just once. Twice ought to have been impossible. Anywhere but here.

The first time was Peter Andersson. That's more than forty years ago now. Sune, who had only just been appointed A-team coach at the time, caught sight of him during skating classes. A scrawny little kid with hand-me-down gloves, a drunk for a father, and bruises everyone saw but nobody asked about. Hockey noticed him when no one else did. Changed his life with colossal force. One day that little kid grew up and raised a bankruptcy-threatened club that everyone had written off to the second-best in the country, and then he raised himself up to the NHL, the impossible path from the forest to the stars. Before fate snatched it all away from him.

It was Sune who called Peter in Canada after the funeral and told him that Beartown needed a general manager. That there was still a club and a town here that needed rescuing. And Peter needed something to rescue. That was how the Andersson family came to move home.

The second time was about ten years ago. Sune and Peter broke away from the search party in the forest because Sune realized they were looking for a hockey player while everyone else thought they were looking for an ordinary boy. They found Kevin out on the lake at dawn, his cheeks touched by frostbite, the look of the bear in his eyes. It was Peter who carried the seven-year-old back home. Sune walked alongside in silence, inhaling deeply through his nostrils. In the depths of winter the town smelled of cherry blossom again.

When a taciturn twenty-two-year-old A-team player that year gave up the fight against recurring injuries and a lack of talent, it was Sune who stopped him in the parking lot. He was the one who saw the makings of a brilliant coach when everyone else saw a failed player. The twenty-two-year-old was called David, and he stood awkwardly in front of Sune and whispered, "I'm no good as a coach," but Sune gave him a whistle and said: "Anyone who thinks they're a good coach never is." David's first team was a gang of seven-year-olds, and one of the players was Kevin. David told them to win. And they won. And didn't stop.

Kevin is seventeen now, David is coach of the junior team, and next season they'll both be on the A-team. Together with Peter, they make up the holy trinity of the future: hands on the ice, heart on the bench, brain in the office. And now Sune's discoveries will be his downfall. Peter is going to fire him, David will take his job, and Kevin will prove to everyone that it was the right decision.

An old man saw the future. And now it's overtaken him. He opens the door to the rink, lets its sounds tumble toward him.

Why does he care about hockey? Because his life will be silent without it.

Why? No one's ever asked Amat that. Hockey hurts. It demands inhuman sacrifices, physically and mentally and emotionally. It breaks feet and tears ligaments and forces him to get out of bed before dawn. It eats all his time, swallows all his energy. So why? Because when he was little he once heard that "there are no former hockey players," and he knows exactly what that means. That was back in skating class, when Amat was five years old. The A-team coach came down onto the ice to talk to the children. Sune was a fat old man even then, but he looked Amat right in the eye when he said: "Some of you were born with talent, some weren't. Some of you are lucky and got everything for free, some of you got nothing. But remember, when you're out on the ice you're all equals. And there's one thing you need to know: desire always beats luck."

It's easy for a child to fall in love with something if they're told that they can be best at it, as long as they want it enough. And no one wanted it more than Amat. Hockey became a way into society for him and his mother. He's planning to turn it into more than that—he's planning to make it the way out as well.

Every part of his body hurts, every cell is pleading with him to lie down and rest. But he swings around, blinks the sweat away, clutches his stick more tightly, and drives his skates across the ice. As fast as he can, as hard as he can. Again. Again. Again.

Everything reaches an age when it no longer surprises us. That applies even to hockey. Most days you'd think there aren't any original ideas left, that everything has already been thought, said, and written by a whole range of coaches, each one more confident than the last. The other sort of day is more rare—the unusual occasions when the ice still manages to reveal things that are beyond description. Things that surprise.

The caretaker is heading toward the stands to put some new screws in an old railing. He sees Sune open the main door and is surprised, because Sune is never here this early.

"You're up bright and early today," the caretaker chuckles.

"You have to work hardest just before the final whistle," Sune smiles wearily.

The caretaker nods sadly. As already noted, Sune's dismissal is the worst-kept secret in town. The old man is on his way up through the stands, heading for his office, when he stops. The caretaker raises an eyebrow. Sune nods toward the boy out on the ice. He squints, his eyes aren't what they were.

"Who's that?"

"Amat. One of the fifteen-year-olds on the boys' team."

"What's he doing here so early in the morning?"

"He's here every morning."

The boy has put his gloves, hat, and jacket down as markers between the lines. He skates as fast as he can until he reaches them, then changes direction without appearing to lose any speed at all, then stops abruptly and explodes. The puck never leaves his stick. Back and forth. Five times. Ten times. Without any loss of intensity. Then the shots. The puck in exactly the same place in the net at the end of each approach. Again. Again.

"Every morning? Is he being punished by someone for something, then?" Sune mutters.

The caretaker chuckles.

"He just loves hockey. You remember how that feels, old man?"

Sune doesn't answer, grunts as he looks at his watch, and heads up through the stands. He's almost reached the top row when he stops again. He tries to take another step but his heart won't let him.

He's seen Amat in skating class; he sees all these boys there, but it wasn't as obvious then. Hockey is a sport that rewards repetition. The same exercises, the same movements, until a player's responses become instinctive, branded into his marrow. The puck doesn't just glide, it bounces as well, so acceleration is more important than maximum speed, hand-eye coordination more important than strength. The ice judges you by your ability to change direction and thought quicker than anyone else—that's what separates the best players from the rest.

There are vanishingly few of them, those days when the game can still surprise us. When it does happen, it comes without warning; we just have to trust that we'll recognize it. So when the echo of the skates cutting into the ice bounds up the banks of seating, Sune stops and pauses for a moment before casting one final glance over his shoulder again. He sees the fifteen-year-old turn, holding his stick lightly in his hand, then set off again at blistering speed, and Sune will remember this as one of the true blessings in his life: seeing the impossible happen in Beartown for a third time.

The caretaker looks up from the screws in the railing and sees the old coach sink onto one of the seats on the top row. At first he seems to be seriously ill. Then the caretaker realizes that it's because he's never seen the old man laugh before.

Sune is breathing through his nose with tears in his eyes, and the whole rink smells of cherry blossom.

Why does anyone care about hockey?

Because it tells stories.

6

Amat leaves the rink with every scrap of fabric on his body transparent with sweat. From the top row of the stands, Sune watches him go. The boy is lucky, he didn't notice the A-team coach sitting there; if he had, his nerves would have sent him diving headfirst onto the ice.

Sune remains seated after Amat's gone. He's been old for a long time, but is really feeling it today. There are two things that are particularly good at reminding us how old we are: children and sports. In hockey you're an experienced player at twenty-five, a veteran at thirty, and pensioned off at thirty-five. Sune is twice that. And with age he has become shorter and broader, he's got more face to wash and less hair to comb, and finds himself getting annoyed by narrow chairs and poor-quality zippers.

But when the door closes behind Amat, the old man can still smell cherry blossom in his nostrils. Fifteen years old. Bloody hell, what a future. Sune is ashamed of the fact that he's only just noticed him; the boy has clearly developed in an explosive fashion recently while everyone else has had their eyes on the junior team, but a few years ago Sune would never have missed a talent like that. He can't blame it all on his old eyes; he's got an old heart as well.

He knows he won't be here long enough to get the chance to coach the boy, but he hopes no one ruins his talent by cutting him down. Or by letting him grow too quickly. But he knows there's no point wishing for anything like that, because when all the others realize how good this boy is they'll want to start squeezing results out of him immediately. The club needs that; the town demands that. Sune has had this argument with the board time and time again over the years, and he always loses.

It would take days to recount the long version of why Sune is being fired from Beartown Ice Hockey Club. But the short version is only two words long: "Kevin Erdahl." The sponsors, the board, and the club's president have all demanded that Sune let the seventeen-year-old wunderkind play in the A-team, and Sune has refused. In his world it takes more than hormones to turn boys into men. Senior hockey requires maturity just as much as it does talent, and he's seen more players crushed by opportunities proffered too early than too late. But no one's listening anymore.

The people of Beartown are proud of being bad losers. Sune knows that he himself bears much of the blame for that. He's the one who imprinted the words "club comes first" into every player and coach since his first day here. The good of the club must always come first, never anyone's ego. They're using that against him now. He could have saved his job by letting Kevin play in the A-team, and he wishes he was certain he's done the right thing. But he genuinely doesn't know any longer. Maybe the board and the sponsors are right—maybe he's just a stubborn old goat who's lost his grip.

David is at home, lying on his kitchen floor. He's thirty-two years old and his red hair is so unruly it looks like it's trying to escape from his head. He got teased about it when he was little; the other kids pretended to burn themselves on him in class. That was where he learned to fight. He didn't have any friends, which was why he was able to devote all his time to hockey. He never bothered to acquire any other interests, which is how he's managed to become the best.

Sweat is dripping on the floor as he frantically performs push-ups under the kitchen table. His computer is on top of it; he's been watching videos of old matches and training sessions all night. Being junior team coach for Beartown Ice Hockey makes him a simple man to understand and an impossible man to live with. When his girlfriend gets annoyed with him, she usually tells him he's the sort of man "who could take offense in an empty room." That could be true—his face looks like he's walking into a headwind. He's always been told that he's too serious; that's why hockey suits him so well.

No one on a hockey team thinks it's possible to take hockey too seriously.

The match tomorrow is the most important in David's life, as well as the juniors'. A more philosophically inclined coach might tell them that those could be their last sixty minutes on the ice as children, because most of them will be turning eighteen this year, then they'll be grown men and seniors. But David isn't philosophical, so he'll just say his usual single word to them: "Win."

He doesn't have the best players in the country, far from it. But they're the most disciplined, and have received the best tactical training. They've been playing together all their lives. And they've got Kevin.

They rarely play beautifully. David believes in detailed strategy and a solid defense, but above all he believes in results. Even when the board and parents keep going on about "letting the players lose" and trying to play "more enjoyable hockey." David doesn't even know what "enjoyable hockey" is, he only knows one sort of hockey that isn't enjoyable—the one where the opposing team scores more points. He's never let anyone else influence him; he's never given a place on the team to the son of a marketing manager at one of the big sponsors like he's been told to. He's uncompromising; he knows that's not going to make him any friends, but he doesn't care. Do you want to be liked? It's easy: just get yourself to the top of the podium. So David does whatever it takes to get up there. That's why he doesn't see his team the same way everyone else does, because even if Kevin is the best player he isn't always the most important.

The computer on the kitchen table is showing a game from earlier in the season, when an opposing player sets off after Kevin with the obvious intention of tackling him from behind, but the next moment is himself lying flat on the ice. Another Beartown player, number sixteen, is standing over him, already missing his gloves and helmet. A torrent of punches rains down on the opposing player.

Kevin might be the star, but Benjamin Ovich is the heart of the team. Because Benji is like David: he's prepared to do whatever it takes. So ever since he was small, the coach has drummed one single idea into him: "Don't pay any attention to what people say, Benji. They'll like us well enough when we start winning."

He's seventeen years old, and his mom wakes him early by saying his full name. She's the only person who uses it. "Benjamin." Everyone else calls him Benji. He stays in bed, in the smallest room in the last row house at the far end of Beartown, just before the start of the Hollows, until she comes in for the third or fourth time. When words from her homeland creep into her exhortations he gets up, because that's when it gets serious. His mom and Benji's three older sisters only slip into the old language when they want to express great anger or eternal love, and this country simply doesn't have sufficiently flexible grammar to express which good-for-nothing part of the laziest useless donkey Benji might be, or how they love him as deeply as ten thousand wells full of gold. His mom can get both elements into the same sentence. It's a remarkable language in that sense.

She watches him as he cycles off. She hates having to force him out of bed before the sun has risen, but she knows that if she goes to work without driving her son out of the house he wouldn't leave it at all. She's a single mother with three daughters, but it's this seventeen-year-old boy who worries her more than anything. A boy who cares too little about the future and frets too much about the past: nothing could depress a mother more. Her little Benjamin, the fighter with whom it's far too easy for the girls of Beartown to fall in love. The boy with the most handsome face, the saddest eyes, and the wildest heart they've ever seen. His mom knows, because she married a man who looked just the same, and nothing but trouble lies ahead for men like that.

David is making coffee in his kitchen. He always brews an extra pot each morning and fills a thermos—the coffee at the rink is so bad you ought to be able to charge someone for assault just for offering it to you. His computer is playing a match from last year, in which Kevin is being pursued by a furious defender until Benji appears at full speed out of nowhere and hits the defender on the back of his neck with his stick, sending him flying headfirst into the opposing team's bench. Half the team storms onto the ice to get revenge on Benji, who is standing there waiting for them without his helmet, fists clenched. It takes the referees ten minutes to get the fight under control. In the meantime Kevin has gone to sit down quietly on his own bench, unharmed and untroubled.

Some people try to make excuses for Benji's temperament by blaming his tough childhood, the fact that his dad died when he was young. David never does that; he loves Benji's temperament. Other people call him a "problem child," but all the characteristics that make him a problem off the ice are what make him so special on it. If you send him into a brawl it doesn't matter if serpents, trolls, and all the monsters of hell are in the way, Benji always comes out with the puck. If anyone gets anywhere near Kevin he'll fight through concrete to place himself in the way, and that sort of thing can't be taught. Everyone knows how good Kevin is—every youth-team coach on each of the top clubs in the country has tried to recruit him—and that also means that every team they play contains at least one psycho who wants to hurt him. So David doesn't accept it when people say that Benji ends up "fighting" in every other match. He's not fighting. He's protecting the most important investment the town has ever seen.

But David has stopped using that particular word in front of his girlfriend: "investment." Because, as she put it: "Is that really any way to talk about a seventeen-year-old?" David has learned not to try to explain it. Either you understand that aspect of hockey or you don't.

On the road that links the row houses to the rest of the town, Benji stops his bicycle at the point where his mother can no longer see him and lights a joint. He lets the smoke fill him, feels the sweet calmness rise and fall. His long, thick hair stiffens in the wind, but the cold has

never bothered him. He cycles everywhere, no matter what time of
year it is. At practice, David often commends him on his calf muscles
and sense of balance in front of the other players. Benji never replies,
because he suspects that saying, "That's what you get if you ride a
bike through deep snow every day when you're high as a kite" isn't
the answer the coach wants to hear.

On his way to his best friend's house he passes through the whole
of Beartown: the factory that's still the largest employer in the town,
but which has "effectivized its personnel" three years in a row now—a
fancy way of saying people have been laid off. The big supermarket
that has closed down its smaller competitors. A street full of stores
in varying states of disrepair, and an industrial area that is just getting quieter and quieter. The sports store, which has one section for
hunting and fishing and another for hockey, but very little else worth
mentioning. A little farther out is the pub, the Bearskin, frequented by
the sort of men who make it such an excellent destination for any curious tourist eager to find out what it's like to get beaten up by the locals.

Toward the forest, off to the west, is a garage and—farther in
among the trees—the kennels that Benji's eldest sister runs. She raises
two types of dogs: hunting dogs and guard dogs. No one around here
wants dogs for pets anymore.

There's not much to love about this place apart from hockey. But
on the other hand, Benji hasn't loved very much else in his life. He
inhales the smoke. The other guys keep warning him he'll get kicked
off the team if David finds out he smokes weed, but Benji just laughs,
secure in the knowledge that would never happen. Not because Benji
is too good to be thrown off the team, definitely not, but because Kevin
is too good. Kevin is the jewel, Benji the insurance policy.

Sune looks up at the roof of the rink one last time. At the flags and jerseys hanging there, memories of men soon no one will be old enough
to remember. Alongside them hangs a shabby banner bearing what
used to be the club's motto: "Culture, Values, Community." Sune

helped hang it there, but he's no longer sure what it means. Sometimes he's not sure if he knew back then either.

"Culture" is an odd word to use about hockey; everyone says it, but no one can explain what it means. All organizations like to boast that they're building a culture, but when it comes down to it everyone really only cares about one sort: the culture of winning. Sune is well aware that the same thing applies the world over, but perhaps it's more noticeable in a small community. We love winners, even though they're very rarely particularly likeable people. They're almost always obsessive and selfish and inconsiderate. That doesn't matter. We forgive them. We like them while they're winning.

The old man stands up and makes his way toward his office, with his back creaking and heart hardened. The door closes behind him. His personal belongings are already packed in a small box that's tucked under the desk. He won't make a scene when he gets fired, won't speak to the press. He's just going to disappear. That's how he was brought up, and that's how he's brought others up. The team comes first.

No one really knows how the pair of them became best friends, but everyone has long since given up any attempt to separate them. Benji rings the doorbell of the house that's more than half the size of the entire block where he lives.

Kevin's mom opens the door with her ever-friendly yet constantly stressed smile, clutching her phone to her ear, while behind her Kevin's dad walks past talking loudly into his. The walls of the front hall are decorated with family photos, but those framed pictures are the only place Benji has ever seen all three members of the Erdahl family side by side. In real life one of them always seems to be in the kitchen, the other in the study, and Kevin in the garden. *Bang-bang-bang-bang-bang.* A door closing, an apology directed at a phone. "Yes, sorry, it's my son. The hockey player, yes, that's right."

No one raises their voice in this house and no one ever lowers it either—all communication has had its emotions amputated. Kevin is simultaneously the most and least spoiled kid Benji has ever met: the fridge is full of prepared meals made in exact accordance with the nutrition plan provided by the team, delivered every three days by a catering company. The kitchen in the Erdahl family's house cost three times more than the whole of Benji's mom's row house, but no one ever prepares a meal in it. Kevin's room has everything a seventeen-year-old could dream of, including the fact that no adult except the cleaner has set foot inside it since he was three. No one in Beartown has ever spent more on their son's sports career, no one has given more to the team in sponsorship than his dad's company, yet Benji can count the number of times he's seen Kevin's parents in the crowd of spectators on the fingers of one hand, and still have two fingers left. Benji asked his friend about it once. Kevin replied: "My parents aren't interested in hockey." When Benji asked what they were interested in, Kevin replied: "Success." They were ten years old at the time.

When Kevin is top of the class in history tests, which he almost always is, and goes home and says he got forty-nine out of fifty questions right, his dad merely asks in an expressionless voice: "What did you get wrong?" Perfection isn't a goal in the Erdahl family, it's the norm.

Their home is white and precise, an advertisement for right angles. When he's sure no one's looking, Benji silently nudges the shoe-rack one inch out of line and touches a couple of the photos on the wall so that they're hanging ever so slightly crooked, and as he walks across the rug in the living room he lets his big toe fleetingly mess up some of the fringe. When he reaches the terrace door he sees Kevin's mom's reflection in the glass. She's going around mechanically putting everything back to how it was, without missing a beat of her telephone conversation.

Benji goes out into the garden, grabs a chair, and goes to sit near Kevin, then closes his eyes and listens to the banging. Kevin pauses, his collar black with sweat.

"Are you nervous?" he asks.

Benji doesn't open his eyes.

"Do you remember the first time you came out into the forest with me, Kev? You'd never been hunting before and held your rifle like you were scared it was going to bite you."

Kevin sighs so deeply that half of the air probably escapes from another bodily opening.

"Aren't you ever going to take anything in life seriously?"

Benji's broad grin reveals an almost imperceptible difference in the color of his teeth. If you send him into a skirmish, he'll come out with the puck, even at the cost of one of his own teeth, or someone else's.

"You almost managed to shoot me in the balls. I take that very seriously."

"So you're really not nervous about the game?"

"Kev, you and a gun anywhere close to my testicles make me nervous. Hockey doesn't make me nervous."

They're interrupted by Kevin's parents calling good-bye. His dad in the same tone he would use to say good-bye to a waiter in a restaurant, his mom with a cautious little "sweetheart" at the end. As if she really is trying but can't quite manage to make it sound like anything more than a line she's learned for a play. The front door closes, two cars start up out in the drive. Benji fishes another joint from the inside pocket of his jacket and lights up.

"Are *you* nervous, Kev?"

"No. No, no . . ."

Benji laughs; his friend has never been able to lie to him.

"Really?"

"Okay, what the fuck, Benji, I'm shitting myself here! Is that what you want to hear?"

Benji looks like he's fallen asleep.

"How much have you smoked already today?" Kevin chuckles.

"Nowhere near enough," Benji mumbles, and curls up on the chair as if he were thinking of hibernating for winter.

"You know we've got to be at school in an hour?"

"All the more reason."

"If David finds out, you'll get kicked off the tea—"

"No, I won't."

Leaning on his stick, Kevin says nothing and just looks at him. Of all the things in the world you can be envious of your best friend for, this is what Kevin would most like to have: the ability that Benji has always had to not give a shit about anything, and to get away with it. Kevin shakes his head and laughs in resignation.

"No, you won't."

Benji falls asleep. Kevin turns toward the goal and his eyes turn black. *Bang-bang-bang-bang-bang.*

Again. Again. Again.

At home in his kitchen David does his last push-ups. Then he showers, gets dressed, packs his case, and grabs his car keys to drive to the rink and start work. But the very last thing the thirty-two-year-old coach does before leaving the house is put his coffee down on the little table beside the door and run into the bathroom. There he locks the door and turns the taps on in both sink and bathtub so that his girlfriend won't hear him throwing up.

7

It's only a game. Everyone who plays it gets told that from time to time. A lot of people try to tell themselves that it's true. But it's complete nonsense. No one in this town would have been the same if that game hadn't existed.

Kevin always goes to the bathroom just before he and Benji go to school. He doesn't like using the bathrooms at school, not because they're disgusting, but because they make him feel stressed. They make him feel anxious in a way he's never quite been able to identify. He can only relax enough at home, surrounded by overpriced tiles and a sink that's as exclusive as it is impractical, carefully selected by an interior designer who invoiced for many more hours than the workmen. This house is the only place in the world he has ever learned to be alone.

Everywhere else, in the rink or at school or even on the way to and from them, he is part of a group. Always in the middle, with the team gravitating toward him in order of their ability on the ice, the best players closest to him. At home Kevin learned to be alone at such a young age that it became natural, but now he can't bear being alone anywhere else.

Benji is waiting outside the house. As always. A boy with less control of his impulses than Kevin would have hugged him. Instead he just nods and mutters, "Let's go."

Maya walks away from her dad's car so fast that Ana has to jog to keep up with her. Ana holds out a plastic cup.

"Do you want some? I'm on the green smoothie diet now!"

Maya slows down and shakes her head. "Why do you keep doing those diets? Why do you hate your taste buds so much? What have they ever done to you?"

"Shut up, this is really good! Try it!"

Warily, Maya puts her lips to the edge of the cup. She takes half a sip before spitting it out.

"It's got *lumps*!"

Ana nods happily.

"Peanut butter."

Disgusted, Maya picks at her tongue with her fingers, as if it were covered with invisible hairs.

"You need help, Ana. Serious help."

Beartown used to have more schools, because there used to be more children. Now there are just two buildings left: one for primary and middle school pupils, and one for high school. They all have lunch in the same cafeteria. The town is no bigger than that anymore.

Amat runs to catch up with Lifa and Zacharias in the parking lot. The three boys have been in the same class all the way through school, and have been best friends since preschool, not because they are particularly similar but because they shared the fact that they weren't like everyone else. In places like Beartown, the most popular children become leaders at a young age; teams are invisibly chosen as early as the playground. Amat, Lifa, and Zacharias were the sort of children who got passed over. They've stuck together ever since. Lifa is less talkative than a tree, Zacharias louder than a radio, and Amat just appreciates the company. They make a good team.

". . . such a clean headshot! He tried to chicken out and hide . . . What the hell? Are you even listening, Amat?"

Zacharias, wearing the same black jeans and black hoodie and black cap that he seems to have been wearing since they were ten years old, interrupts his speech about his evidently extremely impressive performance against a heavily armed sniper in a virtual universe last night and shoves Amat in the shoulder.

"What?"

"Did you even hear what I was saying?"

Amat yawns. "Yeah, yeah, headshot. Amazing. I'm just hungry."

"Did you go training this morning?" Zacharias asks.

"Yeah."

"You're not right in the head, getting up that early."

Amat grins.

"So when did you get to bed last night?"

Zacharias shrugs and massages his thumbs. "Four o'clock . . . Okay, five, maybe."

Amat nods.

"You spend as much time gaming as I do training, Zach. We'll see who turns professional first!"

Zacharias is about to answer when his head is knocked forward hard by the slap of an open palm. Zacharias, Amat, and Lifa know it's Bobo before they even turn around. Zacharias's cap lands on the ground to the sound of laughter from the juniors who have suddenly surrounded them. Zacharias, Amat, and Lifa are fifteen years old, the juniors are only two years older, but they're so much more developed physically that there could easily have been ten years between them. Bobo is the biggest of them, as wide as a barn door and ugly enough to make rats move house. He shoves Zacharias hard with his shoulder as he walks past, and Zacharias stumbles and falls to his knees. Bobo laughs with feigned surprise and the juniors surrounding him join in.

"Nice beard, Zach. You look more like your mother every day!" Bobo smirks, and before the juniors' laughter dies away he goes on:

"Have you got any hair on your balls yet? Or do you still cry in the shower when you realize it's just fluff from your underpants? Fuck, Zach . . . Seriously, though, there's something I've been wondering: the first time you, Amat, and Lifa slept together, how did you work out which of you guys was going to lose his virginity first?"

The juniors head off toward the school. They'll have forgotten the exchange within thirty seconds, but it takes a long while for their laughter to die away for the boys behind them. Amat sees the silent hatred in Zacharias's eyes as he helps him up. It grows stronger each morning. Amat worries that one day it's going to explode.

———

All kinds of things, big and small, can make you love being part of a team. When Kevin was at primary school he went with his dad to the Christmas market in Hed. His dad had a meeting, so Kevin went around on his own looking at the displays and stalls. He got lost and was five minutes late getting back to the car, and his dad had already left. Kevin had to walk all the way back to Beartown on his own in the dark. The snowdrifts by the sides of the road reached his thighs and it took him half the night to get home. He staggered, wet and exhausted, into the silent house. His parents were already asleep. His dad wanted to teach him the importance of being punctual.

Six months later the hockey team was playing in a tournament in another town. The rink was the biggest the boys had seen, and on the way to the bus Kevin got lost. The older brothers of three of the players in a team Kevin had humiliated a couple of hours earlier found him, dragged him into a washroom, and beat him up. Kevin will never forget the look of astonishment on their faces when another primary-school kid showed up and took on all three of them in a storm of kicks and punches. Benji and Kevin were both covered with blood and bruises when they arrived at the bus more than forty-five minutes late. David was standing there waiting. He had told the rest of the team to leave without him; he'd catch the train with Benji and Kevin when they showed up. But every player on the team had refused to get on the bus. They weren't old enough to know their multiplication tables, but they knew that a team didn't mean anything if you couldn't depend on each other. That's both a big and a small thing. Knowing that there are people who will never abandon you.

Kevin and Benji are alone when they enter the school, but exert a magnetic pull as they move along the corridor. Bobo and the other juniors flock around them instantly, and within ten paces they have become a group of twelve people. Kevin and Benji don't think it odd, the way you don't if something's been going on your whole life. It's impossible to say what it is that catches Kevin's attention, because the day before a game there's usually nothing on the planet that can distract him, but as he passes a row of lockers his eyes meet hers. He stumbles into Benji, Benji swears at him, Kevin doesn't hear.

Maya has just put her bag in her locker, and when she turns around and Kevin's eyes meet hers she closes the locker door so quickly she nips her hand. It's over in a moment—the corridor fills with bodies, and Kevin disappears in the crowd. But the friends you have when you're fifteen years old obviously aren't going to miss a thing like that.

"Sooo . . . are you interested in hockey all of a sudden now?" Ana teases.

Embarrassed, Maya rubs her hand.

"Shut up. What the . . . ?"

Then her face breaks into a brief smile:

"Just because you don't like peanut butter doesn't necessarily mean you can't like . . . peanuts."

Ana laughs so hard she ends up spraying the inside of her locker with smoothie.

"Okay, fine! But if you do talk to Kevin, the least you can do is introduce me to Benji, yeah? He's . . . mmm . . . I could eat him all up. Like . . . butter."

Maya's brow furrows with disgust, then she pulls the key from her locker and starts to walk off. Ana watches her and throws her arms out.

"What? So YOU'RE allowed to say things like that, but not me?"

"You know he doesn't come up with those jokes himself, don't you? He's not smart enough. He nicks them from the Internet," Zacharias mutters, humiliated, as he shakes the snow from his clothes.

Lifa picks up his cap and brushes the snow off it. Amat holds his hand out in an attempt to calm his friend down.

"I know you hate Bobo, but next year we'll be juniors . . . It'll be better then."

Zacharias doesn't reply. Lifa flashes him a look, somewhere between anger and resignation. Lifa stopped playing hockey when they were younger. He kept being told he had to be able to handle the "banter" in the locker room, which turned out to be a very useful argument, because when Lifa gave up, everyone could blame that. It was his problem, not hockey's. If Zacharias's parents hadn't loved the game as much as they did, he wouldn't have carried on playing either, and if Amat hadn't been so good, even he might not have been able to summon up the enthusiasm to keep playing.

"It'll be better when we're juniors," Amat repeats.

Zacharias says nothing. He knows very well that he won't get a place on the junior team, and that this is his last year playing hockey. Amat is the only person who hasn't yet realized that he's about to leave his best friend behind.

The silence doesn't bother Amat, who opens the door and turns a corner in the corridor, after which he can only hear a muffled rumble in his ears. She gives him tunnel vision.

"Hi, Maya!" he exclaims, a little too loudly.

She turns around fleetingly, notes his presence, but nothing more than that. When you're fifteen years old, no look can hurt you more.

"Hi, Amat," she replies distractedly, and is gone before she even gets to the end of his name.

Amat stands there, trying not to look at Zacharias and Lifa, knowing they won't be making much effort not to laugh.

"Hiiii, Maayaaa . . . ," Zacharias mimics, as Lifa giggles.

"Fuck off, Zach," Amat mutters.

"Sorry, sorry, but you've been doing this since primary school and I was nice to you for the first *eight* years you were in love with her, so now I think I've earned the right to make fun of you."

Amat walks toward his locker, his heart sinking in his chest like a lead weight. He loves that girl more than he loves skating.

8

It's only a game. It only resolves tiny, insignificant things. Such as who gets validation. Who gets listened to. It allocates power and draws boundaries and turns some people into stars and others into spectators. That's all.

David enters the rink and goes straight to his office, the smallest one at the end of the corridor. He closes the door, switches his computer on, and studies videos of tomorrow's opponents. They're a brilliant team, an imposing machine, and—player for player—only Kevin really matches up against them. It's going to take an immense effort for the team to stand any chance at all, but David knows that they do at least have a chance, and that every single one of his players will work themselves to death out there on the ice if need be. That isn't what's making him feel sick. It's what he's missing from the team. Speed.

For several years the junior team's first line has consisted of Kevin, Benji, and a third player called William Lyt. Kevin is a genius, and Benji a fighter. But William is slow. He's big and strong, and not bad at passing, so David has managed to find tactical solutions to hide his shortcomings when they've been playing less impressive teams, but the team they're about to face is good enough to shut Kevin down unless there's someone else who's quick enough to create space for him.

David rubs his temples. Looks at his reflection in the computer screen, his red hair and exhausted eyes. He gets up and goes out to the bathroom. And throws up again.

In a larger office two doors away, Sune is sitting at his computer. He's watching the same clips as David, over and over again. Once upon a time the two men always looked at events out on the ice the same way, thought the same about everything. But as the years passed, David grew older and more ambitious while Sune became old and stubborn. When David claims that fights ought to be permitted out on the ice because "there'd be fewer injuries if the guys knew they'd get beaten up for bad play," Sune retorts, "That's like saying there'd be fewer road accidents if you banned car insurance, because people would take better care of their cars." When David wants to "increase the load" on the juniors, Sune talks about "quality over quantity." If David says "up," Sune yells "down." When some of the other sporting associations recently proposed that little league games should no longer keep a tally of goals and points, and not have league tables until the age of twelve, Sune thought it sounded "sensible," while David denounced it as "communism." David thinks Sune should let him do his job. Sune thinks David has misunderstood what his job actually is. The two men are stuck in their own trenches, buried too deep even to see each other anymore.

Sune leans back, rubs his eyes, and hears his chair creak under his weight as he lets out a sigh. He feels like explaining to David just how lonely the job of A-team coach can be, how numbingly heavy the responsibility gets. How you need to be ready to see the bigger picture, adapt, change. But David's young, not ready to listen and understand. Sune closes his eyes and swears at himself. Because isn't he just the same? One of the hardest things about getting old is admitting mistakes that it's too late to put right. The worst thing about having power over other people's lives is that you sometimes get things wrong.

Sune has always refused to move young players to older age groups. The old man believes in the principle that players should develop alongside their peers, that being given opportunities too early stifles talent. But as he sits alone in his office watching these videos, he has to admit that he sees the same thing as David right now. Something that hardly anyone else understands: without a bit of pace, the junior team is going to die a death tomorrow.

So even Sune finds himself wondering: what are principles worth, if you don't win?

———

Beartown is just small enough for everyone to recognize almost everyone else, but just big enough to be full of people that no one really notices. Robbie Holts is a few years past forty. His beard has started to turn grey; he scratches it and pulls the collar of his old camouflage jacket tighter around his neck. When the wind blows off the lake at this time of year, it feels like your face is being torn by ghosts. He's walking along the other side of the street, pretending to have important things to do, convincing himself that no one who sees him will realize that he's waiting for the pub, the Bearskin, to open.

He can see the roof of the rink from here. Like everyone else, the junior team's game tomorrow is all he's talked about every waking hour since they won the quarterfinal. It's just that he no longer has many people to talk to anymore, not since the factory got rid of him along with nine other guys. There's a good chance no one was interested in what he was saying before either, but that's only dawned on him recently.

He looks at the time. Another hour before the Bearskin opens. He pretends it's no big deal. Keeps his hands in his pockets when he goes into the supermarket so no one will see them shaking. He fills his basket with things he doesn't need and can't afford, and puts the low-strength beer—the only sort the supermarket is allowed to sell—in last, to make it look like an impulse buy. "This? Oh, it might be useful to have a few beers at home, just in case." He asks if he can use the bathroom in the little hardware store. Downs the beers. Goes out and chats to the sales assistant and buys a few very specific screws that he makes very clear he needs for an item of furniture that doesn't exist. He goes back out onto the street, sees the roof of the rink again. Once upon a time he, Robbie Holts, was king there. Once upon a time he showed more promise than Kevin Erdahl does now. Once upon a time he was better than Peter Andersson.

Peter turns the car around in the parking lot, pulls out onto the road, drums his fingers on the wheel. Now that the children have gone he becomes aware of his pulse again. It's only a junior team game. Only a game. A game. He keeps repeating the mantra but his nerves are eating him up. His lungs seem to be drawing in oxygen through his eye sockets. Hockey is a simple sport: when your desire to win is stronger than your fear of losing, you have a chance. No one wins when they're frightened.

He hopes the juniors are too young to feel fear tomorrow, too naive to understand how much is at stake. Because a hockey crowd knows no nuances, only heaven or hell. Seen from the stands, you're either a genius or utterly worthless, never anything in between. An offside is never a matter for doubt; every check is either perfectly clean or deserves a lifetime ban. When Peter was twenty and team captain and arrived back in Beartown after almost winning the final of the top league in the country, he was met by his dad's voice from the kitchen: "Almost? For Christ's sake, you can't *almost* get on a boat. You're either on the boat or in the water. And when all the other buggers are in the water as well, no one gives a shit that you were the last one to end up there."

When Peter got his contract with the NHL and was about to move to Canada, his dad told him in no uncertain terms not to think he was "anything special." It's possible that the old man meant it more gently than it came out, that he intended to say that humility and hard work would take the boy just as far over there as they had here. It's possible that drink made his words sharper. It's possible that Peter didn't mean to slam the door quite as hard as he did. It doesn't matter now. A young man left Beartown in silence and when he came home again it was too late for words. You can't look a gravestone in the eye and ask its forgiveness.

Peter remembers walking alone down all the small streets where he grew up and realizing that people he had known his whole life looked at him differently now. He remembers how they would suddenly stop talking when he walked in the room. He was relieved when that passed, when they stopped seeing him as a star and started to see him as general manager. Then, as the club went on tumbling down through the divisions and people told the GM what they really thought, he discovered that that part of him wished they still saw him as a star. Because a hockey crowd knows no nuances, only heaven or hell.

So why does he carry on? Because he's never considered any alternatives. It's hard for a lot of people to remember the reasons why they started to love the thing they love, but it's easy for Peter. The greatest reason for his love of hockey, from the very first moment he stood on a pair of skates, was the silence. Everything outside the rink, the cold and the darkness and the fact that his mom was ill and his dad would be drunk again when he got home . . . it all went quiet inside his head when he stepped onto the ice. He was four years old that first time, but hockey told him straightaway that it was going to demand complete devotion from him. He loved it for that. And still does.

A man who is the same age as Peter but looks fifteen years older sees Peter's car pass through the town. He pulls his camouflage jacket more tightly around him and scratches his beard. When they were seventeen years old there was only one person in the whole of Beartown who thought Peter was more talented than Robbie when it came to hockey. "Talent is like letting two balloons up into the air: the most interesting thing isn't watching which one climbs fastest, but which one has the longest string," that old bastard Sune used to say. He was right, of course. The board and the sponsors forced him to move Robbie up to the A-team even though the coach insisted that the boy wasn't ready mentally. Robbie kept getting hammered with hard checks, got injured, got scared, and spent the rest of the season hitting the puck into the boards rather than risk a fight. The first time the crowd booed him, he went home and cried. The second time he went home and got drunk.

When he turned eighteen he was worse than he had been when he was seventeen, while Peter was better than anything this town had ever seen. When Peter was offered the chance to move to the A-team, he was ready. Robbie started to doubt himself every time he stepped out onto the ice, while nothing scared Peter. He went off to the NHL the same year Robbie started work at the factory. There are no almosts in hockey. One player achieved his dreams while the other now finds himself stamping his feet in the snow until the pub door finally opens.

A short flight of stairs leads down to the bar, five steps. From down there you can't see the roof of the rink.

Sune hears David leave his office. He waits until the bathroom door opens and closes, then the old man writes four words on a yellow Post-it note and stands up. He goes into David's office and sticks it onto the screen of his computer. Sune isn't a religious man, but at that moment he prays to all the powers he can think of that he's not making a mistake. That those four words aren't going to wreck another young boy's life.

For a moment he thinks about waiting until David comes back, then looking him in the eye and telling him the truth, as he sees it: "I hope you never stop arguing, David. I hope you never stop telling us to go to hell. That's how you've made it to the top." But he goes back to his own office instead and closes the door. Sports creates complicated men, proud enough to refuse to admit their mistakes, but humble enough always to put their team first.

When David gets back from the washroom he reads the four words on a Post-it note stuck to his computer monitor: *Amat. Boys' team. Fast!!!*

It's only a game. It can only change people's lives.

9

All adults have days when we feel completely drained. When we no longer know quite what we spend so much time fighting for, when reality and everyday worries overwhelm us and we wonder how much longer we're going to be able to carry on. The wonderful thing is that we can all live through far more days like that without breaking than we think. The terrible thing is that we never know exactly how many.

When the members of her family are asleep, Kira still goes around the house and counts them. Her own mother always did that with her children, Kira and her five siblings, counting them every night. Her mother said she didn't understand how anyone could have children and not do that, how anyone could live without being terrified of losing them at any moment. "One, two, three, four, five, six," Kira would hear her whisper through the house, and each child would lie there with his or her eyes closed and feel that they had been seen and acknowledged. It's one of her most treasured childhood memories.

Kira is driving from little Beartown to the larger town beyond the forest. Her commute to work takes longer than most people could bear, but it feels surprisingly quick to Kira, since she has the sense of having crossed the entire universe when she gets out of the car. Even though the larger town is many times smaller than the city where she was born, it's a different world from the one among the trees. A larger world with colleagues to be spurred on by, friends to discuss culture and politics with, opponents to analyze and fight against.

She is often told that it's odd that a woman who doesn't understand hockey ended up marrying a hockey player, but that's not entirely fair. She finds the game perfectly logical, it's just the intensity of the training she doesn't understand. The adrenaline, the hunger teetering on the brink of fear, throwing yourself off the edge of the abyss and either floating or being swallowed up—Kira understands all that. She experiences it in the courtroom, in negotiations. Law is a different sort of game with a different set of rules, but you're either a competitive person or you aren't. Like they say in Beartown: Some people have the bear in them.

Perhaps that's why Kira, who up to the age of nineteen had never lived anywhere with fewer than a million inhabitants, has been able to make a home for herself among the forest-dwellers in spite of everything. She understands their love of the fight, she shares it. She knows that one of the funny things about fighting for success—and God knows, Kira fought her way through her legal training alongside kids from rich families who never had to do the washing up in the family restaurant in the evenings—is that you never really stop fighting. You never stop being scared of falling from the top, because when you close your eyes you can still feel the pain from each and every step of the way up.

Peter already has a pain in his stomach when he steps into the president's office. It's messy, littered with old photographs and cups; there are some expensive bottles of drink on a table in one corner, golf clubs, and a half-open wardrobe containing a spare suit and clean shirts. They're going to be needed—the president is sitting at his desk eating a sandwich the way a German shepherd would try to eat a balloon filled with mayonnaise. Peter tries to stop himself from wiping down both the desk and the president with napkins, and at least manages to stop before he gets to the president.

"Can you close the door?" the president mutters as he chews.

Peter takes a deep breath and feels his guts tie themselves in knots. He knows that everyone in the town thinks he's naive, that he doesn't understand where this is going. But he's really just good at hoping. He closes the door and gives up on that.

"We're going to appoint David as coach of the A-team," the president says, like a training video in how not to be diplomatic.

Peter nods bitterly. The president brushes some crumbs from his tie.

"Everyone knows how close you and Sune are . . . ," he adds by way of an apology.

Peter doesn't respond. The president wipes his fingers on his pants.

"Don't look like that, for God's sake, as if I just stole the presents from under your Christmas tree. We need to put the good of the club first, Peter!"

Peter looks down at the floor. He's a team player—that's how he would describe himself. And the starting point for that is always understanding your own role, and its limitations. He's going to have to tell himself that plenty of times today, force his brain to control his heart. It was Sune who persuaded him to become GM, and it was Sune's door that was always open to him when things got tough.

"With all due respect: you know I don't agree about that. I don't think David's ready," he said quietly.

He doesn't make eye contact with the president and looks around the walls of the office instead, as if he were looking for something. The only time he avoids eye contact is when something feels extremely unpleasant. Kira says he starts "shooting imaginary clay pigeons" as soon as he finds himself in any sort of conflict. He can't even point out that he's been given the wrong change in the supermarket without breaking into a cold sweat and wanting to curl up into a ball. The wall behind the president is decorated with pictures and pennants, and one of them—ancient and faded—reads "Culture, Values, Community." Peter feels like asking the president what he thinks that means now that they're about to fire the man who built up everything surrounding them. But he stays quiet. The president throws up his hands.

"We're aware that David pushes hard, but he gets results. And the sponsors have made a significant investment . . . for God's sake, Peter, they saved us from bankruptcy. And we've got a chance to build something big now, using the products of the junior team."

Peter looks him in the eye for the first time and replies through gritted teeth:

"We're not supposed to develop 'products.' We don't manufacture anything at all. We nurture human beings. Those guys are flesh and blood, not business plans and investment targets. The youth program isn't some factory, regardless of what some of our sponsors seem to think."

He bites his lip hard and stops himself. The president scratches his stubble. They both look tired. Peter looks down at the floor again.

"Sune thinks David is pushing the juniors too hard. I'm concerned about what might happen if he's right," he mutters.

The president smiles. And shrugs his shoulders.

"Do you know what happens to coal if you apply enough pressure to it, Peter? It turns into diamonds."

The Andersson family never plays Monopoly, not because the parents don't want to, but because the children refuse. The last time they tried, Kira ended up holding the board over the open fire, threatening to burn it unless Peter confessed that he had been cheating. Their parents are so competitive that Maya and Leo simply refuse to play. Leo loves hockey because he loves being part of a team, but he would probably have been just as happy being in charge of the equipment as he is being a center. Maya chose the guitar. You can't compete at playing the guitar. Maya's last sporting memory is of the time she lost a game of table tennis when she was six because another girl ran into her and knocked her over, and how the youth-group leader who was supposed to hand out the medals had to lock himself in a cleaning cupboard so Kira wouldn't find him. Maya had to console her mother all the way home. After that she announced that she wanted to learn to play a musical instrument.

Nothing has made Kira more proud or more envious than when she heard her daughter plug in an amplifier for the first time and play David Bowie in the garage with her dad on drums. She hated and loved Peter because he had the sensitivity to learn. So that he could be close to Maya.

The four members of the family are so improbably different, and even if Kira never stops reminding them that Peter actually *confessed* to cheating at Monopoly, she nonetheless thinks about that Monopoly board every now and then and feels . . . ashamed. Not a second has passed since she had children without her feeling like a bad mother. For everything. For not understanding, for being impatient, for not knowing everything, not making better packed lunches, for still wanting more out of life than just being a mother. She hears other women in Beartown sigh behind her back: "Yes, but she has a *full-time* job, you know. Can you imagine?" No matter how much you try to let words like that run off you, a few of them stick.

She's ashamed to admit it to herself, but getting to work feels like a liberation. She knows she's good at her job, and she never feels that way about being a parent. Even on the best days—the tiny, shimmering moments when they're on holiday and Peter and the children are fooling about on a beach and everyone is happy and laughing—Kira always feels like a fake. As if she doesn't deserve it, as if she just wants to be able to show a photoshopped family photograph to the rest of the world.

Her work may be demanding and tough, but it's straightforward and logical. And being a parent is never like that. If she does everything right at work, things usually go as planned, but it doesn't matter if she does absolutely everything in the universe correctly as a mother: the very worst can still happen.

The weight on Peter's chest feels too heavy for him to be able to get up from his chair. The president tries to look authoritative:

"The board wants you to tell Sune the news and deal with the interviews with the press. It's important that we demonstrate that we're all united regarding this decision."

Peter rubs his eyebrows with his knuckles. "When?"

"Right after the juniors' final." Peter looks up in surprise.

"Don't you mean after the semifinal? Tomorrow?"

The president shakes his head calmly.

"No. If they lose the semifinal, David won't be getting the job. The board will select someone else instead. In which case we'll need another couple of weeks."

Peter's world wobbles on its axis.

"Are you kidding? You're seriously contemplating firing Sune and then bringing in someone from *outside*?"

The president opens a small bag of chips, eats a handful, and wipes the salt on his jacket.

"Come on, Peter, don't be naive. If the juniors win the final, we'll get an incredible amount of publicity. The sponsors, the council, everyone's going to want to join in. But the board isn't interested in 'almost'. . . Just look at us, look at the club . . ."

The president throws up his hands a bit too quickly, but carries on talking through the ensuing shower of crumbs:

"Don't be a hypocrite, Peter. You haven't devoted all those hours to this team for 'almost,' you didn't become GM for 'almost.' No one really cares if the guys put up a good fight, they'll only remember the final result. David is completely inexperienced as an A-team coach, but we can overlook that if he wins. But if he doesn't . . . well, you know the rules: either you win, or you're an also-ran."

For a long time they just look at each other, the club president and its GM. They say nothing more, but they both know: if Peter doesn't fall into line behind the board and the sponsors, he, too, can be replaced. Club first. Always.

He leaves the president's office, closes the door behind him, and stands forlornly in the hallway with his forehead against the wall. One harsh lesson that Peter had to learn very quickly when he became GM was that everyone was always unhappy with him. That was hard to accept for someone who has always wanted to keep people happy. It was Sune who told him not to let it bother him, and that his talent for compromise would get him a long way. Then he was able to listen and make difficult decisions with his head rather than his heart.

Perhaps Sune didn't have his own dismissal in mind when he said that. Perhaps he changed his mind when he got older. Perhaps Peter himself has changed, he doesn't know. But he does know the rules, everyone knows the rules. You're either a particular type of club, or you're one of all the rest.

Not that any of this feels the slightest bit better as a result. All he knows is that he keeps disappointing people. Always.

On one corner of the desk in Kira's office there's an increasingly cramped collection of family photographs. One is of her and Peter taken the day they moved to Canada, when he'd only just gotten his NHL contract. She happens to notice it just as she's putting her briefcase down and smiles. God, they were so young then. She had only just qualified as a lawyer, and was pregnant, and he was going to be a superstar. How easy everything was back then, for a few magical weeks. She stops smiling when she remembers how quickly the smiles in that picture had faded.

Peter broke his foot in preseason training, and when he returned he had to fight his way up through the farm team league, only to break his foot a second time when he was finally allowed to play again. After four NHL games. It took him two years to work his way back after that. Six minutes into his fifth game he fell and didn't get back up. She screamed out loud, despite swearing while she was growing up that she would never make a fool of herself for any man. She sat through nine operations, she doesn't know how many hours of rehab, physiotherapists, and specialists. All that talent, all that sweat, all leading up to nothing but tears and bitterness in a man whose heart wanted so much more than his body could handle. She remembers when the doctor told her Peter would never be able to play at elite level again, because no one dared tell Peter directly.

They had a young son at the time, and a daughter on the way. Kira had already decided that she would be called Maya. For several months they had a dad who was present without being present. There are no former hockey players, because they never quite reach the same temperature as the rest of us. It's like trying to rehabilitate returning soldiers: they drift about aimlessly when they don't have anyone to fight with or for. The whole of Peter's life had been divided into times and schedules and bus trips and locker rooms. Meals and training sessions and even regulated times for sleep. One of the toughest concepts to teach someone like that is "everyday life."

There were days when Kira thought about giving up and asking for a divorce. But she remembered one of the stupid slogans written on scraps of paper all over Peter's room when he was growing up: "The only time I'm not moving forward is when I'm taking aim."

Peter is alone in the hallway. The door to Sune's office is closed. It's the first time in twenty years that Peter has seen it like that, and he's never been more grateful. He thinks about the words on the wall of the president's office: "Culture, Values, Community." He remembers something Sune told him during preseason training a lifetime ago: "Culture is as much about what we encourage as what we permit." For Sune the coach, that applied to making them run through the forest until they threw up, but for Sune the man it also applied to life.

Peter gets some coffee and drinks it, even though it tastes like something has crawled into the cup and died there, then stops in front of the team photograph from their silver-medal season, the club's greatest triumph. There are copies of the picture all around the building. Robbie Holts is standing next to him in the middle row. They haven't so much as spoken to each other since Peter came back to Beartown, and hardly a day goes by without Peter wondering what life would have been like if they had changed places. If Robbie had been the more talented one, if he had gone to Canada, if Peter had stayed here and worked in the factory. How different life would have been then.

He remembers one morning in Canada when Kira pulled him out of bed before the children woke up. Forced him to sit and look at them as they slept. "They're your team now," she whispered, over and over again, until tears from his eyes started to run down her cheeks.

That year they built a new life, stayed in Canada, and fought their way through every battle that came their way. Kira got a job in a law firm, Peter worked part-time selling insurance. They made it work, they settled, and then—just as Kira started to make plans for the future—came the nights when they realized something was wrong.

All through their childhood boys are told that all they need to do is their best. That it will be enough, as long as they give their all. Peter looks himself in the eye in the photograph; he's so incredibly young. He met Kira for the first time the evening they lost that last game down in the capital. The fact that they'd made it as far as that was a miracle, but that wasn't good enough for Peter. For him it was more than a game, it was a chance for a small town to show the big city that not everything can be bought. The papers in the capital had patronizingly decided to label the game "The Call of the Wild," and Peter had looked each of his teammates in the eye and roared: "They may have the money, but hockey belongs to us!" They gave it everything they had. It wasn't enough.

That evening the team went out to celebrate winning silver. Peter sat on his own all night in a little family-run restaurant next to the hotel. Kira was behind the bar. Peter broke down in tears in front of her, not for his own sake but because he wouldn't be able to look his town in the eye again. Because he'd let them all down. It was a pretty weird first date, but he's able to smile about it in hindsight. What was it she said to him? "Have you ever considered not feeling so sorry for yourself?" That made him laugh, and he didn't stop for several days. He's fallen for her every day since then.

And once, a long time afterward, when Kira had been drinking and was a bit too loud, the way she gets after too much wine, she held his ears so tightly that he genuinely thought they were going to come off, and when he lowered his head to hers she whispered: "You adorable stupid idiot, don't you realize that's when I fell in love with you? You were a lost little kid from the backwoods, but I knew that someone who was second-best in the country but was still crying because he was worried about disappointing the people he loved, that person was going to turn out to be a good man. He'd be a good father. He'd protect his children. He'd never let anything happen to his family."

Kira remembers every inch of the descent into darkness. The greatest terror of every parent, waking up and listening out for small breaths. And every night you feel so foolish when you hear them, as usual, for worrying about nothing. "How did I become someone like this?" you think. You promise yourself that you'll relax, because of course you know that nothing's going to happen. But the following night you still lie there wide awake, staring up at the ceiling and shaking your head, until you tell yourself, "Just tonight, then." And you creep out of bed and put your palms to your children's little chests to feel them rising and falling. And then one night one of them falls and doesn't rise again as strongly.

And then you fall. All the hours in the waiting room at the hospital, all the nights on the floor beside the boy's bed, that morning when the doctor told Peter because no one dared tell Kira. They simply fell. If they hadn't had Maya, would they have been able to go on living? How does anyone do that?

Kira was so pleased when they moved away; she could never imagine that she would feel so happy to move back. But they could start again there. She and Peter and Maya. And then Leo came along. They were happy, or at least as happy as a family can be when it's burdened by a grief too large to be absorbed by time.

But Kira still doesn't know how to deal with it.

Peter puts his hand on the glass of the frame. Kira never stopped making his pulse throb in his throat; he still loves her the way you do when you're a teenager, when your heart swells in your chest and makes you feel like you can't breathe. But she had been wrong. He couldn't protect his family. And not a single day goes by without him wondering what he could have done differently. Could he have made a deal with God? If he had sacrificed all his talent? Given up all his success? His own life? What would God have given him in exchange? Could he have changed places in the coffin with his firstborn son?

At night Kira still goes around the house, counting their children. One, two, three.

Two in their beds. One in heaven.

10

Say what you like about Beartown, it can take your breath away. When the sun rises above the lake, when the mornings are so cold that the oxygen itself is crisp, when the trees seem to bow respectfully over the ice in order to let as much light as possible reach the children playing on it, then you can't help wondering how anyone could choose to live in places where all you can see are concrete and buildings. Four-year-olds play outdoors on their own here, and there are still people who have never locked their front doors. After Canada, Maya's parents were overprotective to a degree that might have appeared a bit unusual even in a big city, so in Beartown it seemed almost psychotic. There's something very peculiar about growing up in the shadow of a dead older brother: children in that situation become either terrified of everything or nothing at all. Maya fell into the second group.

She parts from Ana in the hallway with their secret handshake. They were in their first year at school when Ana came up with it, but Maya was the one who realized that the only way to keep it secret was to do it so quickly that no one had time to see the different elements: fist up, fist down, palm, palm, butterfly, bent finger, pistols, jazz hands, minirocket, explosion, ass-to-ass, outbitches. Ana came up with the descriptions. Maya still laughs every time they bang their backsides together at the end and Ana turns her back on her, throwing her hands up in the air and yelling: ". . . and Ana is OUT, bitches!" and walks away.

But she doesn't do it as loudly anymore, not when they're at school, not when other people can see her. She pulls her arms in, lowers her voice, tries to fit in. Throughout their childhood Maya loved her best friend because she wasn't like any other girl she had met, but life as a teenager seems to have acted like sandpaper on Ana. She's getting smoother and smoother, smaller and smaller.

Sometimes Maya misses her.

Kira looks at the time, pulls some papers from her briefcase, and hurries off to a meeting, then straight on to another one. She's running late as usual as she hurries back to her office, already behind schedule. There's a label she used to love but which she loathes when it's pronounced in a Beartown accent: "career woman." Peter's friends call her that, some in admiration and some with distaste, but no one calls Peter a "career man." It strikes a nerve because Kira recognizes the insinuation: you have a "job" so you can provide for your family, whereas a "career" is selfish. You have one of those for your own sake. So now she's dangling somewhere between two worlds, and feels just as guilty when she's in the office as she does when she's at home.

Everything has become a compromise. When she was young, she used to dream about criminal trials and dramatic courtroom showdowns, but the reality now is agreements, contracts, settlements, meetings, and emails, emails, emails. "You've overqualified for this," her boss told her when she got the job, as if she had any choice. Her qualifications and skills could have given her a six-figure salary in plenty of places around the world, but this is the only major law firm within commuting distance of Beartown. Their clients are forestry companies and council-run partnerships; the work is often monotonous, rarely stimulating, yet always stressful. Sometimes she thinks to their time in Canada and what all the hockey coaches there kept banging on about: they wanted "the right kind of guy" for their team. Not just someone who could play, but someone who fit into the locker room, who didn't cause problems, who did his job. Someone who played hard and kept quiet. She wonders what it would take for a woman to be the right kind of guy.

Her train of thought is interrupted by a colleague—Kira's best work friend and the antidote to the sickness of boredom:

"I've never been so hungover. My mouth tastes like an ashtray. You didn't see me lick one last night, did you?"

"I wasn't with you last night," Kira says with a smile.

"Weren't you? Are you sure? After-work drinks. You were, weren't you? It was after-work drinks, wasn't it?" her colleague mutters, dropping onto a chair.

She's over six feet tall and carries every inch with pride. Instead of trying to shrink when faced with insecure men in the office, she shows up in bloodred shoes with heels as sharp as army knives and the height of Cuban cigars. She's a comic-book artist's fantasy—no one dominates a room the way she does. Or a party.

"What are you doing?" she asks.

"Work. What are you doing?" Kira counters.

Her colleague waves one hand and holds the other over her eyes, as if trying to pretend it's a chilled towel.

"I'll do some work in a minute."

"I need to get this finished before lunch," Kira sighs, bending over her papers.

Her colleague leans forward and scans the documents.

"It would have taken a normal person a month to grasp all that. You're too good for this firm, you know that, don't you?"

She always says she envies Kira's brain. In return, Kira is envious of her colleague's middle finger, which gets regular use. Kira smiles wearily.

"What is it you usually say?"

"Stop whining, shut up, and send the invoice," her colleague says with a grin.

"Stop whining, shut up, and send the invoice," Kira repeats.

The two women lean across the table and high-five each other.

A teacher is standing in a classroom, trying to get a group of seventeen-year-old boys to be quiet. Jeanette is having one of those mornings when she asks herself why she puts herself through this—not just teaching, but Beartown itself. She raises her voice, but the boys at the back aren't even ignoring her on purpose; she's quite convinced that they genuinely haven't noticed she's there. There are other pupils in the class who want more than this, but they're invisible, inaudible. They just lower their heads and close their eyes tightly and hope that the hockey season will soon be over.

One of the plainest truths about both towns and individuals is that they usually don't turn into what we tell them to be, but what they are told they are. The teacher has always been told she's too young for this. Too attractive. That they won't respect her. Those boys have been told that they're bears, winners, immortal.

Hockey wants them that way. Needs them that way. Their coach teaches them to go hard into close combat on the ice. No one stops to think about how to switch that attitude off when they leave the locker room. It's easier to pin the blame on her: She's too young. Too attractive. Too easily offended. Too difficult to respect.

In a final attempt to get control of the situation, the teacher turns to the team captain; he's sitting in a corner tapping at his phone. She says his name. He doesn't react.

"Kevin!" she repeats. He raises an eyebrow.

"Yes? How can I help you, my lovely?"

The juniors around him laugh as if on command.

"Are you actually following what I'm teaching you here? It's going to be on the exam," she says.

"I already know it," Kevin replies.

It irritates her intensely that he doesn't say this provocatively or aggressively. His voice is as neutral as a weather forecaster's.

"Really? You already know it?" she snorts.

"I've read the book. You're just telling us the same things it says there. My phone could do your job."

The juniors roar with laughter so loudly that the windows rattle, and then of course Bobo sees his chance, the biggest and most predictable boy in the school, always ready to kick someone who's already down.

"Just calm down, sweet cheeks!" he yells.

"What did you call me?" she snaps, then realizes that's exactly the response he wants.

"It's a compliment. I love sweets."

Howls of laughter wash over her. "Sit down!"

"Just calm down, now, sweet cheeks. I said you should be proud."

"Proud?"

"Yes. In a couple of weeks' time you'll be able to go around telling everyone you meet that *you* once taught the legendary junior team who brought the gold back to Beartown!"

A large part of the class roars its approval, hands banging radiators, feet stamping the floor. She knows it's too late even to try to raise her voice now, she's already lost. Bobo stands up on his desk like a cheerleader and sings, "We are the bears! We are the bears! We are the bears, the bears from BEARTOWN!" The other juniors leap up onto their desks and join in. By the time the teacher leaves the classroom they're all standing bare-chested, chanting, "THE BEARS FROM BEARTOWN!" All apart from Kevin, who just sits there quietly looking at his phone, as calm as if he were alone in a dimly lit room.

In Kira's office, her colleague runs her tongue back and forth across her teeth in disgust.

"Seriously, it feels like I've eaten someone's toupee. You don't think I could have ended up sleeping with that guy in accounting, do you? I was planning to sleep with the other one. Whatever his job is. The one with the tight buns and scruffy hair."

Kira laughs. Her colleague is single to the extreme, whereas Kira is fanatically monogamous. The lone she-wolf and the mother hen, doomed to envy each other. Her colleague lowers her voice to ask:

"Okay. Who would you pick from the office? If you had to pick one?"

"Not this again."

"I know, I know, you're married. But if your husband was dead."

"HELLO?"

"Christ, it's hardly that sensitive! Okay, if he was sick. Or in a coma. Better? Who would you sleep with if your husband was in a coma?"

"No one!" Kira hisses.

"If the survival of the human race depended on it? The guy with the buns and the hair, right? Not the badger, surely?"

"Remind me, which one's the badger?"

Her colleague does what Kira has to admit is a fairly impressive impression of a man who has recently been appointed to management and happens to bear a striking resemblance to a badger. Kira laughs so hard she almost knocks her coffee over.

"Don't be mean to him. He's a nice guy."

"So are pigs, but we don't let them inside the house."

Her colleague hates the badger, not as an individual but for what he represents. He got a position in management even though everyone knows it should have gone to Kira. It's a subject Kira tries to avoid discussing, seeing as she can't bring herself to tell her friend the truth: Kira was offered the job, but turned it down. It would have meant too much work in the evenings, too much travelling. She couldn't do that to her family. And now she's sitting here, not daring to tell her colleague because she doesn't want to see the disappointment in her eyes. That Kira was offered the chance but didn't take it.

Her colleague bites off a broken nail and spits it out into the wastepaper basket.

"Have you seen the way he looks at women? The badger? Those beady little eyes. I bet you a thousand kronor he's the sort who'd want you to shove a pen up . . ."

"I'm trying to WORK!" Kira interrupts.

Her colleague looks genuinely baffled.

"What? It's an objective observation. I have extensive experience on the subject of markers, but fine, sit on your high horse and pretend you're morally untouchable just because your husband's in a coma!"

"You're still drunk, aren't you?" Kira says, laughing.

"Does he like that sort of thing? Peter? Pens?"

"NO!"

Her colleague apologizes at once, sounding upset:

"Sorry, is that a sensitive subject? Have you argued about it?"

Kira hustles her out of her office. She hasn't got time for any more laughter today. She's got a schedule to stick to, or at least try to. Then one of the bosses comes along and asks if she's got time to "take a quick look" at a contract, which swallows an hour. A client rings with an urgent problem, which takes another hour. Leo rings and says his training session has been brought forward half an hour because the junior team needs more time on the ice, so she'll have to get home earlier this afternoon. Maya calls and asks her mom to buy new strings for her guitar on the way home. Peter sends a text saying he'll be late home tonight. Her boss comes in again and asks if Kira has time for "a quick meeting." She doesn't. She goes anyway.

Trying to be the right kind of guy. Even if it's impossible to be the right kind of mom at the same time.

Maya can still remember the first time she met Ana. They held hands before they saw each other's faces. Maya was six years old and was out skating on the lake on her own, something her parents would never have allowed, but they were at work and the babysitter had dozed off in an armchair. So Maya grabbed her skates and sneaked out. Perhaps she was looking for danger, perhaps she simply trusted that an adult hand would catch her before anything went wrong, perhaps she was just like most children: born to seek out adventure. Dusk fell sooner than she was expecting, she didn't see the change in the color of the ice, and when it gave way beneath her the water paralyzed her before she even had time to feel frightened. She didn't stand a chance, six years old, with no crampons or studs, and her arms so cold that she could barely cling on to the edge. She was already dead. Say what you like about Beartown, but it can take your breath away. In a single second.

She saw Ana's hand long before she saw Ana. How one six-year-old girl managed to pull out another girl the same age, weighed down by a soaking wet snowsuit, Maya will never understand, but that's what Ana was like. You can't keep two girls apart after a thing like that. Ana, a child of nature who went hunting and fishing but didn't quite understand people, ended up best friends with Maya, who was the exact opposite.

The first time Maya was over at Ana's and heard her parents arguing, she understood that Ana was on thin ice in ways all her own. Ana has spent more nights at Maya's than at home ever since. They came up with their secret handshake to remind each other that it was always "sisters before misters," which Ana used to repeat like a mantra before she even knew what the words meant. She took every chance she got to nag Maya about fishing or hunting or climbing trees. It used to drive Maya crazy, seeing as she would much rather be at home playing her guitar, preferably next to a radiator. But God, she loved Ana!

Ana was a tornado. A jagged, hundred-sided peg in a community where everyone was supposed to fit into round holes. When they were ten years old she taught Maya to shoot a hunting rifle. Maya remembers that Ana's dad always hid the key to his gun cabinet in a box on top of a cupboard at the back of the cellar that stank of mold. Apart from keys and a couple of bottles of vodka, the box was also full of porn magazines. Maya stared at them in shock. Ana noticed and simply shrugged her shoulders: "Dad doesn't understand how the Internet works." They stayed in the forest until the ammunition ran out. Then Ana, who always had a knife with her, made swords for them both out of tree limbs and they fenced among the trees until it got dark.

Now Maya watches her friend walk off down the corridor, sees her pull her arms down as if she's embarrassed, without even daring to yell "OUT," because all she dreams about these days is being as normal as possible. Maya hates being a teenager, hates sandpaper, hates round holes. Misses the girl who pretended to be a knight in the forest.

We become what we are told we are. Ana has always been told that she's wrong.

Benji is slumped so low on his cushion in the headmaster's office that there's more of him on the floor than on the chair. They're going through the motions. The headmaster has to tell him off for being late so often this term when all he really wants to talk about is hockey. Like everyone else. Any thought of expulsion or other disciplinary measures is out of the question.

From time to time Benji thinks about his eldest sister, Adri, the one with the kennels. The further the juniors have progressed in the tournament, the more Benji has realized how similar he is to the dogs: if you make yourself useful, you get a longer leash.

They hear Jeanette long before she storms through the door.

"THOSE ANIMALS . . . THOSE . . . I CAN'T BEAR IT ANY-MORE!" she roars before she's even entered the room.

"Calm down now, sweet cheeks," Benji says with a smile, and is quite convinced that she's going to punch him.

"SAY THAT AGAIN! SAY THAT ONE MORE TIME AND I SWEAR YOU WON'T BE ABLE TO PLAY IN THAT GAME!" she roars at him with her hand raised.

The headmaster lets out an anxious yelp and flies up from his chair, takes her by the arm, and leads her out into the corridor. Perhaps grabbing someone's arm is the correct response. But both Benji and the teacher know that it should have been Benji's.

In a classroom farther down the corridor Bobo slips off his desk and tumbles to the floor, still bare-chested and in the middle of "the bears from BEART . . ." There are two types of seventeen-year-olds around him: those who like hockey, and those who hate it. The ones who are terrified that he's hurt himself, and those who hope he has.

11

A simple truth, repeated as often as it is ignored, is that if you tell a child it can do absolutely anything, or that it can't do anything at all, you will in all likelihood be proven right.

Lars has no leadership style. He just yells. Amat has had him as his coach throughout his time on the boys' team, and there are few things that worry him more than David being given the job of coaching the A-team next season, so that Lars ends up in charge of the junior team just as Amat gets there. Two more years with this man is more than he could handle, even for the sake of hockey. Lars has no grasp of tactics or technique, he just thinks everything is warfare. His only pep talk is bellowing that they "have to win the battle for the fortress!" and that they mustn't "get fucked up the ass!" If the fifteen-year-olds had been clutching axes in their hands instead of hockey sticks, he would have coached them in exactly the same way.

Obviously it's much worse for the others on the team. You can get away with a lot when you're the best, and that's what Amat has become this season. Zacharias has had to suffer one of Lars's patented saliva-fountains as he yells: "Are the scars from your sex-change itching, Zach?" but Amat has sailed through. When he thinks about how close he came to giving up completely twelve months ago, he isn't sure if he should feel happy that he carried on, or aghast at how close he came to not doing so.

He was tired, that's all he can remember. Tired of fighting, tired of everyone shouting at him, tired of dealing with so much crap and abuse, tired of the locker room, where the juniors snuck in during one training session to cut up his shoes and throw his clothes in the shower. Tired of trying to prove he was more than the things they called him: a zero from the Hollow. The cleaner's son. Too small. Too weak.

One evening after training he went home and didn't get out of bed for four days. His mom very patiently left him alone. Only on the fifth morning did she open his door, ready to go to work, and say:

"You might be playing with bears. But that doesn't mean you have to forget that you're a lion."

When she kissed him on the forehead and put her hand on his heart, he whispered:

"It's too hard, Mom."

"Your dad would have been so proud if he could have seen you play."

"Dad probably didn't even know what hockey was," he mumbled.

"That's why!" she replied in a raised voice, and she was a woman who took great pride in the fact that she never raised her voice.

She'd managed to clean the stands and the corridor and office, and had reached the locker room that morning when the caretaker walked past and knocked gently on the doorframe. When she looked up he nodded toward the ice and smiled. Amat had put down his gloves, hat, and jacket between the lines. That was the morning the boy realized that the only way to become better than the bears at their own game was to stop playing it their way.

David is sitting at the top of the stands. Now thirty-two, he's spent more of that time inside rinks than outside them. When David became a coach, Sune forced him to watch every A-team game for an entire season from up here in the nosebleed seats, and now it's a habit he can't shake. Hockey looks different from up here, and the truth is that Sune and David always saw eye to eye about the questions, they just didn't agree on the answers. Sune wanted to keep all the players in their own age group as long as possible, so that they would have time to work on their weaknesses and form rounded, focused teams without any shortcomings. David thought that attitude only led to the creation of teams where no one was exceptional. Sune believed that a player who was allowed to play with older players would only play

to his strengths, and David agreed—he just couldn't see the problem with that. He didn't want a whole troupe of players who were all
pretty good at exactly the same things, he wanted specialists.

Sune was like Beartown: a firm adherent of the old faith that no tree
should grow too tall, naively convinced that hard work was enough.
That's why the club has collapsed at the same rate that unemployment in the town has rocketed. Good workers aren't enough on their
own, someone needs to have big ideas as well. Collectives only work
if they're built around stars.

There are plenty of men in this club who think that everything
in hockey "should be the way it's always been." Whenever he hears
that, David feels like rolling himself up in a carpet and screaming until
his vocal cords give out. As if hockey has ever been constant! When
it was invented you weren't even allowed to pass the puck forward,
and two generations ago everyone played without a helmet. Hockey
is like every other living organism: it has to adapt and evolve, or else
it will die.

David can no longer remember how many years he has been arguing about this with Sune, but on the evenings when he gets home in
his very blackest mood his girlfriend usually teases him, asking if he's
"fallen out with daddy again?" It was quite funny to start with. Sune
was more than just a coach when David himself became one, he was
a role model. The end of a hockey player's career is an endless series
of doors closing with you on the wrong side, and David couldn't have
lived without a team, without feeling he was part of something. When
injury forced him off the ice at the age of twenty-two, Sune was the
only person who understood that.

Sune taught David to be a coach at the same time as he was teaching
Peter to be GM. In a lot of ways they're each other's opposite. David
could get into an argument with a door, and Peter was so averse to
conflict that he couldn't even kill time. Sune hoped they'd comple-
ment one another, but they've developed a mutual loathing instead.

For years David's deepest shame was the fact that he could never get over the jealousy he felt whenever Sune and Peter would go into Peter's office without inviting him along. His love of the camaraderie of the sport was grounded in a fear of exclusion. So eventually he did what all ambitious pupils do to their teachers: he rebelled.

He was twenty-two when he began coaching this group of seven-year-old boys, Kevin, Benji, and Bobo among them. He has been coaching them for ten years now, melding them into one of the best junior teams in the whole country, and he has finally realized that he can no longer stay loyal to Sune. The players are more important; the club is bigger than that.

David knows what people in the town are going to say when he gets Sune's job. He knows a lot of them aren't going to be happy. But they're going to like the results.

Lars blows his whistle to signal the end of the practice so close to Zacharias's ear that the boy trips over his own stick. Lars grins unkindly.

"And worst in training today was, as usual, little Miss Zach. So you get the honor of collecting the pucks and cones!"

Lars leaves the ice with the rest of the boys' team trailing behind him. A few of them laugh at Zacharias and he tries to give them the finger, but it's surprisingly hard to do that when you're wearing hockey gloves. Amat has already started circling the ice to gather the pucks. Their friendship has always been like that: as long as Zacharias is left on the ice, Amat doesn't leave.

Once Lars is out of sight, Zacharias gets angrily to his feet and mimics the coach's exaggeratedly forward-leaning style of skating as he scratches himself hard between the buttocks:

"COLLECT THE PUCKS! DEFEND THE FORTRESS! DON'T GET FUCKED UP THE ASS! NO ASS-FUCKING ON MY ICE! HOLD ON . . . WHAT THE . . . ? WHAT'S THIS? IN MY ASS?! IS IT A FUCK? IS IT A LITTLE FUCK? THERE'S A LITTLE FUCK IN MY ASS, AMAT! I ORDER YOU TO GET IT OUT AT ONCE!"

He tries to reverse into Amat, who slips nimbly out of the way, laughing, leaving Zach to back straight into the open team bench and land in a heap.

"Do you want to stay and watch the juniors practice?" Amat wonders, even though he knows Zach would never do that of his own accord.

"Stop saying 'juniors' when you mean 'watch Kevin.' I know he's your idol, Amat, but I have actually got a life. Carpe diem! Laughter and love!"

Amat sighs.

"Fine, forget it . . ."

"IS THAT KEVIN ERDAHL IN YOUR ASS, AMAT?" Zacharias cries.

Amat taps his stick restlessly on the ice.

"Do you want to do something this weekend, then?"

He really does try to make the question sound nonchalant. As if he hadn't actually been thinking about it all day. Zacharias gets up from the bench with the body language of a baby elephant that's been shot with a tranquilizer dart.

"I've got two new games! But you'll have to bring your own handset, seeing as you broke my other one last time."

Amat looks offended by his friend's recollection of events, given that he had broken the handset with his forehead when Zacharias threw it at him in a fit of temper because he was losing. He clears his throat and collects the last of the pucks.

"I just thought we could go . . . out."

Zacharias looks as if his friend has suggested pouring poison in each other's ears.

"Go out where?"

"Just . . . out. People go . . . out. That's what they do."

"You mean Maya does?"

"I mean PEOPLE."

Zacharias gets up on his skates and starts dancing on tiptoe and singing:

"Amat and Maya, sitting in a treeee, Amat squirts her with his seeeed . . ."

Amat slaps a puck hard into the boards beside him, but can't help laughing.

David is standing with Lars in the corridor outside the locker room. "It's a mistake!" Lars insists.

"However unlikely it might sound, I heard you the first twelve times. Go and get the juniors ready for practice," David replies coldly.

Lars lumbers off. David massages his temples. Lars isn't an entirely useless assistant coach. David can put up with the shouting and swearing because that's part of locker-room culture, and, dear God, some of the guys on the team do need a tyrant at practice to make sure they actually put the pads on the right parts of their body. But sometimes David can't help wondering how the junior team will function if Lars is going to take charge of it. The man knows no more about hockey than the average noisy fan in the stands, and David could go out into the street, throw a stone, and whatever he hit that had a pulse would know as much as them.

Amat and Zach are laughing as they approach but fall silent abruptly when they catch sight of David. The boys squeeze against the wall so as not to get in his way. Amat visibly starts when David holds up his hand.

"Amat, isn't it?"

Amat nods.

"We . . . we were just collecting the pucks . . . we were only messing about . . . I mean, I know Zach was imitating Lars but it was only a j . . ."

David looks baffled. Amat gulps.

"Actually, well, if you didn't see anything, then . . . it was . . . nothing."

David smiles. "I've seen you sitting in the stands during the junior

team's training sessions. You've been there more often than some of
the players."

Amat nods nervously. "I . . . Sorry . . . I just want to learn."

"That's good. I know you've been studying Kevin's moves; he's
a good example. You ought to check out how he always looks at the
defenseman's skates in any one-on-one situation: as soon as they angle
their skates and shift their center of gravity, Kevin taps the puck and
makes his move."

Amat nods dumbly. David is looking him right in the eye, and the
boy isn't used to adult men doing that.

"Anyone can see that you're fast, but you need to practice your
shooting. Practice waiting for the goalie to move, shoot against the
flow. Can you learn that, do you think?"

Amat nods. David slaps him hard on the shoulder.

"Good. Learn it fast, because you're training with the juniors in a
quarter of an hour. Go into the locker room and get a jersey."

Amat's hand moves instinctively toward one ear, as if he needs
to clean it out to make sure he hasn't misheard. David has already
walked off.

Zacharias waits until the coach has swung around the corner before
wrapping his arms around his friend's neck. Amat is hyperventilating.
Zacharias clears his throat:

"Seriously, though, Amat . . . if you had to choose between sleeping
with Maya and sleeping with Kevin, you'd pick . . . ?"

"Shut up," Amat says, laughing.

"I'm just checking!" Zacharias grins, then pats him on his helmet
and growls: "Kill them, my friend. Kill them!"

Amat takes a breath as deep as the lake behind the rink, then for
the first time walks past the boys' team's locker room and steps across
the threshold into the juniors'. He is met instantly by a hurricane of
booing and swearing and a chorus of "GET OUT OF HERE, YOU
FUCKING MAGGOT!" from the older players, but when David

emerges from the hallway a silence so complete settles that you could hear a jockstrap drop. David nods to Lars and Lars reluctantly tosses a jersey at Amat. It stinks. Amat has never been happier.

Standing outside in the hallway is his best friend.

There are no almosts in ice hockey.

12

A long marriage is complicated. So complicated, in fact, that most people in one sometimes ask themselves: "Am I still married because I'm in love, or just because I can't be bothered to let anyone else get to know me this well again?"

Kira knows that her complaining drives Peter mad. That he sometimes feels browbeaten. Sometimes she calls him five times a day simply to check that he's done something he promised to do.

Peter's office is perfectly organized, the desk so clean you could eat off it. The shelves are lined with LPs that he doesn't dare take home because he's worried Kira will force him either to throw them away or buy a bigger house. He orders them online and has them delivered to the rink, effectively turning the receptionist into his dealer. Some people hide the fact that they smoke from their spouse. Peter hides his online shopping.

He buys the records because they calm him down. They remind him of Isak. He's never told her that.

Kira can't remember exactly how old the children were when the snowstorm hit, but they hadn't been living in Beartown long enough for her to get used to the forces of nature. It was around Christmas, the children weren't at school, but there was a crisis at work so Kira had to go off to an important meeting. Peter took Maya and Leo out tobogganing and Kira stood by the car and watched them disappear into the swirling whiteness. It was so beautiful and so ominous at the same time. She felt so bereft once they had vanished from sight that she cried all the way to the office.

When Peter got injured in Canada and Kira started work, Peter was left at home alone with Isak. One day the child had a stomachache and wouldn't stop screaming. Panic-stricken, Peter tried everything. He rocked him and took him out in the stroller and tried all the home remedies he had ever heard of, but nothing worked. Until he put a record on. Perhaps it was something about the old record-player—the crackle in the speakers, the voices filling the room—but Isak fell completely silent. Then he smiled. And then he fell asleep in Peter's arms. That's the last time Peter can remember really feeling like a good father. The last time he had been able to tell himself that he actually knew what he was doing. He's never told Kira that, has never told anyone. But now he buys records in secret because he keeps hoping that feeling might come back, if only for a moment.

After her meeting that morning close to Christmas, Kira called Peter. He didn't answer. The man who otherwise always answers. Then she heard on the radio that the snowstorm had hit the forest and people were being advised to stay indoors. She called a thousand times, left shouted messages for him, no response. She threw herself in the car and drove with her foot to the floor, even though she could barely see a yard in front of the hood. She ran out into the trees where they had left her that morning and started yelling hysterically, then collapsed and dug desperately at the snow with her hands, as if she might find her children there. Her ears and fingertips froze, and afterward she didn't know how to explain what had happened inside her. Only several years later did she realize that it was a nervous breakdown.

Ten minutes later her phone rang. It was Peter and the children, carefree and untroubled, wondering where she was. "WHERE ARE YOU?" she yelled. "At home," they replied, their mouths full of ice-cream and cinnamon buns. When Kira asked why, Peter replied uncomprehendingly: "There was a snowstorm, so we came home." He had forgotten to charge his phone. It was in a drawer in the bedroom.

Kira has never told him, has never told anyone, but she's never really recovered from that snowstorm. From the feeling she had in the car that she'd lost them too. So now she sometimes calls her husband and children several times a day just to complain to them. To reassure herself that they're still there.

Peter puts a record on, but today it doesn't help. He can't stop thinking about Sune. The same thoughts keep going around his head for hours as he stares at a dark computer screen and throws a small rubber ball harder and harder against the wall.

When his phone rings, the interruption is so welcome that he even forgets to be annoyed at his wife for always taking it for granted that he's going to forget everything he's promised to do.

"Did you drop the car off at the garage?" she asks, even though she can already hear the answer.

"Yes! Of course I did!" Peter says, with the absolute conviction he only demonstrates when he's lying.

"How did you get to the office, then?" she asks.

"How do you know I'm at the office?"

"I can hear you bouncing that stupid ball against the wall." He sighs.

"You ought to work as a lawyer or something, has anyone ever told you that?"

The lawyer laughs.

"I'll consider it if I can't go professional with rock-paper-scissors."

"You're a cheat."

"You're a liar."

Peter's voice is shaking when he suddenly whispers:

"I love you so much."

Kira laughs so he won't hear her crying when she answers:

"Same here."

They both hang up. Kira is eating lunch four hours late in front of her computer so she can get her work done and still have time to stop to buy new guitar strings for Maya before she rushes home to take Leo to his evening practice. Peter isn't eating at all—he doesn't want to give his body the chance to throw up again.

A long marriage is complicated.

The juniors' locker room is quieter than usual. The significance of tomorrow's game has started to get under their skin. William Lyt, who's just turned eighteen but has a beard as thick as an otter's coat and weighs as much as a small car, leans toward Kevin and whispers in a voice that suggests he's in a prison film and is asking for a knife made out of a toothbrush, "Have you got any chewing tobacco?"

On one occasion last season David happened to mention to Lars that he had read that a single portion of chewing tobacco did more damage to a person's fitness than a whole case of beer. Since then the juniors have been able to count on being yelled at so hard by both Lars and their parents that their hairline shifts backward if anyone so much as glimpses the telltale signs of wear on the pocket of their jeans from carrying a puck-shaped can of chewing tobacco.

"No," Kevin replies.

Lyt nods gratefully anyway, then sets off around the locker room in search of some. They play in the first line together, but no matter how much bigger and stronger Lyt is, Kevin has always been the obvious leader. Benji, who could perhaps be described as having certain issues with authority figures, is lying half asleep on the floor, but reaches for a stick and pokes Kevin in the stomach with it.

"What the . . . ?" Kevin snarls.

"Give me some chewing tobacco," Benji asks.

"Are you deaf? I just said I've run out."

Benji just lies there calmly on the floor looking at Kevin. Poking him in the stomach with the stick until Kevin snatches it from him, reaches for his jacket, and fishes out an almost full can of chewing tobacco.

"When are you going to learn that you can't lie to me?" Benji smiles.

"When are you going to start buying your own chewing tobacco?" Kevin replies.

"Probably around the same time."

Lyt returns without any chewing tobacco. He nods cheerily at Kevin.

"Are your parents coming to the game tomorrow? My mom's bought tickets for pretty much all my relatives!"

Kevin says nothing and starts to wrap tape around his stick. Benji sees this out of the corner of his eye and knows exactly what it means, so he turns to Lyt and grins:

"Sorry to disappoint you, Lyt, but your family comes to your games to see KEVIN play."

The room bursts into mocking laughter. And Kevin is spared having to say if his parents are coming to the game. Apart from the fact that Benji never has his own tobacco, it would be hard to find a better friend.

Amat is sitting in a corner, doing his very best imitation of an empty corner. As the youngest in the locker room, the maggot, he has good reason to be terrified of attracting attention. He keeps his gaze focused high, to avoid eye contact but still have time to react if anyone throws something at him. The walls of the locker room are covered with posters bearing slogans:

"Train hard, win easy."

"Team before individual."

"We play for the bear on the front of our jerseys, not the name on the back."

A recent addition with extralarge print right in the middle says:

"We're bad losers, because a good loser is someone who's used to losing!"

Amat's concentration wanders for a moment, and a little too late he sees Bobo walking across the floor. When the junior back leans his substantial bulk over him, Amat disappears into his shadow and waits for Bobo to hit him, but instead Bobo smiles. Which is much worse.

"You'll have to excuse the guys here, they haven't been brought up properly, you know."

Amat blinks hard, unsure how to respond. Bobo clearly enjoys this, and turns solemnly to the rest of the players, who are now silent and expectant. Bobo points angrily to the pieces of tape littering the floor.

"Look at this mess! Well? Is this how it's supposed to look? Do you think your mothers work here or something?"

The juniors grin. Bobo marches around demonstratively picking up pieces of tape until they fill his cupped hands. Then he holds them up toward the ceiling like a newborn child and proclaims:

"Guys, you need to remember that Amat's mother works here."

He meets the newcomer's gaze, smiles, and says:

"It's *Amat's* mother who works here, guys."

The pieces of tape hang in the air for a moment before raining down like small, sharp projectiles over the boy in the corner. Bobo's warm breath hits his ear as he commands:

"Can you give your mom a call, maggot? It really is very messy in here."

The locker room empties in ten seconds flat when Lars bellows "TIME!!!" Kevin hangs back till last. He passes Amat, who is on his knees gathering together the pieces of tape.

"It's only teasing," Kevin tells him, without a trace of sympathy.

"Sure. Only teasing," Amat repeats quietly.

"You know that girl . . . Maya . . . don't you?" Kevin says quickly on his way out through the door, as if it had only just occurred to him.

Amat looks up. He's watched every single junior training session this season. Things never just occur to Kevin. Everything he ever does is carefully considered and planned.

"Yes," Amat mumbles.

"Has she got a boyfriend?"

The answer is slow coming. Kevin taps the end of his stick expectantly on the floor. Amat stares down at his hands for a long time before his head finally and reluctantly moves a few inches from side to side. Kevin nods with satisfaction and walks out toward the ice. Amat stays where he is, chewing the inside of his lower lip and breathing hard through his nose, before tossing the tape in the trash and adjusting his pads. The last thing he sees before he goes through the door are words written in almost faded pencil on crumpled yellowed paper: *A great deal is expected of anyone who's been given a lot.*

He joins the juniors at the center circle. In the middle of it is an image of a large, threatening bear. The emblem of the club: strength, size, fear. Amat is the smallest person on the ice; he always has been. Ever since he was eight years old everyone has always told him that he won't be able to handle the next level, that he isn't tough enough, strong enough, big enough. But now he looks around him. Tomorrow this team is playing a semifinal game—they're one of the four best junior teams in the whole country. And he's here. He looks at Lyt and Bobo, at Lars and David, at Benji and Kevin, and thinks that he's going to show them he can play. Even if it kills him.

There's hardly anything that can make Peter feel as bad as hockey can. And, absurdly, there's hardly anything that can make him feel better. He keeps going over and over his situation, until the air in his office seems to run out. When the frustration and nausea start to get unbearable, he gets up and goes out to sit in the stands. He usually thinks better there, so he sits there bouncing his ball up and down on the concrete for so long he doesn't even notice the junior team start their training session down on the ice.

Sune emerges from his office to get some coffee, and on the way back he sees Peter sitting on his own in the stands. Sune knows that the GM is a grown man now, but it's hard for an old coach to stop thinking of his boys as boys.

Sune has never told Peter he loves him. It can be just as hard for father figures to say that as it is for real fathers. But he knows how afraid Peter is of disappointing everyone. All men have different fears that drive them, and Peter's biggest one is that he isn't good enough. Not good enough as a dad, not good enough as a man, and not good enough as GM. He lost his parents and his firstborn child, and every morning he's terrified that he's going to lose Kira, Maya, and Leo. He couldn't bear losing his club as well.

Sune sees him lift his head at last and look out across the juniors on the ice. Absentmindedly to start with—he's so used to following this team now that he counts them without thinking about it. Sune remains standing in the shadows just so he can see Peter's face when the penny finally drops.

For ten years Peter has helped shape this group of boys. He knows all their names, knows the names of all their parents. He ticks them off one by one in his mind to see if anyone's missing, if anyone might be injured, but they all seem to be there. In fact there's actually one too many. He counts again. Can't make sense of it. Until he sees Amat. Shortest and slightest of them all, still in equipment that looks a bit too big, just like in his skating classes. Peter just stares. Then he starts to laugh out loud.

He's been told so many times that the boy ought to stop playing, that he doesn't stand a chance, and now there he is, down on the ice. No one else has fought harder for this opportunity, and David is giving it to him today of all days. It's a small dream, nothing less, and Peter could do with a dream today.

Sune nods with both joy and sadness as he sees this. He goes back to his office and closes his door. This evening he'll hold one of his last training sessions with the A-team, and when the season is over he'll go home and—deep down—will wish what we all wish whenever we leave something: that it's going to collapse. That nothing will work without us. That we're indispensible. But nothing will happen, the rink will remain standing, the club will live on.

———

Amat adjusts his helmet and skates straight at an opponent, is checked and falls, but bounces up again. He gets hit and falls, but bounces up again. Peter leans back, smiling the way Kira says he only smiles when he's starting to fall asleep after a couple of grilled cheese sandwiches and half a glass of red wine. He allows himself fifteen minutes in the stands before he goes back to his office, with his heart feeling much lighter.

Fatima is standing in the washroom stretching her back, slowly and carefully, so no one hears her whimpering in pain. Sometimes she quite literally rolls off the sofa bed in the morning because her muscles refuse to let her body sit up. She hides it as well as she can, always lets her son sit by the aisle on the bus so he's facing away from her when they stand up to get off and can't see the expression on her face. She discreetly lets the ends of the plastic bags in the trash cans at work hang so she doesn't have to bend down quite so far to get hold of them when she empties them. Every day she finds new ways to compensate.

She apologizes as she creeps into Peter's office. If she hadn't he would never even have heard her. Peter glances up from his papers, checks what time it is, and looks surprised:

"But Fatima, what are you doing here now?"

Horrified, she takes two steps back.

"Sorry! I didn't mean to disturb you. I was just going to empty the trash and water the plants. I can come back when you've gone home!"

Peter rubs his forehead. Laughs.

"Hasn't anyone told you?"

"Told me what?"

"About Amat."

Peter realizes far too late that you can't say something like that to a mother. She immediately assumes that her son has either been in a terrible accident or has been arrested. There's nothing neutral when you say "Have you heard about your child?" to a parent.

Peter has to take her gently by the shoulders and lead her through the hallway, out into the stands. It takes her thirty seconds to realize what she's looking at. Then she claps her hands to her face and weeps. A boy training with the junior team, a head shorter than all the others. Her boy.

Her back has never been straighter. She could run a thousand miles.

13

The juniors are taking it easy; they've been told to play at seventy-five percent, no one wants any injuries before the game. Amat doesn't have that luxury. He throws himself into every situation, presses his skates down as hard as if he were trying to cut through to the concrete. He gets nothing for it. The juniors hack and trip him, force him into the boards, bring their sticks down on his wrists, and seek out every little weakness in every piece of equipment in order to hurt him. He gets cross-checked from behind, falls on all fours, sees Lyt's skates swerve, and doesn't have time to shut his eyes before the shower of ice hits his cheeks. He doesn't hear a word from David. After three-quarters of an hour Amat is so sweaty and exhausted and furious that it takes an epic exertion of will not to shriek, "Why am I here? Why did you bring me here if you're not going to let me play?" He hears them laughing behind his back. He knows that saying anything would only make them laugh even louder.

"I said as much. He's too weak," Lars snorts as Amat picks himself up off the ice for the thousandth time.

David looks at the time.

"Let's do some one-on-one. Amat against Bobo," he declares.

"Are you kidding? Amat's done two training sessions in a row, he's on his last legs!"

"Line them up," David replies bluntly.

Lars shrugs and blows his whistle. David stays by the boards. He knows his views on hockey aren't entirely uncontroversial; he knows he has to keep on winning for the club to continue to let him play his way. But it's also the only thing he cares about. And there are no winners without losers, no stars are born without others in the collective being sacrificed.

———

David's one-on-one training is simple: a line of cones is laid out on the ice, from one end all the way to the other, forming a sort of corridor between them and the boards. One defenseman and one forward meet. If the puck leaves the corridor the defenseman wins, so the exercise forces the forward to find a way to get past in a very confined space.

Lars is setting the line up seven or eight yards from the boards, but David tells him to make it even narrower. Lars looks surprised but does as he says, but then David gestures to him to make it even narrower. A couple of the juniors squirm uncomfortably but say nothing. In the end it's so narrow that it's only a couple of yards wide, so narrow that Amat doesn't stand a chance of using his speed against Bobo; there's nowhere for him to escape, he has to meet him, body to body. Amat, some ninety pounds lighter than Bobo, can see this too. His thighs are screaming with lactic acid when he sets off with the puck. The exercise naturally presupposes a certain sporting distance between attacker and defender, but Bobo gives him none. He comes straight at him and hits him with all his weight. Amat lands on the ice like a sack of flour. Loud laughter from the bench. David gives a slight gesture to indicate that they should do it again.

"Stand up like a man!" Lars shouts.

Amat adjusts his helmet. Tries to breathe normally. Bobo approaches faster this time, Amat's vision goes black for a moment, and when he opens his eyes again over by the boards he's not quite sure how he ended up there. He can't hear the laughter from the bench anymore, just a muffled echo in his ears. He gets to his feet and collects the puck. Bobo slams him in the chest with his stick. It's like hitting a low-hanging branch at full speed.

"Get up!" Lars roars.

Amat crawls to his knees. There's blood dripping from his mouth. He realizes he must have bitten his lip or tongue, or both. Bobo is leaning over him, but no longer cruelly. Almost concerned this time. A glimpse of sympathy in his eyes. Or at least humanity.

"What the hell, Amat . . . ? Just lie there. Don't you get it, this is what David wants? This is why you're here?"

Amat glances toward the bench. David is standing there with his arms folded, calmly waiting. Even Lars looks concerned now. And only then does Amat realize what Bobo means. The only thing that matters to David is winning, and only teams with self-confidence win big games. So what do you do the day before the biggest game ever? You let them bulldoze something weaker. Amat isn't here as a player—he's here as a sacrifice.

"Just stay lying down," Bobo tells him.

Amat disobeys him.

"Again," he whispers, his thighs trembling.

When Bobo doesn't reply, Amat hits the ice with his stick and roars: "AGAIN!!!"

He shouldn't have done that. The whole bench hears him. He hasn't given Bobo a choice. The back's eyes darken.

"Okay. Whatever you want. Stupid idiot."

Amat sets off, Bobo waits toward the center, forcing him out toward the boards, and as Amat skates Bobo ignores the puck altogether and goes straight for his body. Amat's head hits the boards, he collapses onto the ice, and it takes him ten seconds before he can even get to his knees.

"Again?" Bobo growls through gritted teeth.

Amat doesn't answer. He leaves a small trail of blood behind him as he goes over to the far blue line, collects the puck, and straightens up. He sees Bobo's body tense as he circles threateningly across the bear in the center circle and into the corridor of cones to put an end to this, once and for all. "Like a man," Amat thinks to himself. Like a man.

He shouldn't have the energy to take off the way he does. He ought to refuse to skate straight at Bobo after the beating he's taken. But at a certain point in a person's life you either sink or swim, and nothing really matters anymore. What else could they do to him now beyond this? Fuck them. Bobo heads toward him at full speed, but at the very

last instant Amat doesn't stand up like a man, he folds himself double.
When he sees Bobo's skates change angle he slips the puck between
them and nimbly spins his body out of and away from the check.

In one stride he's past Bobo, in two he's caught up with the puck,
in three he's inside the offensive zone. He hears Bobo crash into the
boards behind him, but now he only has eyes for the goalie. He pulls
the puck off to the right, left, right, and waits for the goalie to move
sideways, waits, waits, waits, and when he finally sees the goalie's
skates tilt a quarter of an inch he shoots midskate into the opposite
corner. Against the flow.

A lion among bears.

Bobo sets off in blind fury, all the way from the other side of the rink.
He's one of the worst skaters on the team, but when he reaches Amat
with his stick raised he still has enough speed and weight-advantage
to put the boy in the hospital. Bobo doesn't hear the sound of skates
approaching rapidly from off to one side behind him, so the pain in his
jaw when the shoulder hits it is jarring.

Amat slumps in exhaustion some distance away, untouched. Bobo
lies on his back on the ice, blinking up at the lights as Benji's face leans
over him.

"That's enough, Bobo," he says.

Bobo nods stiffly. Benji helps him up and then ruefully rubs his own
shoulder.

The sound of a puck hitting the net can be the most wonderful sound
in the world when you're fifteen. When you're thirty-two as well.

"Write him up for tomorrow," David says as he leaves the bench.

When the juniors head off to the locker room, Amat is still lying on
the ice. Lars's voice reaches him through a milky haze:

"Gather up the pucks and cones. I usually tell the guys that there's
a fuck-embargo the night before a game, but there's no chance of you

getting a fuck so just lay off the wanking, because you're playing to-morrow."

It takes the boy an hour to half crawl, half stagger to the locker room. It's empty. The heating has been switched off. His shoes have been shredded and his clothes are lying soaking wet on the floor of the shower. It's the best day of his life.

14

It's Saturday, and everything is going to happen today. All the very best, and all the very worst.

The time is quarter to six in the morning when Maya is hunting through the kitchen cupboards in search of painkillers. She goes back to bed feeling feverish and full of snot, and curls up next to Ana. She's almost asleep when Ana kicks her and mutters sleepily:

"Play for me."

"Be quiet."

"Play for me!"

Maya grunts:

"All right, I've got a question for you: always hear me play the guitar every time you ask me to, or have me not KILL YOU WITH IT!?"

Ana sulks in silence for a long time. Then she gently touches Maya's thigh with her permanently ice-cold toes.

"Please?"

So Maya gives up and starts playing. Because Ana loves falling asleep to the sound of the guitar, and because Maya loves her. The last thing Maya thinks before she, too, falls asleep, with her headache and cough, is that it feels like she ought to spend the day in bed.

The yard lies in thick darkness as Peter parks the little car outside the garage, beside the last building before the town stops and the forest takes over to the west. He slept for three anxious hours and woke up feeling overwhelmed.

Hog, his childhood friend, is standing in a poorly lit workshop bent over the engine of a Ford so old that it looks like it needs magic rather than a wrench. He's always been known as Hog, because he played like a wild boar. He's the same height as Peter but looks twice as wide. His stomach may have softened a little since their hockey years, but his arms and shoulders still look hard enough to have been beaten out of steel. He's wearing a T-shirt even though the garage door is open, and shakes Peter's hand, unconcerned about the fact that Peter doesn't have anything with which to wipe off the sticky mixture of oil and dirt left on his skin. Hog is well aware that the sticky mess will drive his friend mad.

"Thought Kia said you were going to drop it off yesterday," he says, grinning at the car.

"I was," Peter admits, doing his best not to think about the mess on his fingers.

Hog lets out a dry laugh, hands him a rag, and scratches his beard, which is so thick and unkempt it's started to look like a shaggy ski mask.

"Annoyed?"

"Let's just say she wasn't exactly over the moon," Peter confesses.

"Do you want coffee?"

"Have you got any fresh?"

Hog chuckles.

"Fresh coffee. Have you gone all soft now? There's some instant and a kettle in the corner."

"I think I'll leave it."

Hog pats his hand intentionally as he walks past, and Peter wipes it with an irritated smile. Friends for forty years, still the same joke. Hog grabs a flashlight and heads out into the yard, and Peter stands next to him shivering, full of the sense of inadequacy that only afflicts a man of a certain generation when he watches another man from the same generation repair his wife's car. Hog straightens up and spares Peter any technical jargon.

"Piece of crap. Bobo can do it when he wakes up. You can come pick it up at nine."

He goes back into the garage and absentmindedly picks up one of the Ford's heavy tires, making it look about as challenging as it is for Peter to put paper in the recycling bin. Bobo has unfortunately inherited both his father's raw strength and indifferent skating abilities. Hog was a terrifying defensive player in his day, but Sune always used to sigh: "That lad even manages to trip over the blue lines."

"Maybe you could let Bobo have a bit of a rest today? Big game this afternoon," Peter says.

Hog raises an eyebrow without looking up, then wipes his hand across his face to get rid of the sweat, leaving glossy streaks of oil in his beard.

"It'll take two hours to fix your car. If you're picking it up at nine, Bobo won't have to start until seven. That's a rest."

Peter opens his mouth but says nothing. A game of hockey is a game of hockey, but tomorrow this family will have to get up and earn a living again. Bobo is a solid back, but nowhere near professional standard. There are two younger kids in the family, and the global economy waits for no man. Bears shit in the woods, and everyone shits on Beartown.

Hog offers him a lift home but he's happy to walk. Needs to calm his nerves. He walks past the factory, which provides work for fewer and fewer people. He passes the big supermarket, which has put all the smaller stores out of business. He turns onto the road leading to the center of town, and then onto the main shopping street. The street gets shorter and shorter every year.

Ramona has survived long enough to get her pension, but one of the good things about owning your own pub is that no one can force you to stop working. The Bearskin has been hers since it stopped being her mother's, and before that it belonged to her grandfather. It still looks much the same, but Grandfather used to smoke indoors and now Ramona smokes outside. Three before breakfast; she lights the last of them on the dying stub of the second. The boys who play billiards and drink beer on a tab here every evening affectionately call her "the

Marlboro Mom." She has no children of her own; Holger couldn't have any, and perhaps never needed them either. The only family he wanted apart from Ramona was his sporting family, he used to say. Someone once asked him if there was any sport he didn't like, and he replied "Politics. They should stop showing that on TV." If the house had been on fire he'd have rescued Ramona first of all, but she'd have had to be clutching their Beartown Ice Hockey season tickets when he did so. It was theirs, that ridiculous sport. All his loudest laughter and warmest embraces had been left behind in the stands. She was the one who smoked, he was the one who got cancer. "I'm suffering from an ironic illness," he declared breezily. Ramona refuses to let anyone say that he died; she says he left her, because that's how she sees it. Like a betrayal. She's been left standing in the snow like a bare tree trunk without any bark, unprotected now that he's no longer here.

She has learned how to make the days pass. You just do. When the shift at the factory gets out in the afternoon, the Bearskin fills with young men she calls "the boys," and whom the police and the hockey club call far worse things. They're capable of a lot of crap, but they love Ramona the way Holger loved her. Maybe she's a bit too protective of them. She knows that. Beartown nurtures tough people, and the way life has turned out hasn't made her boys any softer. But they're all she has left of him, as close to her memories as she can bear to go.

Death does strange, incomprehensible things to loving souls. She still lives in the apartment above the pub. Some of the boys who drive forklifts over in the supermarket warehouse buy food for her there now that the little store across the road has closed down, so the old woman no longer goes any farther than the ashtray outside the door. Eleven years have passed since Holger left her, and at every A-team game, even when the rink is sold out, there are always two empty seats in the stands.

Peter sees her from a long way off. She waits for him to get closer.

"Are you looking for something, sir?" Ramona asks.

She's gotten older, but she's like her pub: always the same. The people who don't like the fact that the Bearskin offers a refuge to the town's thugs each evening talk about her as an unpleasant, sociopathic old woman who's losing her marbles, but even if Peter hardly ever sees her these days it still feels like coming home after a long journey each time he does.

"Don't know yet," he smiles.

"Nervous about the game?"

He doesn't have to answer. She stubs her third cigarette out under her shoe, tucks the butt inside the packet, and says:

"Whisky?"

He looks up at the sky. Soon the town will wake up, and even the sun seems to be planning an early appearance. Everyone will wake up to the dream that a junior team game can change everything. Can it make the council turn its gaze toward the forest again? Set up a hockey academy, maybe even build a shopping center? Make it so people giving directions say: *Stay on the road, past Hed,* instead of: *If you get to Beartown, you've gone too far?* Peter has spent so long convincing other people of all that, he no longer knows if he believes it himself.

"A cup of coffee would be good," he says.

She lets out a hoarse chuckle and maneuvers herself down the steps into the pub.

"That's always the way with sons of fathers who liked whisky a little too much: you either drink it all the time or not at all. There's no in-between in some families."

Peter went to the Bearskin more times before he turned eighteen than he's been since. He usually had to carry his dad home; sometimes he had to help him beat up a debt collector from Hed while he was at it. The bar looks the same now as it did back then. Smells a bit less of smoke, and considering what else a basement bar can smell of instead, that isn't altogether a good thing. It's empty now, of course. Peter never comes here in the evening; it isn't a healthy environment for the GM of an underperforming A-team. The old men in the bar have always had a lot to say, but the younger men sometimes go further than harsh words these days. There's a constant threat of violence hidden just beneath the surface of a certain type of person in this town that Peter never noticed when he was growing up, but which struck him all the more plainly after he came home from Canada. Neither hockey nor school nor the economy ever managed to find a way out for these people, and they emanate a silent fury. They're known as "the Pack" now, even if no one ever hears them say that themselves.

The team's official supporters' club has always been called "Ursus Arctos," and technically the men who hang out at the Bearskin belong to nothing but that, along with the pensioners, preschool teachers, and parents of young families in the seats in the stands. The Pack has no membership cards or T-shirts. The town is small enough for big secrets, but Peter knows that even when they are at their strongest there are never more than thirty or forty of them, yet that's enough to require extra police at A-team games in order to guarantee security. Players who have been recruited from other towns and are thought not to have performed well enough on the ice in comparison to their paycheck have occasionally shown up in Peter's office out of the blue, wanting to tear up their contracts and move. Reporters from the local paper ask questions one day and are inexplicably uninterested the following morning. The Pack has scared their opponents away from coming to Beartown, but sadly the same thing applies to sponsors. The twentysomething men at the Bearskin have become the most conservative people in town: they don't want a modern Beartown, because they know that a modern Beartown won't want them.

Ramona pushes the cup of coffee across the bar, then knocks on the wood.

"Is there something you need to talk about?"

Peter scratches his head. The Marlboro Mom was always Beartown's preeminent psychologist. Even if her standard prescription was usually, "Pull yourself together, there's others have got it worse."

"I've just got a lot on my mind, that's all."

He looks at the walls, covered with game jerseys and pictures of players, pennants and scarves.

"When did you last see a game, Ramona?"

"Haven't seen one since Holger left me. You know that, son."

Peter turns the cup between his fingers. Reaches for his wallet. When Ramona waves her hand dismissively he puts the money down on the bar anyway.

"If you don't want it for the coffee you can always put it in the kitty."

She nods appreciatively and takes the notes. The kitty is a box she keeps in her bedroom; she uses it to help when one of the boys loses his job and can't pay the bills.

"The person who needs it right now is someone from your old line. Robert Holts has lost his job at the factory. He's spending too much time here."

"Oh shit," Peter says, because he doesn't know what else to say.

He had meant to call Robbie from Canada; he had meant to call him when he moved home. Good intentions don't count. Twenty years is too long for him to know how to start the conversation now. Should he apologize? What for? How? His eyes roam across the walls again.

"Hockey," he says. "Do you ever think about what a strange sport it is, Ramona? The rules, the rink . . . Who on earth would come up with something like that?"

"Someone who needed to give drunk men with rifles a less dangerous hobby?" the aged landlady suggests.

"I just mean . . . Damn . . . this might sound a bit crazy, but sometimes you can't help wondering if we don't take all this a bit too seriously. If we aren't putting too much pressure on the juniors. They're not really much more than . . . kids."

Ramona pours herself a glass of whisky. Breakfast is, after all, the most important meal of the day.

"That depends what we want from the kids. And what the kids want from hockey."

Peter clutches his cup tighter.

"And what do we want, Ramona? What can the sport give us? We devote our whole lives to it, and what can we hope to get, at best? A few moments . . . a few victories, a few seconds when we feel bigger than we really are, a few isolated opportunities to imagine that we're . . . immortal. And it's a lie. It really isn't important."

Silence settles between them, untouched. Only when Peter pushes his empty cup back across the bar and stands up to leave does the old widow drain her glass and grunt:

"The only thing the sport gives us are moments. But what the hell is life, Peter, apart from moments?"

The best psychologist in town.

Kira gathers together Leo's pads and folds his laundry and packs his bag and puts it in the hall. He's twelve, he ought to do his own packing, she knows that. But she also knows that she's the one who has to drive him to practice and will have to come straight back to pick up half his things if he packs for himself. When she's done she sits down at the computer for half an hour. When Leo was at primary school, his teacher once told them during a parent consultation what he had said when he was asked what his parents did: "My dad works with hockey. My mom writes emails."

She puts the coffee on, ticks a number of things off her lists and on her calendar, takes several deep breaths and feels the heaviness in her chest. "Panic attacks," the psychologist said six months ago, and Kira never went back after that. She felt ashamed. As if life wasn't happy enough, as if she wasn't content, how could she possibly explain that to her family? "Panic attacks," what did that even mean? A lawyer, wife of the GM, hockey mom, and God knows she loves being all three of those, but sometimes she stops the car in the forest going one way or the other and sits in the darkness, crying. She remembers her own mother on those occasions, the way she would wipe the tears from her children's cheeks and whisper: "No one ever said life was going to be easy." Being a parent makes you feel like a blanket that's always too small. No matter how hard you try to cover everyone, there's always someone who's freezing.

She wakes Leo at eight. His breakfast is already on the table; she'll be driving him to practice in half an hour. Then she'll come home and pick up Ana and Maya, so that the three of them can do a voluntary shift in the cafeteria during the juniors' game. Afterward Leo will need driving to a friend's, and Maya to one of hers, presumably. Then Kira hopes Peter will get back from the office in time for them to have a glass of wine together, maybe some heated-up lasagna from the freezer, before he falls asleep from exhaustion and she sits up till midnight answering emails in an inbox that never empties. Tomorrow is Sunday, and there will be hockey clothes to wash and bags to be packed and teenagers to be woken. Then back to work on Monday, and work, quite honestly, has been shit recently. Since she turned down the offer of promotion the demands on her have, ironically enough, gotten worse. She knows she's only allowed to arrive last each morning and leave first in the afternoon because she's the best at what she does. But it's been a long time since she felt she was the best she could be. She doesn't have time. She's not up to it.

When the kids were little she saw so many other parents lose control in the stands at the rink, and she couldn't understand them, but now she does. The children's hobbies aren't only the children's hobbies—the parents put just as many hours into them, year after year, sacrificing so much, paying out such huge amounts of money, that their significance eats its way even into adult brains. They start to symbolize other things, compensating for or reinforcing the parents' own failures. Kira knows it sounds silly; she knows it's just a silly game in a silly sport, but deep down she's nervous too, as well as feeling nervous on behalf of Peter and the juniors and the club and the town today. Deep down she could also do with winning at something.

She goes past Maya's room, picks up some clothes from the floor, and when her daughter whimpers in her sleep she puts her hand on her forehead. It's hot. In a couple of hours Kira will be surprised by the fact that her daughter voluntarily and almost eagerly insists on going with them to the rink, regardless. She usually plays the martyr as hard as she can if she finds so much as a split end in order to have an excuse not to have to go to hockey.

In hindsight Kira will wish a thousand times over that she had forced her daughter to stay at home.

15

There are plenty of things that hurt people without people ever really knowing why. Anxiety can act as internal gravity, shrinking the soul. Benji has always been good at falling asleep and bad at actually sleeping. He wakes up early on the day of the game, but not from nerves—that's never bothered him. He cycles away from home before his mom wakes up, leaves his bike at the edge of the forest, and walks the last few miles to Adri's kennels. He sits in the yard patting the dogs until his other two sisters, Katia and Gaby, also show up. They kiss their little brother on the top of his head, then their elder sister comes out and slaps him hard on the back of the neck with her open hand and asks if it's true that he called his teacher "sweet cheeks." He never lies to Adri. She slaps him on the back of the neck again, then kisses him just as hard and whispers that she loves him and that she'll never let anything bad happen to him, but that she'll kill him if she hears he's spoken to a teacher like that again.

The four of them eat breakfast surrounded by dogs, without saying anything much. They do this once a year, a quiet act of remembrance, always early in the morning so their mother doesn't find out about it. She's never forgiven her husband. Benji was too little when it happened to harbor any hatred, and his three sisters are somewhere in between. Everyone has their own struggle. When Benji gets to his feet he doesn't ask any of them to go with him, and they don't ask where he's going. They just kiss his hair one after the other, tell him he's an idiot, and that they adore him.

He walks back through the snow to his bicycle, then goes off to the cemetery, where he crouches down with his back against Alan Ovich's headstone, smoking joints until the pain is soft enough to let his tears start to fall. The boy's fingertips trace the worn lettering of the name on the stone. On this day fifteen years ago, early one March morning, Alan got out his hunting rifle before his family woke up. Then he took everything that hurt him and went straight out into the forest. It doesn't matter how many times you explain it to a child. No one loses a parent that way without knowing that all the other grownups are lying when they say, "It wasn't your fault."

People feel pain. And it shrinks their souls.

The minutes are creeping toward lunchtime. Kevin is standing in the garden dribbling a puck with soft, controlled movements in complicated patterns between forty glass bottles placed around the ice. To anyone else it would have looked like it was happening incredibly fast, but to him each movement of his wrist feels leisurely. Time moves slower for him than other people, he doesn't know why. When he was little he used to get beaten up by the older kids because he was too good, until Benji showed up out of nowhere at training one day. They slept at each other's houses every day for several months, read Benji's sisters' old superhero comics by flashlight under the covers, and both their lives suddenly made sense. Their own superpowers united them.

"Sweetheart?" Kevin's mom calls from the terrace door, pointing at her watch.

As Kevin approaches she carefully reaches out her hand and brushes some snow from his shoulder, lets her hand rest there for longer than usual, more gently than he's used to. She bites her lower lip.

"Are you nervous?"

Kevin shakes his head. She nods proudly.

"We need to go. Your dad managed to get us on an earlier flight to Madrid. We'll drop you off at the rink."

"You'll have time to watch the first period, though?"

He can see in her eyes that she's going to pieces. But she'd never admit it.

"We're in a hurry, sweetheart. Your dad's got an important meeting with a client."

"It's a round of golf," Kevin snaps. That's as close as he ever gets to answering back.

His mother doesn't reply. Kevin knows it's pointless to carry on: the main hobby of this household isn't hockey, it's avoiding any talk about feelings. If you raise your voice, you lose. All you get is a curt, "There's no point talking to you if you're just going to shout," followed by a door closing somewhere in the house. He starts to walk toward the hall.

His mother hesitates. Reaches her hand out to his shoulder again, but stops herself and touches him tenderly on the neck instead. She runs a large company, and is very popular among her staff precisely because she's so approachable and sympathetic. It's as if it's easier when the people involved have different job descriptions. For years she used to go to bed dreaming of all the things she was going to do when she got older and had more time, and now she sometimes wakes up in despair in the middle of the night because she can no longer remember what those things were. She wanted to give Kevin everything she herself never had as a child, and she always thought she'd have time left over for all the other stuff. Talking and listening. The years have passed too quickly, and somewhere between her work and Kevin's hockey practice he grew up. She never managed to learn how to communicate with her child, and now that she has to tilt her head back to look him in the eye it's even harder.

"We'll come to the final!" she promises, the way only a mother can when she inhabits a world where it would be inconceivable for a final to take place without her son being part of it.

The cafeteria is still empty, even if the rink is beginning to fill with people. Kira is making coffee and getting hot-dog rolls out of the freezer. Maya is gazing out of the window.

"Who are you looking for?" Ana teases.

Maya gives her a hard stare, and Ana cups her hands in front of her mouth and imitates a crackly cockpit announcement:

"Ladies and gentlemen, we ask you not to open any snacks during this flight because we have someone suffering from a peanut allergy on board."

Maya kicks her on the shin. Ana jumps out of the way, and goes on in the same voice:

"We MAY let you lick the salt from the pean . . ."

Kira sees everything, hears everything, and understands almost everything, but says nothing. It's impossible to let your daughter grow up. The only problem is that you're not given a choice. Kira was fifteen once upon a time, and unfortunately still remembers exactly the sort of thing that used to fill her head back then.

"I'm just going to get the milk from the car," she interrupts when she suspects that Ana is about to say something that neither mother nor daughter are ready to hear spoken out loud in each other's company.

Kevin's father is already sitting in the car, and he tells Kevin to sit in the front and starts to quiz him about his English test on Monday. His father's life is all about the quest for perfection, his whole life a chessboard where he isn't happy unless he's two moves ahead of everyone else. "Success is never a coincidence. Luck can give you money, but never success," he often says. His ruthlessness in business frightens people, but Kevin has never seen him raise his hand to anyone, or even his voice. He can actually be quite charming when he wants, without ever needing to reveal anything about himself. He never loses control, never gets excited, because you just don't if you're always living in the future. Today there's a hockey game, but on Monday there's an English test. Two moves ahead.

"My job is to be your father, not your friend," his dad explained when Kevin mentioned once too often the fact that Benji's mother sees almost all of their games. He didn't need to get angry for Kevin to understand his point: Benji's mother doesn't sponsor the team to the tune of several million kronor every year. She doesn't make sure that the lights in the rink stay on. So she probably has rather more time to watch games.

Benji has taken the road by the lake so he can smoke without anyone seeing, which ought to stop Lyt's mother from organizing another petition, the way she did when they were at preschool and Lyt saw Benji eating sweets even though it wasn't a Saturday. She's very keen on justice and equality, Lyt's mother, so long as they're based on her precise interpretation of those words. Almost all the parents are like that. Benji has always thought that this town must be a terrible place to be a grownup. He buries the butt of his joint in the snow, then stands among the trees with his eyes closed and contemplates turning around and walking back the way he came. Away from all this. Then maybe steal a car and leave Beartown in the rearview mirror. He wonders if that would make him happier.

The parking lot in front of the rink is full of people. Kevin's dad stops the car a short distance away.

"We haven't got time to stop and talk today," he says, nodding toward the other sponsors and parents in the parking lot, who are as impressed by the Erdahl family's money as their kids are by the way Kevin plays hockey.

When you grow up in a family that never talks about feelings, you learn to hear the nuances in words like that. There's no need for him to apologize to Kevin for not driving him all the way to the door, because he just did. They pat each other briefly on the shoulder and Kevin gets out.

"You can tell us all about it tomorrow," his dad says.

There are dads who ask "Did you win?" but Kevin's asks "How many did you win by?" Kevin always hears him making notes; a whole section of the basement of the house consists of neatly stacked boxes packed with thick notepads full of careful statistics from every game Kevin has ever played, all the way back to little league. There are probably people who think it's wrong to ask your son, "How many goals did you score?" instead of "Did you score any goals?" but both Kevin's father and Kevin himself would have replied the same way: "How many goals do their sons score?"

Kevin doesn't ask his father if they'll have time to watch the first period, he just shuts the door and hoists his bag onto his shoulder, as if this were just an ordinary Saturday. But as the car pulls away, he turns and watches it until it's gone. There are more parents than players around him in the parking lot. This isn't just an ordinary Saturday for them.

Kevin's mom turns around for some reason and looks through the back window. She usually doesn't do that: like her husband, she places great value on not being sentimental and teaching Kevin to be independent. They've watched spoiled children in the Heights grow up to become triumphs of mediocrity—feeble, whining creatures who are going to need their hands held all their lives—and they're not going to let that happen to Kevin. Even when it hurts, even when Kevin had to walk all the way back from Hed in the dark when he was in primary school because his dad wanted to teach him the consequences of being late, even when his mother had to pretend to be asleep when the boy got home. Even when she wept silently into her pillow. What feels comfortable for the parents isn't what's best for the child, she's convinced of that, and Kevin has grown strong because they've allowed him to.

But Kevin's mother will always remember what she sees through the rear window that Saturday, and how her son looks as he stands in the parking lot. On the biggest day of his life he is the loneliest boy on earth.

Amat tries to make it look like he's only walking past the cafeteria by chance, and succeeds pretty much as well as if he'd tried to claim he'd eaten his best friend's ice-cream by mistake. Kira is heading in the opposite direction, but greets him cheerily and says far too loudly:

"Hi, Amat! Are you looking for Maya?"

Kira gestures brightly toward the cafeteria and disappears down the stairs, but turns back and calls:

"Good luck today!"

Then she tenses her muscles and growls dramatically, the way she's heard teenagers do out in the town when they wish each other luck:

"Knock 'em dead!"

Amat smiles bashfully. In the cafeteria Ana and Maya's voices grow louder in heated debate and Kira hurries down the stairs before one of the girls says something about boys that her mother would have to scrub away from her brain with soap, water, and copious amounts of Riesling.

Benji is suddenly standing next to Kevin without Kevin having heard him arrive. His hand on his friend's shoulder and not a word about the fact that Kevin's eyes look shiny. In return, Kevin says nothing about anniversaries and cemeteries. They've never needed to. They just look each other in the eye and say the only thing they always say before a game:

"What's the second-coolest thing in the world, Kev?"

When Kevin doesn't respond at once, Benji elbows him in the stomach.

"What's the SECOND-coolest thing in the world, hotshot?"

"Fucking," Kevin says, smiling.

"But *first* you have go into that rink and do the *coolest* thing in the world!" Benji cries, swinging his bag so carelessly that Kevin has to duck.

As they head off toward the locker room Kevin raises his eyebrows and asks: "So, Benjamin, have you been to the bathroom?"

When they were little, during one of their very first matches together, Benji wet himself on the team bench. Not because he couldn't get to the bathroom, but because one of the players on the opposing team had been trying to check Kevin all through the game, and Benji refused to leave the bench and risk missing a changeover and leaving Kevin unprotected.

Benji bursts out laughing. As does Kevin. Then they pick up their sticks and set off to go and do the coolest thing in the world.

"Have you heard any of their new tracks, though? They're completely insane! It's like you get high just from listening!" Ana squawks.

"What is it you don't get? I don't like techno!" Maya cries.

"This isn't techno. It's house," Ana snaps, insulted.

"Whatever. I like music where they can play at least one instrument, and with lyrics that contain more than five words."

"God, when are you going to listen to music that isn't a suicide soundtrack?" Ana wonders, letting her hair fall over her face and imitating Maya's music taste with drawn-out air-guitar strumming and groaned lyrics: "I'm so sad, wanna die, because my music suuucks . . ."

Maya laughs loudly and counters with one fist gyrating in the air and the other on an invisible laptop:

"Okay, this is your taste in music: Umph-umph-umph . . . DRUGS! YEAH! Umph-umph-umph-umph!"

Beside them Amat clears his throat. By now they're bouncing around the cafeteria so uncontrollably that Ana knocks over a whole stack of boxes of gummy bears. Maya stops, howling with laughter.

"Are you . . . okay?" Amat asks.

"We just have very, very different taste in music," Maya grins.

"Okay . . . I . . . well, you know . . . I was just passing, I . . . I might be playing today," Amat says.

Maya nods.

"I heard. Congratulations."

"Well, I'll probably be on the bench most of the time. But I'm on . . . the team . . . I . . . But if you're not doing anything afterward. Later, I mean. This evening. Or if you are doing something, then . . . I thought maybe I'd ask if we . . . I mean, if you like . . . with me . . ."

Ana slips on two packets of candies and very nearly brings down the entire soda fountain. Maya is laughing so hard she's almost sick.

"Sorry, Amat, what did you say?"

Amat is about to reply, but isn't quick enough. Suddenly Kevin is standing next to him, not bothering to pretend that he just happened to be passing by. He's here because of Maya. She stops laughing when she sees him.

"Hi," he says.

"Hi," she says.

"Your name's Maya, isn't it?"

She nods warily. Looks him up and down.

"Yes. What's your name?"

It takes Kevin a few seconds to realize that she's joking. Everyone in Beartown knows his name. He laughs.

"Ephraim von Shitmagnet, at your service."

He bows theatrically, even though he hardly ever makes jokes. And she laughs. Amat stands alongside, hating the fact that it's the best sound he knows, and it's not for him. Kevin looks at Maya in fascination.

"We're having a team party at my place tonight. To celebrate our victory. My parents are away."

Maya raises a skeptical eyebrow.

"You seem very sure you're going to win."

Kevin looks like he doesn't understand.

"I always win."

"Really, you do, do you, Ephraim the Shitmagnet?" Maya laughs.

"VON Shitmagnet, please," Kevin grins.

Maya laughs. Ana crawls to her feet and adjusts her hair awkwardly.

"Will . . . will Benji be there? At the party?"

Maya kicks her on the shin. Kevin nods cheerily at Maya.

"There, you see? Bring your friend. It'll be cool."

Then he turns toward Amat for the first time and exclaims:

"You'll come too, won't you? I mean, you're part of the team now!"

Amat tries to look self-assured. Kevin's two years older, and that's crushingly obvious as they're standing next to each other.

"Can I bring a friend too?" he asks quietly.

"Sorry, Ahmed! This is just for the team, yeah?" Kevin replies, slapping him on the back.

"My name's Amat," Amat says, but Kevin has already walked off.

Maya and Ana go back into the cafeteria, still laughing. Amat is left alone in the corridor.

If he gets a single chance to make a decisive move in the match this evening, there's nothing he wouldn't give to make the most of it.

16

Pride in a team can come from a variety of causes. Pride in a place, or a community, or just a single person. We devote ourselves to sports because they remind us of how small we are just as much as they make us bigger.

Kira leaves the girls in the cafeteria, laughing in spite of herself. If Peter had heard the things she herself had said to her friends when she was fifteen he'd have needed a defibrillator. They were so surprised by each other to start with. She told him he was "the only prudish hockey player," and he covered his ears when she joked around with other bar staff. She was so used to being the only girl where she worked—it is the same in law firms as it had been in the restaurant—but testosterone has never been a problem for her. Peter was the one who needed a paper bag to breathe into when one A-team player, sans front teeth, once told Kira gleefully at one of the few team dinners the wives were still invited to that he had "rubbed his knob on every fucking glass in here," in the hope that the GM's wife would be disgusted. She responded by explaining the female equivalent to him in great detail, until the toothless wonder didn't dare look at her again for the rest of the evening. Peter was ashamed at the time. Still is. The last embarrassed Neanderthal. All these years, and they can still surprise each other. That's not such a bad thing.

She walks toward the parking lot through the rink, but stops by the ice and just stares at it. No matter how much she tries, she will never be anything more than Peter's other half in this town. She assumes that all adults occasionally wonder about another life, one they could be living instead of the one they've got. How often they do so probably depends on how happy they are. Her mother always used to say her daughter was an incurable romantic as well as hopelessly competitive, both at the same time. Kira presumes that's true, based on the fact that she and Peter have gone bowling three times and are still married. The third time they ended up googling "emergency marriage counselor" at one thirty in the morning. God, how much he annoys her sometimes, but God, how she loves him. It wasn't a love that developed gradually, it hit her like an affliction. It's an ongoing condition. All she wishes is that each day were forty-eight hours long. But she's not greedy, she'd be happy with thirty-six. She just wants to be able to have a drink and catch up with a TV show, is that really too much to ask? She just wants sufficient time to make a big enough blanket.

She thinks about that other life far too often. The one someone else is living. She was so happy for Peter when he got his professional contract, but she was happy for herself when he stopped playing. When there was space for her. Will she ever be able to admit that to him? The brief period when he was neither a player nor GM, when he sold insurance and simply tried to be happy, is the best time she can remember. How can you tell the person you love something like that?

When Isak died, everyone did everything for them. When their lungs collapsed, they needed a fabricated form of love that could help them breathe. So Kira made the hardest decision she has ever made: she realized she was going to have to give hockey back to Peter.

There's a thin line between living and surviving, but there's one positive side effect of being both romantic and very competitive: you never give up. Kira gets the milk from the car, then stands there just laughing to herself, and realizes that she's learned to laugh that way more and more often. Then she takes out a green scarf emblazoned with the words "Beartown Ice Hockey" and ties it around her neck. On her way back into the rink she greets and hugs other people wearing the same color, and for a few moments everything else seems unimportant. You don't need to understand every aspect of the ice to love it, and you don't have to love the town to feel proud of it.

Peter is wandering around the rink like an exorcised ghost. His entire day so far has been a sequence of moments similar to walking into a room and instantly forgetting why you are there. In the hallway outside his office he absentmindedly walks into Tails, which is no mean feat seeing as there's a lot of Tails not to notice. He's six and a half feet tall and a good deal sturdier around the waist than when they played in the final of the Swedish Championship together. He was always the sort of guy who compensated for a lack of self-confidence by trying to attract as much attention as possible; he talks as loudly as a child with headphones on, and when they were teenagers he always turned up at parties in a suit when everyone else was wearing jeans, because he had read in a magazine that girls liked that. Toward the end of their time in high school, one of the club's sponsors died and the whole team was told to wear suits for the funeral. When he heard that, he showed up in a tailcoat. And that was how he got his nickname.

These days he owns a chain of large supermarkets, one here and one in Hed, and a couple more in places Peter has never really bothered to make a mental note of when Tails has been going on about them. He's managed to get thrown out of every hunting club in the area because he can't even keep quiet in the forest. When they played together he would gesticulate with his long arms every time a call went against him, veering between laughter, tears, despair, and rage so quickly that Sune used to say it was like trying to coach "a mime who can't shut up." Tails was a mediocre player, but he loved the competitive aspect of the game. When his hockey career came to an end, that attitude made him a far-from-mediocre salesman. Now he gets a new car every year and wears a Rolex the size of a blood-pressure monitor. Trophies from a different sport.

"What a day, eh?" the bulky grocer grins, gazing down at him.

They're standing next to the old team photograph, in which they're standing side by side.

"And now you're GM and I'm the main sponsor." Tails smirks in a way that stops Peter from pointing out that he's actually a long way from being the main sponsor.

"Yes, what a day," Peter agrees.

"We look out for each other, don't we? The bears from Beartown!" Tails roars, and before Peter has time to respond he goes on:

"I bumped into Kevin Erdahl yesterday. I asked him if he was nervous. And do you know what he said? 'No.' So I asked him what his tactics were for the game, and do you know what he said? 'To win.' Then he looked me right in the eye and said: 'That's why you sponsor the team, isn't it? To get a return on your investment?' Seventeen years old! Did we talk that way when we were seventeen?"

Peter doesn't answer. He's not sure he can remember ever being as young as seventeen. He goes over to the coffee machine. It's gone wrong again and rattles and hisses before reluctantly emitting a dribble the color of old chewing tobacco and the consistency of glue. Peter drinks it anyway. Tails scratches himself under one of his chins and lowers his voice.

"We've met up with the councilors, some of us sponsors and board members . . . all off the record, of course."

Peter is looking for cream, and is trying to make it clear that he doesn't want to hear this. Tails takes no notice.

"When the juniors win the final, they're going to pick Beartown as the site of the hockey academy. It would look terrible if they didn't, in PR terms, of course. And we've had a bit of a discussion about renovating the rink . . ."

"Also off the record, I assume," Peter grunts, seeing as he knows that "off the record" in the political language of the local council means backs being scratched with one hand while the other stuffs money into a pocket.

Tails slaps him on the back and nods toward his office.

"Who knows, Peter, maybe we'll even be able to afford to get you an espresso machine!"

"Great," Peter mutters.

"I don't suppose you've got anything stronger in there?" Tails says loudly, looking toward Peter's office.

"Nervous about the game, then?" Peter smiles.

"Did da Vinci get a discount on brown when he painted the *Mona Lisa*?"

Peter laughs and nods toward the office next to his.

"The president's bound to have a bottle or two."

Tails brightens up. Peter calls after him:

"You are going to keep your shirt on today, aren't you, Tails? Not like the quarterfinal? The parents weren't happy!"

"Promise!" Tails lies, then adds quickly without turning around, as if it hadn't been his intention all along:

"Let's have a little glass together before the game, eh? I mean, I guess you could have water. Or soda if that's what you drink. I've invited a few of the other sponsors along as well; I thought we could have a little chat. You know . . . off the record."

He returns with both a bottle and the president, whose forehead is already as shiny as freshly polished ice, with dark patches under his armpits. Only then does Peter realize that he's walked into an ambush.

Fatima has never been in the rink when there are so many people in it. She usually sees Amat's games with the boys' team, but those are only watched by the parents of the players and whatever younger siblings have been dragged along. Today grown men are standing in the parking lot begging to buy tickets at four times their face value. Amat bought two well in advance. She had wondered why he didn't want to go with Zacharias like he usually does, but Amat had said he wanted to show her the boys he would one day be playing with. That was only a week or so ago, and back then it would have seemed utterly fantastical that such a day would come so soon. She clutches the tickets tightly in her hand and tries not to get in anyone's way in the throng, but evidently fails to be invisible because someone suddenly grabs her and says:

"You! Are you going to help with this, or what?"

Fatima turns around. Maggan Lyt is waving her arms at her, then points to a glass bottle that someone's dropped on the floor and has broken.

"Can you get a dustpan and brush? Surely you can see that some-one might step on it here! A child!"

The woman who dropped the bottle—Fatima recognizes her as the mother of another player on the team—is showing no sign of picking the glass up herself. She's already started to walk off to her place in the stands.

"Are you listening, or what?" Maggan Lyt exclaims, taking hold of Fatima's arm.

Fatima nods and puts the tickets in her pocket. She goes to bend down by the glass.

She is stopped by another hand on her shoulder.

"Fatima?" Kira says warmly, before turning to Maggan Lyt with noticeably less warmth:

"What's the problem?"

"I don't have a problem. She works here, doesn't she?" Maggan snarls.

"Not today," Kira says.

"What do you mean, not today? So what's she doing here, then?"

Fatima straightens her back and takes such a tiny step forward that it's unnoticed by everyone but her. Then she looks Maggan in the eye and replies:

"I'm not 'she.' I am actually standing here. I'm here for the same reason as you. To watch my son play."

Kira has never seen anyone more proud. And has never seen Mag-gan so speechless. When the crowd has carried mother Lyt away, Kira picks the glass up from the floor. Fatima asks quietly:

"Sorry, Kira, but . . . I'm not used to . . . I wonder . . . would you mind if I sat next to you today?"

Kira bites her lip. Takes a firm grasp of Fatima's hand.

"Oh, Fatima, I should be asking if I can sit next to you."

Sune is sitting at the top of the stands. The sponsors who've passed him on the stairs have pretended they haven't seen him, so he knows precisely what they're on their way to talk about in the office. Oddly enough, he no longer feels angry. Or sad. He just feels tired. Of the politics and money and everything about the club that no longer has anything to do with hockey. He's just tired. So maybe they're right after all. He doesn't fit in anymore.

He looks out across the ice and takes several deep breaths through his nose. A few of the players on the opposing team—ready early the way you are when you're terrified—set out to warm up. No matter how times change, nerves remain the same. Sune finds that comforting, that this is still only a sport, regardless of what the men in the offices are trying to turn it into. A puck, two goals, hearts full of passion. Some people say hockey is like religion, but that's wrong. Hockey is like faith. Religion is something between you and other people; it's full of interpretations and theories and opinions. But faith . . . that's just between you and God. It's what you feel in your chest when the referee glides out to the center circle between two players, when you hear the sticks strike each other and see the black disk fall between them. Then it's just between you and hockey. Because cherry trees always smell of cherry trees, whereas money smells of nothing.

David is standing in the players' tunnel, watching the sponsors go up the steps toward the offices. He knows what they say about him, how they talk about his successes, but he also knows how quickly they'd turn against him next year if the A-team doesn't reach the same heights. And, dear God, does anyone in this town have any idea how utterly improbable this junior team is? There are no Cinderella stories in hockey anymore; the big clubs strip the smaller ones of talent before the players have even reached their teens. And even in Beartown, where—miraculously—all the guys have stayed put, there's only one player of truly elite caliber; the rest ought to be outplayed in a hundred games out of a hundred. But despite that, here they are. This team is like a swarm of hornets.

People keep asking what David's "tactical secret" is. He can't tell them, because they wouldn't understand. The tactical secret is love. He became Kevin's coach when he was a frightened little seven-year-old who would have been flattened by the older kids outside the rink if he hadn't had Benji there to protect him. Even then, Benji was the most courageous little bastard David had ever seen, and Kevin the most talented. David taught them to skate backward as well as forward. He taught them that passes are just as important as shots, he made Benji play for entire practices without his stick, and forced Kevin to play for weeks with a stick that was curved wrong. But he also taught them that they only had each other, that the only person you can really trust in this world is the guy next to you on the ice, that the only people who will refuse to get on a bus before you come back to it are a team.

It was David who taught the boys how to tape their sticks and sharpen their skates, but he also taught them how to knot a tie and shave. Well, their chins, anyway. They taught themselves the rest. He starts to laugh every time he remembers how Bobo, the wayward, hyperactive little fatty, once turned around in the locker room when he was thirteen and asked Benji if they were supposed to shave their backsides at the same time as they shaved their testicles. "Do girls think it's important that they match?" When David himself was a junior, that was part of the younger players' initiation, forcibly shaving their pubic hair off—it used to be regarded as humiliating. He doesn't know what the modern equivalent would be, but he suspects that today's teenagers would only be scared by the prospect of being taped to a chair and having to let their pubes grow out again.

Hockey changes all the time, because the people playing it do. When David was a junior the coach used to demand total silence in the locker room, but David's team has always been full of laughter. He's always known that humor could bring people together, so when the guys were young and nervous he always used to tell jokes just before a game. Their favorite when they were small was: "How do you sink a submarine from Hed? You swim down and knock on the door. How do you sink it a second time? You swim down and knock on the door, because then they open it and say, 'Oh no, we're not falling for that again!' " When the guys grew older, their favorite was: "How do you know you're at a wedding in Hed? Because everyone's sitting on the same side of the church." Then they got old enough to tell their own jokes, and David used to leave the locker room more and more. Because sometimes the absence of the coach can also unite a team.

He looks at the time, counting the minutes until the start of the game. The sponsors in the stands will never understand his tactics, because they could never understand what the guys on the team are ready to sacrifice for each other. While the sponsors have been shouting at David to "let the team loose offensively," David has patiently allocated very clear roles to his players, drilling them on where to pass the puck, on precise positioning, how to direct the play, angles, evaluation, and how to eliminate risk. He's taught them how to disarm any advantage their opponents may have in terms of technique or speed, how to bring them down to their own level, how to frustrate and irritate, because that's when they win, because they have something no one else has: Kevin. If he gets the chance he can score two goals, and as long as he has Benji beside him, he'll always get at least one chance.

"Ignore the stands, ignore what people say," David keeps repeating. His tactics demand subordination, humility, and trust, ten years of training and hard work, and if Beartown loses in every stat except the one indicating the number of goals scored, David will tell each and every one of the players in the locker room that they've done their job. And they trust him. They love him. When they were seven years old, when everyone else just laughed, he told them he would take them all the way here, and he's kept his promise.

Before he turns to go back to the locker room, he sees Sune sitting alone at the top of the stands. Their eyes meet for a moment. No matter how much they have argued, David knows that the stubborn old bastard is the only person in this club who actually still understands the love underpinning what they do.

17

Some people say that everything in hockey is black and white. They're crazy. Fatima and Kira are sitting in their seats when Kira suddenly excuses herself and stands up, makes her way to the steps, and stops a middle-aged man who Fatima knows is in middle management at the factory. Kira grabs at his red scarf irritably.

"Christer, for heaven's sake, take that off!"

The man, who is obviously not used to being scolded, and certainly not by a woman, stares at her.

"Are you serious?"

"Are YOU serious?!" Kira exclaims, loud enough to make the other people on the steps turn toward them.

The man looks around with uncertainty flaring on his cheeks. Everyone is looking at him. He doesn't know who it is, but behind him someone mutters: "For God's sake, Christer, she's right!" and then other voices soon join in. Christer slowly removes his scarf and puts it in his pocket. His wife leans toward Kira apologetically and whispers:

"I tried to tell him. But you know what men are like. Sometimes they just don't understand hockey."

Kira laughs and goes and sits down next to Fatima again.

"A red scarf. He must be mad! Sorry, what were we talking about?"

Nothing is black and white in Beartown. It's red or green. And red is Hed's color.

Amat's fingertips trace the seams of his match jersey. Dark green with silver numbers and the brown bear on the chest. The colors of Beartown: forest, ice, earth. He's wearing number eighty-one. He was number nine on the boys' team, but that's Kevin's number here. The locker room around him is chaotic. Benji, number sixteen, is of course lying in a corner, asleep as usual, but all the other juniors are sitting huddled up on their benches, forced back by parents who are getting louder and more excitable with their advice the closer the start of the game gets. That tendency exists in all sports: parents always think their own expertise increases automatically as their child gets better at something. As if the reverse weren't actually the case.

The noise level is unbearable, and loudest of all is Maggan Lyt, a privilege you can grant yourself when your son plays in the first line. Benji's mom has never set foot inside the locker room, and Kevin's mom hardly ever comes to the rink, so Maggan has ruled the roost here for years. She came and untied little William's skates after every game until he was thirteen, and she and her husband sacrificed their second car and holidays abroad so they could afford to move into the house next to the Erdahl family's, and their sons could become best friends. Her frustration at the fact that William hasn't yet managed to force his way in between Kevin and Benji has started to slip into downright aggression.

When David walks in, the locker room explodes in a torrent of accusations, questions, and demands from all the adults in there. He walks straight through them as though they didn't exist, followed by Lars, who starts shepherding them toward the door. Maggan Lyt is so insulted that she bats his hand away.

"We're here to support the team!"

"That's what we have the stands for," David replies without looking at her.

She loses control at that.

"And as for you, David! What sort of leadership are you showing, making changes to the team before this of all games?"

David raises his eyebrows uncomprehendingly at her. William Lyt looks like he wants to die.

"What's *he* doing here?" Maggan demands, pointing straight at Amat.

Amat looks like he shares William's wish. David keeps his voice quiet on purpose, forcing all the other adults to shut up.

"I don't justify my choice of team to anyone."

The vein on Maggan's forehead is throbbing like a church-bell.

"You'll justify it to ME, I'll have you know! These boys have played for you for ten years and for their biggest game ever you pick someone from the BOYS' TEAM?"

She gestures expansively toward all the other adults in the room, and manages to get them to nod and grunt in agreement, before fixing her eyes on David and demanding:

"Do you have any idea how important this game is for us? For all of us? Do you know what we've had to sacrifice for this sport?"

Amat is squirming, and looks like he'd like to run off down the hall, leave the rink, and never come back. That's not helped when David's face turns red so quickly that even Maggan reverses straight into the wall.

"You want to talk to me about sacrifices?" David hisses, walking right up to her without giving her the slightest chance to reply.

"Look at him!" he says, pointing at Amat, and before Maggan has time to react he's grabbed her by the arm and dragged her halfway across the floor until she's standing right in front of the boy.

"Look at him! Are you seriously standing here saying that your son deserves this more than he does? Are you saying they trod the same path to get here? Are you telling me your family has worked harder than he has? *Look at him!*"

Maggan Lyt's arm is shaking when he lets go of it. David simply gives Amat a quick pat on the shoulder, his thumb nudges the boy's neck, and he looks him in the eye. Not a word. Just that.

Then the coach crosses the room, puts his hand on William Lyt's cheek, and whispers:

"We play for ourselves, William. No one else. You and I, we play for ourselves. Because we got ourselves here. No one else did."

William nods and wipes his eyes.

———

Bobo's feet are drumming the floor relentlessly. He's finding it impossible to sit still. When Lars throws out all the parents, including Maggan, the silence is so intense that it's suffocating. And Bobo can't keep quiet in situations like that; he's never been able to. He isn't Kevin or Benji, he's always had to fight his way to the center of attention, to the middle of the locker room. As long as he can remember he's been terrified of corners, of being forgotten, left unacknowledged. He can see all his best friends' heads hanging on their chests now, and he would desperately love to stand up and give an inspirational speech, the sort you see in films, but he doesn't have the words for it. Nor the voice. He just wants to kill the silence. So he stands up, clears his throat, and says:

"Hey, guys, what did one lesbian vampire say to the other lesbian vampire?"

The juniors look up at him in surprise. Bobo grins.

"See you in a month!"

Some of the team start to laugh, which is all the encouragement Bobo needs to carry on.

"Do you know what the usual cause of death is for lesbians?"

A few more are laughing now.

"Hairballs!" Bobo cries, before launching into his big finale.

"And do you know why lesbians get so many colds? LACK OF VITAMIN D!"

The whole locker room is laughing now. With him and at him, he doesn't care which. As long as they laugh. In a moment of pride he turns to David, whose expression hasn't changed, and bursts out:

"Have you got any good ones, coach?"

The locker room falls silent again. David sits there motionless. Bobo's face turns first red, then white. In the end Lars both saves and destroys him by clearing his throat, getting to his feet, and saying:

"Do you know why Bobo always cries and his ears hurt after he's had sex?"

Bobo squirms anxiously. Some of the guys start giggling in anticipation. Lars's face cracks into an alarmingly wide grin.

"Because of the pepper spray and rape whistle!"

The storm of laughter from all the juniors makes the room shake. In the end even David smiles, and he'll think back to that moment many times afterward: whether a joke is always only a joke, whether that particular one went too far, whether there are different rules inside and outside a locker room, whether it's acceptable to cross the line in order to defuse tension and get rid of nerves before a game, or if he should have stopped Lars and intervened by saying something to the guys. But he does nothing. Just lets them all laugh. He'll think about that when he gets home and looks his girlfriend in the eye.

In the meantime Amat is sitting in the corner, hearing himself laugh. Because it's a release. Because it makes him feel part of the team. Because there's something wonderful about making the same noise as everyone around him. He'll feel ashamed of that forever.

Benji wakes up to find Kevin shaking him. Being able to sleep through both Maggan Lyt's tactical talk and Lars's sense of humor is one of his foremost talents, and getting a chance to do so is definitely a privilege. There have always been parents who have questioned Benji's behavior, both on and off the ice, but David always says the same thing: "If the other players gave me even an ounce of what Benji gives me on the ice every time, I wouldn't give a damn if they all slept on the team bench."

When Bobo sits back down again, destroyed in the way that only a teenager can be by an adult in front of his best friends, another adult sits down next to him with his hand on his shoulder and his thumb against his neck. Bobo looks up. David is smiling at him.

"You're the least selfish player I've got on this team, you know that?"

Bobo presses his lips together. David leans closer to him.

"You're going to be playing in the third defensive pair tonight, and I know that's going to be a disappointment to you."

Bobo fights back tears. Throughout his early childhood he was the best back in this team because of his size and strength, but in the past few years his poor skating has let him down. First he slipped into the second defensive pair. Now the third. David holds his hand gently on his neck and looks at him intently as he says:

"But I need you. Your team needs you. You're important. So I want you to give me everything you've got tonight, at every changeover. I want every last drop of blood. And if you give me that, if you trust me, I promise I'll never let you down."

By the time David stands up Bobo's feet are drumming against the floor again. If David had asked him to go out and kill someone at that moment, he would have done so without hesitation. When the coach stands in the middle of the room, after ten years with them, there isn't a boy in there who doesn't feel the same. He looks each of them in the eye in turn.

"I'm not going to say much. You know who you're up against. I know you're better than them. So I expect just one thing. I will only tolerate one thing. Don't come back to this locker room until you've given it to me."

He seeks out Kevin's gaze and holds it like a vise:

"Win."

"Win!" Kevin replies with dark eyes.

"WIN!" David repeats, punching his clenched fists in the air.

"WIN!!!" the whole locker room roars with one voice.

They fly up from their benches, a stamping, banging, panting horde, ready to be led out by their team captain. David walks past and slaps each of them hard on the helmet, then when he gets to the front and has his fingers on the door handle he whispers so that only boy number nine can hear:

"I'm proud of you, Kevin. No matter what happens this evening, if you play your best match ever or your worst, there isn't another player in the world I'd have picked over you."

The door opens. Kevin doesn't walk out onto the ice.

He takes it by storm.

18

Loneliness is an invisible ailment. Since Holger left her, Ramona has become like the animals in the wildlife documentaries she watches on the nature channels on the nights when the sleeping pills don't work. The ones who have been held in captivity for so long that you can remove all the barriers without them making any attempt to escape. Any living thing that is kept behind bars for long enough eventually becomes more scared of the unknown than its own captivity. At the start she only stayed indoors because she could still hear his laughter in here, his voice, and the way he used to swear when he stubbed his toe on the low step behind the bar. A whole life together in this building, and he still couldn't figure out where that damn step was. But isolating yourself happens faster than you might think: the days blur together when you live more on the inside than outside, and the years continued to pass by on the other side of the street while she desperately tried to make everything inside the Bearskin and the apartment above it carry on exactly as it was when he died. She was frightened she would forget him if she went out into the world, that she might go to the supermarket and come home to find that his laughter was no longer there. Then suddenly one morning, eleven years had passed and everyone but her boys thinks she's lost her mind now. She became a time traveller trapped inside her own machine.

People sometimes say that sorrow is mental but longing is physical. One is a wound, the other an amputated limb, a withered petal compared to a snapped stem. Anything that grows closely enough to what it loves will eventually share the same roots. We can talk about loss, we can treat it and give it time, but biology still forces us to live according to certain rules: plants that are split down the middle don't heal, they die.

She is standing in the snow just outside the door, smoking. Three in a row. The roof of the rink is visible from here, the roar when the Beartown juniors make it 1–0 sounds like it's going to blow every building along the main street apart, as if it's going to pick the whole forest up and dump it in the lake. Ramona tries to take a step toward the street, just one step nearer the pavement. Her whole body is shaking uncontrollably as she fumbles for the wall behind her, sweat drenching her clothes in spite of the sub-zero temperature. She goes back into the warmth, closes the door, switches the lights off, and lies down on the floor in the bar with Holger's photograph in her hands. Right next to the step.

People say she's gone mad, because that's what people who know nothing about loneliness call it.

Amat is terrified, even though he hasn't played for a second. When he followed Kevin and the rest of the team out onto the ice, when the crowd stood up and the roar made his ears pop, he headed straight for the bench absolutely convinced he was about to throw up. One day he'll look back on that moment and realize that the feeling never disappears. No matter how successful you become.

Kevin scores the first goal in the opening minute of the game. That's no coincidence; in every game he seems to get a short window before the defense realizes just how good he is, exactly how fluid his wrist action, how swiftly he can skate around them. He does that with laser-like precision. They won't make that mistake again; for the rest of the game they shut him down by shadowing him so closely they may as well be sharing the same pair of skates. The opposition turns the game around to 2–1. They deserve it, they're astonishingly good, powerfully and methodically mounting attack after attack until Amat ends up surprised that they're only leading by one goal every time he looks up at the scoreboard. They're the strongest and most techni-cally proficient team he's seen; he's pretty sure they could have beaten Beartown's A-team. And everyone can see it. With every line change, the players around Amat slump more heavily on the bench, their sticks pound the boards less often and less aggressively, and even Lars is swearing more quietly. In the second intermission, on his way to the locker room, Amat hears some adults in the stands laugh forlornly: "Well, a semifinal's nothing to be ashamed of. We'll just have to hope for a better team next season." He's surprised at how angry that makes him. It rouses something inside him. By the time he enters the room he's ready to smash something. David is the only person who notices.

Robbie Holts is standing alone in the street, hating himself. He wouldn't have gone outside voluntarily today unless he'd run out of drink at home again. He looks at the roof of the rink, estimates in his head where they ought to be in the game now. It's a peculiar sort of angst, the one he lives with, knowing that you had the greatest moment in your life at the age of seventeen. While he was growing up everyone kept telling him he was going to turn professional, and he believed them so intensely that when he didn't make it, he took it to mean that everyone else had let him down, as if somehow it wasn't his own fault. He wakes up in the mornings with the feeling that someone has stolen a better life from him, an unbearable phantom pain between what he should have been and what he actually became. Bitterness can be corrosive; it can rewrite your memories as if it were scrubbing a crime scene clean, until in the end you only remember what suits you of its causes.

Robbie walks down the steps to the Bearskin but stops himself in surprise. The lights are off inside. Ramona is downing one last glass of whisky and yanking on her outside clothes.

"Good that you came," she whispers.

"Why? Are you going somewhere?" he wonders, confused, because he knows as well as everyone else that the crazy old bag hasn't been farther than a couple of paces from the pub in over a decade.

"I'm going to a hockey match," she says.

Robbie starts to laugh, because there's no other option.

"And you want me to mind the bar for you?"

"I want you to come with me."

He stops laughing then. She has to promise to wipe out his tab for the last four months to get him to take a single step outside the door.

Tails is standing up even though he's paid for a seat. No one in the row behind can be bothered to complain anymore.

"That fucking William Lyt, Christ, there are people in witness protection programs who are easier to find on the ice than that bastard!" he snarls to the other sponsors.

"I beg your pardon?" Maggan Lyt exclaims from two rows below.

"I said WITNESS PROTECTION PROGRAM, Maggan!" Tails repeats.

And everyone sitting between them wishes they could apply to join it.

Bobo is still sitting in complete silence on the bench when the third period begins, and he can count the number of minutes he's played on one hand. He doesn't know how you can be part of a team when you're not part of the game. He's trying to control himself, but he loves this team, he loves his jersey and his number. So when he sees something he can't believe everyone else can't see as well, he grabs hold of William Lyt on the bench and shouts:

"Their backs *want* you to try to cut inside them, can't you see that? They *want* it to be so crowded in the center that Kevin doesn't have any space. Pretend you're heading in and then dart outside just once, and I promise you . . ."

William clamps his glove over Bobo's mouth.

"Shut up, Bobo! Who do you think you are? You're in the third defensive pair, you don't tell the first line what to do. Go and get me my water bottle!"

The look in his eyes is so cold and patronizing that Bobo can hardly hear the mocking laughter from the other players. The most painful fall for anyone is tumbling down through a hierarchy. Bobo has known Lyt all his life, and the way his friend is looking at him now leaves marks, and gives rise to the sort of corrosive bitterness that never leaves some men, that can wake you in the middle of the night and make you think someone has stolen the life you should have had. Bobo goes and gets the water bottle; Lyt takes it without a word. Bobo is the largest player on the team, but when he sits down he is the smallest player on the bench.

Ramona stops outside the rink. Stands in the snow shaking, and whispers:

"I'm . . . sorry, Robert, I can't . . . I can't . . . No farther than this."

Robbie is holding her hand. She's not supposed to be living this way. Holger ought to have been sitting in there, this should have been their moment. He puts his arm around her as only someone else who has been the victim of theft can.

"Let's go back home, Ramona. It doesn't matter."

She shakes her head, fixes her eyes on him.

"The deal is that I wipe your tab if you go to the game, Robert. I want to know what happened immediately afterward. I'll be standing here waiting."

Robbie is many things. But brave enough to argue with Ramona isn't one of them.

There's a distinct moment in a player's life when they find out exactly how good they are. William Lyt's comes halfway through the third period. He's never been quick enough for this level, but now it also becomes clear that he doesn't have the stamina either. He can't keep up, he hasn't got the energy, their opponents can direct him without going anywhere near him. Kevin has two men marking him, four arms across his chest the whole time. Benji is a tornado, flying across the whole of the rink, but Beartown needs more space. Lyt gives all he has. It isn't enough.

David has built his whole philosophy, this team's entire unbelievable season, on not trusting to fate. They never just hope for the best. They don't just dump the puck forward and go for it, they have a plan, a strategy, a purpose with each pattern, each movement. But as Sune, the old bastard, keeps saying, "The puck doesn't just glide, it bounces as well." It's unpredictable.

Lyt is heading for the bench when he gets tripped. He falls to the ice and sees the puck bounce over the blade of one of their opponents and nudges it forward out of reflex. It jumps over another three sticks, Kevin reaches for it but is brought down by a big hit. There's no way for anyone to get around the falling bodies, but as luck would have it, Benjamin Ovich isn't a go-around person. He's a go-through person. When the puck flies into the goal, Benji isn't far behind it, and the crossbar hits him across the neck. You couldn't have gotten him to admit that it hurt even if it had been a medieval broadsword.

2–2. Maggan Lyt is already down banging on the door to the scorekeeper's cubicle, to make sure that William is credited with the assist.

David nods silently to himself and taps Amat's helmet. Lars's pupils widen in pure disbelief when he realizes what's going on.

"For God's sake, David, you can't be serious."

David is as serious as a stray bullet.

"Lyt is one change away from needing oxygen, and two from needing a priest. We need pace."

"Lyt just made an assist!"

"He was lucky. We don't play on luck. AMAT!"

Amat just stares at the coach. David grabs hold of his helmet:

"At the next face-off in our zone I want you to take off. I don't give a shit if you've got the puck or not, I just want them to know how fast you are."

He points toward their opponents' bench. Amat nods hesitantly. David doesn't break eye contact.

"Do you want to be something, Amat? Do you really want to show this whole town that you can be something? Now's your chance to show them."

At the next defensive face-off Benji lines up on one side of Kevin, Amat on the other. Maggan Lyt is now standing with both hands against the glass of the team bench, shrieking that NO ONE pulls her son from a semifinal and goes unpunished. Lars looks at David.

"If we lose this game she's going to castrate you."

David leans nonchalantly against the boards.

"Winners have a tendency to be forgiven in this town."

Out on the ice, Benji does as he's been instructed—he gets the puck and fires it out of the zone, and it glides toward the opposing team's end. Amat does as he's been instructed: he takes off. He gets hacked by one of the backs as he's only just starting to skate away, and by the time he pulls free there's no point chasing the puck. He goes after it anyway. A gasp runs through the spectators who understand hockey. A deep sigh passes through the ones who don't. The opponent's goalie calmly skates out and plays the puck to his defense, who move it up the ice, where their forwards fire a shot at Beartown's goal. When the referee blows for another face-off back in Beartown's end, Amat is standing alone in the opposing team's zone two hundred feet away. The other sponsors are muttering, "Does that one need a compass, or what?" But Tails can see what David sees. What Sune saw.

"Quick as a wolverine with mustard up its ass! They won't catch him!" he smiles.

David leans over the boards and catches Amat by the shoulder when he's on his way back.

"Again!"

Amat nods. Kevin wins the face-off, but Benji doesn't even manage to get the puck out of the zone, but Amat sets off at full speed toward the opponents' goal anyway, and doesn't stop until he reaches the boards at the far end. He can hear booing and mocking laughter from the stands: "Are you lost? The puck isn't anywhere near you!" but he just looks at David. The Beartown goalie smothers the puck, another face-off. David makes a brief circular gesture in the air. "Again."

The third time Amat races across the ice it doesn't matter where the puck is, because there's one person in the rink who sees his pace and realizes what's going on. The coach of the opposing team snatches a sheaf of papers from his assistant and roars:

"Who the hell is that? Who the hell is number eighty-one?"

Amat looks up at the stands. Maya is on the steps just below the cafeteria; she sees him. He's been longing for that since the first day in primary school, and now she sees him. He loses his concentration so much that he doesn't hear Bobo yelling his name until he's right next to the bench.

"AMAT!"

Bobo is hanging over the boards, and grabs him by the collar:

"Fake inside, skate outside!"

For half a second they look each other right in the eye and Bobo doesn't need to say anything to prove how much he would have liked to be on the ice himself. Amat nods in acknowledgment, and they tap each other's helmets. Maya is still standing on the stairs. At the next face-off Kevin and Benji circle the zone, stop in front of Amat, and lean toward him.

"Have you got any strength left in those little chicken-legs, then?" Kevin grins.

"Give me the puck and you'll see," Amat replies with bloodshot eyes.

Kevin wouldn't have lost that face-off even if his hands had been tied behind his back and he had a pistol held to his head. Benji shovels the puck along the boards and chases after it. Tomorrow his thighs won't even let him get out of bed but he feels nothing now, and knocks down two opponents with one hit. Amat feints inside but chips the puck off the boards instead, then blasts past the defenseman on the outside, so quickly that one of the two players covering Kevin has to let go of number nine and chase number eighty-one instead. That's all Beartown needs. A stick hits Amat's lower arm so hard that he thinks his wrist is broken, but he manages to pull the puck from the boards and skate around the net. He has one breath in which to look up, wait until the blade of Kevin's stick hits the ice, then release the puck at the same instant he's knocked to the ice. Kevin gets the puck two inches off the ice, and that's twice as much as he needs.

When the red light goes on behind the net, adults tumble over each other in the stands. The sponsors send each others' cups of coffee flying across the rows of seats as they try to do high fives. Two fifteen-year-old girls bounce around a cafeteria in delight, and up at the back of the stand an old A-team coach who never laughs does so today. Fatima and Kira hug each other until they're lying on the floor and aren't really sure if they're celebrating or crying.

Outside the rink, alone in the snow, Ramona stands and feels the sound wave hit her. "I love you," she whispers to Holger. Then she turns and walks home on her own with a smile in her chest. It is a moment shared between people and hockey, between a town whose inhabitants want to believe and a world that has spent years telling them to give up. There isn't a single atheist in the whole building.

Kevin turns and heads straight for the bench, swatting away every teammate who tries to hug him, climbs over the boards, and throws himself in David's arms.

"For you!" the boy whispers, and David holds him like he was his own son.

Twenty yards away Amat crawls to his feet from the ice. He might as well be in a different rink altogether seeing as no one is looking at him anyway. A moment after his pass, the defenseman's stick and elbow hit him in the neck with all his weight behind them, Amat's head hit the ice as if he'd been knocked into an empty swimming pool, and he didn't even see the goal. By the time he gets to his knees every Beartown player is following Kevin toward the bench, everyone in the stands is watching number nine. Even Maya.

Number eighty-one—the number he chose because his mother was born that year—stands alone by the boards and looks at the scoreboard. It is simultaneously the best and worst moment he has experienced in this rink. He adjusts his helmet and skates toward the bench in a few lonely strides, but someone swings around behind him and taps him twice on the helmet.

"She'll notice you when we win the final," Benji smiles.

He's already skated off and is standing by the center line before Amat has time to reply. Lyt is on his way over the boards but David stops him and calls to Amat to stay on the ice. As Kevin skates out to take the face-off at center ice, they nod briefly to each other, number nine and number eighty-one. Amat is one of them now. It doesn't matter how many people up in the stands actually realize that.

Peter loses his bearings after the final whistle; one moment he's bellowing in an embrace, the next he's tumbling headfirst down an entire section of the stands, and gets to his feet with his ears ringing from all the people shrieking in and around them. Old people, young people, people who love this game, and people who don't even care. He has no idea how it happened, but all of a sudden he finds himself in the middle of a wild, singing embrace with a stranger, and when he looks up he realizes that the man he's dancing with on the steps is Robbie Holts. They stop and look at each other, then start laughing and can't stop. For this one evening they're seventeen years old again.

Hockey is just a silly little game. We devote year after year after year to it without ever really hoping to get anything in return. We burn and bleed and cry, fully aware that the most the sport can give us, in the very best scenario, is incomprehensibly meager and worthless: just a few isolated moments of transcendence. That's all.

But what the hell else is life made of?

19

Adrenaline does strange things to the body. When the final signal sounds, it makes moms and dads jump over the boards, respected entrepreneurs and factory managers slide around on the ice on slippery shoes, hugging each other like overtired toddlers in diapers. When Kevin drapes himself and Benji in a huge green flag and starts skating a lap of honor, the stands are already pretty much empty. The rink has filled up with the entire community. Everywhere people are jumping, slipping, tumbling, laughing, celebrating, crying. Childhood friends, classmates, parents, siblings, relatives, neighbors. How long will the town remember this? Only forever.

When you lose in hockey it feels like having your heart scalded. When you win, you own the clouds. Beartown is a heavenly town this evening.

Peter stops by the boards in one corner. He sits down alone on the ice and just laughs. All those hours in the office, all the arguments, the sleepless nights and angst-ridden mornings, they're all worth it now, every last one of them. He's still sitting there when the rest of the town, one inhabitant at a time, leaves the ice. Robbie Holts comes and sits down next to him. They just grin.

Adrenaline does strange things, especially when it leaves you. When he was a player, Peter kept getting told how important it was to "control your adrenaline," but he never understood that. For him, his complete, unquestioned focus and concentration out on the ice, his ability to live absolutely in the moment, came quite naturally. It was only when he had to watch a game from the stands for the first time that he realized how close adrenaline is to panic. What rouses the body to battle and achievement are the same instincts that instill mortal dread in the brain.

During his career as a player Peter used to think of the final signal at the end of a game as a roller coaster that's come to a halt: Some people think, "Good, that's over." And some think, "Again!" His first wish after every game was always to be allowed to play another one. Now, as GM, he needs migraine pills just to be able to function normally afterward.

When the last supporters, parents, and sponsors, delirious with victory, finally leave the rink over an hour later and spill out across the parking lot, chanting, "WE ARE THE BEARS, WE ARE THE BEARS, WE ARE THE BEARS, THE BEARS FROM BEARTOWN!" Peter, Robbie, and their memories stay behind.

"Do you want to come up to the office?" Peter asks, and Robbie bursts out laughing.

"Bloody hell, Peter, this is our first date—I'm not that kind of girl!"

Peter laughs too.

"Sure? We can have some tea and look at old team photos?"

Robbie holds out his hand.

"Say hi to your lads from me, okay? Tell them a proud old soldier was here watching them this evening."

Peter squeezes his hand.

"Drop around for dinner one evening. Kira would love to see you too."

"Sure!" Robbie lies, and they both know it.

They part. We only get moments.

The locker room is empty. After the adrenaline, after the singing and dancing and jumping on benches and banging on walls, after having just been packed with young and old men alike with bare chests and beer in their hair, it's now numbingly silent. Amat is the only one left, he's going around picking up scraps of tape from the floor. Peter walks down the corridor and stops in surprise.

"What are you still doing here, Amat?"

The boy reddens.

"Don't say anything okay? About me doing a bit of tidying up? I just want to deal with the worst of it."

Peter's throat starts to tighten with shame. He remembers when he used to see the boy collect empty cans from the stand so that Fatima could afford to buy hockey gear for him for the first time, when he was eight or nine years old. They were too proud to accept charity, so Peter and Kira had to place fake adverts in the local paper so that every year some cheap, secondhand equipment in Amat's size would just happen to show up. Kira built up a network of people all the way to Hed who took turns pretending to be the sellers.

"No, no . . . of course not, Amat, it would never even occur to me to say anything to the other players," he mumbles.

Amat looks up, baffled. Then he snorts.

"The players? I don't give a shit what you say to the players. Don't say anything to Mom! She gets really pissed off if I do her job!"

Peter wishes he could say something to the boy just then. Something about how incredibly proud he made him out on the ice that evening. But he lacks the words for that; he doesn't know how to go about it. And feels like a bad actor when he does try. Sometimes he gets so envious of David's ability to make these young guys love him that it drives him mad. They trust David, they follow him, worship him. Peter feels like a forlorn parent at the playground watching some jokey mom or dad farther away who manages to get all the kids roaring with laughter.

So he says none of the things he'd like to say to Amat. Just smiles and nods, and manages to say:

"You must be the only teenager in the world who gets told off by his mom for cleaning too much."

Amat hands him a grown man's shirt.

"One of the sponsors left this."

It smells of alcohol. Peter slowly shakes his head.

"Look . . . Amat . . . I . . ."

Words fail him. All that comes out is:

"I think you should go out into the parking lot. You've never gone out of this rink after a match like this. I think you should, it's quite an experience, one not many people get to have. You can walk through that door as . . . a winner."

Amat doesn't really understand what that means until he actually packs his equipment away, heads out into the corridor, and pushes through the outside door. Grownups cheer and applaud when they see him, a few of the older girls from school shout his name, Bobo gives him a hug, Benji ruffles his hair, and everyone wants to shake his hand. Farther away he can see Kevin being interviewed by the local paper. Then he writes autographs for a sea of children while their mothers nag him to let them take two photographs each: one of Kevin and the child, and one of Kevin and the mother.

Amat bounces around between the hugs and pats on the back, and hears himself join in a shouted rendition of "WE ARE THE BEARS FROM BEARTOWN!" so loudly that his chest stings, and he hears the others singing louder because he does, because they want to feel that they're participating in what he represents now.

The rush lifts him up, his endorphins are bubbling, and afterward he will remember thinking: "How can anyone possibly experience this without thinking he's a god?"

Kira is cleaning the cafeteria. Maya and Ana emerge from the wash-room; they've changed and put on makeup, and are full of laughter and expectation.

"I . . . I'll be staying at Ana's tonight. We're going to . . . study," Maya smiles.

Her daughter is lying, of course, and her mother is lying when she pretends not to understand that. They're balancing on that defining moment in life when they're each equally concerned about the other. The teenage years offer a brief period of equality after childhood, be-fore the balance shifts and Maya becomes old enough to worry about her parents more than they do about her. Soon Maya won't be Kira's little girl anymore, and then Kira will become Maya's little old mom. It doesn't take a lot to be able to let go of your child. It takes everything.

Peter steps into the president's office. It's full of grown men stumbling about, already very, very drunk.

"That's what I've been looking for!" Tails yells, and comes staggering toward Peter, bare-chested, and grabs his shirt from Peter's hand.

Peter glares at him.

"I never want to hear that you've taken alcohol into the players' locker room again. They're kids, Tails."

"Pah, they're not KIDS, Peter, give it a rest! Let the boys celebrate!"

"I let the boys celebrate, I just think that grown men ought to have their limits."

Tails waves his words away as if they were persistent little insects. Two men behind him, clutching cans of beer, are engaged in a heated debate about the club's A-team players. One forward is described as "so fucking thick he can't even go and buy a loaf of bread without someone to hold his hand," a goalie is "soft in the head; you can tell because he married a woman everyone knows slept with half the team before him, and probably the other half afterward." Peter isn't sure if the men are sponsors or just part of Tails's group, but he's heard remarks like that a thousand times and still hasn't gotten used to the hierarchy in these rooms. The players can talk crap about the referee but never the coach, the coach can criticize the players but never the GM, the GM can't criticize the president, the president can't criticize the board, the board can't criticize the sponsors. And at the very top are the men in suits in this office, talking shamelessly about the players as if they were racehorses. Products.

Tails tweaks Peter's ear affectionately to lighten the mood.

"Don't sulk, now, Peter, this is your night! Do you remember ten years ago when you said you were going to develop our youth program? When you said that one day we'd have a junior team that could hold their own against the best in the country? We laughed at you then. Everyone laughed at you. And now here we are! This is YOUR night, Peter. YOU made this happen."

Peter wriggles out of the headlock Tails—drunk and happy—tries to get him in. The other sponsors start loudly comparing scars and capped teeth, trophies from their own hockey-playing days. None of them asks Peter about his. He has no scars, he never lost any teeth, never got into any fights. He has never been a violent man.

One board member, a beer-sodden director of a ventilation company in his sixties, starts bouncing about and slapping Peter on the back as he grins:

"Tails and I met our local councilors! They were here this evening! And off the record I can say that things look pretty damn promising for your new espresso machine!"

Peter sighs and excuses himself, then goes out into the hallway. When he sees David he actually feels relieved, even though the junior coach's constantly supercilious attitude normally drives him mad, because right now he's the only sober person in the vicinity.

"David!" he cries.

David carries on without so much as glancing at him. Peter jogs after him.

"David! Where are you going?"

"I'm going to watch the video of the game," the coach replies mechanically.

Peter laughs.

"Aren't you going to celebrate?"

"I'll celebrate when we've won the final. That's why you appointed me. To win that."

His arrogance is even more pronounced than usual. Peter sighs and stick his hands forlornly in his pockets.

"David . . . come on, now. I know the two of us don't always see eye to eye on everything, but this is your victory. You've earned it."

David's eyes narrow, and he nods toward the office full of sponsors and says:

"No, Peter. Like everyone in there keeps saying, this is YOUR night. After all, you're the star on this team, aren't you? You always have been."

Peter stands rooted to the spot with a growing dark cloud in his stomach, unsure if it's made up mostly of shame or fury. His voice sounds angrier than it should be when he calls after David:

"I only wanted to congratulate you!" David turns around with a bitter little laugh.

"You should congratulate Sune instead. He was the one who predicted that you and I could do this."

Peter clears his throat.

"I . . . He . . . I couldn't find him in the stands."

David holds Peter's gaze until Peter looks down. David nods sadly.

"He was sitting in his usual place. You know that."

Peter swears under his breath and turns away. David's words creep after him:

"I know what we're doing here, Peter, I'm not some naive little kid. I'll be getting Sune's job because the time has come, because I've earned it, and I know that makes me a bastard. But don't forget who's holding the door open for him. Don't try to kid yourself that this isn't your decision."

Peter spins around, fists clenched.

"Be careful what you say, David!"

David doesn't back down.

"Or what? You'll hit me?"

Peter's chin is trembling. David stands motionless. In the end David snorts derisively. He has a long scar across his chin, and another between his chin and cheek.

"No, I thought not. Because you're Peter Andersson. You always let others take penalty suspensions for you."

David doesn't even slam the door behind him when he goes into his office, he just closes it silently. Peter hates him for that more than anything. Because he's right.

Kevin looks completely unmoved when he's being interviewed by the journalist from the local paper. Other boys his age would go to pieces with nerves, but he's calm and professional. He looks at the reporter's face but never in the eye, he fixes his gaze on her forehead or the top of her nose, he's relaxed but not nonchalant, he's not unpleasant, but not pleasant either, and he answers all her questions without saying anything at all. When she asks about the game, he mutters that "it's all about doing a lot of skating, getting the puck in the net, creating chances." When she asks what he thinks victory in the final would mean for the town and the people here, he repeats like a machine: "We're taking each game as it comes, concentrating on the hockey." When she points out that one of the opponents checked by his team-mate Benjamin Ovich toward the end of the game was left concussed, Kevin claims without blinking: "I didn't see that incident."

He's seventeen years old and already as media savvy as a politician. The crowd carries him away before the reporter has time to ask anything else.

Amat finds his mother in the crowd and kisses her on the forehead. She merely whispers, "Go! Go!" with tears in her eyes. He laughs and hugs her and promises not to be late home. She knows he's not telling the truth. And it makes her so happy.

Zacharias is standing at the far end of the parking lot, in the outermost circle of popularity, while his best friend is in the innermost circle for the first time. The adults get in their cars and drive off, leaving the youngsters to enjoy the biggest night ever, and when the stream of players and girls starts to move off toward the party that almost all of them are going to, it becomes painfully obvious who belongs and who's going to be left behind.

Zacharias will never ask Amat if he forgot about him or simply didn't care. But one of them goes, and one stays behind. And nothing will ever be quite the same again.

Peter bumps into Maya and Ana when he's on his way to the cafeteria. To his surprise, his daughter throws her arms around his neck, the way she used to every day when he came home back when she was five years old.

"I'm so proud of you, Dad," she whispers.

Rarely has he let go of her more reluctantly. Once the girls have rushed down the stairs laughing, the entire rink falls silent. A silence only broken by his own breathing, followed by his wife's voice:

"Is it my turn now, superstar?" Kira calls.

Peter's face breaks into a melancholic smile and he walks toward her. Gently they take hold of each other's hands and dance slowly, slowly, in tiny, tiny circles until Kira takes his face in her hands and kisses him so hard that he gets embarrassed. She can still do that to him.

"You don't look as happy as you should," she whispers.

"Oh, I am," he ventures.

"Is it to do with Sune?"

He hides his face against her neck.

"The sponsors want to go public with the news about David taking over after the final. And they want to force Sune to hand in his notice voluntarily. They think it'll look bad in the media if he gets fired."

"It's not your fault, darling. You can't save everyone. You can't carry the weight of the whole world."

He doesn't answer. She tickles his hair and smiles.

"Did you see your daughter? She going to go back to Ana's to 'study.'"

"Quite a lot of makeup for solving equations, eh?" Peter mutters.

"The hardest thing about trusting teenagers is the fact that we used to be teenagers ourselves. I can remember when some boy and I were . . ."

"I don't want to hear this!"

"Don't be ridiculous, darling, I did have a life before I met you."

"NO!"

He sweeps her up off the floor and into his arms, and all the air goes out of her. He can still do that to her. They giggle like a couple of kids.

Through the window of the cafeteria they see Maya and Ana go off down the road with the hockey players and their school friends. The temperature is falling rapidly in the darkness, and snow is swirling around the girls' bodies.

There's a storm brewing.

20

The windows of the Erdahl family house are rattling from over-strained loudspeakers, the ground floor fills with bodies at the same rate as if they were being thrown in through a hole in the ceiling. Most of the players are already hopelessly hammered, and the majority of the other guests aren't far behind. They aren't novices when it comes to parent-free houses. Everyone is drinking from disposable cups, all the pictures have been removed from the walls, fragile objects moved, the furniture covered in plastic. Two of the juniors take turns guarding the staircase all night to stop anyone going upstairs. Say what you like about Kevin, but just like his coach, he believes in preparation and planning, and doesn't leave anything to coincidence. The cleaner is coming first thing tomorrow. She gets paid well not to say anything to his parents, and on a night like this one he knows the neighbors will go to bed with earplugs and pretend they weren't home if anyone asks.

No longer does anyone question the fact that he seems to be the only person not enjoying his own party. In the living room teenagers are drinking and singing as they shed their clothing at an ever-increasing rate, but on the other side of the thick, heavily insulated walls, the garden is almost silent. The sweat is dripping from Kevin's face as he goes on firing shot after shot after shot at the goal. He can never wind down after a match, but at least he's not so violent if they've won. If they've lost, the terrace and little rink end up littered with broken sticks and shattered glass. As usual, Benji is sitting perfectly calm at a cast-iron table, rolling cigarettes nimbly between his fingers to get the tobacco out without breaking the paper. He fills the empty tube with weed, twists the end shut, carefully puts the filter between his teeth, removes it, and replaces it with a thinly rolled piece of cardboard. He has to do it this way because the woman who owns the tobacconist's in Beartown is the sister of the school's headmaster, so he can't buy loads of cigarette papers but not an equivalent quantity of tobacco without questions being asked. Ordering online would be pointless; Benji's mother checks all the mail that arrives at the house like a sniffer dog. So, even though no one has ever seen Kevin smoke, a few years ago he started to charge an admission fee of two cigarettes from everyone attending his parties, so that Benji has something to roll his joints with. Oddly enough Kevin finds it relaxing, watching his idiotic best friend focus so intently on his drugs.

Kevin grins and says, "I'm going to sell you into child labor in Asia—those agile fingers could stitch footballs faster than any other little kid's."

"Do you want me to sew a bigger net for you so you can actually hit the goal every now and then?" Benji wonders, then ducks down like a shot without even looking up to avoid the puck that Kevin fires over his head. It hits the fence behind him, making it sway for several minutes.

"Don't forget to roll some for the housecleaner," Kevin reminds him. Benji hasn't forgotten. This isn't the first party they've hosted.

Amat walks into the house and can't help gawking.

"Okay, seriously? Just ONE family lives here?"

Bobo and Lyt laugh and push him toward the kitchen. Lyt is already so drunk that he couldn't put a magnet on a fridge door. They're drinking "knockshots." Amat doesn't know what's in them, but they taste of moonshine and throat lozenges, and every time you down one you have to beat your fists on each other's chests and roar "KNOCK-SHOT!" It feels a lot more logical after five or six of them. Most of the kids are doing it.

"You can fuck *any* girl you like here tonight; they're *all* hockey-whores when we win," Lyt slurs, gesturing toward the throng of bodies inside the house, then, just a moment later, violently grabbing hold of Amat's top and bellowing:

"Unless Kevin or Benji or I want her. The first line has first pick!"

Amat will later remember Bobo looking as uncomfortable as him when Lyt says this. It's the first time he's ever seen Bobo look uncertain about anything. As Lyt lurches away, shouting, "I got an assist tonight! Who wants to fuck?" the other two boys are left forlornly facing each other in the kitchen. They drink more, beat each other's chests, and yell, "KNOCKSHOTS!" to avoid having to talk, because they're both convinced you can tell from a man's voice if he's a virgin.

Maya and Ana are among the last to arrive at the house, because Ana insisted on stopping to check her makeup a couple of dozen times during the walk over. Every month she becomes obsessed with a different part of her body, and right now it's her cheekbones. Not long ago it was her hairline. That time she very solemnly asked Maya to help her find out if it was possible to have plastic surgery to make it lower.

Before they go inside the house Maya stops on the road to admire the view. From the street where the Erdahl family lives you can see right across the lake, all the way to the forest on the other side. It's more of a wilderness there; the trees grow more densely and even the snow seems to gather in deeper drifts. Beyond it lie open white spaces so vast that you could stand there as a child convinced you were the last person on the planet. Kids in Beartown soon learn that that's the place to go if you want to get up to no good out of sight of any adults. Maya knows that Ana came close to getting them both killed over there when they were little. When they were twelve she stole a snowmobile and drove Maya around all night. Maya has never admitted it, but she's never felt more liberated than she did then.

A year later Ana stopped googling how to hot-wire snowmobiles and started googling diets instead. So Maya takes a moment now to mourn the girls who used to play on the other side of the lake before she goes into the party.

———

Kevin is standing on the terrace and sees Maya walk into the hall through the big windows. He's looking right at her, and doesn't notice Benji watching him, reading his reaction. As Kevin moves quickly toward the terrace door, Benji irritably packs his things in his backpack and follows him. They push their way through the living room without a word, toward different goals. Kevin stops in front of Maya and makes a real effort to stop the pounding of his heart being visible through his shirt, and she does her best not to show how happy she is, or how much she's enjoying the fact that a whole gaggle of older girls in the kitchen are looking over and hating her.

"Madame," Kevin smiles theatrically and gives a deep bow.

"Herr von Shitmagnet, how delightful to see you!" she laughs, bowing to him in return.

Kevin opens his mouth but stops himself when he sees Benji disappear through the front door. He looks almost as disappointed as the girls in the kitchen and Ana do.

Out in the street Benji pulls his backpack onto his shoulders, shields his lighter from the wind, and waits for the smoke to curl its way into his lungs. He hears Kevin call but doesn't turn around.

"Come on, Benji, you freak! Don't be stupid!"

"I don't party with little girls, Kev, you know that. What are they? Fifteen?"

Kevin throws his arms out.

"Come off it, it wasn't even me who invited them!"

Benji turns around and looks his best friend in the eye. It takes almost ten seconds before Kevin starts laughing. Nice try.

"You can't lie to me, Kev."

"Stay anyway?" Kevin asks with a grin.

Benji calmly shakes his head. Kevin blinks sadly.

"What are you going to do, then?"

"Have my own party." Kevin looks at the backpack.

"Don't smoke so much that you start seeing little pixies with knives and shit in the forest again, okay? I don't want to have to come looking for you because you're sitting huddled up in some fucking tree shouting and crying."

Benji bursts out laughing.

"That happened *once*. And it wasn't weed."

"Do you remember how you phoned me and screamed, 'I'VE FORGOTTEN HOW TO BLINK'?"

"Don't joke about that. It was seriously fucking nasty."

Kevin looks like he wants to touch him. He doesn't.

"And if you're going to steal a car, don't do it on this street, okay? Dad would get seriously pissed off."

Benji nods, but doesn't make any promises. Then he pulls a joint from his pocket and tucks it gently behind Kevin's ear.

"For later. With a bit of tobacco, just the way you like it."

Kevin gives him a quick hug, so fleeting that no one would notice, but still so hard that it speaks volumes. He can never sleep after games, and that's the only time he smokes. Only best friends know that sort of thing about each other. Only two boys who once lay side by side under the covers, reading comics by flashlight and realizing that the reason they always felt like outsiders was because they were superheroes.

As Benji walks off into the darkness Kevin watches him go for a long time, feeling envious. He knows the girls fall for him because he's good at hockey; without it he'd only be an average, mediocre seventeen-year-old. But not Benji. They fall for him for completely different reasons. He's got something everyone wants, something completely independent of anything he does on the ice. His eyes always let you know that he could leave you any moment if he felt like it, without so much as a backward glance. He isn't tied to anything, he just doesn't care. Kevin is terrified of loneliness, but Benji embraces it as a natural state. All through their childhood Kevin has been scared that one day he'll wake up and discover that the other superhero is gone. That this friendship never meant anything to him.

Benji's blood is different from other people's. He disappears into the forest on the road down toward the lake, and Kevin can't help thinking that Benji is the only truly free individual he knows.

That's the last time they see each other in their childhood. That ends tonight.

21

Maya watches Kevin's every move when he comes back into the house. At first he looks like a kitten that's been left out in the rain. Abandoned and forgotten, even though she's never encountered anyone who's at the center of things as much as him. Then he downs two drinks out in the kitchen and roars, "KNOCKSHOTS!" with Bobo and Amat, and jumps up and down with his arm around Lyt, so hard that the floor vibrates, singing, "WE ARE THE BEARS!"

She isn't sure when he gives her the first alcoholic drink, but the second one isn't anywhere near as repulsive. He keeps making bets with Lyt about who can finish their drink first, and Kevin wins every time, and Maya smiles indulgently and says:

"Honestly! You hockey guys can't even drink without turning it into a competition!"

Kevin looks directly at her, as if they were alone, and seems to take her comment as a challenge.

"Get more shots," he tells Lyt.

"Yes! Run, Lyt, I'll time you!" Maya laughs sarcastically, clapping her hands.

Lyt runs straight into a wall. Kevin laughs so hard that he's left gasping for breath. Maya is fascinated by the way he always seems to be living in the moment. On the ice he doesn't seem to think about anything but hockey, and off it he doesn't seem to think about anything at all. He lives on instinct. She wishes she could be like that.

She doesn't know how much they drink; she can remember beating Lyt at drinking three shots in a row, then standing on a chair with her arms raised in triumph as if she were holding a giant trophy.

Kevin likes the fact that she's different. That her eyes never quite stop moving, that she's always watching. That she seems to know who she is. He wishes he could be like that.

Ana stops drinking after the first shot. She doesn't really know why, but Benji has disappeared and he was the reason she wanted to come. She's standing in the kitchen with Maya, but people keep getting in between them. Ana can see the way the older girls look every time Kevin laughs at something Maya says, somewhere between derision and a death threat. She feels Lyt's hands on the base of her spine and moves farther and farther into the corner. No matter how hard she sandpapers herself, how small she makes herself, she's never going to fit in here.

Benji walks across the ice until he reaches the middle of the lake. He stands there smoking, and watches as the town goes out, one house at a time. The hard shell beneath his feet is rocking slightly; it's late in the year to be this far out alone at night, even for Beartown. He's always liked toying with the idea of falling through and disappearing into the cold darkness beneath, even when he was a child. Wondering if everything painful would cause less pain down there. Perhaps surprisingly, his dad's suicide didn't make him frightened of death, but the reverse. The only thing Benji doesn't understand is why his dad felt obliged to use a rifle. The forest, the ice, the lake, the cold—this town offers thousands of ways to die a natural death.

He stands out there until the smoke and sub-zero temperature have numbed him inside and out, then he walks back to the town, heads into one of the smaller residential areas, and steals a moped. He rides off toward Hed.

"Why don't you like hockey players?" Kevin asks.

"You're not particularly smart," Maya laughs.

"What do you mean by that?" He seems genuinely interested.

"You discovered the jockstrap seventy years before you invented the helmet," she says.

"We know how to prioritize," he says with a big smile.

They drink some more. When they have bets, he wins. He never loses.

"The Barn" is a poor name for a bar, possibly all the more so if it is actually in a barn. But, as Katia's boss usually puts it: no one has ever looked at anyone in Hed and said, "You know what, you've almost got *too much* imagination!" A band is playing on the stage in front of a handful of spectacularly uninterested men in varying stages of middle age and intoxication. Katia is standing at the bar when the bouncer comes over to her.

"Does your brother own a moped?"

"No."

The bouncer chuckles.

"In that case I'll tell him to park it around the back."

Katia, the second-eldest big sister of the little brother who is bound to be the death of them all one day, merely sighs when Benji walks in. She doesn't know if he goes looking for trouble or if it seeks him out, she just knows that you never find one without the other. Lucky for him that his eldest sister isn't here, she thinks, because she'd have broken his neck by now. But Katia can't be angry, not with him, she's never been able to.

"Calm down, I'm going to take the moped back," Benji promises, and tries to smile even though she can see he's in a foul mood.

"I heard you won today. What are you doing here?" his sister asks.

"I'm celebrating, you can see that," he replies bitterly, and she leans forward and kisses the top of his head hard.

"Did you go to see Dad?"

He nods. Her beloved little brother—she can see why all the girls fall for him. "Sad eyes, wild heart, nothing but trouble lies ahead for that sort," their mother says, and she knows from experience. Katia has never been to their father's grave, not once, but she thinks of him sometimes, and how it must have felt to be so unhappy and not be able to tell anyone. It's a terrible thing to have to keep a big secret from the people you love.

When Benji is angry with something he shows up at his youngest older sister, Gaby's, and plays with her children until he gets over it. When he wants to be quiet and think, he goes to see his eldest sister, Adri, over at her kennels. But when he's feeling bruised, he comes here. To Katia. So she pats his cheek gently instead of yelling at him.

"If you can watch the bar for a bit, I can sort things out in the office. Then you can come back to my place with me. The guys will sort out the moped thing," she says, nodding toward the bouncers.

First thing tomorrow morning two men you really wouldn't want to get into an argument with will return the moped to its owner, explaining to him that "he must have left it in Hed by mistake." When it gets taken to the garage to be repaired, the garage will do the work free of charge. That's pretty much all anyone needs to know around here.

"And don't touch the damn beer!" Katia orders.

Benji goes around the bar and waits until his sister has gone into the office before opening a bottle of beer. The band onstage are playing covers of old rock songs, because that's what you have to play if you want to play in Hed. They look the way you'd expect: overweight and undertalented and distinctly average. All but the bass player. There's nothing average about him at all. Black hair, black clothes, but he still stands out. The others are giving it their all, but he looks like he's just playing. He's standing there, squeezed into one and a half square yards between an amp and a cigarette machine, but he's dancing in his own little kingdom. As if this barn weren't at the end of the world but at its beginning.

The bass player notices the young bartender with the messy hair in the silence between two songs. And at that moment the rest of the room might as well have been empty.

Ana comes out from the bathroom. Lyt is standing right outside the door. He leans his bulky frame toward her and tries to bundle the two of them back through the doorway. If he weren't already drunk he might have succeeded, but Ana slips nimbly out of the way and darts out into the hall as he grasps for the sink to keep himself upright.

"Come on! Fuck it, I got an assist today, don't I get anything for that?"

Ana backs away, glancing instinctively to her right and her left along the narrow hallway, like an animal in the forest evaluating escape routes. Lyt holds his arms out and slurs heavily:

"I saw the way you looked at Benji. That's fine. But he won't be coming back here tonight. He's a pothead . . . right? So he won't be back on this PLANET tonight! So forget about him and fosus . . . fosuc . . . foscus on ME instead! I got a fucking ast . . . astist . . . fucking ASSIST tonight and WE WON!"

Ana slams the door in his face and runs toward the kitchen, looking for Maya. She can't see her anywhere.

Benji is pouring beer at the bar. The band has stopped playing; Katia's put some country music on instead. Benji turns toward the next customer so quickly that he almost hits him in the face with a glass. The bass player smiles. Benji raises his eyebrows.

"Wow, a musician in my bar. What would you like? It's on the house." The bass player tilts his head.

"A whisky sour?"

Benji's grin stretches from ear to ear.

"And where the hell do you think you are? Hollywood? You can have a JD and coke."

He mixes the drink as he talks and slides the glass across the bar with a practiced hand. The bassist gives it a long stare without touching it, then admits:

"Sorry, I don't even like whisky. I was just trying to sound like a rocker."

"Whisky sour isn't all that fucking rock'n'roll," Benji informs him.

The bass player runs his hand through his hair.

"I met a bartender once who said that if you stand on that side of the bar long enough you start to see everyone as a type of drink. Like some warped version of that 'spirit animal' thing fortune tellers go on about. Know what I mean?"

Benji laughs out loud. He doesn't often do that.

"Well, your spirit animal isn't whisky, I can tell you that much."

The bassist nods and leans forward discreetly.

"I'm actually more interested in something veiled in smoke than drowned in coke. I heard from someone that you might be able to help me with that?"

Benji downs the bass player's drink and nods.

"What did you have in mind?"

Amat and Bobo never actually decide to go out into the garden. It just happens. They're both bad at parties, they don't know what to do, so it's natural that they should seek out something that they do understand. Something they know how to do. So they end up standing in the garden, each clutching one of Kevin's sticks and taking turns firing pucks at the goal.

"How do you get to be so fast?" Bobo asks drunkenly.

"You spend a lot of time running away from people like you at school," Amat replies, half joking and half serious.

Bobo laughs, half properly and half not. Amat notes that he shoots harder than you might think, when he can stand still and calmly take aim.

"Sorry . . . I . . . You know it's just a joke, don't you? You know . . . it's a thing . . . the A-team shit on us and we shit on you."

"Yeah, yeah. Just a joke," Amat lies.

Bobo shoots harder. Full of guilt.

"You're in the first line now. You get to throw my clothes in the shower from now on, not the other way round."

Amat shakes his head.

"You smell far too bad for me to want to touch your clothes, Bobo."

Bobo's laughter echoes between the houses, genuine now. Amat smiles at him. Bobo suddenly lowers his voice.

"I need to get quicker before autumn. Or I won't be allowed to play anymore."

This is Bobo's last season before he gets too old for the junior team. In other towns there are junior teams that go up to twenty-one, but not in Beartown, where there aren't enough young men left in town after they graduate from high school. Some move away for school, others for work. The best players move up to the seniors, the rest get left over.

"But then there's the A-team!" Amat says brightly, but Bobo lets out a dry snort. "I'll never make the A-team. This is my last season if I don't get faster. Then there's just repairing cars with Dad for the rest of my life."

Amat doesn't say anything more; he doesn't need to. Everyone who's played hockey for as much as five minutes as a child knows that there's no better sport. No greater rush. Amat takes a deep breath and says something he will never admit to anyone else:

"I was frightened today, Bobo. I was terrified the whole way through the game. I wasn't even happy when we won, just relieved. I . . . Shit, do you remember when you were little and used to play out on the lake? That was nothing but fun. You didn't even think, it was just the only thing you wanted to do. It's still the only thing I want to do. I have no idea what I'm going to do if I can't do this; hockey's the only thing I'm any good at. But now . . . it just feels like . . ."

"Work," Bobo concludes, without even looking at him.

Amat nods.

"I was scared the whole time. Does that sound sick?"

Bobo shakes his head. They don't say any more about it. They just fire their pucks without speaking. *Bang-bang-bang-bang-bang.*

Bobo nods and grins. They're fifteen and seventeen years old, and in ten years' time they'll remember this evening, when all the others were inside having a party, and they stood out here and became friends.

The night is clear and full of stars, the trees are still, and they're standing behind the barn smoking. Benji never usually gets high with strangers, because most of the time it's an intimate and solitary act for him, and he doesn't really know why tonight should be an exception. The way the bass player made his own space on the stage, maybe. Like he was in some other dimension. Benji recognized it. Or longed for it.

"What have you done to your face?" the bass player asks, pointing at the scar on his chin.

"Hockey," Benji replies.

"So you're a fighter?"

His accent betrays the fact that he's not from this part of the country. The question reveals that it's probably his first visit.

"If that's what you want to know, you shouldn't look for scars on people's faces. You should be looking for scars on their knuckles," Benji replies.

The bassist takes some deep drags, blows his bangs from his eyes.

"Of all the sports I don't understand why anyone would play, hockey is the one I understand least."

Benji snorts.

"Isn't the bass what people who can't play the guitar play?"

The bass player laughs loudly, and the sound sings between the trees and hits Benji in his head as quickly as in his chest. Very few people have that effect. Very few people are tequila and champagne at the same time.

"Have you always lived here in Hed? Don't you get cabin fever in a town this small?" the bassist smiles.

His gaze alternates between shy and greedy as it roams across Benji's lips. Benji lets the smoke filter up over his cheeks.

"I live in Beartown. Hed is big in comparison. What are you doing here?"

The bassist shrugs his shoulders, tries to sound nonchalant, but all the hurt inside him shines out.

"My cousin sings in the band. Their bass player went off to college somewhere and they asked if I wanted to move here and play for a couple of months. They're really shit and we get, like, a crate of beer in return for playing, but I'd just . . . I was in a bad relationship. I needed to get away."

"It's hard to get any farther than this," Benji says.

The bass player listens to the trees, feels tentative snowflakes land on his hands. His voice trembles in the darkness.

"It's more beautiful than I thought. Here."

Benji goes on smoking with his eyes closed. He wishes he'd smoked some more. Or was drunk. Maybe then he would have dared. But now he just says:

"Not like where you're from."

The bass player inhales Benji's smoke. Nods down toward the ground.

"We'll be playing here again next Sunday. If you want to come. It would be . . . I'd like to get to know someone. Here."

His black clothes fall gently over his thin frame. His movements are soft and light, so free from exertion that he seems weightless. In a forest full of predators he stands above the covering of snow like some sort of bird. His breath is cold as it reaches Benji's skin. Benji extinguishes the glow in his hand and takes two steps back.

"I need to go in before my sister sees me standing out here."

"Big, tough hockey player, but you're scared of your sister?" the bass player smiles.

Benji shrugs his shoulders lightly. "You would be too. Who the hell do you think taught me to fight?"

"See you next Sunday, then?" the bass player calls.

He doesn't get an answer.

Maya is standing in the kitchen when she suddenly realizes that Ana is gone. She goes to look for her. The guys see her leaning against the wall to keep her balance as the alcohol tosses her around inside, like a penguin on an unsteady piece of ice. Lyt leans closer to Kevin's ear and whispers:

"The GM's daughter, Kev, Christ, you'll NEVER get to fuck her!"

"Want to bet?" Kevin grins.

"A hundred kronor."

Lyt nods. They shake on it.

Afterward Maya will remember bizarre details, like the fact that Kevin had spilled a drink on his shirt and the stain looked like a butterfly. No one will want to hear her talk about that. The only thing they'll ask about that night is how much she'd had to drink. If she was drunk. If she held his hand. Gave him signals. If she went upstairs voluntarily.

"Lost?" he smiles when he finds her beside the stairs.

By that point she's been around the ground floor three times without finding the bathroom. She laughs and throws her arms out. Forgets Ana.

"This is a completely crazy house. It's like you live in Hogwarts."

"Do you want to see upstairs?" he asks.

She'll never stop wishing that she hadn't gone with him up the stairs.

Katia's car starts reluctantly on the eighth or ninth attempt.

"You can sleep over at the kennels with Adri tonight."

"No, drive me home," Benji says sleepily.

She pats him on the cheek.

"No, because you see, sweetie: Adri and I love our little brother. And if you go home to Mom smelling of beer and weed one more time, we won't have a little brother anymore."

He grunts and shrugs his jacket off, and makes a pillow out of it against the window. She pokes him on his arm, just below the sleeve of his T-shirt, where the tattoo of the bear peeps out, and says:

"That bass player was sweet. But I suppose you're going to tell me he isn't your type, the way you do about everyone?"

Benji replies with his eyes closed:

"He didn't like hockey."

She laughs at that, but as her little brother falls asleep Katia blinks away tears. Throughout his childhood, ever since the sandboxes and swings, she has seen girls look at him. As much because they dream of being able to rein him in as because they suspect it wouldn't be possible. But they never understand why.

With each passing year, as Benji has grown older, Katia has wished him a different life. In a different place, another time, maybe he would have been a different boy. Milder, more secure. But not in Beartown. Here he is burdened with too much that no one sees, and here he has hockey. The team, the guys, Kevin. They mean everything to him, so he is everything they want him to be. And that's a terrible thing.

Having to keep a secret from those you love.

Everyone talks about what it's like. The school nurse, the poor teacher in charge of the sex education lessons, anxious parents, moralizing television programs, the entire Internet. Everyone. All your life you're told exactly what happens. Even so, no one tells you it's going to be like this.

Maya is lying on her back on Kevin's bed. It's her first time smoking marijuana. It feels different from how she's imagined it—as if warmth has a flavor. The smoke seems to fly straight up into her head instead of down her throat. Kevin has posters of hockey players on the walls, trophies on all the shelves, but in one corner is an old record-player. She will remember that because it doesn't fit in.

"It's my dad's old one. I like the way it sounds . . . the way it crackles when you switch it on," he says, almost apologetically.

He puts some music on; she doesn't remember what, just remembers the crackle. In ten years' time she will hear the same crackle from a record-player in the corner of a bar or in a clothing boutique on the other side of the world and will be instantly transported back to this place, this moment. She feels the weight of his body on top of hers and she laughs—she'll remember that. They kiss each other, and she'll get these two questions more than any other she ever gets asked in her life: Who kissed whom? Did you kiss him back? He's the one kissing her. And yes, she kisses him back. But when he forces her jeans down she stops him. He seems to think it's a game, so she catches his hand and holds it tight.

"I don't want to, not tonight, I've nev . . . ," she whispers.

"Of course you want to," he insists.

She flares up.

"Are you deaf or what? I said no!"

His grip on her wrists tightens, first almost imperceptibly, then to the point where it hurts.

Katia turns the car onto the little road that leads up into the forest just after the "Welcome to Beartown" sign. Drives toward the kennels. There are no lights out here, so when Benji wakes up and looks out through the window, he doesn't realize what it is before they've already gone past.

"Stop," he mutters.

"What?" Katia replies.

"STOP!" Benji shouts.

Shocked, she brakes hard. Her little brother has already opened the door and run out into the darkness.

Everyone talks about what it's like. All your life you're told exactly what happens: you get assaulted on a jogging trail, beaten and dragged into an alleyway on a package holiday, drugged in a bar and locked up by unknown adult men in a slum in a big city. Everyone warns you, time and time again, they warn all girls: This can happen! This is how it happens!

It's just that no one tells you it can be like this: with someone you know. Trust. Have laughed with. In this boy's room, beneath the posters of hockey players with the entire floor below full of classmates. Kevin kisses her neck, moves her hand out of the way. She will remember the way he touched her body as if it didn't belong to her. As if it were a thing he had earned, as if her head and the rest were two separate objects, independent of each other. No one will ask her about that. They'll just ask how much resistance she put up. If she was "clear" enough.

"Stop playing hard to get—you came upstairs with me, didn't you?" he laughs.

She tries to pull his hand away, but he's infinitely stronger than her. She tries to twist out of his grip and get up from the bed, but his knee is locked around her waist.

"Stop it, Kevin, I don't wa . . ." His breathing echoes in her ear.

"I'll be careful, I promise. I thought you liked me."

"I do . . . but I've never . . . Stop it, please!"

She tries so desperately to move his hand that her nails tear two deep scratches in his skin. She will remember seeing drops of blood seep out, slowly, slowly, slowly, and the way he doesn't even seem to notice. He is holding her down with his weight alone; he doesn't even have to put any effort into it, and his tone changes instantly:

"Come on, for fuck's sake! Stop playing hard to get! I can go downstairs and get whatever girl I want and fuck her instead!"

With a last effort Maya manages to pull one hand free, and hits him as hard as she can across the cheek.

"Go on, then! Do that!!! And LET GO OF ME!!!"

He doesn't let go. His eyes just turn black. It's as if he's no longer in there anymore, the guy she had spent all evening joking around with. When she tries to stop his hand he closes his other fist tightly around her throat like a vise, and when she tries to scream his fingers are covering her lips. Lack of oxygen makes her slip in and out of consciousness, and in the midst of everything she will remember peculiar details that no one asks about: a button coming off her blouse when he tears it open, and the fact that she hears it land and bounce across the floor somewhere in the room. And she will remember thinking: "How am I going to find that later?"

They will ask her about the alcohol and marijuana. They won't ask about the bottomless terror that will never leave her. About this room with its record-player and posters, from which she will never really escape again. One blouse-button somewhere on the floor, and a sense of panic that will be with her forever. She sobs noiselessly beneath his body, and screams silently behind his hand.

For the perpetrator, rape lasts just a matter of minutes. For the victim, it never stops.

22

It's Saturday night, and everything is different now. Ana just doesn't know it yet. All she knows is that the older girls in the kitchen laugh at her cruelly when she asks after Maya.

"That little whore? She went off with Kevin. Don't worry, sweetie, he'll throw her back when he's finished with her. No one on the team holds on to second-rate bitches!"

Their laughter tears holes in Ana's lungs and her throat tightens. Granted, she could have gone off to look for her best friend, and stands there with her phone in her hand for several minutes without actually calling. But anger gets the better of her. Few disappointments can compare with the way you feel the first time your best friend dumps you for a boy, and there's no more silent walk than the one that takes you home alone after a party when you're fifteen years old.

Ana and Maya found each other as children when they saved each other's lives. One pulled the other out of a hole in the ice, and in return she pulled the other out of her loneliness. They were opposites in many ways, but they both liked dancing badly, singing loud, and going fast on snowmobiles. That goes a long way. Best friends. Sisters before misters. And of all the things they've promised each other, the most important: we never desert each other.

The girls in the kitchen are still laughing at Ana. They're saying something about her clothes and her body, but she's no longer listening; she's already heard it all in the school corridors and in comments online. Lyt staggers around a corner and catches sight of her, and Ana mutters: "Fuck off." Because they all can. The whole lot of them.

As she walks out of the front door, she stops one last time and considers calling Maya. Maybe going upstairs to look for her. But she's not going to beg and plead for attention. Even in a town that's covered with snow three-quarters of the year, it's unbearably cold standing in the shade of someone who's a bit more popular than you are. Ana puts her phone on silent and drops it in her bag. Humanity has many shortcomings, but none is stronger than pride.

She sees Amat and grabs hold of his shoulder. He's so drunk he couldn't even read the top line of an optician's chart. Ana sighs.

"If you see Maya, tell her I couldn't be bothered to wait for her to decide if she likes peanuts or not."

Amat stammers at her in confusion. "Where . . . I mea . . . Wha . . . I mean . . . Who?" Ana rolls her eyes.

"Maya. Tell her I've gone."

"Where . . . Where is she?"

The question makes his brain clearer, his voice more sober. Ana almost feels sorry for him.

"Oh, Amat, don't you get it? Try looking in Kevin's bedroom!"

Amat shatters into a thousand invisible pieces, but Ana doesn't feel like staying, doesn't want to be in this house when she herself falls apart. She slams the front door behind her and the night cold strokes her cheeks. Her breathing becomes easier immediately; her heartbeat calms. She grew up outside, and being stuck behind windows has always felt like being imprisoned. Social relationships, trying to make friends, be accepted, always starving and sandpapering herself smaller—it makes her feel claustrophobic. She takes the path through the forest in the darkness and feels infinitely safer there than in a house full of people. Nature has never done her any harm.

Behind a closed door on the upper floor of the Erdahl family house stays the only secret Maya has ever kept from her best friend: that right up to the last moment, when she could no longer breathe beneath Kevin, she kept telling herself one single thing: "I mustn't be frightened. Ana will find me. Ana won't desert me."

Amat will never be able to explain his reasons. Jealousy, maybe. Pride, probably. An inferiority complex, possibly. Infatuation, definitely.

There are two juniors sitting guarding the stairs, and when they tell him he can't go upstairs he roars at them, surprising not just them but himself: "And which fucking line do YOU play in?"

During all those years in little league and the boys' team, people kept saying his feet were superior, but that wasn't what took him all the way. It was the way he saw things. His eyes were always faster than everyone else's, he managed to see more than everyone else, re-membered every detail of every attack. The position of the backs, the movements of the goalie, the tiniest shift in the corner of his eye when a teammate put his stick on the ice.

Intimidated, the juniors get out of the way. There are three sections to the staircase. On the upstairs landing there are photographs of the entire Erdahl family, and beside them pictures of Kevin alone. Pictures of him everywhere. In hockey gear when he was five. When he was six. When he was seven. The same smile every year. The same look in his eyes.

They will ask Amat exactly what he heard. Exactly where he was. He will never be able to say if it was a "no" or a "stop," or just a desperate, muffled scream from behind the palm of a hand that made him react. Maybe none of those. Maybe he opened the door out of sheer instinct. They will ask him if he was drunk. They will glower at him accusingly and say: "But is it not the case that you are, and have been for many years, in love with the girl in question?" The only thing Amat will be able to reply to that is that his way of seeing was superior. Faster than his feet, even.

He pushes the door handle down and stands in the doorway to Kevin's room and sees the violence and torn clothes. The tears and the fiery red marks left by the boy's fingers on the girl's neck. One body taking the other against its will. He sees everything, and afterward he will dream about the most peculiar details: exactly which posters of exactly which NHL players were on the walls. Amat will remember that for the simplest possible reason. He has the same posters on the wall above his own bed.

———

Kevin loses his concentration for two seconds when Amat rushes through the door. That's twice as much time as Maya needs. She won't remember it as a reaction but as a fight to the death. A survival instinct. She manages to knee Kevin hard enough to get a tiny gap in which to push his body out of hers. She hits him as hard as she can in the neck, and runs. She doesn't know how she gets out of the room, who she passes on the way, if she hits or kicks the juniors guarding the stairs. Perhaps everyone at the party is too drunk to notice her, perhaps they only pretend not to see. She tumbles out through the door, and just runs.

The year is halfway into March, but the snow still embraces her feet as she marches along the side of the road in the darkness. Her tears are hot when they leave her eyelids but already frozen by the time they fall from her chin. "You can't live in this town; you can only survive it," as her mom says. Never has that been more true than tonight.

Maya tugs her jacket tighter around herself; she'll never know how she managed to take it with her—her blouse is torn to shreds, the skin on her neck and wrists already black with finger-shaped bruises. She hears Amat's voice behind her but doesn't slow down. The boy stumbles a few last breathless steps in the snow before falling to his knees in it. He's drunk and crushed as he calls her name. In the end she stops, turns with her fists clenched, and stares at him, her tears now caused by equal parts exposure and fury.

"What happened?" Amat whispers.

"What the hell do you think happened?" she replies.

"We need to . . . You need to . . ."

"What? What do I need to do, Amat? What the hell do I need to do?"

"Talk to someone . . . the police . . . anyone, you need to . . ."

"It won't make any difference, Amat. It won't make any difference what I say, because no one will believe me anyway."

"Why not?"

She rubs the back of her glove across her eyes, and it comes away stained with eyeliner. Amat is crying, too, now. They are fifteen years old and the entire world has collapsed in the course of a single evening. A solitary car passes them; Maya's eyes flare with the reflection of the headlights. When it's gone past, something goes out inside both her and her eyes.

"Because this is a fucking hockey town," she whispers.

Amat is left kneeling in the snow as she disappears down the road. The last thing he sees before night swallows her is her silhouette against the sign that says, "Welcome to Beartown."

Soon she won't be anymore.

Ana opens the door to the house. It swings open without a sound on freshly oiled hinges. Her dad is asleep; her mom no longer lives here. She walks through the kitchen toward the storeroom. The hunting dogs greet her with cold noses and warm hearts. She does what she has done a thousand times in her childhood when the house stank of alcohol and her parents were screaming at each other. She sleeps with the animals. Because the animals have never done her any harm.

For people who have never lived where darkness and cold are the norm, where anything else is the exception, it is hard to understand that it is possible to find someone who has frozen to death with their jacket open, or even naked. But when you get really cold your blood-vessels contract and your heart does all it can to stop blood reaching the frozen parts of your body and then coming back to your heart cold. Not unlike a hockey team suffering a penalty and playing at a numerical disadvantage: prioritize resources, play defensively, defend the heart, lungs, and brain. What happens when the defense finally collapses, when you get cold enough, is that your box play falls apart, your goalie does something stupid, your backs stop communicating with each other, and the body parts that were previously shut off from circulation are suddenly switched back on again. And then, when warm blood from your heart flows back to your frozen feet and hands, you experience an intense rush of heat. That's why you suddenly imagine that you're overheating and start to take your clothes off. Then the chilled blood goes back to your heart and it's all over. Every couple of years or so, someone in Beartown goes home drunk after a party and takes a shortcut across the ice, or gets lost in the forest, or sits down to rest for a moment, and is found lifeless in a snowdrift the following morning.

When Maya was little she often used to think how strange it was that her mom and dad, the two most overprotective parents in the universe, chose to settle here, of all places. Somewhere where even nature itself tried to murder their daughter every day. As she's gotten older she's come to realize that the admonitions "don't go out on the ice alone" and "don't go into the forest on your own" are almost designed to promote team sports. Every child in Beartown grows up with the constant warning that the threat of death is ever-present if you're alone.

She tries calling Ana, but gets no answer. She can't force herself to walk down the main street through town, so she wraps her jacket more tightly around herself and takes the narrow road through the forest instead.

When the car drives past her in the darkness and stops abruptly fifty yards ahead of her, panic hits her with full force. The adrenaline in her body reacts instantly, convincing her that someone is about to run up and grab her and do it to her all over again.

One of the many things snatched from the girl that night is the place where she never needed to feel afraid. Everyone has a place like that, until it gets taken away from us. You never get it back again. Maya will feel afraid everywhere from now on.

Benji sees her through the car window with newly woken eyes. No one walks this way of their own volition at night, and he can see that she's limping. He makes Katia stop, and is out in the darkness before the car comes to a halt. Maya is hiding behind a tree. You can't do that for more than a minute or so in sub-zero temperatures—the cold forces you to move about in order to keep your circulation going, whether you want to or not. Benji has been hunting in these forests with his sisters since he was big enough to hold a rifle, so he sees her. Maya knows he's seen her. Katia calls from the car, but to Maya's surprise Benji shouts back:

"It's nothing, sis. Sorry, I saw . . . I thought I saw . . . Oh, I've probably just smoked too much."

Maya looks directly at him then; he's standing ten yards away. Her tears are freezing at the same rate as his. But he merely gives a curt nod to the darkness, then turns around and disappears.

He knows too much about how it feels to have to hide to give away someone else doing the same.

As the red taillights of the car fade into the night, Maya stays where she is, with her forehead against the tree trunk, sobbing hysterically without making a sound, with no tears.

There are thousands of ways to die in Beartown. Especially on the inside.

23

Peter and Kira wake up happy. Laughing. That's what they will remember about this day, and they will hate themselves for it. The very worst events in life have that effect on a family: we always remember, more sharply than anything else, the last happy moment before everything fell apart. The second before the crash, the ice-cream at the gas station just before the accident, the last swim on holiday before we came home and received the diagnosis. Our memories always force us back to those very best moments, night after night, prompting the questions: "Could I have done anything differently? Why did I just go around being happy? If only I'd known what was going to happen, could I have stopped it?"

Everyone has a thousand wishes before a tragedy, but just one afterward. When a child is born, its parents dream of it being as unique as possible, until it gets ill, when suddenly all they want is for everything to be normal. For several years after Isak died, Kira and Peter felt a terrible, lacerating guilt every time they laughed. Shame can still catch them when they feel happy, making them wonder if it's a betrayal of their child that they didn't disintegrate entirely when he left them. One of all the terrible effects of grief is that we interpret its absence as egotism. It's impossible to explain what you have to do in order to carry on after a funeral, how to put the pieces of a family back together again, how to live with the jagged edges. So what do you end up asking for? You ask for a good day. One single good day. A few hours of amnesia.

So today, the morning after a hockey game, Peter and Kira wake up happy. Laughing. He whistles as he potters about in the kitchen, when she gets out of the shower they kiss each other the way adults do when they forget that they're parents. Leo, twelve years old, runs from the table in disgust. His mom and dad laugh into each other's mouths. One single good day.

———

Maya hears them from her room; she's lying deeply cocooned under the covers. They haven't even discovered that she's home yet; they think she spent the night at Ana's. When they open the door and look surprised, she will explain that she isn't well, she's wearing two pairs of jogging clothes to make sure her forehead feels warm enough. She can't tell her parents the truth. She hasn't got the heart to do that to them; she knows they wouldn't survive. She's not thinking like someone who's been the victim of a crime, she's thinking like someone who's committed one: all she can think is that no one must ever know, that she must get rid of all the evidence. So when her dad drives Leo to practice and her mom goes to the supermarket, Maya creeps out of bed and washes the clothes she was wearing yesterday, so that no one will see the stains. She will put her shredded blouse in a plastic bag and walk toward the door. But there she will stop, and she will stand there in the doorway shaking with terror, unable to bring herself to walk to the garbage bin.

A thousand wishes yesterday, one single one today.

Benji's three sisters have always communicated in different ways. His youngest sister, Gaby, talks, and his middle sister, Katia, listens. His eldest sister, Adri, shouts. If you have three younger siblings when your dad goes out into the forest with a rifle, you grow up faster than you should, and maybe become harder than you would really like to be.

Adri doesn't let Benji sleep off his hangover, and forces him to get up and help her with the dogs all morning. When that's done, she drags him over to the outbuilding that's been fitted out as a small gym, and makes him pump weights until he throws up. He doesn't complain. He never does. Adri could lift more than him until a couple of years ago, but when he passed her he did so at astonishing speed. She's seen him take down three fully grown men over at the Barn when they've said something inappropriate to Katia. The sisters often talk about it when he isn't there, the things they see in their little brother's eyes when he gets really angry. Their mom always says that she doesn't know what would have happened to the boy if he hadn't found hockey, but his sisters know all too well what would have happened. They've seen men like that, in the Barn and at the gym and in a thousand other places.

Hockey gave Benji a context, a structure, rules. But above all it rewarded the best sides of him: his boundless heart and unshakeable loyalty. It provided a focus for his energy, channeling it into something constructive. All through his childhood he used to sleep with his hockey stick beside him, and sometimes Adri is pretty sure he still does.

When her little brother lets go of the bar and rolls off the bench to throw up for the third time, she hands him a bottle of water and sits down on a stool next to him.

"So. What's the problem?"

"I'm just hungover," he groans.

His phone rings. It's been doing that all day but he refuses to answer it.

"No. Not the problem with your stomach, you donkey, what's the problem up here?" She sighs, and points to his temple.

He wipes his mouth with the back of his hand and drinks small sips of water.

"Oh . . . just a thing. With Kev."

"Argument?"

"Sort of."

"So?"

"Just crap."

His phone goes on ringing. Adri shrugs and lies back on the bench. Benji stands behind her and spots her as she lifts the bar. He has always wished she could have played hockey longer; she would have beaten the shit out of the whole junior team. She played for the girls' team in Hed for a few years when she was young, until driving there and back several evenings a week got too much for their mother. There was no girls' team in Beartown, never has been. Sometimes Benji wonders how good his sister could have been. She gets the game—she yells at him for making the same sort of tactical mistakes that David tells him off for. And she loves it. The way her brother loves it. When she's done she pats him on the cheek and says:

"You hockey boys are like dogs. To do something stupid, all you need is the opportunity. To do something good, all you need is a reason."

"So?" he mutters.

She smiles and points at his phone.

"So stop being such an old woman, little brother, and go and talk to Kevin. Because if I have to listen to that ringtone one more time, I'm going to drop the bar on your face."

Amat calls Maya's number ten times. A hundred times. She's not answering. He can still see every detail, thinks about it so intently that he starts trying to convince himself that he might have imagined it all. A misunderstanding. God, how wonderful that would be, if everything he thought he'd seen hadn't happened. He was drunk, after all. Jealous. He calls Maya's number, over and over again, doesn't leave any messages on voicemail. Sends no texts. He goes out running in the forest until he's too tired to think, running all day so he can collapse with exhaustion that evening.

Kevin is standing in the garden. All hockey players are used to playing through pain. There's always some little injury somewhere. A groin-strain, a sprain, a fractured finger. Not a week passes in the junior team without someone talking about how they can't wait until they're old enough to play without a grille on their helmet. "Get rid of the shopping cart," they plead. Even though they've all seen A-team players who've been hit in the face with pucks and sticks, they're not afraid of it, but are actively looking forward to it. When they were small they all saw a player standing after a game with twenty stitches in his lip from splitting his cheek open. But when asked, "Doesn't it hurt?" he merely grinned and said, "Can't pretend it doesn't sting a bit when I chew tobacco."

It's Sunday afternoon and the Erdahl house, empty and silent, has been cleaned to perfection. Kevin is standing in the garden firing puck after puck after puck. Even in little league he learned to play through any pain. Even to enjoy it. Blood blisters, fractures, cuts, concussions: they never affected his game. But this is different. Now two deep scratches on one hand are making him shoot his pucks high above the net.

The front door is unlocked. Benji walks through the house and notices that apart from a mark on the door to the basement, the house looks like it always does. As if no one had ever lived there. He stands in the terrace doorway and watches Kevin spray pucks all over his neighbors' flowerbeds as if he were firing blind. Kevin's eyes are bloodshot and furious when they meet his.

"There you are! I must have called you a thousand times!"

"And now I'm here," Benji replies.

"You need to answer when I call!" Kevin snarls.

Benji's words come slowly, his eyebrows lower threateningly.

"I think you must be confusing me with Lyt or Bobo. I'm not your slave. I answer when I feel like it."

Kevin points at him with the tip of his stick. It's quivering with rage.

"Have you finished taking drugs now, then? We're playing in the final next week and everyone's acting like we've done enough just getting there. We need to get the guys together and make them all understand what I demand from them this week! So you need to be available! I won't tolerate the fact that when the team needs you most, you vanish in a puff of smoke!"

Benji doesn't know if he means "puff of smoke" as a joke, or if Kevin's too stupid to appreciate the double meaning. It's always hard to tell with Kevin. He's both the smartest and stupidest person Benji knows.

"You know why I left the party."

Kevin snorts.

"Yeah, because you're a fucking saint, right?"

Benji's eyes stare at Kevin's, intently and without looking away. When Kevin eventually averts his gaze and looks away, his friend asks:

"What happened last night, Kev?"

Kevin lets out a curt laugh and throws his arms out.

"Nothing. Everyone was drunk. You know what it's like."

"What happened to your hand?"

"Nothing!"

"I saw Maya in the forest. It didn't look like nothing."

Kevin spins around as if he were about to hit Benji with his stick. His lips are quivering, his pupils burning.

"So NOW you give a damn? What the hell does it matter to you anyway? You weren't even here! You'd rather go to Hed and get wasted than stay here with your best friends! Your TEAM!"

Benji's eyes are staring intently at the way Kevin's are moving. Kevin looks away again, fires a puck so high above the net that it should be recategorized as a hunting weapon, and mumbles:

"I needed you yesterday."

Benji doesn't answer, which always makes Kevin lose his temper with him, and he roars:

"You weren't HERE, Benji! You're NEVER here when I need you! Lyt was sick all over the fucking kitchen and someone banged into the cellar door and left a huge mark on it! Have you got any idea what's going to happen when my dad gets home and sees it? Do you have any idea, or have you smoked away all . . . ?"

"I don't give a shit about your dad. I want to know what happened last night," Benji interrupts.

Kevin takes five quick steps and breaks his stick on the top of the goal, and it snaps into two razor-sharp projectiles, one of which misses Benji's face by a hand's width, but he doesn't blink.

"REALLY? YOU DON'T GIVE A SHIT ABOUT MY DAD'S . . . ? You ungrateful fucking . . . Who's been paying for your skates and sticks and gear for the past ten years? Didn't you give a shit about him then either? Do you think your mom could have afforded all that? Christ, my dad's right about you. He's ALWAYS been right about you! You're a virus, Benji, a fucking virus. You can't live without some sort of host!"

Benji takes two steps forward, just two. His face is expressionless.

"What happened last night, Kev?"

"What do you want? Is this some fucking police interrogation? What's your problem?"

"Don't be a coward, Kev."

"You want to lecture ME about being a coward? You want to talk about COWARDICE? For fuck's sake, you're the one who's a fucking . . . a fucking . . ."

Benji moves so fast that Kevin breathes the last words into his face. Their eyes are just a few inches from each other's. Benji's are wide open.

"What? What am I, Kev? Tell me."

Kevin's skin is pulsating, his eyes running, his neck is red and blue on one side, as if he's been punched hard by someone with small hands. He backs away and picks up part of the broken stick and slams it into the goal, making the metal sing.

"Get out of my house, Ovich. You've sponged off my family for long enough."

He doesn't turn around to watch Benji go. Nor when he hears the front door slam shut.

They get home late. The house looks like it did when they left it. Their son is pretending to be asleep; they don't knock on his door. Kevin's father finds two sheets of paper on the kitchen counter on which Kevin has given a careful account of all the statistics of each period of the game. Minutes played, shots, assists, goals, numerical superiority and inferiority, possession, penalties, mistakes. His father spends a couple of minutes sitting in the glow of a single lamp and smiles in a way that he doesn't let anyone see anymore. So proud. A man with less impulse control would have gone upstairs and kissed his sleeping son on his forehead.

His mother notices things that his father misses. She sees the pictures that the cleaner has mixed up and hung in the wrong order. The table that is slightly askew in the living room. A scrap of the plastic covering that has caught beneath one corner of the sofa. But above all, she sees the mark on the cellar door.

While her husband is sitting in the kitchen, she takes a deep breath and slams her suitcase into it as hard as she can. He comes running and she apologizes, saying she tripped and let go of the case. He helps her up and holds her and whispers:

"Don't look so upset, it's only the cellar door, it's just a little mark, darling."

Then he shows her the sheets of paper and says:

"They won!"

She laughs into his shirt.

24

When the burglar alarm goes off at the school early on Monday morning, the security company doesn't call the police, because it could take them hours to get there. They call one of the teachers instead. Not any teacher, they call the one whose little brother works for the security firm, so that her brother won't have to go to the trouble of fetching his own keys. Jeanette gets out of her car in the deserted parking lot, pulls up the collar of her coat, and blinks tiredly:

"Sometimes you're so lazy I'm starting to think your kids must be adopted."

Her brother laughs.

"Come on, Sis, stop whining, you're the one who always says I don't call you often enough!"

She rolls her eyes, takes his flashlight off him, and unlocks a side door to the school.

"It's probably just snow that's slid off the roof onto the sensors around the back again."

They go into the corridor without turning the lights on, because if anyone has broken in, the lights will have come on automatically in that section. But what sort of idiot would break into a school on a Monday morning?

Benji is woken by a bright light, even though the lamps in the ceiling are already on. His back aches. His mouth tastes of moonshine and cheap beer nuts, which troubles him, because he has no memory of having eaten beer nuts. He blinks sleepily, holds up his hand, and tries to squint at the person who's shining a light in his eyes.

"You've got to be kidding," the teacher sighs.

Benji pushes himself into a sitting position on top of the two desks he's been sleeping on in the classroom. He throws his arms out like the world's most exhausted magician.

"The headmaster did tell me I needed to start showing up on time in the morning. So . . . ta-dah! Actually . . . what time is it?"

He feels his pockets. Can't find his watch. His fractured memories of the previous night suggest that he may well have drunk that away too. Precisely what train of thought led him to conclude his little odyssey trying various substances with a break-in at his school is also a little vague in hindsight, but he's sure it must have seemed a superb idea at the time.

The teacher leaves him without a word, and he sees her talking with a security guard out in the corridor. The guard will write this off as a false alarm, seeing as brothers do what their big sisters tell them, no matter how old they get. The teacher comes back into the classroom and opens two windows to air out the room. She sniffs at Benji's jacket and makes a face.

"Please don't tell me you've brought drugs into the school."

Benji does a poor job of wagging his finger at her.

"It would NEVER even occur, occur . . . occur to me! Drugs in school are no good. I keep my drugs in my body. Do you want to dance?"

He falls off the desk with a giggle and lands on the floor on his back. The teacher crouches down beside him and looks at him somberly until he falls silent. Then she says:

"If I report this to the headmaster, he'll have to suspend you. Maybe even expel you from school. And shall I tell you something, Benjamin? Sometimes I think that's what you want. It's as if you're trying to prove to the whole world that there's nothing in your life that you aren't destructive enough to have a go at wrecking."

Benji doesn't answer. She hands him his jacket.

"I'm going to switch the alarm off, then I'm going to let you into the gym so you can have a shower. To be honest, you smell so terrible that I should probably call pest control as well. Have you got any clean clothes in your locker?"

He tries to smile when she helps him up.

"So that I look presentable when the headmaster arrives?"

She sighs.

"I'm not going to report you. You're going to have to ruin your life on your own. I'm not going to help you."

He meets her gaze and nods gratefully. Then his voice suddenly becomes adult, his eyes a man's instead of a boy's:

"I'm sorry I called you sweet cheeks. That was disrespectful. I won't do it again. Nor will anyone else on the team."

He rubs his neck, and Jeanette almost regrets telling the truth when she met up with Adri at the pub in Hed and was asked what his behavior in school was like. But she knows he's telling the truth when he says that no one on the team will call her that again, and she wonders how he has come to have such authority over the others. That a single word from Benji can make any hockey player in the entire school start or stop doing anything. It almost makes her miss playing the game herself. She and Adri were childhood friends, and they used to play together over in Hed. Sometimes she feels that both she and Adri stopped too soon, and wonders what would have happened if there had been a girls' team in Beartown.

"Go and shower," she says, patting Benji's hand.

"Yes, miss," he smiles, his eyes a boy's again.

"I'm not hugely fond of being called 'miss' either," she grunts.

"What would you like to be called, then?"

"Jeanette. Jeanette will do absolutely fine."

She fetches a towel for him from the gym bag in her car, and he follows her to the gym. After she's switched the alarm off and unlocked the door for him, he stands in the opening and says:

"You're a good teacher, Jeanette. You just had really bad timing, getting us in your class when we were at our best."

At that moment she understands why the team follows his lead. The same reason why the girls fall for him. When he looks you right in the eyes and says something, no matter what crap he may have done immediately before, you believe him.

———

Kevin's dad knots his tie, adjusts his cuff links, and picks up his brief-case. At first he considers calling good-bye to his son from the door like he usually does, but he changes his mind and goes out through the terrace door instead. He puts his briefcase down and picks up a stick. They stand side by side and take turns firing shots. It must be ten years since the last time.

"I bet you can't hit the post," his dad says.

Kevin raises his eyebrows, as if it's a joke. When he sees that it isn't, he pulls the puck back a couple of inches, flexes his wrists gently, and sends the puck flying into the metal. His dad taps his stick on the ground approvingly.

"Luck?"

"Good players deserve luck," Kevin replies.

He learned that when he was little. His dad has never let him win so much as a table- tennis match in the garage.

"Did you see the statistics from the match?" the boy asks hopefully.

His dad nods and looks at his watch. Walks toward his briefcase.

"I hope you don't imagine that the final is an excuse for you not to put one hundred percent into your schoolwork this week."

Kevin shakes his head. His dad almost touches his cheek. Almost asks about the red marks on his neck. But instead he clears his throat and says:

"People in this town are going to try to stick to you more than usual now, Kevin, so you need to remember that viruses make you sick. You need to be immune to them. And the final isn't just about hockey. It's about what sort of man you want to be. A man who goes out and grabs what he deserves, or one who stands in a corner waiting for someone to give it to him."

The father walks off without waiting for a reply, and his son stands there with scratch-marks on his hand and a heartbeat that won't stop throbbing in his neck.

———

His mom is waiting in the kitchen. Kevin stares at her uncertainly. There's freshly made breakfast on the table. A smell of bread.

"I . . . Well, it's probably a bit silly . . . but I took this morning off," she says.

"What for?" Kevin wonders.

"I thought we could . . . spend some time together. Just you and me. I thought we could . . . talk."

He avoids her gaze. She looks a little too desperate for him to be able to handle eye contact.

"I have to go to school, Mom."

She nods, her teeth biting into her lower lip.

"Yes. Yes. Of course . . . it was silly. I'm silly."

She feels like going after him and asking a million questions. Late last night she found sheets in the dryer, and he's never washed so much as a sock for himself before. There was a T-shirt there too, with bloodstains that hadn't quite come out. When he was in the garden this morning firing pucks she went into his room. Found the blouse-button on the floor.

She wants to go after him, but she doesn't know how to talk to an almost grown man through a closed bathroom door. She packs her briefcase and gets in her car and drives half an hour into the forest before stopping. She sits there all morning, so that no one at work will ask why she's there so early. Because she told them she was going to be spending the morning with her son.

Kira is standing with her hand against the door of Maya's room, but she doesn't knock again. Her daughter has already said she's ill, and Kira doesn't want to be that mother. The nagging, uncool, anxious "helicopter parent." She doesn't want to knock again to ask if there's actually something else wrong. You can't do that; nothing makes a fifteen-year-old girl clam up more than the words "Do you want to talk?" You can't just open the door and ask why she has suddenly started washing her own clothes of her own volition. After all, what is Kira? The secret service?

So Kira does the not-nagging, not-anxious, not-helicopter, cool-mom thing. She gets in her car and drives off. Forty-five minutes into the forest she stops the car. Sits there alone in the darkness and waits for the pressure on her chest to subside.

Lyt opens the door and looks like he's just seen a cake.

"Kevin! Hi! Er . . . what . . . ?"

Kevin nods at him impatiently.

"Ready?" Lyt asks.

"For . . . what? School? Now? With you? You mean . . . do I want to walk to school? With you?"

"Are you ready or not?"

"Where's Benji?"

"Fuck Benji," Kevin snaps.

Lyt stands there in shock with his mouth open, unable to think of anything to say. Kevin rolls his eyes impatiently.

"Are you waiting for Communion or what? Shut your mouth, for fuck's sake. Let's go."

Lyt stumbles off and hurries to make sure he's got his shoes on the right feet and his outdoor clothes at least relatively close to the appropriate body parts. Kevin doesn't say a word all the way, until his outsize teammate grins and pulls out a hundred-kronor note.

"So do I owe you this or not?"

He starts giggling uncontrollably when Kevin takes it. Kevin tries to look nonchalant as he says:

"But keep your mouth shut about it, okay? You know what women are like."

Lyt has never looked more euphoric than when he was given the chance to share a secret with his team captain.

Maya's phone rings, and she wishes with all her soul that it might be Ana, but it's Amat again. She hides the phone under her pillow as if she were trying to smother it. She doesn't know what to say to him, and she knows that Amat will primarily be wishing he hadn't seen anything at all. If she doesn't answer the phone, maybe the two of them can find some way of pretending that nothing happened. That it was just a misunderstanding.

She removes the batteries from all the fire alarms and opens all the windows before putting her blouse on the floor of the shower and setting light to it. Then she sets light to a carton of cereal, letting the top burn before putting it out and leaving the remains on the kitchen counter. When her mom, a woman with the nose of a hungry grizzly bear, comes home and wonders why there's a smell of smoke, the explanation will be that Maya managed to knock the carton of cereal onto a lit burner on the stove.

She carefully sweeps up the remains of the blouse from the shower and only then does she realize that the buttons have melted and stuck to the drain, and the synthetic material hasn't turned to ash the way she had hoped. If Ana had been there, she would have said: "Shit, Maya, if I ever murder anyone, remind me NOT to ask you for help!" She misses her. God, how she misses her. For several minutes she sits on the bathroom floor crying and trying to make herself phone her best friend, but she can't do that to her. Can't drag her into this. Can't force her to carry this secret.

It takes more than an hour to clean the bathroom and get rid of the remains of the burned blouse. She puts them in a plastic bag. Stands shaking in the doorway and stares at the garbage bin ten yards away. It's light outside now, but that doesn't make any difference. She's scared of the darkness, in the middle of the day.

25

Ana is walking to school alone. Holding her phone in her hand like a weapon. Maya's number on the screen, her finger on the button, but she doesn't call. The most important promise they made was never to leave each other, not because of safety but because the promise made them equals. They've never been equals in any other way. Maya still has two parents. A brother. A home that doesn't smell of cigarettes and vodka. She's smart, funny, popular. Gets better grades. She's musical. Brave. She can get better friends. And she gets guys.

If Ana left Maya alone in the wilderness Maya would die. But what she didn't realize when she left Maya alone at a party was that it amounted to the same thing.

Ana keeps her finger on the button, but doesn't call. In a few years' time she'll read an old newspaper article about research showing that the part of the brain that registers physical pain is the same part that registers jealousy. And then Ana will understand why she hurt so badly.

Amat and Fatima are standing at the bus stop as usual, but nothing else is the same. When Fatima was out shopping yesterday everyone said hello to her. When she went to the cash register, Tails, who owns the whole store, came over and tried to give her everything free of charge. She didn't let him, of course, no matter how wealthy he was, and in the end the huge man threw up his hands and said with a chuckle, "You're as stubborn as winter; I can see where Amat gets it from!"

His white car is coming along the road now, a couple of minutes ahead of the bus. He stops and says he's been to one of his other stores and just happened to be passing. Fatima doesn't know if it's true. At first she declines his offer of a lift to the rink, but changes her mind when she sees the way Amat is looking at the car. Tails is driving,

Fatima is sitting in the passenger seat, and in the rearview mirror she can see how proud that makes her son. That he has been able to make this happen.

As the boy practices on his own that morning, Tails sits in the stands alongside the A-team coach and the GM. When Fatima goes into the club president's office to empty the trash can, the president stands and picks it up off the floor for her. Shakes her hand.

The school corridor is already full of people when the boys walk in. Everyone turns to look at them, and Lyt has never been so happy that Benji isn't around. The attention from people who think he's Kevin's new best friend is dizzying. That's why he doesn't react when Kevin mutters that he "needs to shit," goes into one of the bathrooms. His old best friend would have known that Kevin never does that at school if he can possibly help it.

Inside, in the dark, Kevin tears the hundred-kronor note into tiny pieces and flushes them down the toilet. He doesn't switch the light on. Doesn't look at himself in the mirror.

Amat catches up with Zacharias at the lockers. They haven't seen each other since the game, and only now does it occur to Amat that perhaps he should have called. When he sees the disappointment and anger in Zacharias's eyes, he realizes he should have done more than that.

"Hi . . . sorry about Saturday, everything happened so fast, I—"

Zacharias slams his locker shut and shakes his head.

"I get it. Team party. With your new team."

"Look, that's not what I meant—" Amat says, but Zacharias doesn't let him get as far as an apology.

"It's okay, Amat. You're a star now. I get it."

"Come on, Zach, I . . ."

"My dad said to congratulate you."

This last remark hurts Zacharias most of all. His dad works at the factory. Everyone loves hockey there; because the team was founded by factory workers they still feel that it belongs to them. Zacharias would have done any number of ridiculous things to be able to send his dad off to work as the father of a junior team player. The fact that his son is friends with one of them was enough to put a smile on his dad's face all way there.

Amat swallows the words he feels like saying and tries to find others instead, but doesn't have time before Zacharias's cap flies off his head and his body thuds into the lockers. Two final-year pupils whose names Amat doesn't know laugh loudly.

"Oops! Didn't see you!" one of them grins.

"That must be the first time someone hasn't seen you, eh, fatty? How much have you eaten? Another fat kid?" the other one leers, pinching Zacharias's stomach.

This sort of thing happens to Zacharias a lot. It's been going on for years, so the shock for all concerned is almost unimaginable when he suddenly flashes forward and headbutts one of them in the chest as hard as he can.

The older boy staggers, as if a sandbag had just hit back, and it takes a moment for him to come to his senses. But then his fist smashes straight into Zacharias's mouth. Amat cries out and throws himself between them. The two final-year pupils evidently don't go to hockey matches because they don't hesitate to knock him to the floor.

"What have we got here, then? A little terrorist? You're from the Hollow, aren't you?" Amat says nothing. The older boy goes on:

"There's nothing but terrorists and fucking camels in the Hollow. Is that where you're from?"

Amat doesn't answer back. He's had a whole lifetime to learn that it only makes things worse. One of the older boys drags him up by his top and snarls:

"I said: Where. Do. You. Come. From?"

No one has a chance to react. The noise when the back of a head hits a locker is so deafening that at first Amat thinks it must be his. Bobo picks one of the final-year pupils off the floor. Even though he's a year older than Bobo, he must be at least twenty pounds lighter. Bobo's voice is on fire when he clarifies:

"Beartown. His name is Amat, and he's from Beartown."

The older boy's eyes flit about until Bobo lets go of him, only to slam the back of his head into the locker again. With his face pressed up against the older boy's, he asks:

"Where's he from?"

"Beartown! Beartown! Fuck . . . it was only a joke, Bobo!"

Bobo lets go of him, and he and his friend run off. Bobo helps Amat up, and tries to hold out his hand to Zacharias too, but Zacharias brushes it aside. Bobo says nothing.

"Thanks," Amat says.

"You're one of us now. No one touches us," Bobo smiles.

Amat looks at Zacharias. There's blood seeping from his friend's nose.

"I . . . I mean . . . we . . ."

"I've got a class. See you at lunch. Everyone on the team always sits at the same table. Come and find us," Bobo interrupts, then disappears.

Amat nods as he walks off. When he turns around Zacharias has already taken his jacket and bag from his locker and is heading for the exit.

"What the hell, Zach? Wait! Come on, he HELPED you!"

Zacharias stops but doesn't turn around. He refuses to let Amat see his tears when he says:

"No, he helped you. So run along, big shot. Your new team is waiting for you."

The door closes after him. Amat's conscience and a sense of guilt and injustice wash over him. If he hadn't been so worried about getting injured and missing the final, he would have slammed his fist into one of the lockers. He picks up his phone from the floor. Calls no one.

Benji is on his way to the classroom, but he happens to pass the bathrooms just as Kevin emerges from one of the cubicles, and it throws him off balance like an elbow from out of nowhere. Kevin hurries past, but Benji stops dead. He's not easily surprised, but he's left standing with his mouth half-open and his eyes half-closed. Kevin avoids looking at him, as if he didn't exist.

As long as the two friends can remember, anyone who has seen them play has said that they seem to be on the same wavelength, a secret frequency that only they can access. They don't need to look at each other on the ice to know where the other is. Neither of them has ever been able to put it into words, but whatever it was, there's nothing but static now. Kevin brushes the wall of the corridor, sheltered by Lyt, and the other juniors automatically fall in on all sides. Benji has never known who he would have been if he didn't have his team, but he's starting to realize that he's about to find out now.

When Kevin, Lyt, Bobo, and the others go into the classroom, Benji stands outside trying hard not to prove to the whole world that there is nothing in his life that he isn't destructive enough to have a go at wrecking. He really does try.

When Jeanette takes attendance, she looks out of the window and sees Benji light a cigarette in the schoolyard, get on his bicycle, and ride off. The teacher hesitates for a moment. Then she marks him as present anyway.

Ana turns up the brightness of the screen to maximum, opens all her apps, and starts a film before leaving her phone in her locker. She treats herself like an alcoholic emptying her home of bottles. She knows that before the morning is over she won't be able to resist calling Maya any longer. She wants to make sure that the battery will be exhausted by then, making it impossible.

It doesn't matter who sits together that day. Everyone eats lunch on their own.

26

Peter is sitting on a bench in the juniors' empty locker room. One of the posters with a quote meant to inspire has fallen to the floor; it's crumpled and marked with footprints. Peter reads it over and over again. He can remember when Sune pinned it up. Peter had only just learned to read.

He had been a child heading straight into darkness when hockey found him. Sune dragged him to the surface and this team kept him afloat. With a mom who died when he was in primary school and a dad who was always teetering on the brink between happy drunk and cruel alcoholic, when Peter as a little boy found something to cling on to, he held on until his knuckles turned white. Sune was always there, through the wins and the losses, in Beartown and on the other side of the world. When the injuries piled up and his career came to an abrupt halt, when Peter buried his father and his son within the space of a year—it was Sune who called him then and told him there was a club here that needed help. And Peter needed to feel that he could keep something alive.

He knows how quiet it gets when hockey tells you you're finished. How quickly you start to miss the ice, the locker room, the guys, the bus trips, the gas-station sandwiches. He knows how as a seventeen-year-old he would look at the tragic former players in their forties who used to hang around the rink going on about their own achievements in front of an audience that got smaller and smaller each season. The job of GM gave him a chance to live on as part of a team, to build something bigger, something that could outlast him. But with that came responsibility: make the difficult decisions, live with the pain.

He picks up the poster that's fallen to the floor. Reads it one last time. *A great deal is expected of anyone who's been given a lot.*

Today he will persuade the man who dragged him to the surface to resign of his own free will. The sponsors and the board don't even want to fire Sune, they don't want to give him a redundancy pay-off. Peter is expected to tell him to leave in silence, because that would be best for the club.

Sune wakes early in the little row house where he's always lived on his own. He rarely has visitors, but those who do come are often surprised by how tidy it is. No piles of clutter, newspapers, beer cans, and pizza boxes as some people might expect of an old man who has been a bachelor all his life. Neat, tidy, clean. Not even any hockey posters on the walls or trophies on the shelves. Sune has never been very fond of objects; he has his plants in the windows and during the summer recess he grows flowers in the narrow garden at the back. And the rest of the time he has hockey.

He drinks his instant coffee and washes the cup straight afterward. He was once asked what the most important requirement was if you wanted to become a successful hockey coach. He replied: "Being able to drink really bad coffee." All those early mornings and late nights in rinks with scorched coffeepots and cheap coffee machines, bus trips and isolated roadside cafés, camps and tournaments with school refectories—how could anyone with an expensive espresso machine at home ever put up with that? You want to be a hockey coach? Get used to not having the things other people have. Free time, a family life, decent coffee. Only the toughest of men can handle this sport. Men who can drink terrible coffee cold, if need be.

He walks through the town. Says hello to almost all the men over thirty; at some point over the years he's coached pretty much every single one of them. The teenagers are a different matter altogether, because each year he recognizes fewer and fewer of them. He no longer shares a language with the boys in this town, which makes him as obsolete as a fax machine. He doesn't actually understand how he's expected to believe that "children are the future" when more and more of them are choosing not to play hockey. How can you be a child and not want to play hockey?

He takes the road leading up through the forest, and when he reaches the turning to the kennels he sees Benjamin. The boy stubs his cigarette out too late to avoid being seen, but Sune pretends not to have noticed. When he himself was a player his teammates used to smoke in the breaks between periods, and some of them would drink export-strength beer. Times change, but he isn't sure that the game has actually changed quite as much as some coaches think.

He stops by the fence and looks at the dogs rushing about. The long-haired boy stands beside him, uncomprehendingly, but doesn't ask what he's doing there. Sune pats him lightly on his shoulder.

"Fantastic game on Saturday, Benjamin. Fantastic game."

Benji looks down at the ground and nods silently. Sune doesn't know if it's shyness or humility, so the old man points through the fence and adds:

"You know, when David first became a coach I always used to say to him that the best hockey players are like the best hunting dogs. They're born egotists; they always hunt for their own sake. So you need to nurture them and train them and love them until they start hunting for your sake too. For their teammates' sake. Only then can they become really good. Truly great."

Benji brushes his bangs from his eyes.

"Are you thinking of getting one, then?"

"I've been thinking about it for years. But I always thought I didn't have time for a puppy."

Benji puts his hands in his jacket pockets and stamps some snow from his shoes.

"And now?"

Sune starts laughing.

"I have a feeling that I might have a bit more free time than I'm used to fairly soon." Benji nods and looks him in the eye for the first time in the conversation.

"Just because we love David doesn't mean that we wouldn't have played for you."

"I know," the old man replies, and pats the boy on the shoulder again.

Sune doesn't say what he's thinking, because he isn't sure if it would actually do Benjamin any favors. But the whole time David and Sune have been arguing about whether a seventeen-year-old could be ready to play in the A-team, they've really always been in total agreement. Just not about which of the seventeen-year-olds it should be. Kevin may have the natural talent, but Benjamin has all the rest. Sune has always been more interested in the length of the string than the size of the balloon.

Adri comes out of the house, ruffles her little brother's hair, and shakes Sune's hand.

"I'm Sune," he says.

"I know who you are," Adri replies, then asks immediately: "What do you think about next season? Have we got a chance of going up? You need to get a couple of decent skaters into that team, surely? Get rid of the donkeys in the second and third lines."

It takes Sune a few moments to realize that she's talking about the A-team and not the juniors. He's so used to the juniors' relatives only wanting to talk about the junior team that it catches him off guard.

"There's always a chance. But the puck doesn't just glide . . . ," Sune says.

"It bounces as well!" Adri grins.

When Sune looks bemused, Benji explains helpfully:

"Adri used to play. In Hed. She was rough as hell, got more penalties than me." Sune laughs appreciatively. Adri gestures toward the fence.

"So what can we do for you?"

"I'd like to buy a dog," Sune says.

Adri holds out her hand and presses his shoulder, with a stern face but a friendly smile.

"I'm afraid I can't let you buy one, Sune. But I can give you one. For building up this club, and for saving my little brother's life."

Benji is breathing through his nose and concentrating on the dogs. Sune's lips quiver gently. When he's composed himself he manages to say:

"So . . . which puppy would you recommend for a retired old guy, then?"

"That one," Benji says, pointing at one without hesitation.

"Why?"

Now it's the boy's turn to pat the old man on the shoulder. "Because he's a challenge."

David is sitting on his own in the stands in the rink. For once he is looking up at the roof, not down at the ice.

He's got a migraine, is under more pressure than ever, can't remember the last time he slept right through the night. His girlfriend can't even be bothered to try communicating with him at home anymore seeing as she never gets any response. He's living inside his own head, and in there he's on the ice twenty-four hours a day. In spite of that, or perhaps precisely because of it, he can't take his eyes off the worn old banner hanging above his head: "Culture, Values, Community."

He's due to give an interview to the local paper today; the sponsors have arranged it. David protested but the club's president just grinned: "You want the media to write less about you? Tell your team to play worse!" He can already imagine all the questions. "What is it that makes Kevin Erdahl so good?" they'll ask, and David will reply the way he always replies: "Talent and training. Ten thousand little things that he's repeated ten thousand times." But that isn't really true.

He'll never be able to explain it properly to a journalist, but when it really comes down to it, a coach can never create a player like that. Because what makes Kevin the best is his absolute desire to win. Not that he hates losing, but that he can't even begin to conceive of trying to accept not winning. He's merciless. You can't teach someone that.

How many hours do these guys put into it? How much did David himself sacrifice? Their whole lives up to the age of twenty, twenty-five, are nothing but training, training, training, and what do they get for that if it turns out that they're not good enough? Nothing. No education, no safety net. A player who's as good as Kevin is might turn professional. Might earn millions. And the players who are *almost* as good? They'll end up in the factory just the other side of the trees from the rink.

David looks at the banner. As long as his team carries on winning, he'll have a job here, but if they lose? How many steps away from the factory is he? What can he do apart from hockey? Nothing.

He was sitting in this precise spot when he was twenty-two, thinking exactly the same things. Sune was sitting beside him then. David asked about the banner, asked what it meant to Sune, and Sune replied: "Community is the fact that we work toward the same goal, that we accept our respective roles in order to reach it. Values is the fact that we trust each other. That we love each other." David thought about that for a long while before asking: "What about culture, then?" Sune looked more serious, choosing his words carefully. In the end he said: "For me, culture is as much about what we encourage as what we actually permit."

David asked what he meant by that, and Sune replied: "That most people don't do what we tell them to. They do what we let them get away with."

David closes his eyes. Clears his throat. Then he stands up and walks down toward the ice. Doesn't look up at the roof again. Banners have no meaning this week. Only results.

Peter passes the president's office. It's full of people even though it's still morning. Enthusiastic sponsors and board members are abuzz. One of the board members, a man in his sixties who made his money in three different construction companies, is making wild, thrusting movements with his hips to illustrate what he thinks Beartown did to their opponents in the semifinal, then yelps:

"And the whole third period was one big ORGASM! They came

here thinking they were going to fuck US! They won't be able to put their legs together for WEEKS!"

Some of the men laugh, some don't. If any of them is thinking anything, they don't say it. Because it's only a joke, after all, and the board members are like a team, you take the good with the bad.

Later that day Peter will drive to the big supermarket owned by Tails. He'll sit in his old friend's office and talk rubbish about old matches, telling the same jokes they've told since they first met in skating class when they were five years old. Tails will want to offer whisky, Peter will decline, but before he leaves he'll say:

"Have you got any jobs in the warehouse?"

Tails will scratch his stubble hesitantly and wonder:

"Who for?"

"Robbie."

"I've got a waiting list of a hundred people who want warehouse jobs. Which Robbie are you talking about?"

Peter will stand up and cross Tails's office to an old photograph hanging on the wall, a photograph of a hockey team from a small town in the forest who got to be second-best in the country. First Peter will point at himself in the photograph. Then at Tails. And then, in between the two of them, at Robbie Holts.

" 'We look after each other,' isn't that what you said, Tails? 'The bears from Beartown.' "

Tails will look at the photograph and lower his chin in shamefaced agreement. "I'll check with personnel."

Two men in their forties will shake hands in front of a picture of themselves in their twenties.

The locker room fills with juniors without filling with noise. They put their gear on in silence. Benji doesn't show up. Everyone notices, no one says anything.

Lyt makes a halfhearted attempt to break the silence by telling them how he got a blowjob from a girl at Kevin's party, but when he won't say who the girl was it becomes obvious that he's lying. Everyone knows Lyt can't keep a secret. Lyt looks as if he wants to say something else, but glances toward Kevin with an anxious look on his face and says nothing. The players move out toward the ice, Lyt tapes his pads and tears the loose scraps of tape and throws them on the floor. Bobo waits until almost all the others have left the locker room before bending over, picking them up, and dropping them in the garbage. He and Amat never talk about it.

They're halfway through the training session before Kevin finds a way to end up close enough to Amat during a break in play to be able to talk without being overheard. Amat is leaning forward on his stick, staring at his skates.

"What you think you saw . . . ," Kevin begins.

He's not threatening. Not hard or commanding. He's almost whispering.

"You know what women are like."

Amat wishes he knew what he is supposed to say. Wishes he had the courage. But his lips remain sealed. Kevin pats him gently on the back.

"We're going to make a fucking good team, you and me. In the A-team."

He glides away toward the bench when Lars blows his whistle. Amat follows, still staring at his skates but unable to look right at the ice. Frightened of seeing his reflection in it.

The lump in Kira's stomach refuses to give up its grasp. She keeps telling herself that there's nothing wrong with Maya, that she's just a normal teenager, that it's just a phase. She keeps telling herself to be the cool mom. It's not working.

So when her colleague blunders in through the door, Kira feels grateful rather than annoyed. Even though she's got an ocean of work to drown herself in, she's relieved to see her standing there shouting that she needs "help crushing these bastards!"

"Didn't this client agree to a settlement?" Kira asks as she scans the document her colleague tosses onto her desk.

"That's the problem. They want me to back down. Like some sort of coward. And do you know what the Badger says?"

"Do as the client sa . . . ," Kira suggests.

"DO AS THE CLIENT SAYS! THAT'S WHAT HE SAYS! Can you believe that he's in charge? IN CHARGE! What is it with men? Have they got a different density from women, or what? How come anyone with a dick always rises to the top of every single organization?"

"Okay . . . but if your client accepts the terms, then . . ."

"Then that's my job? Go to hell! Isn't it my job to look after my client's best interests?"

Kira's colleague is bouncing up and down with anger, her heels leaving little marks in the floor of the office. Kira rubs her forehead.

"Well, yes, but maybe not if the client doesn't actually want you to . . ."

"My clients have no idea what they want!"

Kira looks at the document, sees the name of the firm representing the other party. And starts to laugh. Her colleague applied for a job there once, and didn't get it.

"Okay, but the fact that you want to win this particular case . . . that

wouldn't be because you just happen to hate this particular firm . . . ?"
Kira mutters.

Her colleague grabs her over the desk, her eyes flashing:

"No, I don't just want to win, Kira. I want to crush them! I want to give them an existential crisis. I want them to walk out of the nego-tiation room and think that they might like to move to the coast and renovate an old school and open a bed-and-breakfast. I want to hurt those bastards so badly that they start meditating and trying to FIND THEMSELVES! They'll turn vegetarian and be wearing socks with sandals by the time I'm finished with them!"

Kira sighs and laughs.

"Okay, okay, okay . . . give me the rest of the file and let's take a look . . ."

"Socks with SANDALS, Kira! I want them to start growing their own tomatoes! I want to ruin their self-confidence until they stop being lawyers and try to be HAPPY and shit like that instead! Okay?"

Kira promises. They close the door. They're going to win. They always do.

Peter closes the door behind him. Sits down at his desk. Stares at the resignation papers that are waiting for Sune's signature. If Peter has learned one thing about human nature during all his years in hockey, it's that almost everyone regards themselves as a good team player, but that very few indeed understand what that really means. It's often said that human beings are pack animals, and that thought is so deeply embedded that hardly anyone is prepared to admit that many of us are actually really rubbish at being in groups. That we can't cooperate, that we're selfish, or, worst of all, that we're the sort of people other people just don't like. So we keep repeating: "I'm a good team player." Until we believe it ourselves, without actually being prepared to pay the price.

Peter has always existed on various teams, and he knows the sac-rifices that being on a team truly demands. "The team is greater than the individual" is just a cliché for people who don't understand sports; for those who do, it's a painful truth because it hurts to live in accordance with it. Submitting to a role you don't want, doing a crap job in silence, playing on defense instead of getting to score goals and be the star. When you can accept the worst aspects of your teammates because you love the collective, that's when you're a team player. And it was Sune who taught him that.

He stares at the space on the forms where Sune has to sign his name, so absorbed in his thoughts that he jumps when the phone rings. When he sees that it's a Canadian number, he smiles as he answers:

"Brian the Butcher? How are you, you old rogue?"

"Pete!" his former teammate exclaims at the other end.

They played in the farm team league together. Brian never made it all the way to the NHL as a player, but became a scout instead. Now he identifies the most talented teenagers for one of the best teams in the league. Every summer when he hands in his report ahead of the NHL draft, he fulfills and crushes lifelong dreams the whole world over. So he isn't just calling for Peter's sake.

"How's the family?"

"Good, good, Brian! How about yours?"

"Oh, you know. The divorce went through last month."

"Shit, I'm sorry."

"Don't be, Pete. I've got more time for golf now."

Peter laughs halfheartedly. For a few years over in Canada, Brian was his best friend. His wife was close to Kira, and the children used to play together. They still call each other, but at some point they started to talk less and less about each other's lives. In the end there was only hockey left. Peter is about to ask *Are you okay?* but doesn't have time because Brian has already exclaimed:

"How's your boy getting on?"

Peter takes a deep breath and nods.

"Kevin? Fantastic, really great. They won the semifinal. He's been brilliant."

"So I won't regret it if I tell my people to include him in the draft?"

Peter's heart starts to beat faster.

"Seriously? You're thinking of drafting him?"

"If you can promise me that we won't be making a mistake. I trust you, Pete!"

Peter has never been more serious when he replies:

"I can promise you that you'll be getting a fantastic player."

"And he's . . . the right sort of guy?"

Peter nods hard, because he knows what that means. Drafting one player instead of another is an immense financial investment for an NHL team. They take absolutely everything into account. It's no longer enough just to be good on the ice; they don't want any unpleasant surprises from the player's private life either. Peter knows it shouldn't be like that, but those are the rules of the game these days. A few years ago he heard about a hugely talented youngster who slid down the draft because the scouts found out his dad was an alcoholic with a criminal record. That was enough to scare them off, because they had no way of knowing how the teenager would behave if he became a hockey millionaire overnight. So Peter tells the truth, a truth he knows Brian wants to hear:

"Kevin is the right sort of guy. He gets top grades in school. He comes from a stable family, well brought up. There are definitely no 'off ice' problems."

Brian murmurs happily at the other end.

"Good, good. And he wears the same number you used to wear, right? Number nine?"

"Yes."

"I thought they'd have retired that number and hung it from the rafters."

Peter grins.

"They will. Only it'll have Kevin's name on it when they do."

Brian laughs loudly. They hang up with a promise to be in touch again soon, that Peter will go over to Canada with his family, that the children will get to see each other again. They both know it will never happen.

Amat is gathering up the pucks and cones after practice. Not because anyone's told him to, but because it comes naturally to him and because it gives him a chance to avoid the others. He's expecting the locker room to be empty when he gets there, but is met by Bobo and Kevin. The two seventeen-year-olds are picking scraps of tape from the floor and throwing them in the garbage.

Amat stands in the doorway and is amazed at how easy it is, the bit that comes next. Kevin says it as if it were the most natural thing in the world:

"Lyt has borrowed his dad's car. Let's go to Hed and catch a film!"

Bobo slaps Amat happily on the back.

"Didn't I say? You're one of us now!"

Twenty minutes later they're sitting in the car. Amat realizes he's sitting in Benji's place, but doesn't ask. Lyt is boasting about a blowjob again. Kevin asks Bobo to "tell some jokes" and Bobo is so excited to be asked that he snorts Coke out of his nose all over the car seat, infuriating Lyt. They roar with laughter. Talk about the final, about the long bus trip to the city where it's going to be taking place, about girls and parties, and how things are going to be when they're all playing in the A-team. Amat slides into the conversation, at first reluctantly, then with a wonderful warm feeling of being allowed to belong to something. Because that's much easier.

Even in Hed people recognize them, and they get slaps on the back and congratulations. After the movie, when Amat thinks they're on the way home, Lyt turns off the main road just after the Beartown sign. He stops by the lake. Amat doesn't understand why until Kevin opens the trunk of the car. They've got beer, lights, skates, and hockey sticks in the back. They put their woollen hats down to mark the goals.

They play hockey on the lake that night, four boys, and everything feels simple. As if they were children. Amat is amazed at how straightforward it is. Staying silent in return for being allowed to join in.

Peter throws his rubber ball at the wall again. Tries not to look at the resignation forms on the desk, tries not to think about Sune as a person and only as a coach. He knows that's what Sune would want. Club first.

The board and sponsors can be assholes. Peter knows that better than anyone, but they only want the same as him and Sune: success for the club. Success demands that we see beyond ourselves. Sometimes Peter has had to keep his mouth shut when the board has demanded new recruitments that he knows are stupid, and then he has had to keep his mouth shut all over again when it turns out he was right. Sometimes he has been instructed only to sign seven-month contracts with players, so that the club won't have to pay their wages during the summer. The players in turn sign on as unemployed for the rest of the year and are given public assistance, and every so often Tails provides fake certificates declaring that they've done "work placement" in his supermarket when they were actually training with the team all summer. Then, when the season starts again, they sign new seven-month contracts. Sometimes you have to skirt around a few moral issues in order to survive financially as a small club. Peter has had to accept that as part of the job. Kira once told him that the club had an unpleasant culture of silence, the sort of thing you find among soldiers and criminals. But sometimes that's what it takes, a culture of silence to foster a culture of winning.

Peter has spent more time than any other coach trying to reduce the Pack's violence in the stands, as well as their menacing hold over the town, and that's made him a hated figure in the Bearskin, but sometimes even he has trouble working out who the worst hooligans in the Beartown Ice Hockey Club are: the ones with tattoos on their necks, or the ones with neckties.

He puts the rubber ball down. Picks up a pen from a neatly organized box in his desk drawer and writes his signature on the line where it says "Representative of the club" on the resignation form. When Sune signs immediately below, it will officially look like he has resigned of his own accord. But Peter knows what he's done. He's just fired his idol.

Lars is standing in David's office, hesitating as long as possible before eventually clearing his throat and asking:

"How do you want to punish Benji?"

David doesn't look up from his computer screen.

"We won't be punishing him."

Lars's nails tap the wood of the doorframe with pent-up frustration.

"He didn't show up for a training session less than a week before the final. You wouldn't tolerate that from anyone else."

David looks up, straight at him, so abruptly that Lars jerks back.

"Do you want to win the final?"

"Of course!" Lars gasps.

"Then let this go. Because I may not be able to guarantee that we're going to win with Benji, but I can damn well guarantee that we won't win without him."

Lars leaves the room without further protest. When David is alone he switches off his computer, sighs deeply, picks up a large marker pen, and goes and gets a puck. He writes three large letters on it.

Then he drives out to the cemetery.

Maya is lying in her bed, slipping so sleeplessly in and out of consciousness that she sometimes thinks she's hallucinating. She's stolen some of her mom's sleeping pills from the bathroom cabinet. Last night she stood alone with them lined up neatly on the sink and tried to work out how many it would take for her not to have to wake up again. Now, as she blinks up at the ceiling, it's as if she's still hoping everything might be a dream, as if she could look around the room and realize that she's back in reality: that it's Friday, and nothing has happened yet. When awareness hits her, it's like having to live through it all again. His grip on her throat, the bottomless fear, the absolute conviction that he was going to kill her.

Again. Again. Again.

Ana is eating dinner with her dad in that very specific silence they've been practicing for fifteen years. Her mom always hated it. It was the silence that made her leave. Ana could have gone with her. But she lied and said she couldn't imagine living anywhere where there were no trees, and the only trees where her mom lives now are planted outside shopping malls as decoration. But of course really she stayed because she couldn't abandon her dad, even if she doesn't know if that was mostly for his sake or hers. They've never talked about it. But at least he's drinking less than he did when her mom lived here, and Ana loves both parents more as a result.

She offers to take the dogs out. That obviously strikes her dad as odd, because he usually has to nag her to do it. But he says nothing. Nor does she.

They live in the old part of the Heights, in one of the houses that was here before the more expensive ones started to be built. They became Beartown aristocracy by association. She takes the long way around, via the illuminated jogging trail that the council is so proud of having built so that "the women of the district can exercise in safety." By sheer coincidence the lights were, of course, first installed next to the Heights rather than in the forest beyond the Hollow. And by another fortunate coincidence, the two companies that won the contract from the council were both owned by men who lived in houses right next to the trail.

She lets the dogs off their leashes under the lamps and lets them play. Trees and animals—they always help.

———

Kevin comes home, passes his parents in the kitchen and living room without having to look them in the eye. He goes upstairs and closes the door to his room, and does push-ups until his vision starts to fade. When the house falls silent and the door to his parents' bedroom is closed, he puts on his tracksuit and creeps out. He runs through the forest until he has no energy to think anymore.

Ana follows the dogs as they zigzag across the running track. Kevin stops abruptly fifteen yards away. At first she barely reacts, thinking that he must have been startled by the dogs. But then she sees that it's her presence that's made him stop. A couple of days ago he wouldn't have been able to pick her out of a class photograph, even if she were the only person on it, but now he knows who she is. And he looks neither proud nor embarrassed, which are the only two facial expressions she's ever seen on a guy from school after he's slept with a girl on the weekend.

He's scared. She's never seen a man look so terribly scared.

Maya tries to play her guitar, but her fingers are shaking too much. She's sweating under her big grey hoodie, but when her parents ask she says she's shaking with fever. She pulls the hood tighter around her neck, to hide the bruises. Pulls the sleeves halfway down over her hands to conceal the blue-black marks on her wrists.

She hears the doorbell ring; it's too late to be one of Leo's friends. She hears her mom talking outside, relieved and anxious at the same time, the way only her mom can. There's a knock on her bedroom door and Maya pretends to be asleep, until she sees who's standing in the doorway.

Ana closes the door gently behind her. Waits until she hears Kira's footsteps go off toward the kitchen. She's out of breath. She ran all the way here from the Heights, in a mixture of rage and panic. She sees the marks on Maya's neck and wrists, no matter how her friend tries to hide them. When she finally looks Maya in the eye, tears find their way into every crease in their skin, every furrow, running in streams and dripping from their chins. Ana whispers:

"I saw him. He was scared. The bastard was scared. What did he do to you?"

It's as if the event hasn't properly existed for Maya herself until she says the words out loud. And when she does, she's back in that boy's bedroom with its trophies and hockey posters. Sobbing, she fumbles her hands over her hooded top for a blouse-button that was never there.

She falls apart in Ana's arms, and Ana holds her as if her life depends on it, and wishes with all her being that they could change places with each other.

Never again do you find friends like the ones you have when you're fifteen years old.

28

When Ana and Maya were children—it feels like only yesterday—they always talked about how they would live in New York when they were rich and famous. Maya was the one who wanted to be rich, Ana the one who wanted to be famous, which surprised anyone who had spent time with them. They had strikingly different dreams: Maya dreamed of a silent music studio, Ana a noisy throng of people. Ana wanted to be famous as a form of affirmation, Maya wanted to be rich so she didn't have to care what anyone else thought. They are both unfathomably complex, the pair of them, and that's why as different as they are, they understand each other.

When she was very little, Ana wanted to be a professional hockey player. She played one season on the girls' team in Hed, but she was too restless to do what the coaches told her and kept getting into fights the whole time. In the end her dad promised to teach her to hunt with a rifle if she stopped making him drive her to training sessions. She could see he was ashamed of the fact that she was so different, and the offer of learning how to shoot was too good to turn down.

When she got a bit older she wanted to be a sports commentator on television, then high school started and she learned that girls were more than welcome to like sports in Beartown—just not the way that she did. Not that much. Not to the point where she would lecture the boys about rules and tactics. Teenage girls were primarily supposed to be interested in hockey players, not hockey.

So she bowed her head and devoted herself to Beartown's real traditional sports: shame and silence. They were what drove her mom mad. Ana very nearly went with her when she moved away, but changed her mind and stayed. For Maya's sake, for her dad's sake, and perhaps because she loved the trees at least as much as she sometimes hated them.

She always thinks it was the forest that taught the people of

Beartown to keep their mouths shut, because when you hunt and fish you need to stay quiet so as not to scare the animals, and if you teach people that lesson since birth, it's going to color the way they communicate. So Ana has always been torn between the urge to scream as loud as she could, or not at all.

They're lying next to each other in Maya's bed. Ana whispers:

"You've got to tell."

"Who?" Maya breathes.

"Everyone."

"Why?"

"Because otherwise he'll do it again. To someone else."

Over and over again they have the same quiet argument, with themselves and each other, because Ana knows it's an unreasonable demand to make of another person: that Maya of all people should feel some sort of responsibility for anyone else right now. That she, of all people, should stand up and shout in the quietest town in the world. Scare the animals. Ana hides her face in her hands so that Maya's parents won't hear anyone crying in here.

"It's my fucking fault, Maya, I should never have left you at the party. I should have known. I should have looked for you. I was so fucking, fucking, fucking weak. It's my fault, it's my f . . ."

Maya cups her friend's face gently between her hands.

"It's not your fault, Ana. It's not our fault."

"You've got to tell," Ana sobs desperately, but Maya shakes her head.

"Can you keep a secret?"

Ana nods and sniffs and promises: "I swear on my life."

"That's not enough. Swear on techno!"

Ana starts to laugh. How much wouldn't you love someone who could make you do that at a time like this?

"I swear on all forms of electronic music. Apart from really shit Euro techno from the nineties."

Maya smiles and wipes Ana's tears, then looks her friend in the eye and whispers:

"Right now, Kevin has only hurt me. But if I talk, I'll be letting him hurt everyone I love as well. I can't handle that."

They hold each other's hands. Sit beside each other in bed and count sleeping pills, wondering how many it would take to end their lives. When they were children everything was different. It feels like only yesterday, because it was.

Benji sees it from a distance, the black object on top of the headstone. It's been there a couple of hours. He shakes the snow off it and reads what's written on it. One single word.

When Kevin, Bobo, Lyt, Benji, and the other players were young, David used to give them pucks before the games, with short messages that he wanted them to think about extra carefully. *Backcheck harder* or *use your skates more* or *be patient*. Sometimes he wrote things just to make them laugh. He could hand a puck to the most nervous player on the bus and look deadly serious, until the player glanced down and saw that it said: *Zipper's open. Cock hanging out.* He had a sense of humor that only his players were allowed to see, and it made them feel special. Jokes are powerful like that, they can be both inclusive and exclusive. Can create both an Us and a Them.

More than anything else, David could give his players the feeling that he saw every single one of them. He invited the whole team to dinner and introduced them to his girlfriend, but when the club organized a "fathers against sons" game for all the boys' teams, David was the only coach who didn't show up. He went and picked up Kevin and Benji, one from his garden and the other from the cemetery, and drove them down to play on the lake instead.

He fought for them, literally. When Benji was nine or ten he already had a style of playing that used to make his opponents' parents furious. In one away game against the little league team in Hed, one player shouted that he was going to get his dad after

Benji had checked him. Benji thought no more about it until a large man appeared in the darkened players' tunnel after the game and picked him up from the floor by the scruff of his neck and threw him violently against the wall, yelling: "Not so tough now, are you, you little gypsy brat?" Benji wasn't scared, but he was convinced he was going to be killed at that moment. There were plenty of other adults who saw the incident and didn't intervene. Benji never knew if it was because they were scared or because they thought he deserved it. All he can remember is David's fist, knocking the father to the floor with a single punch.

"If I see a grown man lay one finger on a small child in this rink, I'll kill him," David said, not to the father specifically, but to all the adults who had stood there in silence.

Then he leaned toward Benji and whispered in his ear:

"Do you know how to save someone from Hed if they're drowning?"

Benji shook his head. David grinned.

"Good."

In the locker room David wrote a single word on a puck and tucked it in Benji's bag. *Proud.* Benji still has it. In the bus on the way home that evening, all his teammates were telling jokes. The laughter got louder and louder, the punch-lines cruder and cruder. Benji can only remember one of the jokes, one that Lars told:

"Boys, how do you fit four gays on a chair at the same time? You turn it upside down!"

Everyone laughed. Benji remembers glancing surreptitiously at David, and saw that he was laughing, too. It's just as easy to be exclusive as it is to be inclusive, just as easy to create an Us as a Them. Benji has never been worried about being beaten up or hated if anyone finds out the truth about him; he's been hated by every opposing team since he was a child. The only thing he's scared of is that one day there will be jokes that his teammates and coach won't tell when he's in the room. The exclusivity of laughter.

He stands by his father's grave and weighs the puck in his hand. David has written a single word on it.

Win.

Benji doesn't go to school the following day, but he does attend the training session. His jersey is sweatiest of all. Because when he no longer knows what anything in the world means, this is the only thing no one can take from him. The fact that he's a winner. David pats his helmet twice without needing to say anything more.

Lyt had been sitting in Benji's place in the locker room, next to Kevin. Benji didn't use words, he merely stood in front of Lyt until Lyt gathered his things together and skulked unhappily back to the opposite bench. Kevin's face remained motionless, but his eyes betrayed his feelings. They've never been able to lie to each other.

David has never seen his two best players perform better in a practice session.

Saturday comes. The day of the junior team's final. Everywhere grown men and women wake up and put on green jerseys and scarves. In the parking lot in front of the rink stands a bus emblazoned with proud banners, ready to carry a team to the capital, with a spare seat ready for the trophy that will be coming back with them.

Early in the morning three girls of primary school age are playing in a street in the middle of town. They're chasing each other, fencing with sticks, throwing some of the last snowballs of this long winter. Maya is standing at her bedroom window watching them. She and Ana used to babysit the girls a few years ago, and Ana sometimes still rushes out to have a snowball fight with them when she gets bored of Maya's guitar-playing, making them laugh so hard that they fall over. Maya's arms are wrapped tightly around her body. She's been awake all night and every minute of it she was certain that she would never tell anyone about what had happened. It takes three little girls playing in the street outside her window to make her change her mind.

Ana is asleep in her bed, exhausted, so incredibly slight and fragile, with her eyes closed beneath the thick quilt. It will be a terrible story to tell about this town and this day: that Maya finally decided to tell the truth about Kevin, not because she wanted to protect herself, but because she wanted to protect others. And that she already knew, as she stood there at the window that morning, what the town would do to her.

29

The most dangerous thing on the ice is being hit when you're not expecting it. So one of the very first things hockey teaches you is to keep your head up, always. Otherwise—bang.

Peter's phone is busy all morning, sponsors and board members and players' parents; the nerves of the whole town are exposed. In a few hours' time he's going to be on the bus with the junior team, heading to the game, even though he hates travelling. It used to be such a natural part of the family's life, the fact that he used to be away roughly a third of all nights each season, and he was ashamed to admit it but sometimes he almost thought it was a good thing. Then Isak got sick on one of those nights, and since then he hasn't been able to sleep in a hotel bed.

Leo has pestered his way to a seat in someone's car. Peter objected at first, but it actually makes the whole thing feel a bit better. They're going to be staying in the capital overnight, a huge adventure for a twelve-year-old boy, and Leo is so keen to go. In secret, Peter wishes Maya were too. He stands outside her door and has to summon up all his self-restraint to keep himself from knocking.

He once heard that the best way to prepare mentally for becoming a parent is to stay in a tent at a weeklong rock festival with a load of fat friends who are smoking hash. You blunder about in a permanent state of acute sleep deprivation wearing clothes covered with stains from food that is only very rarely your own, you suffer from tinnitus, you can't go near a puddle without some giggling fool jumping in it, you can't go to the bathroom without someone standing outside banging on the door, you get woken up in the middle of the night because someone was "just thinking about something," and you get woken up the next morning to find someone pissing on you.

It may be true, but it doesn't help anyone. Because the thing you can never be prepared for when you have children is your increased sensitivity. Not just feeling, but hypersensitivity. He didn't know he was capable of feeling this much, to the point where he can hardly bear to be in his own skin. After Isak was born the slightest sound became deafening, the slightest worry became terror, all cars drove faster, and he couldn't watch the news without going to pieces. When Isak died Peter thought he would be left numb, but instead it was as if all his pores opened up, so that the air itself started to hurt. His chest can be ripped open by a single unhappy glance from either of the children, particularly his daughter. All the time he was growing up, the only thing he wanted was for life to speed up, and now all he wants is for it to slow down. For the clocks to stop, for Maya never to grow up.

He loves her so much because she always makes him feel a bit stupid. He hasn't been able to help her with her homework since primary school, but sometimes she still asks, just to be kind. When she was little she used to pretend to fall asleep in the car so that he would carry her into the house. He always complained when he had to carry both her and the shopping, as well as steer Leo's stroller, but he secretly loved the way his daughter would cling tight to his neck. That was how he knew she was only pretending, because when she was really asleep it was like carrying a bag of water, but when she was pretending she would bury her nose deep against his neck and wrap her arms around him as if she were afraid of losing him. When she got too big for that, he missed it every day. A year ago she sprained her ankle on a field trip and he had to carry her from the car to the house again. He has never felt more like a bad parent than when he admitted to himself that he wished she could sprain her ankle more often.

He stands with his hand on her door, but doesn't knock. His phone goes on ringing. He's so distracted that he's still clutching his coffee cup in his hand when he goes out to the car.

———

Kira is cruising around the supermarket, sticking to her list, which is written in the exact order in which everything is located in the aisles. Not like Peter's lists, which are entirely random, and which always lead to him shopping as if he were planning to fill a bomb shelter before the apocalypse.

Everyone says hello to her; some shoppers wave from the other side of the store. Tails comes trotting out from his office wearing a Beartown jersey with the number "9" and the name "Erdahl" printed on the back. He's on his way to the rink, but he can't stop talking and she listens patiently with one eye on the time; she doesn't want Peter and Leo to leave before she gets home.

When she's loading the bags into the car, the bottom of one of them gives way. People in the parking lot fight for the right to help her pick up her avocados. They all know her husband, the GM, so well. And yet they don't know him at all.

"He must be so pleased he's going to this game!" someone says, and Kira nods even though she knows he hates travelling. He has hardly left Maya and Leo overnight since the night Isak fell asleep for the last time. Kira has had to travel far more with her work, and for a while she always kept a ready-packed bag in the hall cupboard. Peter used to joke about it, saying he was worried that she also had "a safe-deposit box containing hair dye, fake passports, and a pistol." She never told him how much that hurt her. She knows she's being selfish and hates herself for it, but she almost wishes Leo weren't going along on this trip. Because it's something that Peter is doing as a dad, it's not just a work trip, it doesn't balance out any of the times she's been away. It doesn't make her the slightest little bit less self-absorbed.

She picks up an avocado from the ground and puts it in another bag. When Isak fell ill the family slipped into an almost military routine: doctor's appointments, dates of operations, journey times, waiting rooms, treatments, lists, and protocols. After the funeral Peter couldn't find a way back out of himself—the pain became too great for him to move at all. Kira carried on taking Maya to play in the park, carried on cleaning and making dinner, carried on going to the store with her list. She once read a book that said that after a deeply traumatic event, like an assault or a kidnapping, the victim often doesn't break down until much later—in the ambulance or police car—when everything is over. Several months after Isak's death Kira suddenly found herself sitting on the floor of a supermarket in Toronto with an avocado in each hand, unable to stop crying hysterically. Peter came and carried her home. For weeks after that he was like a machine: cleaning, preparing meals, looking after Maya. That may have been how they survived, Kira realizes: thanks to their ability not to fall apart at the same time.

She smiles in the car on the way home. Puts on the louder-louder playlist. She's going to have a whole weekend with her daughter, and what a blessing that is. It's no time at all since Maya was a little red raisin wrapped up in a blanket, with Kira staring at the nurses in the hospital as if they'd told her they were going to dump her and the baby alone in the Indian Ocean on a raft the size of a postage stamp made of beer cans when they suggested it might be time to go home. Then the little whining bundle suddenly became a complete person. Developed opinions and characteristics and her own taste in clothes and a dislike of soda. What sort of child doesn't like soda? Or sweets? She can't be bribed with sugar and, dear God, how can anyone function as the parent of a child who can't be bribed? It's no time at all since she needed help to burp. Now she plays the guitar. Dear God. Will this love for her daughter ever stop being unbearable?

The sun has settled above the treetops, the air is clear and light, it's a good day. One single good day. Kira gets out of one car just as Peter and Leo are getting into the other. Peter kisses her, taking her breath away, and she pinches him and makes him embarrassed. He's still clutching his coffee cup, and she picks up the bags of shopping and wearily shakes her head, and holds her hand out to take it from him just as Maya comes out onto the steps. Her parents turn toward her, and they will remember this moment. The very last moment of happiness and security.

The fifteen-year-old girl closes her eyes. Opens her mouth. Speaks. Tells them everything.

When the words stop, there are avocados on the ground among the fragments of a dropped coffee cup. On one of the biggest pieces you can still see parts of the pattern from the front of the cup. A bear.

30

Words are small things. No one means any harm by them, they keep saying that. Everyone is just doing their job. The police say it all the time. "I'm just doing my job here." That's why no one asks what the boy did; as soon as the girl starts to talk they interrupt her instead with questions about what she did. Did she go up the stairs ahead of him or behind him? Did she lie down on the bed voluntarily or was she forced? Did she unbutton her own blouse? Did she kiss him? No? Did she kiss him back, then? Had she been drinking alcohol? Had she smoked marijuana? Did she say no? Was she clear about that? Did she scream loudly enough? Did she struggle hard enough? Why didn't she take photographs of her bruises right away? Why did she run from the party instead of saying anything to the other guests?

They have to gather all the information, they say, when they ask the same question ten times in different ways in order to see if she changes her answer. This is a serious allegation, they remind her, as if it's the allegation that's the problem. She is told all the things she shouldn't have done: She shouldn't have waited so long before going to the police. She shouldn't have gotten rid of the clothes she was wearing. Shouldn't have showered. Shouldn't have drunk alcohol. Shouldn't have put herself in that situation. Shouldn't have gone into the room, up the stairs, given him the impression. If only she hadn't existed, then none of this would have happened, why didn't she think of that?

She's fifteen, above the age of consent, and he's seventeen, but he's still "the boy" in every conversation. She's "the young woman."

Words are not small things.

Kira shouts. Makes calls. Causes trouble. Gets told to calm down. Everyone is actually just doing their job here. Peter sits with his hand on top of Maya's fingers at the little table in the interview room in the police station in Hed, and he doesn't know if his daughter hates him because he isn't shouting too. Because he hasn't had legal training, he doesn't know what to shout about. Because he isn't out trying to kill someone, anyone. Because he's powerless. When he takes his hand away from hers, father and daughter are both freezing.

Maya sees the nameless fury in the eyes of one of her parents, the eternal emptiness in the other's. She goes with her mother to the hospital. Her dad heads in the other direction, toward Beartown.

There will be days when Maya is asked if she really understood the consequences of going to the police and telling the truth. She will nod. Sometimes she will believe that she was actually the only person who did understand. Much later, in ten years' time, she will think that the biggest problem here was actually that she wasn't as shocked as all the adults were. They were more innocent than she was. She was fifteen and had access to the Internet; she already knew that the world is a cruel place if you're a girl. Her parents couldn't imagine that this could happen, but Maya simply hadn't expected it to happen to her.

"What a terrible thing to realize," she will think, in ten years' time, and then she will remember the most peculiar details. Like the fact that one of the police officers was wearing a wedding ring that was too big, so it kept slipping down and hitting the table. And the fact that he never looked her in the eye, just kept his gaze focused on her forehead or mouth.

She remembers sitting there and thinking of a physics lesson in high school about liquids and cold. Water expands when it freezes; you need to know that if you build a house in Beartown. In the summer the rain seeps into the cracks in the bricks, then when the temperature slips below zero the moisture freezes to ice, and the bricks break. She will remember that that's how it felt to grow up as the little sister of a dead big brother. A childhood that was one long, desperate attempt not to be liquid, not to seek out the cracks in your parents.

When you grow up so close to death, you know that it can be

many different things to many different people, but that for a parent, death, more than anything else, is silence. In the kitchen, in the hall, on the phone, in the backseat, on Friday evening, on Monday morning, wrapped in pillowcases and crumpled sheets, at the bottom of the toy box in the attic, on the little stool by the kitchen counter, under damp towels that no longer lie strewn across the floor beside the bath. Everywhere, children leave silence behind them.

Maya knows all too well that this silence can be like water. If you let it make its way too far in, it can freeze into ice and break your heart. Even then, in the police station in Hed, she knew she would survive this. Even then she knew that her mom and dad wouldn't. Parents don't heal.

What an uncomfortable, terrible source of shame it is for the world that the victim is so often the one left with the most empathy for others. There will be days when Maya is asked if she really understood the consequences, and she will nod yes, and of all the feelings inside her then, guilt will be the greatest. Because of the unimaginable cruelty she showed toward the people who loved her the most.

They sat there in the police station. She told them everything. And she could see in her parents' eyes how the story made the same terrible sentence echo through them, over and over again. The one every mom and every dad deep down most fear having to admit:

"We can't protect our children."

There's a bus, painted green, parked outside the rink. There's already a large crowd—parents and players and sponsors and board members. They're all hugging and waving.

Kevin's dad drives right up. Gets out and shakes people's hands, takes time to talk. Kevin's mom hesitates for a long while before putting her arm around her son's shoulders. He lets her do it. She doesn't say she's proud, he doesn't say he knows.

———

Fatima is standing unhappily in the hall, asking Amat several times if there's something wrong. He promises that there isn't. He walks out of the apartment with his skates in his hand. Lifa is waiting outside the door; he looks like he's been waiting for a while. Amat smiles weakly.

"Do you want to borrow some money, or what? You don't usually wait for me."

Lifa laughs and holds out his clenched fist, and Amat touches his to it.

"Kill them!" Lifa demands.

Amat nods. He pauses, perhaps thinking about saying something, but decides against it. Instead he asks:

"Where's Zach?"

Lifa looks surprised.

"At training."

Amat's face fills with red shame. Now that he's been promoted to the juniors, it's taken no longer than this for him to forget that the boys' team always has a training session at this time. Lifa holds out his fist again, then changes his mind and hugs his childhood friend hard.

"You're the first person from the Hollow to play with the juniors."

"Benji's from the Hollow, sort of . . . ," Amat says, but Lifa shakes his head firmly.

"Benji lives in a row house. He's not one of us."

Amat thinks of how he can see Benji's house from his balcony, but that's not enough. Lifa arrived in Beartown a few years after Amat. His family lived in Hed first, but the apartments here were cheaper. He played hockey with Amat and Zacharias for a couple of years, until his older brother told him to stop. It was a snobs' game; only rich men's kids played hockey, according to his brother. "They'll hate you, Lifa. They hate us, they're not going to want someone from around here to be better than them at anything." He was right. They kept hearing that in the locker room and on the ice when they were young. No one in Beartown ever lets you forget where you're from. Amat and Zacharias put up with it, Lifa didn't. While they were at middle school some of the older players snuck into the locker room with markers, scribbled out *Beartown Ice Hockey* from their tracksuits, and wrote *Shantytown Hockey* instead.

All the boys knew who had done it. No one said anything. But Lifa never played again. Now he stands outside an apartment block in the Hollow, hugs Amat with tears in his eyes, and whispers:

"I saw some little kids, six or seven, playing with hockey sticks outside my block yesterday. They were pretending to be their idols. One was Pavel Datsyuk, one was Sidney Crosby, one was Patrick Kane . . . and you know what the last one shouted? He shouted, 'I'M AMAT!'"

"That's a load of crap," Amat says with a smile, but Lifa shakes his head, holds his friend tight, and says:

"Kill them, bro. Win the final and turn professional and kill them all. Show them you're one of us."

"You can tell the guys there's a surprise in the locker room," Kevin's dad says surreptitiously into his son's ear.

"Thanks," the boy replies.

They shake hands, but the father puts his other hand on the back of the boy's shoulder as they do so. Almost a hug.

The locker room is already echoing with cheerful swearing when Kevin arrives, his teammates bouncing about like sparky little fireworks. Bobo slaps Kevin on the back, clutching his new stick happily in the other hand, and roars:

"Do you have any idea what these cost? Your dad's a fucking LEGEND!"

Kevin knows exactly what the sticks cost. And there's one for every player on the team in the box on the floor.

Zacharias is last to leave the ice after the boys' team's training session; he's gathered the pucks and cones on his own. He manages to duck at the last moment, and the impact behind him makes the Plexiglas sway.

He looks around wildly. The puck came whistling toward him from the wrong direction—from the corridor rather than out on the ice.

"Watch out, fatso!" Lyt mocks, waving his new stick.

Zacharias knows exactly how much it cost; if there's one thing teenagers know the price of, it's all the things they can't afford.

"Suck cock," he mutters.

"What did you say?" Lyt snarls instantly, his face darkening.

"I said: Suck. Cock."

Bobo is standing behind Lyt in the corridor, and mumbles something like, "It's only a joke," and tries to hold him back. Says something like, "Think of the final." Lyt restrains himself, at least superficially, and snorts derisively toward Zacharias.

"Nice stick! Did Social Services buy it for your mom, or what?"

Zacharias raises his head instead of bowing it.

"Has your mom been in the locker room putting your jockstrap on again, little Willy? Does she cup your balls carefully, the way you like it? Does she still buy far too big . . ."

Lyt rushes at him with his stick at head height before he can finish the sentence, and if Bobo hadn't gotten in the way he would have sent a player two years his junior to the hospital. Amat rushes in behind them, panic-stricken, and stands between them, addressing Lyt as much as Zacharias.

"For fuck's sake . . . STOP IT! PLEASE, STOP!"

Lyt thrusts his arms out, making Bobo let go of him, then he casts a quick, evaluating glance at Amat before he goes over to Zacharias, grabs his stick from him, and smashes it against the wall as hard as he can, breaking it. He drops the pieces on the floor in front of Zacharias and snarls:

"You'll have to tell Social Services to buy a better-quality one next time. Someone could get hurt."

Lyt turns and goes into the locker room and is met by the jubilant cries of his teammates who are chanting "the bears from Beartown" and each others' names in turn.

Amat picks up the pieces of the broken stick. Zacharias doesn't help.
"It's broken, you idiot . . ."

Amat loses his cool and flies up, yelling:

"What the FUCK is wrong with you, Zach? Well? What's got into
you? Why do you have to provoke everyone the whole time?"

Zacharias just glares back. Years of friendship fall from his eyes.

"Good luck today, big shot."

Amat walks off. Zacharias stands there watching him. When Amat
goes into the locker room and throws the pieces of an old stick in the
trash, a new stick is waiting for him by his place. It's the first time in
his life he's had one that isn't secondhand.

Bobo sits down in the bus, two rows in front of Lyt. He hears Lyt
telling the story of Zacharias's stick, to the accompaniment of jokes
about "benefit scroungers" and the "little bastard." Zach's mother is
on disability benefits. Before that she worked on the same ward of the
hospital as Bobo's mom. When Amat gets on the bus, Bobo makes
space for him.

"I tried to stop him," Bobo mutters.

"I know."

They both remember the tracksuits with *Shantytown Hockey*
scrawled on them. It was Lyt's idea. And Bobo did the writing. Lyt
lives in the Heights, Bobo lives one minute away from the Hollow.
Bobo feels like saying something to Amat about that, but he doesn't
have time to finish the thought. Because a moment later someone cries,
"What the hell are the cops doing here?" as a police car rolls into the
parking lot and blocks the bus's exit.

David is late. It's actually the first time he's ever been late for anything. Yesterday he threw up three times, and even tried to persuade
his girlfriend to have a glass of wine with him to help him calm down.
And he never drinks. He has always felt like an outsider in every team
he has ever played in, precisely because that seemed to be a ritual that

everyone followed, drinking themselves senseless at least a couple of times a year. It was like David became less trustworthy in their eyes because he wasn't prepared to vomit alongside a teammate on the parquet floor of a hotel bar somewhere.

His girlfriend looked so surprised. David shrugged his shoulders.

"People always say it calms the nerves."

She started to laugh. Then she started to cry. Then she leaned her forehead against his and whispered:

"Idiot. I didn't want to say anything. But I can't drink wine."

"What?"

"I didn't want to say anything until after the final. I didn't want . . . to distract you. But I . . . I can't drink."

"What are you talking about?"

She giggled between his lips.

"You're as thick as a brick sometimes, you know. Darling, I'm pregnant."

So today David is late, and confused, and happy. He walks straight into the tumultuous chaos in the parking lot, and almost gets run down by the police car. It's simultaneously the happiest and the unhappiest and the most peculiar day of his life.

If it had been a home game maybe they would have let Kevin play. But the final is taking place several hours away, in another city, and they use words like "security" and "risk of absconding." They're all just doing their jobs. The police push their way through the surprised parents in the parking lot and climb onto the bus. All the boys start shouting when they ask Kevin to get out. A heavily built man in uniform grabs Kevin's arm and lifts him up from his seat, and the whole bus explodes in fury. Bobo and Lyt try to block the policeman's path, and they're big enough to require four more officers just to get him off the bus. Kevin looks so small in the confusion, vulnerable, defenseless. Perhaps that's why all the adults around react the way that they do, or perhaps there are thousands of other reasons.

———

Kevin's dad grabs the policeman holding his son and yells at him, and when another officer pulls him off, Tails gets the police officer in a headlock. One board member slams his fist as hard as he can into the hood of the police car. Maggan Lyt takes photographs of all the police officers from a distance of less than half a yard, and promises them all personally that they'll lose their jobs.

Amat and Benji are the only ones who sit quietly in their seats on the bus. Words are difficult things.

Peter is standing at the far side of the parking lot, where the pavement stops and the trees begin. He hates himself intensely for driving here. Because what's he going to do? Violence is like whisky: children in homes that have too much of it grow up either full of it, or entirely without it. Peter's dad was capable of murder, but his son can't fight. Not even on ice. Not even now. Not even Kevin. Peter can't harm anyone, but he stands here anyway, because he dearly wants to watch when someone else does.

David is the only person who notices him. Their eyes meet. Peter lowers his.

31

What makes someone a leader?

Maya undergoes all the obligatory examinations at the hospital. Answers all the questions. Doesn't cry, doesn't complain, doesn't argue, is helpful, accommodating. Kira, on the other hand, is so beside herself that at times she can't even be in the same room. Her phone rings nonstop. She has activated her whole legal practice now, and her daughter is lying on a cold bed in a bare room and knows that she's started a war. Her mother needs to take command, charge the enemy, act—she won't be able to cope otherwise. So Maya gets her own phone and sends Ana a text message, saying: "War now." A few seconds later the reply arrives: "You and me against the world!"

David has seen hundreds of leaders during the course of his career in hockey. Formal ones and natural ones, those who shout, and those who keep quiet. He didn't know he could be one himself until Sune sent him out onto the ice with a whistle and a gang of seven-year-olds. "I'm not a good coach," David said, and Sune ruffled his hair and replied: "People who think they're good coaches never are." The old bastard was both right and wrong.

After the police car drove off with Kevin, it took an hour for David to get all the players back on board the bus, and to get all the parents to realize that nothing was going to get better as a result of them standing there shouting. Now they've been driving for three hours and the bus is still vibrating with cell phones, rocking as the juniors rush up and down reading each others' screens. So far no one in Beartown seems to know why Kevin was taken away—the police are refusing to give any information—so the rumor mill rolls on between the seats with greater and greater intensity. Even the adults are involved; Lars is so agitated that he's salivating.

David, on the other hand, sits alone and silent at the front, staring at the text on his own phone. It's from Kevin's dad. He's just found out what his son is accused of. One of the first things you learn as a leader, whether you choose the position or have it forced upon you, is that leadership is as much about what you don't say as what you do say.

A mother is sitting beside a bed, holding her daughter's hands tightly in hers, all four of them shaking. The daughter leans her forehead against her mother's.

"We're going to survive this, Mom."

"Darling child, you're not supposed to be consoling me, I'm the one who ought to be consoling you."

"You are, Mom. You are."

Kira's phone rings again. Maya realizes it's the law firm. She nods to her mother and strokes her cheek, and her mother kisses her and whispers:

"I'll be just outside in the hallway. I'm not leaving you."

All four hands are still shaking.

For ten years David has nurtured these players for this precise moment. He has gotten them to sacrifice everything, burn themselves out; he has taught them to stand tall under pressure even when their shoulders and necks are howling with pain. What's that worth if they don't win the final now? What is a game if you don't want to be the best at it?

David's strongest belief about hockey has always been that the world outside the rink mustn't encroach upon the world inside it. They need to be separate universes. Outside, real life is complicated and frightening and hard, but inside the rink it is straightforward and comprehensible. If David hadn't kept the worlds so clearly divided,

these guys, with all the shit they've had to deal with out in the real
world, would have been broken even as little kids. But the rink was
their refuge. Their one happy place. No one could take that from
them: the fact that they were winners there.

That doesn't just apply to the boys. David himself has often felt
odd and out of place, but never on ice. It's the last place where the
collective functions, where the team takes precedence over the self. So
how far are you allowed to go to protect your universe? How much
of leadership is what you say, and how much is what you don't say?

The nurse is well aware of who Maya is, but she tries not to let it show.
The nurse's husband, Hog, is one of Peter's best friends, and played
hockey with him half his life. But just now, when she came along the
corridor, it was as if Peter and Kira didn't even recognize her. They
spoke to her as if through glass, but she didn't take offense. She's seen
it before; it's caused by trauma, and means that they only register her
uniform when they talk to her, not her face. The nurse is used to being
seen as a function to the point where patients and relatives forget that
she's a person. It doesn't bother her. In fact, if anything, it actually
makes her take greater pride in her work.

When she's alone in the room with Maya, she leans forward and
says:

"I know this is really unpleasant. We're trying to do everything as
quickly as we can."

The girl looks her in the eye and nods, biting hard on the inside of
her lip. The nurse is usually very careful to maintain a professional
distance; that's what she teaches her younger colleagues. "There'll be
people here that you know, but you need to treat them as patients. It's
a question of leadership," she usually says. But the words catch in her
throat now.

"My name is Ann-Katrin. My husband is an old friend of your
dad's."

"Maya," Maya whispers.

Ann-Katrin puts her hand tenderly against the child's cheek.

"I think you're very brave, Maya."

Peter drives back to Hed from Beartown. He walks into the hospital ready to announce triumphantly to Maya that Kevin has been picked up by the police. That she's going to get justice. Then he walks into the room and sees her. Nothing in the world is as small as your own child in a hospital bed. There's no justice to be had. He sits beside his daughter and cries, because he isn't the sort of person who can kill someone. In the end he asks:

"What can I do, Maya? Tell me what I can do . . ."

His daughter pats her dad's stubble.

"Love me."

"Always."

"Love me like you love hockey and David Bowie?"

"So much more, Pumpkin, much, much more."

And she laughs. It's funny that a ten-year-old nickname, "Pumpkin," is the thing that does that. When she was nine she made him stop calling her that, but ever since then she's missed it, the whole time.

"I need two things," she whispers.

"Let me guess: Ana and your guitar?" he says.

She nods. Kira comes back into the room. The parents' hands touch fleetingly. When Peter reaches the door, his daughter calls out:

"And you need to talk to Leo, Dad. He's going to be petrified."

The mom and dad look at each other. How many years will the stab in their chests feel like a heart attack when they think of this moment? Of all people, the only one who hasn't forgotten Leo today is his big sister.

Ann-Katrin is sitting in the staffroom staring at the wall. Like everyone else, she's heard that the police have picked Kevin up, but she's one of the few who knows why Maya is at the hospital, who makes the connection. Maya didn't recognize Ann-Katrin. Nor, if he'd been there, would Kevin, even though she's been sitting in the crowd watching almost every match he's played since little league. Some parents remain faceless to other children.

She sends her son a text: "Good luck today." Bobo replies almost immediately: "Kev?? Heard anything??" His mother writes back: "No. Nothing. Try to concentrate on hockey now, darling!" It takes a few minutes before he replies: "Going to win for Kev!!" She swallows hard and writes: "I love you." Bobo replies like teenage boys do: "OK."

Ann-Katrin leans back in a hard chair, looks up at the ceiling of the staffroom, and thinks about all the children who are in such pain. You see a lot of it at this hospital. That's why so many of her colleagues are on sick leave. Nurses and doctors have no break for summer training like in hockey, no finals, no time-outs. Their season just goes on, day after day after day, and that can break even the very toughest. Even people from Beartown.

And when even the toughest can't handle it: Who's going to be the leader then?

David starts to get up, clearing his throat to attract the boys' attention, then stops when he sees that they've already begun to sit down. Not because of David, but Benji. The boy is standing in the middle of the bus, and looks each of them straight in the eye in turn, before finishing up in front of Filip, a soft-spoken boy who's a year younger than most of the team, and who lives three houses away from Kevin in the Heights.

"When we were little, Filip, and you were upset because you were smallest and worst on the team; when you couldn't even shoot above the yellow strip at the bottom of the boards, what did David say to you then?"

Filip looks down at his lap, embarrassed, but Benji puts his palm under his chin and tips his head back. Filip wasn't just a year younger, he was also far behind players like Bobo in purely physical terms for so many years that no one even noticed how good he was at everything else. He's the type of guy who disappears in a locker room, never says anything, never causes problems, just goes along with things. In the past three years he has, in his usual unassuming way, become by far the best back on the team without anyone really noticing it happening.

"Ignore everything else, just concentrate on the things you can change," Filip replies quietly.

Benji nods and pats him on the head. Then he turns to William Lyt.

"And what did David say to you, Lyt, when all the others learned to skate backward before you, and you didn't think you'd be allowed to carry on playing?"

Lyt blinks hard and wipes his cheeks angrily.

"Concentrate on the things you can change."

Benji takes hold of Lyt by the shoulders and looks into his eyes as he quotes their coach again:

"We're a team. We give each other power. When one man falls, another steps up."

Lyt rubs his eyes with his sleeve and goes on:

"Team before self. Club before individual."

When no one else can hear, Benji whispers to him:

"We're relying on you now, Lyt, you're our star today. You have to lead us."

If Benji had asked Lyt to kill someone at that moment, the boy would have done it without hesitation. No social scientist nor any member of a sports team really knows what makes them who they are, the leaders we follow. Only that we don't hesitate when we see them.

Benji stops in front of Bobo, the giant who was the best back on the team until all the others learned to skate better than him.

"What's the second-best thing in the world, Bobo?"

It takes a moment before Bobo replies hesitantly:

"Fucking?"

Some of the juniors giggle. Benji lowers his head to Bobo's big face.

"But first we're on our way to do the best thing in the world, Bobo. And do you know how many things I want from you right now?"

Bobo stands up. "Just one, eh?"

"Win," Benji says.

"Win!" Bobo shouts.

"WIN!" the whole bus roars.

David sits down in his seat. "WIN! WIN! WIN!" the team is chanting, and David deletes the text from Kevin's father. When Lars comes over and asks if he's heard anything about why Kevin was taken away by the police, David shakes his head and replies:

"No. Nothing. Now we're going to concentrate on the things we can change, Lars."

Benji goes and lies down at the back of the bus. Sleeps the rest of the way.

32

There's a town in a forest that loves a game. There's a girl sitting on a bed playing the guitar for her best friend. There's a young man sitting in a police station trying not to look scared. In a hallway in a hospital, a nurse walks past a lawyer talking loudly into her cell phone. In the stands in an ice rink in a capital city grown men and women are on their feet, shouting that they are the bears from Beartown, along with sponsors and board members who ten years before laughed at a GM who said that one day they would have the best junior team in the country. Now everyone who is connected to the club is here except the GM.

A team is waiting in a locker room, sticks in hand, waiting for a game to start. A little brother is waiting on a bench with a phone in his lap, waiting to see what his friends will write about his sister on the Internet when they find out what's happened. A law firm gets a call from a wealthy client, and at another law firm a mother starts a war. The girl goes on playing her guitar until her best friend falls asleep, and in the doorway stands a father, thinking that the girls will survive this. They'll be able to deal with it. That's what he's afraid of. That that's what's going to make the rest of the world go on thinking that everything is okay.

There's a player with the number "16" on his back who, ever since he learned to skate, has had to learn exactly what it takes to win. He knows that games are won as much in the head as they are on the ice, and his coach has taught him how hockey is musical: every team has a rhythm and a tempo they like playing in. If you disrupt that rhythm, you disrupt their music, because even the best musicians in the world hate being forced to play out of time, and once they've started it's hard to stop. An object in motion wants to keep going in the same direction, and the larger a rolling snowball gets, the more of a fool you have to be to dare to stand in its path. That's what sportspeople mean by "momentum," whereas in physics lessons at school teachers talk about the "principle of inertia." David was always rather more blunt when he used to talk to Benji: "When something goes right for a team everything feels easy, so it automatically goes even better. But if you can cause a bit of trouble for them, only a very little bit, you'll soon see that they manage to create a lot more trouble for themselves." It's about balance. The slightest puff of wind can be all it takes.

An opposing team arrives at an arena to play against Beartown Ice Hockey, but everyone on the team scornfully calls them "Erdahl Ice Hockey." They already knew long before the match that they were light-years better than the peasants from the forest, but now they've just found out that Kevin isn't even going to be playing. Beartown is nothing without him. A joke. Roadkill at the side of a freeway. As they arrive at the arena the players are confident and calm; they know that all they have to do to win is to play their game. Have ice in their stomachs. Keep themselves balanced.

Their coach is still outside, but the players are hyped up with pride; they want to see their opponents, so they go into the rink ahead of him. The lights in the corridor to the locker rooms are broken; someone jokes that "the poor peasants have probably nicked the bulbs," and someone else replies: "What for? They don't have electricity in Beartown!" At first they think the unmoving shape outside their locker room is just a shadow—their eyes haven't gotten used to the gloom yet—so the first player walks straight into him. Benji's chest is concrete; the whites of his eyes swivel toward each of the twenty players in turn. If they'd had time to react, they might have laughed nervously, but now they just stand silent in the darkness, their eyes darting about.

Benji doesn't move. Just waits in the doorway. Forces them to come at him in order to get into their locker room. They should have waited for their coach, they should have gone to get a referee, but they're too proud for that. When they lose their temper it's predictable; he's already identified which two it will be. One gives him a shove, the other hits him in the shoulder with his fist. Benji soaks up the first and responds to the second by hitting him so quickly on his ear that he falls to the ground with a yelp. Benji twists toward the first again and hits him twice in the ribs, not hard enough to break anything but enough for him to double up, whereupon Benji elbows him in the back of the neck so that he collapses on top of his friend. When a third player rushes toward him, Benji darts out of the way and shoves him in the back, sending him flying into the unlit locker room. The fourth makes the mistake of grabbing hold of Benji's clothes with both hands; Benji headbutts him in the cheek and he falls backward with no one to catch him.

Obviously there's no way he could have taken on the whole team in a well-lit room, but in a cramped, dark corridor where no more than one or two can attack him at a time, they all need to ask themselves the question: Who goes first?

The answer is that no one does. That's enough—that single second's hesitation from a whole group. Benji grins at them, then calmly walks off before anyone thinks of anything to say. When he opens the door to his own team's locker room, "WE ARE THE BEARS!" from two dozen crazed voices echoes into the corridor, and the beam of light lasts just long enough for everyone on the opposing team to see exactly how off balance their teammates suddenly are.

They won't say anything to their coach, because what would they say? That they let a single guy take out their four strongest players while the rest of them stood and watched? "What the fuck was that?" someone mutters. "Head case," another one declares. When they switch the lights on, they try to laugh it off. They try to convince each other that they're going to get number sixteen later, that it doesn't matter, that they're too good to care about something like that. When the game starts it's very obvious that they haven't succeeded. Rhythm, tempo, balance. Puffs of wind.

Benji pulls on jersey number sixteen. David stands in front of his team with his hands behind his back and his eyes on the floor. He has spent the whole journey here thinking about what leadership actually means to him, and has reached one single, shimmering conclusion: Sune has been his mentor, and Sune's greatest strength was always that he nurtured leaders. His problem was that he never let them lead.

The players are holding their breath, but when David looks up at them he is almost smiling.

"Do you want to hear the truth, guys? The truth is that no one believed you could get here. Not your opponents, not the association, not the national coaches, and certainly not any of the people out there in the stands. For them this was a dream, for you it was a goal. No one did this for you. So this game, this moment . . . it belongs to you. Don't let anyone tell you what to do with it."

He wants to say so much more, but they're in the final now. He's done all he can. So he turns and walks out of the locker room. A few seconds later Lars follows, bewildered. The team sits there, at first just staring at each other in surprise. Then they stand up, one by one, and tap each other twice on the helmet. Of all people, the quietest of them is the first to raise his voice:

"Where are we from?" Filip asks.

"BEARTOWN!" the locker room replies.

Lyt climbs onto a bench and bellows: "FOR KEVIN!"

"FOR KEVIN!" the locker room replies.

Benji is already standing on the ice when they come out. Alone in the center circle, number "16" on his back, eyes black. The last to emerge from the Beartown locker room are the team's largest player and its smallest. Bobo taps Amat on the shoulder and asks:

"Where are you from, Amat?"

Amat looks up with his jaw trembling:

"The Hollow."

Bobo nods and holds up his gloves. He's written *Shantytown Hockey* on them with a marker pen. It's a clumsy gesture from a clumsy boy.

Sometimes they're worth the most.

Why does anyone care about sports? There's a woman in the stands who cares because they're the last thing she's got that gives her straight answers. She used to be a cross-country skier at the elite level. She sacrificed all her teenage years to skiing long-distance trails, evening after evening with a headlamp and tears streaming from cold and exhaustion, and all the pain and all the losses, and all the things other high school kids were doing with their free time that she could never be part of. But if you were to ask her now if she regrets anything, she'd shake her head. If you were to ask what she would have done if she could go back in time, she'd answer without hesitation: "Train harder." She can't explain why she cares about sports, because she's learned that if you have to ask the question, you simply wouldn't understand her answer.

Her son Filip is playing in the first line defense pairing, but she knows what he's had to do to get there. All the running in the forest in the light of two headlamps, all the hours on the terrace firing pucks while his mom stood in goal. All the tears when he was the smallest on the team and used to measure and weigh himself every morning because the doctor had promised that his body would catch up with the others in the end. The pencil marks on the doorframe that his mom can't bring herself to paint over now. The crushed little heap that she had to pick up from the kitchen floor every day when he realized he was just as short as the day before. Just as light. No one else may have noticed when he made himself into the best back on the whole team, but his mom was there every step of the way.

———

Tails has spent the entire warm-up with his phone in his hand, trying to find out what's happened to Kevin. Still nothing. He suspects that David is the first person Kevin's dad will contact when they know anything, but he can't get in touch with the coach from here.

The sponsors and board members around him are angry about the lack of information. They're already talking about which lawyers to contact, which journalists to share the story with, who's going to be punished for this.

Tails isn't angry; his emotions have reached another level now. He looks at the parents in the stands. Tries to add up all the days and evenings and nights they've devoted to this team. He feels the weight of his own silver medal from another age around his neck. He doesn't know who's snatched their chance of victory from them, but already he hates them.

It's Benji who tells David and Lars to let Lyt play in the center in place of Kevin. There will never be enough words to describe what that would mean to Lyt. Before the first face-off Benji stops in front of Amat and asks:

"Have you got your fast skates on today, then?"

Amat grins and nods. Their opponents are already talking loudly on their bench about "making number sixteen take his penalty calls." They're not idiots; they've seen Benji for the violent lunatic he is. So when the other team wins the face-off, Benji skates at full speed with his stick raised toward the player who gets hold of the puck, and everyone who saw number sixteen in the darkened corridor a while back obviously realizes that he's going to ignore the puck and go straight in for the hit. His opponent braces his skates and tenses his body to absorb the impact.

It never comes. Benji goes straight for the puck and pokes it between the defenseman's skates into the offensive zone, Lyt takes a hit in the neutral zone and is sent sprawling across the ice like a shot seal—a center sacrificing himself to give the third player in the line enough space. They get one single tiny chance in this game before their opponents realize how fast Amat is.

They take it.

Tails screams until his voice gives out when Amat waits out the goalie and lifts the puck into the top of the net. Parents rush down the stands as if they were going to vault the boards. Amat glides around the net with his arms in the air but doesn't get far before he is engulfed by Benji, Lyt, and Filip. The whole team is on the ice in moments, under and over and on top of each other. Tails grabs hold of someone's mother—he doesn't know whose—and screams:

"WHERE ARE WE FROM?"

A moment ago they were all atheists. None of them is now.

They're leading 1–0 after the first period. David doesn't say anything to them; he doesn't even go into the locker room. He stands in the corridor with Lars without a word. Hears the players tapping each other's helmets. Their opponents pull back to 1–1, then go ahead 2–1, but just before the second intermission, Bobo gets one of his few shifts, and the puck finds him at the offensive blue line. He tries to pass but the puck hits an opposing player's skate and bounces back toward Bobo. If the boy had had time to think, he would of course have realized that it was an idiotic idea, but no one has ever accused Bobo of being quick-witted. So he shoots. The goalie doesn't even move, and when the net behind him does Bobo is left standing there, staring in shock. He sees the lamp light up, the numbers on the scoreboard change to 2–2. He hears the celebrations from the Beartown section of the stands, but his brain doesn't register the sequence of events. The first one to reach him out on the ice is Filip.

"Win!" he yells.

"For Kevin!" Bobo howls, and throws himself at the glass with such mad pride that he forgets to take his stick back to center ice when play resumes.

Filip loves hockey, and so does his mom. And not like some vaguely interested parent who barely knows the rules. She worships this sport for all that it is. Tough. Honest. Definite. True. Straight answers, straight questions.

Maggan Lyt is standing next to her. She and Filip's mom have known each other since they were children, and now live two houses apart. They used to go skiing together, got married the same year, had their sons just a few months apart, have stamped the numbness out of their toes in stands just like this one for more than a decade. Do you want to try telling them that hockey parents are fanatical? They'll tell you to go to a junior cross-country skiing tournament and listen to the spectators there. Or talk to the slalom dad who rushes out onto the course and sabotages a whole tournament because he thinks the course has been set up to disadvantage his daughter. Or talk to the figure skater's mom about how much a nine-year-old really ought to train. There's always someone who's worse. You can get almost anything to look normal if you make enough comparisons.

Filip's mom never screams. Never shouts. Never criticizes the coach and never goes into the locker room. But she would defend Maggan to the end of the world and back if anyone criticized her friend's behavior. Because they're also a team. Filip's mom has learned that you can't ask parents to devote their whole lives to their children's sport, risk the family finances, and then expect that passion never to overflow occasionally.

So when Maggan screams, "Are you blind!?" at the referee, Filip's mom is quiet. When another parent screams, "For God's sake, Ref, did you get dropped as a baby, or what? Does your wife make all the decisions at home?" she says nothing. Then someone says, "What kind of old woman's pass was that?" and a man farther up the stands throws his arms up and yells, "Are we playing basketball now?" When one of the other team's players holds a Beartown player a little too long against the boards without getting penalized, one parent yells, "Are you a homo or number twenty-two?" when the boy returns to the bench.

A mom with two small children farther down in the stands turns around and says: "Can you think about what you're saying, please? There are children here!"

But Maggan replies, her voice dripping with derision:

"Well, sweetie, if you're so worried about them leaving their cozy little nest and hearing something terrible, maybe you shouldn't bring them to HOCKEY games!"

If you were to ask Filip's mom why she doesn't protest, she would say that you can love something without loving everything about it. You don't have to feel embarrassed about not being proud. That applies to hockey, but it also applies to friends.

The mother with the young children demonstratively takes them by the hand, goes off to the steps, and sits down farther away. Out on the ice, Filip is chasing an opponent all the way across the ice, throwing himself forward to block a pass, and getting him off balance. Benji sets off toward them.

One sponsor higher up in the stands turns to Tails, nods toward the mother with the children, and snarls:

"Have we got the fucking morality police in today? What's she doing here?"

The third period has only just started. Tails's reply gets drowned out by the roar of the crowd when number sixteen steals the puck in the neutral zone, fakes out two opponents with a technique no one knew he had mastered, and slams a shot into the net that the goalie gets nowhere near.

Benji brushes aside the other players when they try to hug him, gets the puck from the net, and goes straight over to the Beartown parents.

He stops by the boards a short distance away and waves to two ecstatic little children, then throws the puck to their mother.

The sponsor turns to Tails and asks: "Who . . . who's that, did you say?"

"That's Benji's sister, Gaby. And those children's uncle has just made it 3–2 for us," Tails replies.

33

When Maya was little she always used to go to bed when she was sad. She always slept her way through anything that upset her. When she was eighteen months old her mom was driving a rental car with her in the backseat through the center of Toronto when it broke down at one of the city's biggest intersections. There were buses blowing their horns, taxi drivers swearing, while Kira swore at some poor receptionist at the car-rental company on the phone. In the meantime the toddler looked around calmly, gave a big yawn, and fell asleep, and continued to sleep soundly until they got back home six hours later.

Kira is now standing in the hall of their house looking through the doorway at her daughter in her bed. Fifteen years old, she still sleeps whenever she's in pain. Ana is lying next to her under the covers. Perhaps it's different when you've had to bury one of your own children, or perhaps all parents feel this way, but the only thing Kira has ever wanted for her kids was health, safety, and a best friend.

You can get through anything then. Almost.

David will always remember this game. He will talk about the final minutes to his girlfriend throughout whole nights, tapping her stomach and whispering: "Don't fall asleep! I haven't got to the best bit yet!" Over and over again he will relate the story of how Amat threw himself down and blocked so many shots with his helmet that the referee eventually forced him off the ice to investigate whether it had been cracked. How Lyt played more minutes than anyone, and in the minutes he wasn't on the ice he was a colossus on the bench: no one slapped more backs, shouted more encouragement, or lifted the spirits of more exhausted teammates. When a shattered Bobo stumbled over the step on his way off the rink and collapsed facedown, it was Lyt who caught him and fetched his water bottle. Meanwhile Filip played like an experienced senior out there, no mistakes at all. And Benji? Benji was everywhere. David saw him use the side of his skate to block one shot that was so hard his assistant coach, Lars, clutched his own foot on the bench and yelped:

"Shit, I felt that!"

Benji played through the pain; the whole team hit the wall and smashed through it with their foreheads and just carried on. Every one of them overperformed. Every one of them was the very best version of themselves. They gave their all. No coach could possibly have asked for more. They did their absolute, absolute, absolute best.

It wasn't enough.

When the other team makes it 3–3 with under a minute to go, a team falls to the ice, two dozen parents collapse in the stands, and so does a town in the forest. In the break before overtime three players throw up. Another two barely make it back to the ice because their muscles are cramping. Their jerseys are soaked through, every cell in their bodies drained. But it still takes more than fifteen extra minutes for the opposing team to break them down one last time. They play around, around, around, and in the end Benji can't get there in time, Filip loses his man for the first time, Lyt's stick is too short, Amat is a fraction too late down onto the ice to block the shot.

The entire Beartown Ice Hockey team is lying on the ice while their opponents dance around them, when their parents and friends storm in to celebrate. Only when the winners' shouting and singing have moved to the locker room do Filip, Bobo, Lyt, and Amat begin to head toward theirs, inconsolable. Grown men and women are still sitting in the stands with their heads in their hands. Two children are crying uncontrollably in their mother's arms.

———

This planet knows no greater silence than two dozen hearts after a loss. David steps into the locker room to see the players lying bruised and battered on the floor and benches, most of them so tired they don't even have the energy to take their equipment off. Lars is standing alongside, waiting for the coach to say something, but David just turns around and disappears.

"Where's he going?" one parent asks.

"We're bad losers, because a good loser is someone who loses a lot," Lars mutters.

It's the captain of the opposing team who finally holds his hand out. He's freshly showered and changed, but his jersey is covered with champagne stains. Beartown's number sixteen is still lying on his back on the ice with his skates on. The stands are almost empty.

"Good match, man. If you ever want to change teams, you'd be welcome to come and play with us," the captain says.

"If you ever want to change teams, you're welcome to come and play with ME," Benji replies.

The captain laughs and helps him up, then sees Benji grimace.

"Are you okay?"

Benji nods distantly, but lets his opponent support him all the way into the corridor.

"Sorry I . . . you know . . . ," Benji says, making a slight gesture toward the broken lights in the ceiling.

The captain laughs loudly.

"Really? I wish we'd thought of doing something like that to you guys. You're a hard bastard. You need some serious help, man, but you're a hard bastard."

They part with a firm handshake. Benji creeps into the locker room and lies down on the floor, without making the slightest effort to take his skates off.

Gaby is walking through the corridor with her two children, past all the other adults in green scarves and jerseys with bears on them, nodding to some, ignoring others. She hears one father call the referee "mentally retarded." Then another mutters that "the bastard really needs to put his handbag down." She takes the children straight to the car instead of waiting for Benji. She doesn't want them to hear that sort of thing, and she knows what she'll get called if she protests.

Another quarter of an hour passes before David returns with a plastic bag full of pucks. He goes around the locker room, giving one to each of the players. In turn his boys read the eight letters that are written on them. Some of them smile, some of them start to cry. Bobo clears his throat, stands up, looks at his coach, and says:

"Sorry, Coach . . . but I've got to ask . . ."

David raises his eyebrows, and Bobo nods toward the puck.

"You haven't . . . you know . . . gone gay on us or anything, have you?"

Laughter can be liberating. Roaring with laughter can unite a group. Heal wounds, kill silence. The locker room rocks with giggles until David, with a broad smile, nods and replies:

"Extra cross-country running in the forest tomorrow when you get home. Thanks to Bobo."

Bobo is already crouching beneath a hailstorm of rolled-up balls of tape from the others.

The second from last to get a puck in his hand is Benji. The last is Lars. David pats his assistant coach on the shoulder and says:

"I'm going to take the night train back, Lars. The hotel's all booked for you; I'm trusting you to look after the boys."

Lars nods. Looks at the puck. Reads the words as tears run down onto his tracksuit top: *Thank you.*

———

Gaby jumps when Bobo taps on her window. The kids have fallen asleep in the backseat, and she was at the point of doing the same.

"Sorry . . . you're Benji's sister, aren't you?" Bobo says.

"Yes? We're waiting for him, he said he wanted to come home with us rather than stay the night in a hotel. Has he changed his mind?"

Bobo shakes his head.

"He's still in the locker room. We can't get his skates off. He asked us to get you."

When Gaby finds Benji she starts by telling him she loves him. Then she says it's damn lucky for him that their mom had to work today and couldn't come, because if she'd known that her son had played almost the entire third period plus fifteen minutes of overtime with a broken foot, yet still skated more than anyone else, she'd have killed him.

Filip stands for a long while next to his mother outside the bus in the parking lot. She wipes his cheeks. He whispers:

"Sorry. It was my fault. That last goal. I was marking him. Sorry."

His mom hugs him as if he were little again, even though he's now so big that he could have picked her up with one hand.

"Oh, sweetheart, what on earth have you got to apologize for? What have you ever had to apologize for?"

She pats his cheek. She knows how it feels; she's stood there crushed at the end of a cross-country skiing race until the drops of sweat turned to ice crystals, feeling just the same. She knows what hockey can give, and what it takes in return. All the setbacks her son has overcome pass before her eyes: all the elite teams he didn't get picked for, all the national teams he was never considered for, all the tournaments he's had to watch from the stands. His mom holds a sixteen-year-old boy who has trained every single day of his life for this game. Tomorrow he will wake up, get out of bed, and start again.

———

In a room in a house on the floor beside her best friend's bed, Ana is sitting curled up with a computer on her lap. Every so often she glances anxiously over the edge of the bed to make sure Maya hasn't woken up. Then she goes back into all the places in the Internet where she knows everyone at school will go when they find out what's happened. She plots a silent course via as yet un-updated statuses, a few pictures of cats and smoothies, the occasional disappointed account of the junior team's loss in the final. But nothing else. Not yet. Ana refreshes all the pages again. She's lived here all her life, she knows how quickly information spreads. Someone will know someone who has a brother who's a cop or has a friend who works at the local paper or a mom who's a nurse at the hospital. Someone will say something to someone. And all hell will break loose. She refreshes all the pages again, again, again. Hitting the keyboard harder and harder.

Bang. Bang. Bang. Bang. Bang.

Lars tells the team that the hotel is booked, paid for by the sponsors, and that the boys can order as much room service as they like, get some rest, and go home tomorrow. The players ask where David is. Lars says the coach has gone home to be there when the police release Kevin.

"What if any of us want to go home?" Lyt asks.

"We can arrange that, if that's what you decide," Lars says.

Not one single player chooses to stay. They're a team, and they head home to their team captain. They're halfway home that night when the news finally breaks on their cell phones. Why Kevin was picked up by the police, what he's been accused of, and who it was who reported him. First one player says: "What are they talking about? I saw them at the party. SHE was the one who had the hots for HIM!" Then another says: "Fucking bullshit! I saw them go up to his room, she went FIRST!" And a third declares: "As if she didn't want it! Did you see how she was dressed!? Little bitch."

———

In a bed in a room surrounded by sticks and pucks and match jerseys, a little brother is woken up by the sound of his sister's best friend in the next room, smashing a computer against the wall with full force. As if she hopes that the people who have written what's inside it might shatter into a thousand pieces along with it.

34

Kira and Peter are sitting on the little step outside the house. They're not touching each other. Peter remembers this distance so clearly. There were some days when he thought that grief was the only thing keeping them together, that Kira stayed with him even though he didn't deserve it because she didn't have anyone else to share the memory of Isak with. But other days, the opposite happened. Their grief split them apart, became an invisible barrier between them. It's back now.

"It's my fault," Peter whispers.

Kira shakes her head hard.

"Don't say that. It isn't your fault. It isn't hockey's fault. Don't give the bast . . . Don't give . . . Don't make excuses for him!"

"The club has nurtured him all his life, Kira. My club."

Kira doesn't answer. Her fists have been clenched so tight for so long that the marks her fingernails have left won't fade for several days once she finally opens them. Throughout her whole working life she has lived for justice and the law, has believed in fairness and humanism, has stood against violence and revenge. So she is now using all of her inner strength to fight off the feeling that is overwhelming her now, but she can't stop it, it just sweeps in with full force and destroys everything she believes in.

She wants to kill him. She wants to kill Kevin.

Ann-Katrin and Hog are standing in the parking lot waiting for the team bus to get back from the final. Ann-Katrin will always remember how it sounds, the silence in the town tonight that still hums like a dense buzz of voices, the darkened houses all around where she just knows people are awake, phones and computers sending words to each other, more and more angry, more and more vile. People don't talk much in Beartown. Even so, sometimes it feels like it's the only thing they do. Hog touches her arm gently.

"We have to wait, Ann-Katrin. We can't get involved in this until . . . we really know."

"Peter's one of your best friends."

"We don't know what happened, darling. No one knows what happened. We can't get involved."

Ann-Katrin nods. Of course they can't get involved. There are always two sides to every story. You have to listen to Kevin's version. She tries to convince herself of that. By every god and heaven and all the holy mothers of eternity, she really does try.

Ana is standing on the floor with her hands covering her face in shame. Maya is sitting in bed, shocked, and the remains of the computer are spread about the room. Kira goes in and takes each of their hands in hers.

"Ana, you know how much I love you. Like one of my own."

Ana wipes her face as big drops fall to the floor from her nose. Kira kisses her hair.

"But you have to go home for a little while, Ana. We need to be . . . on our own as a family."

Maya wants to protest on Ana's behalf, but she's too tired. When the front door closes again, Maya lies down and goes back to sleep. And sleeps and sleeps and sleeps.

Peter drives his daughter's best friend home. The houses are all dark, but he can still feel eyes looking out of the windows. When Ana gets out he wishes he could say something, be a wise parent offering comfort and encouragement and instruction. But he has no words. So all that comes out is:

"It's going to be okay, Ana."

Ana tugs her jacket tight around herself and pulls her woolly hat down over her forehead, and tries to look like she believes it, for his sake. She doesn't succeed. Peter can see the girl shaking with silent rage, and thinks back to a time, several years ago, when Kira and Maya had had an argument. Their daughter had one of her first teenage outbursts, and Kira was left sitting in the kitchen, crushed, sniffing: "She hates me. My own daughter hates me." Peter held his wife tight and whispered: "Your daughter admires you and needs you. And if you ever doubt that, just look at Ana. Of all the people your daughter could have chosen as her best friend, she's picked one who's just like you. One who wears her heart on her sleeve." Peter feels like getting out of the car and giving Ana a hug now, telling her not to be frightened, but he's not that sort of person. And he's too frightened himself to be able to lie.

When the car has gone Ana creeps into the house and wakes the dogs, then takes them as far out into the forest as she can. Then she sits there with her face buried in their fur and cries. They breathe on her neck, lick her ear, nudge her with their noses. She will never understand how some people can prefer other people to animals.

The Ovich family house has no empty beds tonight. Gaby's two children are sleeping in their uncle's bed, Adri and Katia in their mother's, their mother on the sofa. The daughters insist that they can sleep on the furniture in the living room, but their mother yells at them until they back down. When Gaby gets back from the hospital with Benji early the next morning, his sisters and mother look at his crutches and his foot in a cast and hit him over the head and shout that he'll be the death of them and that he means the world to them and that they love him and that he's an imbecile.

He sleeps on the floor beside his bed, below his sister's kids. When he wakes up the pair of them have both moved down with their covers and have curled up next to him. They're sleeping in their hockey jerseys. Number "16" on the back.

———

Kira is sitting on the edge of her daughter's bed. When Maya and Ana were children, Peter used to joke about how different they were, especially when they were asleep. "When Maya's slept in a bed you don't even have to make it afterward. When Ana's slept there you have to start by moving it back to the right side of the room." Maya would wake up with the body language of a sleepy calf; Ana like a drunk, angry middle-aged man who was trying to find his pistol. The only thing anyone could think of that the two little girls had in common was how protective they were of their names. Maya has never been more angry than the first time she realized there were other children with her name, which is saying a lot seeing as she was at the age when it was perfectly normal to demand that the plastic handles on her cutlery always matched the color of the food, or to have a tantrum at bedtime because "Daddy, my feet are the same size and I DON'T WANT THAT!!!" Nothing made her more angry than the fact that she wasn't alone in being called what she was called. For both her and Ana, a name was a personal possession, physical property in the same way as lungs and eyeballs, and in her world all the other Mayas and Anas were thieves. These girls wanted to be anything but ordinary.

People grow up mercilessly fast.

Peter closes the door without a sound. Hangs the keys to the Volvo on the hook in the hall. He sits in the kitchen with Kira for a very long time without a word being spoken. Eventually Kira whispers:

"This isn't about us now. It's all about how she's going to get through this."

Peter stares fixedly at the table.

"She's so strong," he says. "I don't know what to say to her; she's already stronger than me."

Kira's fingernails dig fresh grooves in her skin.

"I want to kill him, Peter. I want . . . I want to see him die."

"I know."

Kira is shaking as he crosses the force field and holds her, and they whimper and sniff together, holding back hard so as not to wake the children. They will never stop blaming themselves for this.

"It's not your fault, Peter. It wasn't hockey's fault. What is it they say . . . 'it takes a village to raise a child'?" she whispers.

"Maybe that's the problem. Maybe we picked the wrong village," he replies.

The juniors are picked up from the rink by their parents. They go home in silent cars to silent houses where the only lighting comes from an assortment of screens. Before dawn, Lyt goes over to Bobo's. They don't talk much, just share the feeling that they have to do something. Have to act. They walk through the town, picking up more juniors outside their homes. Like a black swarm they move between gardens, fists clenched under the dark sky, wild eyes staring out across empty streets. Hour after hour, until the sun goes up. They feel threatened, feel that they're under attack. They want to shout out to each other what this team means to them—loyalty and love—and how much they love their team captain. But they don't have the words, so they try to find other ways to show it instead. They walk side by side, like a menacing army. They would dearly like to rescue something. Damage something. Destroy. They're on the hunt for an enemy, any will do.

Amat gets home and goes straight to bed. Fatima sits quietly in the other room. The next morning they take the bus to the rink. No one says a word there either. Amat puts his skates on, picks up his stick, and skates furiously across the ice, hurting himself by crashing into the boards at the other end. He doesn't allow himself to cry until he's sweating so much that no one can see.

In a house a mom and a dad are sitting at a kitchen table.

"I'm just saying . . . what if . . . . . .?" the mother says.

"Do you believe that of our SON!? What sort of mother are you if you can seriously BELIEVE THAT OF OUR CHILD!" the father roars.

She shakes her head in despair, staring down at the floor. He's right, of course. What sort of mother is she? She whispers, "Of course not," of course she doesn't believe that of their son. She tries to explain that everything's just so mixed up, no one's thinking rationally right now, we just need to try to get some sleep.

"I'm not going to sleep as long as Kevin's being held by the police, you can be very fucking clear on that point!" the father declares.

She nods. She doesn't know if she's ever going to sleep again.

"I know, darling. I know."

In another house, another mom and another dad are sitting at another kitchen table. Ten years ago they left Canada and moved to Beartown, because it was the safest, most secure place they could think of. Because they so desperately needed somewhere in the world where it felt as if nothing bad could happen.

They're not talking now. They don't say a word all night long. Each of them knows what the other is thinking anyway. "We can't protect our children."

We can't protect our children we can't protect our children we can't protect our children.

35

Hate can be a deeply stimulating emotion. The world becomes much easier to understand and much less terrifying if you divide everything and everyone into friends and enemies, we and they, good and evil. The easiest way to unite a group isn't through love, because love is hard. It makes demands. Hate is simple.

So the first thing that happens in a conflict is that we choose a side, because that's easier than trying to hold two thoughts in our heads at the same time. The second thing that happens is that we seek out facts that confirm what we want to believe—comforting facts, ones that permit life to go on as normal. The third is that we dehumanize our enemy. There are many ways of doing that, but none is easier than taking her name away from her.

So when night comes and the truths spread, no one types "Maya" on their cell phone or computer in Beartown, they type "M." Or "the young woman." Or "the slut." No one talks about "the rape," they all talk about "the allegation." Or "the lie." It starts with "nothing happened," moves on to "and if anything did happen, it was voluntary," escalates to "and if it wasn't voluntary, she only has herself to blame; what did she think was going to happen if she got drunk and went into his room with him?" It starts with "she wanted it" and ends with "she deserved it."

It doesn't take long to persuade each other to stop seeing a person as a person. And when enough people are quiet for long enough, a handful of voices can give the impression that everyone is screaming.

Maya does everything she has to do, everything everyone asks her to do. She answers all the questions from the police, goes for all the tests at the hospital, spends several hours travelling in the car to see a therapist who keeps wanting her to remember, over and over again, the things she just wants to forget. Wanting her to feel what she wants to suppress, cry when she wants to scream, talk when she wants to die. Ana calls her, but Maya's switched off her phone. It's full of anonymous text messages. People were so quick to decide what the truth was that they bought pay-as-you-go phones just to be able to tell her what she is without her knowing who they are.

She gets home and her jacket slips off onto the hall floor, as if she has shrunk out of it. She becomes smaller and smaller, her organs deserting her one by one. Lungs, kidneys, liver, heart. In the end there is only poison left.

Leo is sitting at his computer when he hears her stop in the doorway of his bedroom. She hasn't been in here since they were little.

"What are you doing?" she asks, barely above a whisper.

"Playing a game," Leo replies.

He's disconnected his computer from the Internet. His phone is lying at the bottom of his backpack. His big sister is standing a couple of yards away with her arms clasped tight around her, looking at the bare walls where there were jerseys and posters hanging yesterday.

"Can I play?" she whispers.

He fetches an extra chair from the kitchen. They play without talking for hours.

Kira is at the office. Sitting in meeting after meeting with other lawyers. Fighting. Peter is at home cleaning every square inch of it, scrubbing the sink until he can feel the lactic acid, washing all the bedclothes and all the towels, washing every glass they have by hand.

When they lost Isak there were moments when they wished they had an enemy, someone who was guilty, just to have someone to punish. There were people who advised them to talk to God about it, but it's hard to maintain an ordinary conversational tone with God when you're a parent, hard to believe in a higher power when your fingertips are tracing the years marked on a gravestone. It's not the fault of mathematics; the equation for calculating a lifetime is simple: take the four-figure number to the right of the stone, subtract the number to the left, and multiply the result by 365, then add an extra day for each leap year. But however you do it, it doesn't make sense. You count, count again, count again, but it never comes right. However you do the sums it's never enough. The days are too few to amount to a whole life.

They hated it when people spoke of "the condition," because conditions are untouchable. They wanted to have a face, a perpetrator. They needed someone to drown under the weight of all the guilt, because otherwise they themselves would be dragged beneath the surface. They were so selfish, they know that, but when they didn't have anyone to punish there was only the sky left to scream at, and then their rage was too great for any human being to bear.

They wanted an enemy. Now they've got one. And now they don't know if they ought to sit next to their daughter or hunt down the person who harmed her, if they ought to help her live or see to it that he dies. Unless they're the same thing. Hate is so much easier than its opposite.

Parents don't heal. Nor do children.

Every child in every town in every country has at some point played games that are dangerous to the point of being lethal. Every gang of friends includes someone who always takes things too far, who is the first to jump from the highest rock, the last to jump across the rails when the train comes. That child isn't the bravest, just the least frightened. And possibly the one who feels he or she doesn't have as much to lose as the others.

Benji always sought out the strongest physical sensations because they displaced other feelings. Adrenaline and the taste of blood in his mouth and throbbing pain all over his body became a pleasant buzz in his head. He liked scaring himself, because when you're scared you can't think of anything else. He's never cut his own skin, but he understands those who do. Sometimes he has longed so much for a pain he can see and focus on that he's taken the train to a town several hours away, waited until dark, and then sought out the biggest bastards he could find to start a fight with, and then fought until they had no choice but to give him a serious beating. Because sometimes, when it seriously hurt on the outside, it hurt a little bit less in other places.

The bass player sees him before he gets off the stage. He's so surprised that he forgets to hide his smile. He's wearing the same black clothes.

"You came."

"The entertainment on offer around here is pretty limited."

The bass player laughs. They drink beer three steps apart, and overweight, drunk men come up from time to time and slap Benji on the back. Praise him on account of his broken foot, curse the fact that the referee was evidently a bastard. Then they mutter, "And that business with Kevin, that's a fucking disgrace." The same back-and-forth with seven or eight men of varying ages. They all want to buy number sixteen a beer. The bass player thinks he's probably imagining it, but for every slap on the back, it feels as if Benji retreats slightly. The bass player has been here before; this isn't the first boy he's met who behaves like he's living under an assumed identity. And perhaps it is different in a place like this, where you don't want to let anyone down.

When they're alone at last, the bass player empties his glass and says quietly:

"I'm gonna get going. I can see you've got . . . a lot of people who want to talk about hockey."

Benji grabs hold of his arm and whispers, "No . . . let's go somewhere," and he catches fire.

The bass player goes out into the night and takes the path off to the right of the building. Benji waits ten minutes before going outside and heading off to the left, taking a shortcut up through the forest before limping back to meet the boy among the trees, swearing and stumbling.

"Are you sure you know how to play hockey? You look like you've been doing something wrong," the bass player says, smiling at Benji's crutches.

"Are you sure you know how to play the bass? It sounded like you were tuning up the whole way through the gig," Benji retorts.

They smoke. The wind gets up in the darkness, whistling across the snow, but at the last moment it seems to decide to leave the boys alone. Only touches them fleetingly, tentatively, like hesitant finger-tips touching someone else's skin for the first time.

"I like your hair," the bass player says, breathing through it.

Benji shuts his eyes, lets go of his crutches; he wishes he'd had more to drink. Smoked more. He's misjudged his impulse control, left the little bastard awake when he should have knocked it out properly. He tries to let everything happen, but when he lays his palms on the other boy's back they clench automatically. The boy jerks in surprise, Benji's body tenses, and he purposefully puts his weight on his broken foot until the pain fires burning arrows up through his whole skeleton. Gently he pushes the bass player away from him. Picks up his crutches and whispers:

"This was a mistake . . ."

The bass player stands alone in the darkness among the trees with his feet lost in the snow while number sixteen limps back toward the Barn. He says:

"Big secrets turn us into small men."

Benji doesn't answer. But he feels small.

Monday morning comes to Beartown without ever really granting them daylight, as if it were as reluctant to wake up as the inhabitants.

A mother is sitting in a Volvo, trying to convince her daughter that she doesn't have to do this. She doesn't have to go in. Not today.

"Yes, I do," the daughter says, stroking her mother's hair.

"You . . . You don't know what they've been saying online," Kira says quietly.

"I know exactly what they've been saying. That's why I have to go in. If I wasn't ready for this, I wouldn't have reported him to the police, Mom. Now, I can't . . ."

Her voice cracks. Kira's nails dig tiny pieces of rubber from the steering wheel.

"You can't let them win. Because you're your father's daughter."

Maya reaches out her hand and brushes two stray strands of hair from Kira's cheek and tucks them behind her ear.

"My mother's. Always my mother's."

"I want to kill them, darling. I'd like to kill the whole lot of them. I've got the whole firm involved in this; there's not a chance in hell that I'm going to let them wi . . ."

"I've got to go, Mom. This is going to get a lot worse before it gets better. So I need to get going."

Kira watches her daughter go. Then she drives as far out into the forest as possible with the stereo turned up as loud as possible. She gets out and screams until her voice gives out.

36

The simplest and truest thing David knows about hockey is that teams win games. It doesn't matter how good a coach's tactics are: if they're to stand any chance of working, first the players need to believe in them. And each one of them needs to have the same words imprinted in his head a million times: Play your part. Focus on your task. Do your job.

David is lying in bed beside his girlfriend, his hand on her stomach.

"Do you think I'm going to be a good dad?" he asks.

"You're going to be a really, really, really annoying dad," she replies.

"That's mean."

She tweaks his earlobe between her thumb and forefinger. He looks so sad that she starts giggling.

"You'll have a tactical plan for the birth, and you'll try to set up a contraction strategy with the midwife because there's bound to be some sort of record to try to beat. You'll get it into your head that the length and weight percentiles are a competition. You'll be the most annoying, argumentative, best dad in the world."

His fingers trace the outline of her navel.

"Do you think he . . . or she . . . the child . . . do you think it will like hockey?"

She kisses him.

"It's really hard to love you without loving hockey, Dave. And it's really, really, really hard not to love you."

He's lying on his back with her legs gently twined around his.

"This business with Kevin. With . . . everything. I don't know what to do."

She whispers without hesitation:

"Your job, darling. You can't get involved in that; you're not a policeman and you're not a lawyer. You're a hockey coach. Do your job. Isn't that what you always say to the guys?"

"I don't know what you want me to do," the headmaster says into the phone. He's already lost track of how many similar calls he's received this morning.

"I WANT YOU TO DO YOUR JOB!" Maggan Lyt shrieks at the other end.

"You have to try to understand that I can't preempt a police inves . . ."

Saliva spatters the phone when Maggan replies:

"Do you know what this is? It's a CONSPIRACY against the whole hockey team! This is all about JEALOUSY!"

"So . . . what do you want me to do?"

"Your job!!!"

Bobo is stacking car tires in the garage. He's stressed and angry as he puts the tools back in their places on the wall and pulls off his dirty overalls.

"I have to go to school now, Dad."

Hog scratches his beard, looks at his son, and perhaps he feels like saying something, without actually knowing what that thing might be.

"You'll have to help me finish this later."

"We've got practice this evening."

"This evening? But the season's over!"

"It's not obligatory. But everyone will be there. For the team's sake. Lyt says we have to stand united for Kevin."

"Lyt says that? William Lyt?" Hog exclaims. He's never heard anyone in that family talk about standing united on any subject, but he can see in his son's eyes that there's no point discussing this unless he wants an argument, so he merely grunts:

"Just don't forget that you've got things to do here too."

Once Bobo has showered he runs out to the road. Ann-Katrin and

Hog watch him from the kitchen window. They can see Lyt and at least ten more juniors standing there waiting. They go everywhere together now.

"We've got to talk to him. I saw Maya at the hospital, I SAW her, and she didn't look like a girl who was lying," Ann-Katrin says, but her husband shakes his head.

"We can't get involved in this, Anki. It's none of our business."

Jeanette is fighting against the black lump in her stomach, trying to suppress the heartburn and migraine she always gets when she's not sleeping properly.

"I'm just saying, we ought to talk to the students about it. We can't just pretend nothing's happening."

The headmaster sighs and waves his phone.

"Please, Jeanette, you've no idea of the pressure I'm under here. The phone's been ringing all morning. The parents have gone mad. I've even had journalists calling! We're simply not equipped to handle something like this!"

Jeanette cracks her knuckles; she does that when she's nervous, an old habit from her hockey days.

"So we just stay quiet?"

"Yes . . . No . . . We . . . Christ, we can't add to the rumors and speculation. What's wrong with people? Why can't we all just wait until the investigation is finished? That's why we have courts, isn't it? We can't set ourselves above the law, Jeanette, that isn't our responsibility. If it turns out . . . If what this student is saying about Kevin . . . if it's true . . . then time will tell. And if it isn't, then we need to be sure we haven't done anything stupid."

Jeanette wants to scream, but doesn't.

"What about Maya? If she comes to school today?"

The headmaster's facial expression goes from sure to unsure to panic-stricken in the space of just a few words.

"She won't, obviously. She wouldn't. Do you think she will?"

"I don't know."

"She won't. Surely she won't? You don't have her in any of your classes, do you?"

"No, but I've got half the players on the team. So exactly what do you want me to do?"

The headmaster throws his hands up in resignation. "What do you think?"

They're sitting in the cafeteria, chairs touching, heads together. There's fire in William Lyt's eyes.

"Where the fuck is Benji? Has anyone seen him?"

They shake their heads. Lyt jabs his index finger down hard on the table.

"My mom's arranged for us all to get a lift to Hed today, okay? We're leaving just before lunch. Don't mention it to anyone not on the team. If the teachers make a fuss, they'll just have to talk to our parents. Okay?"

They nod. Lyt bangs his fist on the table.

"We're going to show the bastards doing this, all of them, that we stand together. Because you know what this is, don't you? It's a conspiracy against the whole team. It's jealousy. A conspiracy, and fucking jealousy."

The boys nod in agreement, determined. They've all got dark circles under their eyes. Several of them have been crying. Lyt slaps them on the shoulder, one by one.

"We have to keep the team together now! The whole team!"

He looks directly at Bobo as he says this.

Amat is standing by his locker. It looks like he's about to be sick inside it. Bobo heads toward him from the cafeteria and stops awkwardly behind him.

"We have to . . . keep the team together, Amat. Kevin is being re-leased by the police today, so we're going to our first classes, but then the whole team's going to Hed together. It's important that we all go as a group. To . . . show."

They both avoid looking toward the row of lockers where Maya has hers. All the pupils going past stare at it without actually looking in that direction, a trick you soon pick up when you're a teenager. The door of the locker is covered in black ink. Five letters. All she is to them now.

Kevin is led out through the door of the police station in Hed, hands holding onto him carefully as if he can't walk on his own. On one side his dad, on the other his mom, and around them like a protective wall of flesh and blood is a group of middle-aged men in jeans and smart, tailored jackets, ties knotted as tightly as their fists are clenched. Most of them are sponsors of the club, two are board members, several are prominent businessmen and entrepreneurs in the region, one a local politician. But if anyone asks, they would never present themselves that way, just say: "Friends of the Erdahl family. Just friends of the family." A few steps behind comes the junior team. One or two of them still look a bit boyish, but en masse they're men. Silent and menacing. There to prove something, to someone.

Kevin's mom tenderly wraps a blanket around his shoulders as they help him into the car. The men surrounding them don't slap him on the back the way they usually do, they pat his cheek lovingly instead. Perhaps that makes it feel easier for them. As if it's the boy who's the victim.

Benji is sitting on a low wall twenty yards away. His cap is pulled down low over his forehead, his hood pulled up so that the shadows hide his face. None of the adults even notice him, but Kevin does. For a single second, just as his mother is wrapping the blanket around him and before the car door closes, his eyes meet those of his best friend. Until Kevin looks down.

———

By the time the cavalcade of cars following Kevin's dad leaves Hed, Benji is already long gone. The only person left on the street outside the police station is Amat. He puts his headphones in, raises the volume, sticks his hands hard in his pockets, and sets off to walk all the way back to Beartown on his own.

Ana walks into the school dining room, the same storm of shrieks and clattering as usual. On a desert island in the corner sits Maya, alone, so isolated that no one has even sat down at the tables next to hers. Everyone is staring without looking. Ana walks toward her but Maya looks up, like a creature caught in a trap warning another not to get too close. Maya shakes her head softly. Ana's footsteps shift the gravity of the whole planet with each step she takes, as she lowers her head and goes and sits down at another table, in a different corner. The shame of that moment will follow her until her dying day.

A group of older girls—Ana recognizes them from the kitchen at Kevin's party—head toward Maya. First as if they're pretending she doesn't exist, then, in a flash, as if she's the only thing that does. One of them steps forward with a glass in her hand. Maya sees the others position themselves as a barrier toward the rest of the room, so that even if everyone sees exactly what happens, everyone will be able to claim afterward, when the teachers ask, that their "view was obscured." That they "didn't see the incident."

"As if anyone would want to rape YOU, you disgusting little bitch . . ."

Milk runs down Maya's hair, drips down her face and down inside her top. The glass doesn't break when the girl hits her across the brow with it, nor does her brow. For a fleeting moment Maya sees the fear in the girl's eyes when she starts to worry she's gone too far, that Maya might start bleeding and collapse on the floor. But Maya's skin is thick. And her attacker's eyes are soon filled with derision again. As if the person she attacked is no longer human.

———

Everyone sees it but no one sees it. The dining room is simultaneously filled with noise and utterly silent. Maya hears the giggling as
a muffled roar in her ears. She sits there calmly with pain throbbing
through her brow and forehead, and slowly wipes herself with the few
small napkins on her tray. They quickly run out. She refuses to look
around for more, but suddenly someone puts a thick pile down next
to her. A different hand, almost as big as her own, starts wiping the
table. She looks at him and then shakes her head, almost beseechingly.

"It'll only get worse for you if you sit here," she whispers.

"I know," Leo says.

Her little brother sits down beside her and starts to eat. In a sea of
stares, he seems unconcerned.

"So why do it, then?" his big sister asks.

Leo looks at her with their mother's eyes.

"Because you and I aren't like them. We aren't the bears from
Beartown."

37

Sooner or later, almost every discussion about the way people behave toward one another ends up becoming an argument about "human nature." That's never been an easy thing for biology teachers to explain: on the one hand, our entire species survived because we stuck together and cooperated, but on the other hand we developed because the strongest individuals always thrived at the expense of the weak. So we always end up arguing about where the boundaries should be drawn. How selfish are we allowed to be? How much are we obliged to care about each other?

People say, "But what about a sinking ship? What about a burning house?" because those are dramatic scenarios to imagine. It's hard to win a debate against that. Because if it were a life-and-death situation, who would you save if you could only choose one? Who would you pull out of the freezing water first if the lifeboat only had a limited number of places?

Your family. You always start with your family. That's what she tells herself. She's freezing; she turned up the heat and is wearing four layers, but she's still shaking. She's gone from room to room in the house. She's cleaned Kevin's room, has gotten rid of all the sheets and pillowcases, has dumped all the T-shirts and jeans from the washing basket into charity collection boxes many miles away from the house. She's vacuumed up all potential blouse-buttons and flushed any traces of marijuana down the toilet.

Because she's his mom. And that's where you start.

When the police arrived she was standing tall in the doorway. Their lawyers had pointed out that they could object, delay, make things difficult, that the search of the house and any forensic evidence could be deemed inadmissible given that the police only showed up a whole week after the alleged offense. But his mom insisted on letting in the men in uniform. She repeated time and time again that her family had nothing to hide, although she was unable to stop wondering if she was trying to convince them or herself. She can't stop shivering. But she's his mom. So where do you start, if not there?

Kevin's dad is sitting in the kitchen, now the command center, making call after call, as more and more men gather in the house. They're all very understanding, sympathetic, angry. They are hurt. Aggressive. They're ready for war, not because they've chosen it, but because they don't believe they have a choice. Kevin's dad's childhood friend, Mario Lyt, is the loudest of them all:

"Do you know what? That girl's family could have come and talked to us. They could have tried to resolve this privately. But instead they waited a whole week, until the moment when they knew it would do us the MOST harm, then went to the police with their lies IMMEDI-ATELY before the final! If it was actually true, why wasn't it reported at once? Why wait a week? Eh? Should I tell you why? Because some people in this town can't control their own jealousy!"

He could have called "that girl's family" by their name. Andersson. But that would have been less effective. He needn't have said anything more, because soon the theory is spreading on its own:

"This is what happens when you let a GM get too big for his boots, isn't it? We've given him too much influence, he thinks he owns the club. So now he can't handle the fact that he's losing his own power, right? And the fact that Kevin is better that he ever was, and the board and the sponsors are going against his wishes and demanding that David take over from Sune as A-team coach. Right? So now the GM is trying to drag his family into it . . ."

When David arrives at the house there are three middle-aged men standing outside, as if on guard. Tonight there will be players from the junior team there instead, David already knows that. As if the house needed protecting.

"Looks like a scene from *The Godfather*," David mutters.

Tails answers him. The big man looks embarrassed and therefore laughs a bit too loudly:

"Yes, it does, doesn't it? Like Don Corleone needs our help. As if a bunch of fat sponsors could make any real difference."

He chuckles and pats his own stomach, trying to appear nonchalant, but eventually gives up and puts a huge hand on David's shoulder, saying:

"Oh, David, you know, we just want to support the family. You can understand that, can't you? We just want to show that we . . . that we stand united. You can see that? I mean . . . no one knows Kevin better than you. Christ, you've practically raised the boy, and do you think one of the boys on your team could do what he's been accused of? Eh? One of your own lads? You can understand why we're here, can't you?"

David doesn't reply. That isn't his job. Not his place. Because who do you start with? If you really had to choose, who do you save first? Whose word do you believe?

Kevin is sitting on his bed. He looks small beneath the posters on the wall—his hoodie looks too big for him. He's spent two nights in the police station. It doesn't matter how comfortable the bunk is or how friendly the staff is to you: when you hear the door lock from the outside before you go to bed, it does something to a person. That's what he tells himself. That he has no choice, that it isn't his fault, that this may not even have actually happened. His parents' house is full of men who have known him since he was a child. They know him. All his life he has been special, chosen, has been expected to do something out of the ordinary. So they don't believe this of him, how could they even entertain the possibility? They're not going to let him down. And if enough people stand behind you, you can start to believe almost anything that comes out of your mouth.

That's what he tells himself.

David closes the door behind him, stands in front of the bed, and looks the boy right in the eye. All the tens of thousands of hours they've spent on the ice together, all the weekends on the team bus, driving up and down the country, all the gas station sandwiches and poker parties. He was a child until recently. Until very recently.

"Just look me in the eye and tell me you didn't do it. I'm not asking for anything else," David says.

And Kevin looks him straight in the eye. Shakes his head as he cries. Whispers with wet cheeks:

"I slept with her, because that's what she wanted. She asked me to! Ask anyone who was at the party . . . Shit, Coach . . . really? You seriously think *I* could rape someone? Why would I do THAT!?"

All the "fathers against sons" days at the rink that David has spent down on the lake with Kevin and Benji. All that he's taught them. All that they've shared. Next year they'll be taking over the A-team, together. Who do you start with? If the water is freezing but you know the boat won't be able to carry everyone to the shore? Who do you sacrifice first? Who do you protect unto the last? Kevin isn't the only one who'll suffer if he confesses. Everyone he loves will. That's what David tells himself.

David sits on the boy's bed and hugs him. Promises that everything will be okay. That he'll never let him down. That he's proud of him. The boat may be rocking, but it's not letting in water. All the feet in the house are dry. Kevin turns to his coach and whispers, like he was a primary school pupil again:

"The team are training, today, aren't they? Can I come?"

On a stool in her bedroom sits a mother, thinking about a childhood. How she and her husband used to come home from trips abroad when

Kevin was ten or eleven and find the house in a complete mess. His father always swore, even though he never seemed to appreciate how calculated the chaos was, but his mom soon learned to understand the pattern. The same things had moved, the same pictures would be hanging crookedly, the bin full of prepared meals whose contents had obviously been opened at the same time.

When Kevin became a teenager and started having parties, his mother started to come home to a house where the boy had obviously done all he could to make it look like he hadn't even been there. But before that, when he was little, when he proudly promised his dad that he wasn't scared of being on his own, he always had to come back on that last evening and mess up the whole house so that no one would know he had slept at Benji's the whole time.

On a chair in his kitchen sits a father, and all around him his friends and business partners are talking, but he no longer hears the words. He knows he occupies his position in this town, his status among this group of men, purely because of his money. None of these men play golf with poor guys, and he's been poor. All his life he has strived for perfection, not out of vanity, but as a survival strategy. He has never been given anything for free, he's never cut himself any slack, the way men who are born rich can. He's convinced that's the reason for his success: the fact that he's been prepared to work harder and fight more ruthlessly than everyone else. And continuing to hunt perfection in all things means never being satisfied, never resting on your laurels. You can't live that sort of life half the time, your work and private life become the same thing. Everything in his life has become a reflection of him as a person. Even his son. Any crack in the façade could lead to an avalanche.

He may have wanted to talk to Kevin when he picked him up from the police station, but every word came out as a roar. A man who takes great pride from the fact that he never loses his temper, never raises his voice, screaming so loudly that the car shook. He may have wanted to scream about what had happened, but it was easier to scream about why:

"HOW THE HELL COULD YOU LET YOURSELF GET DRUNK A WEEK BEFORE THE FINAL?"

It's easier to talk about a cause rather than a problem. For a dad who works with numbers, mathematics provides a more bearable explanatory model: if only X hadn't existed, Y would never have happened. If Kevin hadn't had a party despite promising his parents that he wouldn't, if he hadn't gotten drunk, if he hadn't take a girl up to his room, then they wouldn't have had to deal with this problem.

But now the father has no choice. He can't afford to let anyone tell lies about his son; he can't accept the idea of anyone attacking his family. When the police became involved, when they dragged Kevin off the bus in front of the whole town, when the reporters from the local paper started to call, that was when things passed the point where there could have been a peaceful solution. Now it's too late. The father has a business that consists of his name, and if that name gets sullied, it could destroy the entire life of the family. So he can't let them win, he can't even let them exist. It's not enough merely to hurt them. He has to hunt them down with every weapon he can find.

There's no right or wrong in this house anymore, just survival.

David and Kevin are still sitting on the bed when Kevin's father opens the door. He stands in front of them, tired and pale, and explains in a very controlled voice:

"I understand that you only want to think about hockey right now, but if you want there even to be an A-team to coach and play in next season, you need to listen very carefully now. Either the two of you stay at the club, or Peter Andersson does. There's no middle way. His daughter is lying, and there may be a thousand reasons for that. Maybe she had sex because she's in love and when she discovered that her feelings weren't reciprocated, she invented the story about rape. Maybe her dad found out and got angry, so she lied to protect herself, because she wants to go on being Daddy's innocent little girl. Who knows? Fifteen-year-old girls aren't rational."

David looks down at the floor. He can remember when Kevin was receiving offers from all the big teams but chose not to go, because he didn't want to leave Benji and his home, because he was scared. It was David who persuaded Kevin's dad to let him stay in Beartown. He promised that the boy would develop just as well here, would get to play on the A-team early, and would achieve even greater things once he did turn professional. His dad agreed because David was going to be A-team coach, and because the decision simultaneously made his company even more popular in the district. Kevin was a Beartown kid, his dad a Beartown man, and that looked good. His dad has invested a lot of money in that image. So now he points at Kevin and sternly says:

"This isn't a game anymore. Peter Andersson waited a week before going to the police, because he *wanted* the police to drag you off that bus. He wanted everyone to see that. So either he forces us out of this club, or we force him out. Together. There are no other options."

David says nothing. He's thinking about his job. His team. All those hours. And one single memory refuses to leave him: he saw Peter in the parking lot when the police came to the bus. He saw him standing there waiting. Kevin's dad is right. Peter wanted to see it happen.

Kevin lifts his head and snot and tears drip onto the floor when he says:

"Someone needs to talk to Amat. He . . . I didn't do anything . . . you know I didn't do anything . . . but maybe Amat thinks . . . He came into the room and saw us . . . She just got SCARED, okay? She rushed out, but maybe Amat thinks . . . you know."

David doesn't look up, because he doesn't want to see the way the father is looking at the son.

38

There are damn few things in life that are harder than admitting to yourself that you're a hypocrite.

Amat is walking along, half on the edge of the road and half in the ditch. He's wet and cold and his brain went numb long before his feet. He's halfway between Hed and Beartown when an old Saab drives past and stops ten yards ahead of him. It waits for him as he walks slowly toward it. There are two men in their late twenties or early thirties sitting in the front seats. Black jackets, wary eyes. He knows who they are. He doesn't know which is more dangerous: looking them in the eye or avoiding doing so.

A few months ago the local paper interviewed a player from a team that was due to play Beartown's A-team. The player came from the south—he didn't know any better—so when the reporter asked if he was frightened by the violent reputation of the Pack, the passionate supporters up in Beartown, he said he certainly wasn't frightened of "a few forest gangsters from a dying town."

When the team's bus was driving through the forest the next day, they found the road in front of them blocked by a couple of vans. Out of the trees stepped thirty or forty masked men in black jackets, armed with tree branches. They stood there for ten minutes, let the team on board prepare themselves for the moment when the door was smashed in and the bus invaded, but nothing happened. Suddenly the forest swallowed the men up again, the vans reversed out of the way, and the bus was allowed through.

The player who had talked to the paper turned to an older player and gasped: "Why didn't they do anything?" The older player replied: "They were just introducing themselves. They want you to think about what they could do when the bus is going back the other way."

Beartown lost the match, but the player who had talked to the paper played his worst ever match. When he got back to his own town, someone had already been there and smashed the windows of his car, filled it with branches and leaves, and set fire to it.

"You're Amat, right?" the man in the driver's seat asks.

Amat nods. The driver nods toward the back door.

"Want a lift?"

Amat doesn't know if it's more dangerous to say yes or no. But in the end he shakes his head. The men don't look insulted, the driver even smiles when he says:

"Nice to have a bit of a walk, yeah? We get it."

He puts the car in gear, slowly releases the clutch, but before it starts to move he leans out of the window and adds:

"We saw you play in the semifinal, Amat. You've got heart. When you and the other juniors make it to the A-team, we can build something really good around here again. A real Beartown team made up of real Beartown guys. You get it? You, Benji, Filip, Lyt. Kevin."

Amat knows that the expression on his face is being scrutinized by the men in the car when Kevin's name is mentioned. That this was the whole reason why they stopped. His chin moves quickly up and down, their eyes meet very briefly. They know that he understands.

They wish him a pleasant walk and pull away.

Peter is sitting in his office staring at a black computer screen. He's thinking about "the right sort of guy." He's said those words hundreds of times in hundreds of different rooms, and hundreds of men have nodded in agreement, even though he is certain that no one can explain exactly what they mean. It's a pointless term to use in hockey, because it suggests that who you are off the ice says something about who you are on it. And that's a difficult thing to acknowledge. Because if you love hockey, if you love anything, really, you'd really prefer it to exist inside a bubble, unaffected by anything happening outside. You want there to be one place, one single place, which will always be exactly the same, no matter how much the world outside might change.

That's why Peter likes to say: "Hockey and politics don't belong together." When he said that during an argument with Kira a few years ago, his wife snorted and said: "No? What do you think gets rinks built, if not politics? Do you think it's only people who like hockey who pay taxes, then?"

A few years ago there was an incident at one of the A-team's away games. A Beartown player lost his temper and brought his stick down on the head of an opponent, a promising twenty-year-old. He was ejected for the rest of the game, but escaped a longer suspension. When he left the ice and was on his way to the locker room, he was confronted by two men: the assistant coach of the other team and one of their sponsors. An argument and a clumsy fight ensued. The player hit the coach in the face with his glove, and the sponsor pulled the player's helmet off and tried to headbutt him, before the player smashed his stick into the sponsor's knee and knocked him to the floor. No one suffered any serious injury, but the player was reported to the police and was fined several days' wages. As for the player who got hit in the head while on the ice during the game, the resulting concussion and neck injury ended his career.

Peter remembers the incident because Kira brought it up again and again for the rest of the season. "So when someone gets into a fight three yards from the ice, it's okay to report them to the police. But a minute and a half earlier when the same man hits a twenty-year-old over the head with a stick in the middle of a match, he just has to go and sit and feel embarrassed for a little while?"

Peter couldn't win against her, because he didn't want to say what he really felt: that he didn't think what had happened in the players' tunnel should have been reported to the police either. Not because he liked violence, and not because he was in any way trying to defend what the player had done, but because he wanted hockey to solve hockey's problems. Inside the bubble.

He's always felt that it's impossible to explain that to anyone who doesn't love hockey. Now he's no longer sure he can even convince himself. And he doesn't know what that says about him.

Hypocrisy is a damn hard thing to admit.

The club's president wipes his hands on his pants and feels the sweat trickling down the base of his spine. He's spent all day talking on the phone, trying to put this off as long as possible, but he no longer has a choice. The threats of withdrawn sponsors' money and resigned memberships have grown too strong, and everyone is asking the same thing: "Whose side are you really on?"

As if a hockey club is supposed to choose a side. The president is proud to represent a popular movement that is independent of ideologies, religions, and other faiths. He doesn't believe in God, but he does believe in hockey, and he believes in the unifying strength of a hockey club precisely because it only defines itself as a hockey club. The stands are unique—they contain rich and poor alike, high and low, right and left—and how many places like that does society have left? How many troublesome guys has hockey kept away from addiction and prison? How much money does hockey save society? How come everything bad that happens is "hockey's problem," but everything good is thanks to something else? It drives the president mad, that people don't appreciate how much work goes on behind the scenes. You need more diplomacy here than in the headquarters of the United Nations.

The phone rings again. Again. Again. In the end he stands up and goes out into the hallway, where he tries to breathe normally in spite of the pressure in his chest. Then he goes and stands in the doorway to Peter's office and says quietly:

"Maybe you should go home, Peter. Until this blows over."

Peter sits on his chair without looking at him. He's already packed his things away in boxes. Hasn't even switched his computer on. He's just been waiting.

"Is that what you think, or are you just scared about what other people think?"

The president frowns.

"For God's sake, Peter, you know perfectly well that I think this whole . . . situation . . . is terrible! Just terrible! What . . . What . . . What your daughter is going through is . . ."

Peter stands up.

"Maya. You can say her name. You come to her birthday party every year. You taught her to ride a bike, do you remember? Right here, in front of the rink."

"I'm just trying . . . Please, Peter . . . the board is just trying to handle this . . . responsibly."

Peter's eyebrows quiver; that's the only physical sign of the unbearable firestorm raging inside him.

"Responsibly? Let me guess. The board would rather we had dealt with this 'internally.' That we hadn't involved the police and the media, and just 'looked each other in the eye and talked about it.' Is that more or less what people have been telling you over the phone today? It was RAPE! How do you deal with that INTERNALLY!?"

When Peter picks up his boxes and walks out into the hallway, the president gets out of the way, then clears his throat unhappily and says:

"It's her word against his, Peter. We have to think of the team first. You of all people ought to understand that. The club can't take a position on this."

Peter doesn't turn around when he replies:

"The club has taken a position. It just did."

He dumps his boxes in the back of his car, but leaves it in the parking lot. He walks slowly through the town without knowing where he's going.

The school headmaster hardly has time to put the phone down before it rings again. Voice after voice, parent after parent. What answers do they want? What do they expect? This is a police matter, let the courts decide, as if running a school isn't hard enough. The girl's mother is a lawyer, the boy's father one of the most powerful men in the entire district, one person's word against another's. Who'd want to get in the middle of that? That can't be the task of the school, surely? So the headmaster says the same thing again, over and over again, to everyone:

"Please, let's not make this political. Whatever you do, don't make this political!"

One advantage of having a brother who works for the security company is that all her nocturnal outings as a result of false alarms have given Jeanette a specialist's knowledge of the architecture of the school. For instance, she knows where on the top floor to find the small cubbyhole containing the narrow staircase that the chimney sweeps once used to reach the roof. And up there, behind an air vent just above the dining room, a teacher can have a cigarette without being spotted by either the headmaster or any students. And that's needed more on some days than others.

That's how Jeanette happens to see Benji walking across the schoolyard just after lunch. All the other players in the junior team are playing truant to be with Kevin, so the fact that Benji is here of his own volition can only mean that he's looking for the opposite.

Ana is sitting alone in a classroom full of students who are talking about nothing but Maya and Kevin. Maya is sitting alone in another classroom where no one is talking at all. She sees the notes they pass across each other's desks, the phones they conceal on their laps.

She will always be this to them now: at best the girl who got raped, at worst the girl who lied. They will never let her be anyone but that. In every room, on every street, in the supermarket and at the rink, she will walk in like an explosive device. They will be scared to touch her, even the ones who believe her, because they don't want to risk getting hit by shrapnel when she detonates. They will back away in silence, turn in a different direction. They will wish that she would just disappear, that she had never been here. Not because they hate her, because they don't, not all of them: they don't all scrawl *BITCH* on her locker, they don't all rape her, they aren't all evil. But they're all silent. Because that's easier.

She gets up in the middle of the class and leaves the room without a word of protest from her teacher. She crosses an empty hallway, goes into a bathroom, stands in front of the mirror, and smashes her fist into it as hard as she can. The glass shatters and it takes a few seconds for the pain to reach her brain, and she has time to see the blood before it actually hurts.

Benji sees her go in. He does his best to persuade himself to go in the other direction. Keep quiet. Don't get involved. But then he hears the crash and the tinkling sound as pieces of glass hit the porcelain sink, and he's broken enough mirrors himself to recognize the noise.

He knocks on the door. When she doesn't answer he says:

"I can kick it in, or you can unlock it, your choice."

She's standing there with toilet paper wrapped clumsily around her knuckles. It's slowly turning red. Benji closes the door behind him, nods toward the mirror:

"Seven years' bad luck."

Perhaps Maya ought to be frightened, but she hasn't got the energy. She can't even be bothered to feel hate. She doesn't feel anything at all.

"Hardly makes any difference to me now, does it?"

Benji sticks his hands in his pockets. They stand in silence, the victim and the best friend. The bitch and the brother. Maya clears her throat to stifle her sobs and says:

"I don't care what you want. I get that you hate me. You think I'm lying to get your best friend in trouble. But you're wrong. You're fucking wrong."

Benji takes his hands out of his pockets, carefully picks some pieces of glass out of the sink, and drops them, one by one, into the trash.

"You're the one who's wrong."

"Screw you," Maya hisses, and moves toward the door, and the boy slips nimbly out of the way so she doesn't have to come into physical contact with him, and only much later will she realize what a considerate gesture that was.

Benji utters the words so quietly that at first she thinks she's misheard:

"You're the one who's wrong, Maya. Because you think he's still my best friend."

Jeanette has an hour between lessons. She takes the opportunity to go to the bathroom to wash the smell of cigarettes off her fingers while the hallway is empty. She stops when she sees Maya come out, in tears and with her knuckles bleeding, as if she's smashed something. The girl doesn't see the teacher, just runs off in the other direction, toward the exit.

The next moment the washroom explodes with noise as a sink is torn from the wall and thrown to the floor, a toilet is kicked to pieces, a trash can thrown straight through the window. It doesn't take long for the hallway to fill with adults and pupils, but by then everything inside the bathroom has already been systematically smashed and demolished. It takes one headmaster, one caretaker, and two gym teachers to grab hold of Benji and get him out of the bathroom.

The school will describe this later as "an emotional outburst from a student with a well-documented history of problems with aggression." They will say that it is "understandable, considering his relationship to the boy who had been accused of . . . you know."

Jeanette stands and stares at the wreckage, meets Benji's gaze, and watches as he is led away. The boy smashed up an entire bathroom and accepted both suspension and liability for the cost of repairs without blinking, all because he didn't want anyone to know that Maya had smashed a mirror. He decided that she had already bled enough. The only adult who will know this is Jeanette, and she will never say any-thing. She knows a thing or two about keeping secrets herself.

She goes back up onto the roof. Smokes the rest of the pack.

Kira is in her office, buried in printouts of previous judgments and precedents from sexual assault cases, in constant discussion with her colleagues, total mobilization for war. She is feeling everything all at the same time: rage, grief, impotence, a desire for vengeance, hatred, terror. Yet it still falls away from her in an instant when her phone vibrates and her daughter's name illuminates the screen. Four little words. "Can you come home?" Never has a mother driven a car faster through that forest.

Maya is sitting on the floor of the bathroom at home, rinsing the blood from her hand before finally collapsing altogether. Everything she has held back, everything she has tried to stifle, everything she has tried not to show in order to protect the people she loves, to stop them hav-ing to feel as much pain as her. She can't bear their pain as well. She can't handle the weight of other people's sorrow on top of this.

"I didn't want the bastards to see me bleed," she whispers to her mother.

"Sometimes I'm afraid that they're going to have to. To understand that you're a real person," her mother sobs, clutching her daughter so very, very tightly in her arms.

39

What is a community?

Amat sees it from a long way off. No one in the Hollow has such an expensive car, and no one who has such an expensive car drives to the Hollow voluntarily. The man gets out, self-assured and straight-backed.

"Hi there, Amat. Do you know who I am?"

Amat nods. "You're Kevin's dad."

Kevin's dad smiles. Looks at Amat. He sees the boy glance at his watch, and presumes that he's trying to figure out how many months of his mom's wages one like it would cost. The man remembers what he was like at that age, when he didn't have a damn thing and hated anyone who did.

"Can we have a little chat, Amat? Just you and me . . . man to man?"

Tails is sitting in his office at one end of the supermarket. His chair creaks beneath his bulky frame as he rests his forehead on his palm. The voice on the phone is unhappy but not sympathetic.

"It's nothing personal, Tails. But you must see that we can't build a hockey academy in Beartown after all this. We can't let the media make it look like we . . . you know."

The man on the phone is a local councilor, Tails an entrepreneur, but they're also two boys who used to play hockey together down on the lake. Sometimes their conversations are on the record, sometimes off, and today's is floating somewhere in between the two.

"I have a responsibility to the council, Tails. And to the party. You can understand that, surely?"

Tails understands. He's always been a man who believed in difficult questions and simple answers. What's a business? It's an idea. What's a town? A collection of individuals. What's money? Possibilities. Behind his back, on the other side of the wall, someone is banging with a hammer. Tails is expanding his supermarket, because growth means survival. An entrepreneur who isn't moving isn't actually standing still, he's going backward.

"I've got to go, Tails, I've got a meeting," the voice on the phone says apologetically.

A phone hangs up. An idea is gone. A hockey academy no longer exists. What does that mean? When Tails was young there were three schools in Beartown, now there's one. Once the hockey academy has been built in Hed, how long will it be before the council shuts the last school here? And when the best juniors from here train in the rink in Hed all day, it will be only natural for them to play in Hed's A-team in the evenings. When Beartown's A-team can't recruit the best youngsters in the area, the club will collapse. The rink won't be renovated, there won't be any new employment opportunities, which would have been a natural step toward other developments: a conference center, a shopping mall, a new industrial estate, better links to the freeway, maybe even an airport.

What's a hockey club? Maybe Tails is a hopeless romantic—his wife often says he is—but to him a hockey club is what makes everyone in this town remember, once a week, all the things they have in common instead of what divides them. The club is proof that they can work together to become something greater. It teaches them to dream.

He believes in difficult questions and simple answers. What happens to a town that doesn't grow? It dies.

Peter comes into the store. Everyone sees him, but no one does. Staff and customers, young and old, his childhood friends and neighbors, they all slide away as he approaches. Disappear behind shelves and into aisles, pretending to be absorbed in their shopping lists and comparing prices. Only one man looks straight at him.

———

Tails stands in the doorway to his office. Meets Peter's gaze. What
is a GM? What is a team captain? What is a childhood friend? Tails
puts one foot hesitantly in front of the other, opens his mouth as if
to say something, but Peter merely shakes his head slowly. He will
never know that his daughter shook her head at Ana in the school
dining room because she didn't want the hatred directed at her to hit
her friend, but he does the same thing here.

And when he goes back inside his office and closes the door, Tails's
shame is the same shame all friends feel when they fall short. People
are good at feeling shame in this town. They start training early.

Kevin's dad doesn't wait for an answer, just rubs his hands and chuckles.

"Still cold in March; I never get used to it. Shall we sit in the car?"

Amat sits in the seat in silence, closes the door as if he's afraid it
might break. The car smells of leather and perfume. Kevin's dad looks
at the blocks of apartments.

"I grew up in a block that looked almost exactly like these. I think
maybe mine was one story smaller. Your dad doesn't live with you,
does he?"

He asks the questions directly, without any complication. The same
way he conducts all his business.

"He died in the war, just after I was born," Amat replies, blinking
more quickly. The man notices even though he's not facing him.

"My mom was on her own too. Me and three brothers. The hardest job on the planet, isn't it? Your mom's got trouble with her back,
hasn't she?"

Amat tries to hide it, but the man sees his eyebrows twitch. So he
goes on sensitively:

"I know a good physiotherapist. I can arrange for her to get seen."

"That would be very nice of you," the boy murmurs, without making eye contact. The man holds out his hands briefly.

"I'm actually surprised that no one else has already helped her with that. Someone who works at the club ought to have asked how she was, surely, don't you think? She's been working there long enough, hasn't she?"

"Since we moved here," Amat admits.

"We're supposed to look after each other in this town, Amat, don't you think? In our town and our club we take care of each other," the man says, handing him a business card.

"Is this the physiotherapist's number?" Amat asks.

"No. That's the number of the personnel manager of a business in Hed. Tell your mom to call and arrange an interview. Office work, no cleaning. Light admin, filing, that sort of thing. She knows the language well enough?"

Amat nods a little too quickly, a little more eagerly than he would have liked.

"Yes! Yes . . . of course!"

"Well, then. Just call that number," Kevin's dad says.

Then he says nothing for a long time. As if that were the whole purpose of his visit.

What is a Pack? Nothing, if you ask its members. It doesn't exist. The men sitting around the tables in the Bearskin have nothing in common apart from the fact that they're men. The oldest are over forty, the youngest not even able to vote. Some have the bear tattooed on their necks, others on their arms, many not at all. Some have good jobs, others bad jobs, many no job at all. Some have families, children, mortgages, and go on package holidays, and some live alone and have never set foot outside Beartown. That is precisely the problem when the police try to identify them as "the Pack": they only have something in common when you see them together. As soon as they're a few feet away from each other, they're just individuals.

And what is a club? If you ask them, it belongs to them. Not the old bastards, the men who wear smart jackets to games, the sponsors and board members and president and GM—they're all the same. In a single season all those old bastards could disappear, but the club would still be there, the Pack too. It's a thing that doesn't exist and always exists.

They're not always threatening. Rarely violent, unless it's a match day and there are opposing fans in the vicinity. But they make a point of showing the old bastards who the club really belongs to, every now and then. And what happens if you jeopardize its survival.

Ramona is standing behind the bar. The men in black jackets are sitting at her tables. They're the most considerate lads she knows. They buy her food and put in new bulbs up in the apartment without her even having to ask. When she once asked why they hate Peter so much, their eyes darkened and one of them replied: "Because that fucker never had to fight for hockey. He got it all on a plate. So he's frightened. The sponsors have got him on a leash; he puts their fucking logos ahead of what's best for the club. Everyone knows he grew up in the standing section, but when the sponsors want to drive out those of us standing there now and replace us with the fucking hot-dogs-and-Coke audience, he doesn't say a word. Everyone knows he loves Sune like a father, and that he doesn't want David to be A-team coach, but he just keeps his mouth shut. What sort of man is that? How can we let him be GM of our club?"

Ramona fixed her eyes on them and hissed: "And what about you, then? How many people in this town would dare to disagree with you? Do you think that means you're right, every single fucking time?"

They fell silent then. Ramona could, perhaps, have been proud of that. If it weren't for the fact that through the small windows facing the street she now sees Peter walking along. Slowly, as if he doesn't know where he's going. He stops and looks in through the window with a bag of groceries in his hand, hesitating.

Ramona could have gone out and gotten him. Offered him a cup of coffee. It would have been so simple. But she looks around her inside the Bearskin, at the men at the tables, and the only thing that is simpler than offering Peter coffee in this town right now is not doing so.

How big is the world when you're twelve years old? Both infinite and infinitesimal. It's all your wildest dreams, but it's also a cramped locker room in an ice rink. Leo is sitting on a bench. The front of his jersey has a large bear on it. No one is looking at him, but everyone is. His best friends get up and move to another bench when he sits down. He doesn't get a single pass all session. He wishes someone had checked him. He wishes they'd thrown his clothes in the shower. He almost wishes that they'd shouted something horrible about his sister.

Just to escape the silence.

Amat's fingers can't stop feeling the edge of the business card. Kevin's dad looks at the time, as if he's in a hurry to leave, and smiles at Amat as if they're done. Amat even has time to reach for the door handle before the man pats him paternally on the shoulder and says, as if the thought has only just occurred to him:

"By the way . . . At the party, my son's party, I know you think you might have seen something that night, Amat. But I think you also know that an awful lot of people saw how much alcohol you drank at that party, right?"

The quivering business card betrays how much he is shaking. Kevin's dad puts his hand on his.

"You can get so many ideas in your head when you've been drinking, Amat, but that doesn't mean that they're true. People do stupid things when they're drunk. Trust me, I've done plenty!"

The man laughs, warmly and self-deprecatingly. Amat is still staring at the business card. The name of a personnel manager, a big company, a different life.

"Are you in love with Maya?" the man asks so abruptly that Amat nods before he has time to think.

It's the first time he's admitted it to anyone. Tears are pricking the backs of his eyelids. The man is still holding his fingers gently and says:

"She's put you in a terrible situation, you and Kevin. A goddamn terrible situation. And do you think she cares about you, Amat? Do you think she would have done this if she did? It's hard for you to understand now, but girls need attention in a different way than boys. And they do goddamn weird things to get it. Little girls gossip and spread rumors, but men don't. Men look each other in the eye and sort things out without involving everyone else. Don't you think?"

Amat glances at him. Bites his lip and nods. Kevin's dad leans over confidentially and whispers:

"That girl chose Kevin. But believe me, there'll soon come a time when she'll wish she'd picked you instead. When you're playing in the A-team, when you turn professional, the girls will flock to you. And then you'll understand that some of them can't be trusted. They're like a virus."

Amat sits in silence, feeling the weight of the man's hand on his shoulder.

"Is there anything you want to tell me, Amat?"

The boy shakes his head. Sweat from his fingers is starting to stain the business card. The man takes out his wallet and hands him five thousand-kronor notes.

"I heard you might need new skates. From now on, whenever you need anything, you can just call me. We take care of each other, in this town and on this team."

Amat takes the money and folds the notes around the business card, opens the door, and gets out. The man rolls down his window and calls:

"I know that tonight's training session is voluntary, but it would be good if you were there. The team needs to stick together, right? People are nothing when they're alone in this world, Amat!"

The boy promises to go. The man laughs, pretends to be angry and frowns, hunches his shoulders and growls:

"Because we are the bears, the bears from Beartown!"

The expensive car turns around and disappears out onto the road. A considerably cheaper car is parked at the other end of the parking lot, an old Saab with its hood open. Its owner, a young man in a black jacket with a bear tattooed on his neck, is leaning over it, tinkering with the engine.

He pretends not to notice either the expensive car or the boy it leaves behind in front of the apartment blocks. But when Kevin's dad has gone, Amat drops something in the snow. The boy stands for a long time, staring down, as if he were trying to decide whether to pick it up again. In the end he wipes his face with the back of his hand and disappears into one of the stairwells.

The young man waits a minute before leaving the Saab and going over to pick up the five thousand-kronor notes from the ground. They're crumpled from having been clenched in a sweaty palm.

The man puts them in the pocket of his black jacket.

Amat closes the door of the apartment behind him. Looks at the business card. Hides it in his room and fetches his skates. They're too small, and so worn that the paint is peeling off them. He knows exactly what sort he could buy with five thousand kronor. All the children in the Hollow know the price of things they can't afford. He packs his bag and goes out, runs down the stairs, opens the door.

The money's gone. He will never be able to say for sure if that made him feel disappointed or relieved.

Peter is standing on a quiet street. He can see the roof of the rink from here. What is a home? It's a place that belongs to you. So can it still be your home if you're no longer welcome there? He doesn't know. He will talk to Kira this evening, she'll say, "I can get a job anywhere," and Peter will nod. Even though he can't get a job anywhere. They will talk about moving, and he will decide seriously to try to live without hockey.

He doesn't notice, but when he starts walking again an old Saab drives past him.

Kira is taking the trash out. That's her daughter's job—they agreed on that when she got her guitar—but things are different now. Not even the summer will help cure her daughter's fear of the dark.

There's a smell of fresh coffee coming from their neighbor's window. God, how Kira used to sigh about all the coffee when the family moved to Beartown. "Coffee, coffee, coffee, don't people do anything but drink coffee here?" she grumbled to Peter, and Peter shrugged and said: "They just want to show that they'd like to be your friends. It's hard to say, 'Can I be your friend?' It's much easier to say, 'Would you like coffee?' This is a town where people . . . well . . . I don't really know how to explain it. A town where people believe in difficult questions and simple answers."

Kira got used to it. All the things they expressed with a drink in this place in the forest. Whenever they wanted to say, "Thanks," or "Sorry," or "I'm right there with you," they would say, "Would you like coffee?" or "Can I get you a beer?" or "Two shots, please, on my tab."

Kira drops the garbage in the bin. There are lights on in the neighbor's windows. No one opens the door.

David leads the team out of the locker room, out of the rink. They're training in the forest this evening. He gets them to do push-ups, and no one fights harder than Bobo. The boy who may not even get to play hockey next season—he's too old for the juniors and too bad for the seniors, but he's here of his own accord, sweating blood. David gets them to run, and Filip comes in first every time. Next season will be his biggest, the year when everyone else sees how good he really is. They will say that he is an "overnight success." Sure, it's only taken all his time since he was five years old, only taken everything he and his mom had. "Overnight." Christ. It's only taken his whole life.

David gets them to play tug-of-war, and Lyt almost dislocates his shoulder trying to win. And Amat? He doesn't say a word to anyone, but he completes every exercise, does everything asked of him.

The club's president is standing at the edge of the forest, close enough to see but far enough away not to be easily spotted. He's sweating. When the big car stops down in the parking lot in front of the rink and Kevin and his dad get out, it's the first time anyone has ever seen his dad attend a training session. Kevin is already in his equipment and jogs toward his team in the forest, and the cheers ring out among the trees as they greet him like a king.

The president remains standing on the edge of the tree line as David stands in the middle of his boys and shakes Kevin's dad's hand. The president's eyes meet those of the coach across the distance, just for a moment, then the president turns and goes back to his office.

If Kevin had come into the rink, the club would have been forced to talk about principles and consequences. The president might have had to ask him to go home, "just until this blows over." But he can't stop the boys from training in the forest.

That's what they all tell themselves.

In another part of town, outside a house in the Heights, Kevin's mom takes the garbage out. She looks grey, from exhaustion as much as anything else, but new makeup has hidden the signs of crying. She opens the bin, her back straight, her gaze fixed. There are lights on in the windows all around.

A door opens. A voice calls out to her: "Would you like to come over for coffee?"

Another door opens, in the next house. Then another. Then another.

Difficult questions, simple answers. What is a community?

It is the sum total of our choices.

40

There's an old saying that Sune loves: "What do you call it when a man goes out into the forest and other men follow him? Leadership. What do you call it when a man goes out into the forest alone? A walk."

Peter walks into the house. Puts the milk in the fridge, the bread on the countertop, drops the car keys in a bowl. Only then does he remember that he's left the car outside the rink. He wonders calmly if he's going to find it burned out tomorrow, full of charred branches. He picks up the keys, removes the key ring they're attached to, puts the keys back in the bowl, and drops the key ring in the garbage.

Kira comes into the kitchen. Stands on top of his feet, and he dances slowly, whispering in his wife's ear:

"We can move. You can get a job anywhere."

"But you can't, darling. You can't just get another job in hockey somewhere else."

He knows. He knows that all too well. But he's never been more certain of anything than when he says:

"You moved here for me. I can move away from here for her."

Kira holds his face in the palms of her hands. She sees his car keys in the bowl. For as long as she's known him, all his keys have been on a bear-shaped key ring. Not anymore.

Ana is sitting on her bed; the room no longer feels like it's hers. When her mom was at her angriest, when she was most hurt that her daughter hadn't moved with her after the divorce, she said Ana was "a classic case of codependency." That she was staying for her dad's sake, because she knew he wouldn't manage without her. Maybe it was true, Ana doesn't know. She's always wanted to be close to him, not because he understood her but because he understood the forest. That was her big adventure, and no one knew more about that than he did—there was no better hunter in the whole of Beartown than her dad. As a child she would lie awake in bed at night with her clothes on, hoping that the phone would ring. Whenever there was a car accident involving a wild animal anywhere in the district, which happened fairly regularly in winter, and the driver informed the police that the animal had disappeared into the forest, injured, it was Ana's dad who they called.

His stubbornness and obstinacy and taciturnity were poor qualities in life, but perfect in the forest. "The pair of you can just sit here for the rest of your lives, then, never saying a word!" her mom yelled when she left, so they did. They just didn't see anything wrong with it, that's all.

Ana has very clear memories of always nagging her dad to take her with him at night when she was little, but she never got her way. It was always too dangerous, too late at night, too cold. And she knew that meant he had been drinking. Her dad always trusted his daughter in the forest, but not himself.

Adri is going around the kennels feeding the dogs. She can see Benji in the gym in the outbuilding; his crutches are on the floor while he's on the bench press. He's lifted ridiculous amounts of weight this evening, even allowing for the fact that he's her crazy brother. She knows that the team is having a voluntary training session today; she heard in town that they were out running in the forest. And that Kevin was there too.

But she doesn't ask Benji why he'd rather be alone. She doesn't want to be that sort of nagging sister. She may not have been born here, but she's still a Beartown girl. As tough as the forest, as hard as the ice. Work hard, keep your mouth shut.

Ana is standing naked in front of the mirror in her room, counting. She's always been good at that. Top grades in math all her life. When she was little she used to count everything—stones, blades of grass,

trees in the forest, tracks on the ground, empty bottles in the cupboard under the sink, freckles on Maya's skin, even breaths. Sometimes, when she felt really bad, she counted scars. But mostly she just
counted faults. She would stand in front of the mirror and point at
them: all the things that were wrong about her. Sometimes that made
it feel more bearable, when she had already said them out loud to herself before anyone at school did.

Her dad knocks on her door. He hasn't done that in years. Since her
mom left, father and daughter have had separate apartments, separate
lives. She quickly gets dressed and opens the door in surprise. He's
standing in the hall looking bewildered. Not drunk-bewildered, not
the sad, lonely man who used to sit up all night; he's sober now. He
reaches out his hand without touching her, as if he no longer knows
how to say he cares. He says the words slowly:

"I spoke to some of the guys on the hunting team. The hockey
club's called its members to a meeting. There's a group of parents and
sponsors who are demanding a vote about Peter."

"About . . . Peter?" Ana repeats, because the meaning of the words
isn't sinking in.

"They're going to demand that the club fire him."

"What? WHY?"

"The police weren't called in until a week after the party. Some
people are saying that . . . what happened . . . is . . ."

He can't say the word "rape" in front of his daughter, doesn't want
her to see how relieved and happy he is that it wasn't her. Scared that
she'll hate him for that. Ana's fists hit the edge of the bed.

"A lie? They're saying it's a lie? And now they think Peter waited
a week to report it to the police because he wanted to get at KEVIN?
As if KEVIN'S the goddamn VICTIM HERE!?"

Her dad nods. He stands in the doorway for so long without knowing what to say that all he eventually comes out with is:

"I've made elk burgers. They're in the kitchen."

He shuts the door behind him and goes back downstairs.

———

Ana calls Maya a hundred times that evening. She can understand why she's not getting any answer. Knows Maya hates her. Because precisely what did Maya predict? This. If she hadn't told the truth, Kevin would only have hurt her. But now he's hurt everyone Maya loves too.

The doorbell rings. Peter opens the door. It's the club's president. He looks so sad, so crumpled and sweaty and dirty, so drained and broken by stress that Peter can't even bring himself to hate him.

"There's going to be a meeting and a vote. The club consists of its members, and if they demand that the board dismiss you . . . then . . . it's out of my hands, Peter. But you can be there to speak up for yourself. That's your right."

The girl walks into the hall, behind her dad. At first Peter holds out his arm, as if to protect her, but she calmly pushes it aside. She stands in the doorway and looks the president in the eye. And he looks back at her.

At least he does that.

It's late when Benji's crutch knocks on Adri's bedroom door. He's standing outside with his arms shaking from muscle fatigue. Adri only knows three phases of exercise in normal people: when you put up with the pain, when you learn to enjoy it, and when you start to look forward to it. Her brother is way beyond that. He needs the pain. Has become dependent on it. Can't survive without it.

"Can you give me a lift?" he asks.

There's so much she wants to ask, but she says nothing. She's not that sort of sister. If he wants someone to nag him, he'll have to call Katia or Gaby.

Peter shuts the door. He and Maya are standing alone in the hall. His daughter looks up:

"Is it the board or the parents who want to fire you?"

Peter gives a melancholy smile.

"Both. But it's easier for the board if the members demand it. It's always easier to let someone else take the penalty minutes for you."

She puts her hands on his.

"I've ruined everything, I've ruined everything for everyone, I've ruined everything for you," she sobs.

He brushes her hair from her face and answers calmly:

"Don't say that. Don't even think that. Never again. What could those bastards ever give me? An espresso machine? They can stick their espresso machine up their asses!"

She starts giggling, like when her mom tells rude jokes and her dad gets embarrassed.

"You don't even like espresso. You used to call it 'expresso' until last year or something . . ."

He rests his forehead against hers.

"You and I know the truth. Your family and you and all decent, sensible people know the truth. And we're going to get justice, some-how, I promise you that. I just . . . I just want . . . You mustn't . . ."

"It's okay, Dad. It's okay."

"No, it's not! It never will be! You must never, ever think it's okay, that what he did . . . I'm scared, Maya, I'm so scared that you think I don't want to kill him, that I don't want to kill him every minute of every day, because I do."

The father's tears trickle down his daughter's cheeks.

"I'm scared too, Dad. Of everything. Of the darkness and . . . everything."

"What can I do?"

"Love me."

"Always, Pumpkin."

She nods.

"Can I ask for something, then?"

"Anything."

"Can we go out to the garage and play Nirvana?"

"Anything except that?"

"How can you not like Nirvana?"

"I was too old when they made it big."

"How can you be too old for NIRVANA? How old ARE you?"

They laugh. How powerful that is, the fact that they can still make each other do that.

Kira is sitting alone in the kitchen, listening to her husband and daughter play in the garage. Maya is so much better than him now; he keeps losing the beat but she matches him to stop him feeling stupid. Kira is longing for alcohol and cigarettes. Before she has time to look for any someone puts a pile of playing cards on the table. Not the normal sort, but the children's version they had in the trailer they rented when the children were small. Naturally, the children stopped playing because their mom and dad could never agree on the rules.

"Let's play. I might even let you win," Leo says, sitting down.

He puts two sodas on the table. He's twelve years old, but he lets his mom hug him fairly hard anyway.

In a run-down rehearsal space on the edge of Hed, a single lamp is shining above a boy in black leather, sitting on a chair playing the violin. He's still holding the instrument in his hand when someone knocks on the doorframe. Benji stands there leaning on his crutches with a bottle in his hand. The bass player tries to be fetchingly silent and mysterious, but his smile is having none of it.

"What are you doing here?"

"Went for a walk," Benji replies.

"Don't tell me that's moonshine," the bass player smiles at the bottle.

"If you're going to live around here, you're going to have to learn to drink it sooner or later," Benji says.

The bass player assumes that means "sorry" in these parts. He's noticed that they like communicating through the medium of drink.

"I have no intention of settling down here," he promises.

"No one does. They just get stuck here," Benji says, hopping into the room.

He doesn't ask about the violin. The bass player likes that, the fact that Benji's the sort of person who isn't surprised that someone can be more than one thing.

"If I play, you can dance," the bass player offers, moving the bow gently across the strings.

"I can't dance," Benji replies, without realizing it was a joke about his crutches.

"Dancing's easy. You just stand still, then stop standing still," the bass player whispers.

Benji's chest muscles are shaking with exhaustion. That helps. It makes his insides feel calm by comparison.

Ana is woken by the phone. She snatches it up from the floor but it's not hers ringing. It's her dad's. She hears his voice; he's talking as he gets dressed, fetches the dogs and the key to the gun cabinet. The sounds are like a familiar tune to her, a childhood lullaby. She waits for the finale. The front door closing. The key in the lock. The rusty old pickup starting up. But they don't come. Instead, a gentle knock. His voice, tentative, her name, a question through the door:

"Ana. Are you awake?"

She's dressed before he finishes the sentence. Opens the door. He's holding a rifle in each hand.

"There's a search, up by the north road. I could call some good-for-nothing in town, but . . . seeing as I've already got the second-best hunter in Beartown in the house . . ."

She feels like hugging him. Doesn't.

The boys are lying on their backs on the floor of the rehearsal room. The bottle is empty. They take turns singing the worst drinking songs they know. Roar with laughter for hours.

"What is it with hockey?" the bass player asks.

"What is it with violins?" Benji counters.

"You have to switch off your brain in order to play it. Music is like taking a break from yourself," the bass player replies.

The answer is too quick, too straightforward, too honest for Benji to retort with something sarcastic. So he tells the truth.

"The sounds."

"The sounds?"

"That's the thing about hockey. When you go into a rink. All those sounds you only recognize if you play. And . . . that feeling when you walk from the locker room to the rink, that last inch when the floor turns to ice. The moment when you glide out . . . you have wings then."

The boys say nothing for a while. They daren't move, as if they were lying on a glass roof.

"If I teach you to dance, will you teach me how to skate?" the bass player smiles eventually.

"Don't you know how to skate? What the fuck's wrong with you?" Benji exclaims, as if the bass player has just said he doesn't know how to make a sandwich.

"I've never seen the point. I've always thought that ice is nature's way of telling people to stay away from the water."

Benji laughs.

"So why do you want me to teach you, then?"

"Because you love it so much. I'd like to understand . . . something you love."

The bass player touches Benji's hand. Benji doesn't pull away, but he sits up and the spell is broken.

"I have to go," Benji says.

"No," the bass player pleads.

Benji goes anyway. Out through the door without another word. The snow falls with his tears, the darkness takes him, and he gives up without a fight.

———

When a window breaks, a room can be filled with such an astonishing amount of broken glass that it seems impossible that it all came from a single pane. Not entirely unlike the way a small child can turn a carton of milk upside down and flood an entire kitchen, as if the liquid expands to infinity the moment it leaves the carton.

The person throwing the stone was close to the wall, almost right next to it, and threw the stone as hard as they could to get it to fly as far into the room as possible. It hits a chest of drawers and lands on Maya's bed. The glass follows, raining so gently, light as a butterfly, as if it were ice crystals or tiny, shimmering fragments of diamond.

Peter and Maya hear it above the guitar and drums. They rush out from the garage and into the house. Freezing wind is blowing into Maya's room, and Leo is standing openmouthed in the middle of the floor, looking at the stone. *BITCH* has been written on it in red letters.

Maya is the first to realize what the real danger is. It takes Peter a few more seconds to figure it out. They rush for the front door together but it's too late. It's wide open. The Volvo has already pulled out of the drive, Kira at the wheel.

There are four of them, two on foot and two on bicycles, and the ones on bikes have no chance. The snow is still ankle-deep on the sidewalks, so they can only cycle on the plowed furrow in the middle of the road. Kira presses the accelerator to the floor of the Volvo so hard that the big car lurches out onto the road behind with a howl, and she's caught up with them in twenty yards, and her foot is nowhere near the brake. They're only children, thirteen or fourteen at most, but the mother's eyes are empty. One of the boys turns around and is dazzled by the headlights, and throws himself, terrified, off his bike at speed, and crashes headfirst into a fence. The other boy just manages to do the same before the front bumper of the Volvo smashes into his rear wheel and the bicycle flies across the road.

His pants are torn and his chin grazed when Kira stops the car, opens the door and gets out. She gets one of Peter's golf clubs from the trunk. Gripping it with both hands, she marches toward the boy on the ground. He's crying and screaming, but she doesn't care, doesn't feel anything.

Maya rushes out of the house and down the street in just her socks. She hears her dad call her name but doesn't look back. She hears the crash as the car hits the bicycle, sees the body sail weightless through the air. The Volvo's red brake lights jab at her eyes and she sees her mother's silhouette as she gets out. The trunk opens, a golf club is taken out. Maya is slipping on patches of ice in her soaking-wet socks, her feet are bleeding, and she screams until her voice is nothing but a croak.

Kira has never seen anyone so frightened. Small hands grab the golf club from behind and wrestle her to the ground, and when Kira looks up Maya holds her tight and screams, but at first Kira can't hear what. She's never seen such terror before.

The boys on the road crawl to their feet and limp away. Leaving a mother and a daughter, both crying hysterically, the mother still clutching the golf club in her clenched fists, the daughter soothing her over and over in her rocking arms:

"It's okay, Mom, it's okay."

The houses around them are still dark, but they know that everyone in the street is awake. Kira feels like standing up and bellowing at them, throwing stones at THEIR windows, but her daughter holds her tight and they just sit there in the middle of the road, trembling as they inhale each other's skin. Maya whispers:

"You know, when I was little all the other parents at preschool used to call you 'wolf mother,' because they were all scared of you. And all my friends wanted a mom like you."

Kira sniffs in her daughter's ear:

"You don't deserve this damn life, darling, you don't deserve . . ."

Maya holds her mother's cheeks and kisses her forehead softly.

"I know you'd have killed for me, Mom. I know you'd have given your life for me. But we're going to get through this, you and me. Because I'm your daughter. I've got wolf's blood."

Peter carries them to the Volvo. First his daughter, then his wife. He reverses the car slowly back along the street. Home.

The bicycles are left lying in the snow; the next day they are gone. No one who lives on the street will ever talk about it.

41

Morning comes to Beartown, unconcerned about the little lives of the people down below. A sheet of cardboard has been taped up on the inside of a broken window; a sister and a brother are sleeping, exhausted, side by side on mattresses in the hall, far from any other windows. In his sleep Leo curls up close to Maya, the way he used to when he would creep into her room when he was four years old and had a bad dream.

Peter and Kira are sitting in the kitchen, holding each other's hands.

"Do you think I'm less of a man because I can't fight?" he whispers.

"Do you think I'm less of a woman because I can?" she asks.

"We have to get the kids away from here," he whispers.

"We can't protect them. It doesn't matter where we are, darling, we can't protect them," she replies.

"We can't live like that."

"I know."

Then she kisses him, smiles, and whispers:

"But you're not unmanly. You're very, very, very manly in lots of other ways. For instance, you NEVER admit that you're wrong."

He replies into her hair:

"And you're very womanly. The most womanly woman I've ever met. For instance, you can NEVER be trusted with rock-paper-scissors."

They laugh, the pair of them. Even on a morning like this. Because they can, and because they must. They still possess that blessing.

Ramona is standing outside the Bearskin smoking. The street is empty, the sky is black, but she still sees the puppy from a long way off, even though the weather is bad. She starts to cough hoarsely as Sune rolls out of the darkness; it might have been a chuckle if she'd smoked less. Forty or fifty years less.

Sune calls out, and the puppy totally ignores him. It jumps up at Ramona's jeans, eagerly demanding attention.

"You silly old fool, have you got a puppy now?" she says with a grin.

"A disobedient little shit, too. I'll be filling my sandwiches with him soon," Sune mutters, but his love for the furry creature is already obvious.

Ramona coughs. "Coffee?"

"Can I have a splash of whisky in it?"

She nods. They go inside and stamp their feet and drink while the puppy very methodically sets about eating one of the chairs.

"I assume you've heard," Sune says sadly.

"Yep," Ramona says.

"Shameful. Shameful, that's what it is."

Ramona pours more drink. Sune stares at the glass. "Has Peter been in?"

She shakes her head. "Have you spoken to him?"

Sune shakes his head. "I don't know what to say."

Ramona says nothing. She understands that all too well. It's both easy and difficult to offer someone coffee.

"The club isn't your job anymore, Sune," she murmurs.

"I haven't formally been dismissed yet. They seem to have forgotten about that in the midst of all this. But, sure. You're right. It's not my job anymore."

Ramona pours more whisky. Tops it up with a splash of coffee, sighs deeply.

"So what do we talk about, then? An old bag and an old bastard, sitting here babbling. For God's sake, just spit it out instead."

Sune gives her a wry smile.

"You've always been a bit of a psychologist, you have."

"Just a bartender. You were always too cheap to pay for the real thing."

"I miss Holger."

"You only miss him when I'm shouting at you."

Sune guffaws so loudly that the puppy jumps. It lets out an irritable yap before getting back to chewing the furniture.

"I really just miss you shouting at Holger."

"Me too."

More whisky. A touch more coffee. Silence and memories, withheld words and suppressed sentences. Until Sune eventually says:

"It's shameful, what Kevin did. Utterly damn shameful. And I'm worried about the club. It's been here almost seventy years, but I wouldn't like to bet that it will be here next year. I'm worried people will try to blame the boy's actions on hockey, if he gets found guilty. It's going to be all hockey's fault."

Ramona slaps him so quickly and hard across his ear with the palm of her hand that the fat old man almost falls off his barstool. The angry old bag on the other side of the bar snarls:

"Is that why you're here? To talk about that? Sweet Jesus . . . you men. It's never your fault, is it? When are you going to admit that it isn't 'hockey' that raises these boys, it's YOU LOT? In every time and every place, I've come across men who blame their own stupidity on crap they themselves have invented. 'Religion causes wars,' 'guns kill people,' it's all the same old bullshit!"

"I didn't mea . . . ," Sune tries, but has to duck when she tries to slap him again.

"Keep your trap shut when I'm talking! Fucking men! YOU'RE the problem! Religion doesn't fight, guns don't kill, and you need to be very fucking clear that hockey has never raped anyone! But do you know who do? Fight and kill and rape?"

Sune clears his throat. "Men?"

"MEN! It's always fucking men!"

Sune squirms. The puppy curls up, shamefaced, in a corner. Ramona adjusts her hair, carefully and thoroughly, empties her glass, and admits to herself that perhaps it isn't so complicated after all, this business about coffee.

Then she fills both their glasses, fetches a bit of salami for the puppy, goes around the bar, and sits down next to the old man. She sighs deeply and reluctantly admits:

"I miss Holger too. And do you know what he would have said if he was here?"

"No."

"That you and I already know what's right. So there's no need for him to tell us."

Sune smiles.

"He always was a smug bastard, that man of yours."

"That he was."

In another part of town, Zacharias creeps out of his family's apartment without waking anyone. He's carrying a bag on his back and a bucket in his hand. Headphones in his ears, music in his whole body. He turns sixteen today, and all his life he has been teased and rejected. About everything. His looks, thoughts, manner of speech, home address. Everywhere. At school, in the locker room, online. That wears a person down in the end. It's not always obvious, because the people around a bullied child assume that he or she must get used to it after a while. Never. You never get used to it. It burns like fire the whole time. It's just that no one knows how long the fuse is, not even you.

Jeanette is woken by a call from her brother telling her that the alarm has gone off again. Bleary-eyed and annoyed, she drives to the school. Searches the whole building with her flashlight without finding anything. She's just about to tell her brother it's time to give up, thinking it must have been snow on one of the sensors again, when she puts her foot down in something wet.

———

The second-best hunter in Beartown is washing the elk blood off the back of a rusty pickup truck. The girl and her dad followed the trail all night, until they found the badly wounded animal lying down; it had dragged itself deep into the darkness of the forest. They gave it a humane and painless end. Ana closes the tarpaulin over the bed of the truck and gets the two rifles from the cab, and checks them with the practiced hands of a far older hunter.

A few boys of about seven or eight are playing hockey farther down the street. One of the neighbors, a man in his eighties, is standing by his mailbox. His rheumatism makes movement painful, as if he were dragging invisible blocks of stone behind him as he reaches for his newspaper. He's on his way back to the house when he suddenly stops and looks at Ana. They have lived next to each other all Ana's life. The neighbor used to go hunting with her dad until just a few years ago; when she was little he used to give her homemade toffee at Christmas. Neither of them says anything now, the man just spits derisively on the ground in front of him. When he goes back into his house he slams the door so hard that a green flag just outside with a bear logo on it sways on its hook.

The boys playing hockey look up. One of them is wearing a jersey with the number "9" on it. They look at Ana with expressions that reveal what their parents are talking about at home. One of the boys spits on the ground as well. Then they turn their backs on her.

Ana's dad walks over and puts his hand on his daughter's shoulder. He feels her shaking beneath his fingers, and doesn't know if it's because she's about to cry or scream.

For almost half his life, Zacharias has thought about ending it. He has been through the details time and time again in his head. Somewhere they can see it. Force the bastards to live with that image of him. "You did this." You don't need much: a rope, a few tools, something to stand on. A stool would be good, but an upside-down bucket would do just as well. He's holding it in his hand. He's got everything else he needs in his backpack.

The only thing that's stopped him from doing it earlier, several years ago, was Amat. One single friend like him—that can be enough. Lifa and Zacharias were never friends in the same way, only through Amat, so when Amat was moved up to the juniors and chose a different life, everything disappeared for Zacharias.

Amat was the reason he stayed alive. Amat was the one who told him, on all the darkest, hardest nights: "One day, Zach, you'll have more money and influence than all those bastards. And then you'll do great things. Because you know how much it hurts to have no power. So you won't hurt them, even though you could. And that will make the world a better place."

Never again do you have the sort of friends you have when you're fifteen. Zacharias turns sixteen today. He breaks into the school without caring if he sets the alarm off. Puts the bucket down on the floor.

Jeanette looks down at the floor with her heart practically bursting out of her chest. It's a large puddle, spreading out slowly in front of her. She standing close to the entrance, near the rows of lockers belonging to the high school students. There's an acrid smell; it catches in her nostrils. Her brother comes closer; two flashlights point in the same direction.

"What's that on the floor?" he asks.

Ana is grinding her teeth so hard that her dad can hear it. He whispers:

"They're just frightened, Ana, they're just looking for a scapegoat."

Ana wants to scream. She wants to yank open the door of the neighbor's house, tear down the green flag, and shout: "Why isn't KEVIN the scapegoat, then? WELL?" She wants to scream so loud that all the other neighbors here in the Heights can hear it too. Scream that she loves hockey. LOVES hockey! But she's a girl, so what happens if she says that to a boy? He says: "Really? You're a girl and you like hockey? Okay! Who won the Stanley Cup in 1983, then? Well? And who came seventh in the league in 1994? Well? If you like hockey you ought to be able to answer that!"

Girls aren't allowed to like hockey even just a little bit in Beartown. Ideally they shouldn't like it at all. Because if you like the sport you must be a lesbian, and if you like the players you're a slut. Ana feels like pushing her neighbor up against the wall and telling him that the locker room where those boys sit telling their stupid jokes ends up preserving them like a tin can. It makes them mature more slowly, while some even go rotten inside. And they don't have any female friends, and there are no women's teams here, so they learn that hockey only belongs to them, and their coaches teach them that girls are a "distraction." So they learn that girls only exist for fucking. She wants to point out how all the old men in this town praise them for "fighting" and "not backing down," but not one single person tells them that when a girl says no, it means NO. And the problem with this town is not only that a boy raped a girl, but that everyone is pretending that he DIDN'T do it. So now all the other boys will think that what he did was okay. Because no one cares. Ana wants to stand on the rooftop and scream: "You don't give a shit about Maya! And you don't really give a shit about Kevin either! Because they're not people to you, they're just objects of value. And his value is far greater than hers!"

She wants so much. But the street is empty, and she stays silent. She hates herself for that.

Ana's dad still has his fingers resting clumsily on her shoulder as they go inside the house, but she slides away from his hand. He watches her as she carries the rifles down to the cellar. Sees the hatred in her. He will remember thinking: "Of all the men in the world that I wouldn't like to be, he's the one I'd like to be least of all: the one who hurt that girl's best friend."

"What's that on the floor?" her brother repeats.

"Water," Jeanette replies.

She knows there aren't many pupils at the school who know how to break in here, whether or not they set the alarm off. She doesn't know if the person who did this managed to get out before she and her brother showed up, or if they just didn't care.

Jeanette's first lesson that morning is substitute teaching with a grade-nine class. She sees that Zacharias has ink on his hands. He smells faintly of solvent. In the corridor there's a locker on which the word *BITCH* is no longer scrawled, because he spent part of the night scrubbing it clean. Because he knows what it's like to be the one other people hurt, just because they can. Because he knows what the strong do to the weak in this town.

Jeanette doesn't say anything to Zacharias. She knows this is his silent protest. And her decision not to tell anyone about who broke in last night becomes her own silent protest.

42

When a child learns to hunt, they are taught that the forest contains two different sorts of animal: predators and prey. The predators have their eyes close together, facing the front, because they only need to focus on their prey. Their prey, on the other hand, have their eyes wide apart, on either side of the head, because their only chance of survival is if they can see predators approaching from behind.

When Ana and Maya were little they used to spend hours in front of the mirror trying to work out which of them they were.

Tails is sitting in his office. The supermarket isn't open yet, but the room is full. The men have come here because they don't want anyone to see them meet at the rink. They're nervous and paranoid. They talk about journalists snooping around. Use words like "responsibility" several times, explain to Tails that they "have to stick together now, so that this doesn't get out of hand." They are sponsors, board members, but today, of course, they are just concerned friends, dads, citizens. They all just want what's best for the town. For the club. They all just want the truth to come out. One worried voice says: "Anyone can see . . . I mean, why would Kevin do a thing like that? It's obvious it was voluntary, then she changed her mind. If only we could have dealt with this internally." Another says: "But of course we need to think about both families, of course we do. The girl must be scared. They're only children, after all. But the truth needs to come out. Before this gets out of hand." At the end of the meeting, Kevin's dad gets up and walks into town with Tails. Knocks on door after door.

Maya is awake early. She's standing in the garage on her own, playing the guitar. She will never be able to explain what's happening to her. How she went from being so destroyed that she was just lying on the bathroom floor in her mother's arms, crying and screaming, to . . . what she feels now. But something happened last night. The stone through the window, the broken glass on the floor. *BITCH* in red letters. In the end, that does something to a person. Maya is still so scared of the dark that it feels like it's clutching at her clothes if she so much as enters a room where the lights are out, but she realized something this morning: the only way to stop being afraid of the darkness out there is to find a darkness inside yourself that's bigger. She's never going to get any justice from this town, so there's only one solution: either Kevin must die, or Maya must.

Ramona is drinking her breakfast when they arrive. Kevin's dad, that Erdahl guy, walks in the way he walks into every room: as if it belongs to him. Tails comes stumbling after him, as if his shoes were too big for him.

"I'm closed," Ramona informs them.

Tails grins. Just the way his dad used to, Ramona thinks. He was just as tall and just as fat and just as stupid.

"We just want a little chat," he says.

"Off the record," Erdahl adds.

His eyes are set close together.

Kira's office is full of boxes, her desk drowning in paper. Her colleague puts a cup of coffee down and promises:

"We're going to do everything we can, Kira. Everyone in the firm will do all that we can. But you need to be prepared that most cases like this, where it's one person's word against another's . . . you know how they end."

Kira's eyes are bloodshot, her clothes are creased. That's never happened before.

"I should have become a proper lawyer. I should have specialized in this. I should have . . . I've wasted my whole life on business law and crap like that when I should have . . ."

Her colleague sits down opposite her.

"Do you want to hear the truth?"

"Yes."

"You could bring in the world's foremost expert in cases involving sexual offenses, Kira. But there's no guarantee that would make any difference. It's one person's word against another's, the police weren't told until a week later, there's no forensic evidence, no witnesses. In all likelihood the police will shut down their preliminary investigation within the next couple of days."

Kira flies up from her chair angrily and only just manages to stop herself hurling the coffee cup at the wall.

"I'm not going to let them win! If I can't win in court, I'll have to find another way!"

"What do you mean by that?" her colleague asks anxiously.

"I'll go after his dad's company, their friends' companies, I'll dig up all the crap they've ever buried, every set of accounts, every tax return, and I am going to hurt them. If they forgot to pay the tax on a single pen ten years ago, I'll take them down!"

Her colleague says nothing. Kira's voice fills the office:

"I'm going to attack everything and everyone they love, and I am going to protect my children, do you hear? I'M GOING TO PRO-TECT MY CHILDREN!"

Her colleague stands up. There's a trace of disappointment in her voice when she says:

"That's how wars start. One side protects itself, so the other side has to protect itself even more, and then we start swapping our own fear with their threats. And then we start firing at each other."

The coffee cup hits the wall at that.

"SHE'S MY FUCKING CHILD!"

Her colleague closes her eyes. They're spaced far apart.

"Maybe that's when you really need to know the difference between vengeance and justice."

———

Ana opens the door. Her dad has taken the dogs to the vet; the house is empty. Maya is standing outside with her arms wrapped tightly around her chest. It's hard for both of them to know if they should cry or laugh, scream or joke—which of those will give them the best chance of survival.

"I miss your annoying face," Maya eventually whispers.

Ana smiles.

"I miss your horrible taste in music."

Maya's lower lip quivers.

"I don't want you to get caught up in this. I'm just trying to keep you out of it all."

Ana puts her hands on Maya's shoulders.

"I'm your sister. How much more caught up in it can I get?"

Maya stares at her until her eyes sting.

"I'm just trying to protect you."

"You've been trying to protect me all my life, and can I tell you something? You're really shit at it! I'm obviously completely screwed up in the head, so how well do you think your protection has been working?"

They start laughing, both of them. "You're such an idiot," Maya sniffs.

"But no one else loves you like I do, you idiot. No one!" Maya exclaims.

"I know."

Maya's eyes are shimmering when she asks:

"Can we go out into the forest and do some shooting? I just need to get away, Ana. I just need . . . It's just that shooting's kind of relaxing. I thought it might help me get rid of some of my . . . aggression."

She's lying now; she's never done that to Ana. Ana looks at her for a long time. But she's a real friend, so she goes and fetches two rifles without asking any questions.

Ramona puts her hands down on the bar. Observes the two men.

"This is a business."

"What?" Tails wonders.

Erdahl, on the other hand, sits calmly on his chair and smirks tolerantly.

"She wants us to order something," he says. Okay, two large whiskies, the best you've got, then we'll talk."

She pours the drinks and Erdahl wastes no time. "You know who I am?"

She snorts and drains her own glass. Erdahl interprets that as a yes. He raises his glass and very nearly spits the contents across the bar when it hits his tongue.

"What the . . . This is your BEST whisky?"

Ramona shakes her head.

"It's my worst whisky."

Tails empties his glass without any change of expression. He looks almost pleased with it. But his taste buds are as dysfunctional as the volume control on his voice. Erdahl pushes his own glass away in disgust.

"In that case, can we have your best whisky, please? This one tastes like something you'd use to clean a boat."

Ramona nods obligingly. Gets out new glasses. Pours whisky from the same bottle as before. Erdahl stares at her. Tails can't help grinning.

"There's only one sort of whisky at the Bearskin."

Maya and Ana walk until the forest swallows them up. So far that even Ana's dad would have needed several days to find their bodies. There they stand and fire their guns, shot after shot. Ana adjusts Maya's posture occasionally, angling her shoulder and elbow, reminding her about how to hold her breath without actually stopping breathing. Ana asks:

"Okay . . . what about this one? Live your whole life in Beartown until you get old, or move anywhere in the world but die within a year?"

Maya answers by frowning, her whole face crumpling like a used napkin.

"Stupid question?" Ana asks.

"Pretty stupid."

"We're going to get out of here, Maya. I'm not going to let us get stuck here. We're going to move to New York, you're going to get a recording contract, and I'm going to be your manager."

Maya starts to giggle; she didn't believe she still had that sort of laughter left in her, but it just bubbles out.

"No, no, no, you're never going to be my manager."

"What? I'd be a BRILLIANT manager!" Ana retorts, insulted.

"You'd be a terrible manager. Terrible. You can't even look after your own cell phone."

"Yes, I can!"

Maya raises her eyebrows.

"Okay. So where's your phone?"

Ana starts feeling her body frantically.

"Maybe not right NOW! But . . . Fine! I can be your stylist instead. Believe me, you NEED a stylist!"

"What's wrong with my style?" Maya wonders.

Ana looks her up and down.

"Sorry. You can't afford my consultation fee. Get in touch when you've got your recording contract."

Maya roars with laughter.

"You're totally crazy."

"Or I could be your nutritionist! I've found a new juice diet that cleans out the whole intestine! What happens is that . . ."

Maya covers her ears, turns around, and walks deeper into the forest. "Sorry, the reception's really bad out here . . . shkkkrrrr . . . Hello? Hello?"

She holds a phone to her ear, pretends to talk into it.

Ana squints at her.

"Is that my phone? Where did you find it?"

"I'm driving into a tunnel now!" Maya shouts.

Ana runs to catch up with her. They wrestle and hug each other. Watch the sun go up. Maya whispers:

"Can I sleep at your place one night?"

Ana doesn't know what to say. Maya has never slept at her place, not once; it's always been the other way around. But she's a true friend, so of course she answers:

"You don't have to ask."

Ramona empties her glass. Tails empties his. Erdahl's eyes narrow.

"Well, then. Let's skip the pleasantries. You know why I'm here?"

Ramona looks curious.

"No, but I bet you've brought some gold with you. Tails has brought frankincense. And there's a third wise man standing outside the door with his pants stuffed full of myrrh. Is that more or less right?"

Erdahl breathes hard through his nose and makes a short, disgusted gesture toward the room.

"This . . . pub . . . is one of Beartown Ice Hockey's oldest sponsors. Obviously it doesn't contribute a significant amount, but we all respect tradition. And I presume you've been informed that there's to be an extraordinary meeting of members . . . in light of what has happened."

Tails coughs distractedly and adds:

"We just want to talk, Ramona. The sponsors, all of us, feel that it's important that we stand united at the meeting. For the sake of the club."

"And what does that mean?" Ramona wonders out loud with feigned docility.

Erdahl is already fed up. He gets to his feet and informs her:

"Some of the management needs to be changed. Peter Andersson is going to be voted out as GM and will be replaced by a more suitable person. Both the board and all the sponsors agree on that, but we respect the members and want the proposal to come directly from them. We're here as a gesture of goodwill."

Ramona smiles sarcastically.

"Yes, you strike me as the sort of person who's always doing things as a gesture of goodwill. What's Peter done that's so unsuitable, if I might ask?"

Erdahl growls through his teeth.

"You know perfectly well what's happened."

"No I don't. And I don't think that you do either. That's why there's a police investigation."

"You know what my son has been accused of," Erdahl says.

"You make it sound like he's the victim," Ramona points out.

Erdahl finally loses his composure. Tails has never seen it happen, and he gets so scared that he knocks over his own and Ramona's glasses. Erdahl screams:

"My son IS the victim! Have you got any fucking idea at ALL what it's like to be accused of this? HAVE YOU?"

Ramona doesn't move a muscle when she replies:

"No. But, off the top of my head, it strikes me that the only thing that might be worse than being accused of rape is being raped."

"So you're going to stand here and assume that that damn girl is telling the truth?" Erdahl snarls.

"I'm thinking of standing here and allowing myself the liberty of not assuming that the girl is for some reason lying just because your son happens to play hockey. And she has a name. Her name is Maya," Ramona replies.

Erdahl laughs condescendingly.

"So you're one of the people who are going to try to blame this on hockey?"

Ramona nods seriously and asks:

"Have you ever played hockey?"

"I stopped when I was twelve," Erdahl admits.

"In that case, you're right. In that case, I do blame hockey. Because if it had kept hold of you for another couple of years, you might have learned to lose like a man. You might have learned that your son can make mistakes, and when he does you ought to stand up like a man and take responsibility for that. Not come here and dump all the blame on a fifteen-year-old girl and her father."

Erdahl knocks his chair flying when he throws his arms out in exasperation. It might not have been intentional, but he makes no move to pick it up. He's breathing hard through his nose, his eyes are hunting hers, he tosses a thousand-kronor note on the bar, and concludes, with equal measures of scorn and threat:

"You might own this bar. But you don't own the building. I'd think about that, if I were you."

He slams the door hard, making the windows rattle.

Ana and Maya go into the house, Ana gets the key to her dad's gun cabinet and puts back the rifles they've been shooting with. Maya notes every detail, how they're arranged, where the key is.

"What's that?" she asks innocently, pointing to a double-barreled shotgun.

"A shotgun," Ana replies.

"Is it hard to load?" Maya wonders.

At first Ana laughs, then she gets suspicious:

"Why do you ask?"

Maya shrugs.

"What are you, the cops? I'm just wondering. It looks cool; can't we try shooting with that one sometime?"

Ana grins and nudges her shoulder.

"*You* can be the cop, you lunatic!"

Then she fetches cartridges and shows Maya how to break open, load, and release the safety-catch of the shotgun, because she loves the rare occasions when she's better at something than her friend. She adds, patronizingly, that, "It's so easy that even you could do it." Maya laughs.

"How many cartridges does it hold?" she asks.

"Two," Ana replies.

She breaks the gun open again and unloads it, puts the cartridges back, and locks the gun cabinet. The girls leave the cellar. Maya says nothing. But all she is thinking is: "I only need one."

Tails is still standing in the Bearskin, and carefully picks up the glasses, one after the other.

"It's just a . . . discussion, Ramona," he whispers.

"Your father would have been ashamed," she snaps.

"I'm just trying . . . not to pick a side."

Ramona snorts.

"You're doing it very badly."

Tails turns, wraps his coat unhappily around himself, and walks out. A couple of minutes later he comes back. Stands on the floor in front of the bar like the unhappy little boy he once was, when he used to come in with Peter before they were even teenagers to fetch their drunk fathers.

"Does Robbie Holts still come in here?" he mutters.

"Almost every day since he lost his job," Ramona nods.

Tails nods.

"Tell him to call in to the store and talk to my warehouse manager. I'll see to it that he gets an interview."

Ramona nods. They could have said more to each other. But they're from Beartown.

Late in the afternoon Kevin is running along the jogging track around the Heights. Faster and faster, with his cap pulled down deep across his forehead and his hood pulled up. He's even wearing bulky clothing with no bear logos, so that no one will recognize him. There's no need, of course; everyone from the Heights has gone to the meeting at the rink to vote. But Kevin still feels like he's being watched from inside the forest. Imagination, of course. He's just being paranoid. That's what he tells himself.

———

The sun has already gone down. Maya is standing in the forest shaking, but the trees hide her. The dark still leaves her panic-stricken but she's determined to make it her friend. Her ally. She stood here watching Kevin move about inside the illuminated house; he couldn't see her but she could see him, and that gave her a sudden sense of power. It's intoxicating.

When he came out onto the jogging track, she timed him. One circuit took three minutes and twenty-four seconds. Another circuit: three minutes and twenty-two seconds. Another circuit. Another circuit. Again, again, again.

She writes down the times. Raises her arms as if they were holding an invisible rifle. Wonders where she ought to stand.

One of them is going to die. She still hasn't decided who.

43

Fighting isn't hard. It's the starting and stopping that are hard. Once you're actually fighting, it happens more or less instinctively. The complicated thing about fighting is daring to throw the first punch, and then, once you've won, refraining from throwing that very last one.

Peter's car is still parked in front of the rink. No one has set fire to it, even if he suspects that one or two people have thought about it. He scrapes the windows and gets in, without switching on the engine.

He's always envied good hockey coaches more than anyone; the ones with that ability to stand in front of a group and carry everyone with them. He doesn't have that sort of charisma. He was a team captain once upon a time, but he led through his play, not by his words. He can't explain hockey to anyone, he just happened to be good at it. In music it's called "perfect pitch," and in sports, it's sometimes called "physical intelligence." You see someone do something, and your body instantly understands how to do the same thing. Skating, shooting a puck, playing a violin. Some people train all their lives without learning, while others have just got it.

He was good enough that he didn't have to learn how to fight. That was his salvation. He doesn't have a philosophical position; he hasn't reasoned his way to not believing in violence. He just doesn't have it in him. He lacks the instinct.

When Leo started to play hockey, Peter got into a discussion with a coach who kept shouting and yelling the whole time. The coach said:

"You have to frighten the little buggers to get them to listen!"

Peter said nothing. But in the car on the way home he turned to Leo and explained: "When I was little, my dad used to hit me if I spilled my milk, Leo. That didn't teach me not to spill things. It just made me scared of milk. Remember that."

The parking lot around him gradually fills with cars. People are arriving from all directions. Some of them see Peter but pretend they haven't. He waits until they've gone inside. Until the meeting has started. He considers simply starting the car and driving home, packing up his family and belongings and driving as far away from here as he can. But instead he gets out of the car, walks across the parking lot, opens the heavy door of the rink, and walks inside.

Fighting isn't hard. It's just hard to know when to throw the first punch.

Ann-Katrin is sitting close to Hog in one of the last rows of chairs. It feels like the whole town is gathered in the cafeteria of the rink. All the chairs are taken but people are still pouring in, lining up along the walls. Up at the front, on a little platform, sit the board members. In the first row of seats the sponsors and parents of the juniors. In the middle: Kevin's parents. Ann-Katrin watches as people she's known all her life go up to Kevin's mom as if this were a funeral, as if they were offering their condolences for the terrible tragedy she's suffered.

Hog holds Ann-Katrin's hand tightly when he sees what she's looking at.

"We can't get involved, Anki. Half the people in here are customers of ours."

"This isn't a vote, it's a lynch mob," Anki whispers.

"We need to wait until we know what happened. We don't know everything, Anki. We don't know everything," her husband replies.

She knows he's right. So she waits. They wait. Everyone waits.

Tails is standing in the middle of the parking lot on purpose, not hidden in the shadows or behind a tree. The last thing he wants, obviously, is to appear threatening.

When the little car with the logo of the local newspaper on the door pulls into the parking lot, he gives a cheery wave. A journalist and a photographer are sitting inside it, and he gestures to them to roll the window down.

"Hello, hello! I don't think we've met? I'm Tails—I own the supermarket!"

The journalist shakes his hand through the window.

"Hello, we're just heading to the meet . . ."

Tails leans forward, scratching his stubble hard.

"Yes, the meeting, eh? I just wanted to have a few words with you about that. Sort of . . . off the record, if you get my meaning."

The journalist tilts her head.

"No."

Tails clears his throat.

"Oh, you know how it is. People sometimes get a bit nervous when a reporter shows up. What's happened has been pretty traumatic for the whole town, as you obviously appreciate. So we'd just like to know that your article . . . well . . . that you haven't come here looking for problems where there aren't any."

The journalist has no idea how she's supposed to respond to that, but the way the huge man is leaning over her door as he says it makes her feel uncomfortable. Tails, of course, just smiles, wishes her a nice day, and walks off.

The journalist and photographer wait a couple of minutes before following him. When they open the door to the rink and start to walk down the hallway, two men step out from the darkness. In their late twenties, black jackets, hands in pockets.

"This meeting is for members only," one of them says.

"We're journalists . . . ," the journalist begins to say.

The men block their path. They're a head taller than the photographer, two heads taller than the journalist. They say no more; one just takes half a step forward and stops, a subtle indication of his potential for violence. The rink is poorly lit, and the part they are in is silent and deserted.

The photographer takes hold of the sleeve of the journalist's jacket.

She sees how white his face is. The journalist isn't from around here, she's only got a temporary contract with the paper, but the photographer lives in Beartown. He has his family here. He pulls her away and walks back to the car. They drive off.

Fatima is sitting in her kitchen. She hears the doorbell ring, but Amat insists on answering it himself. As if he already knows who it's going to be. There are two huge boys outside. Fatima can't hear what they're saying, but she sees one of them put his index finger on Amat's chest. When her son closes the door again he refuses to tell his mother what it was about. Just says, "It was to do with the team," and goes into his room.

Bobo is walking a little way behind William Lyt. He doesn't feel comfortable with what they're doing, but doesn't know how to object.

"Amat's one of us, isn't he, so why are you so angry?" he asked on the way here.

"He needs to prove that now," Lyt snapped.

When Amat opens the door, Lyt jabs him in the chest with his finger and commands:

"There's a members' meeting at the rink. The whole team's going to stand outside to show our support for Kevin. You too."

"I'll try," Amat mutters.

"You won't try. You'll do it! We stick together!" Lyt declares.

Bobo tries to make eye contact with Amat before they leave but doesn't succeed.

The meeting goes the way meetings like that always go. It starts hesitantly, then quickly gets out of hand. The club's president clears his throat and asks for everyone's attention, in a feeble attempt to calm the anxiety.

"First, I would like to clarify that only the board can dismiss the general manager. The members can't start unilaterally getting rid of members of staff, that's not how the statutes of the club work."

One man flies up from his chair, forefinger raised:

"But the members can depose the board, and you need to be very clear that we're going to do that if you go against the wishes of the town!"

"This is a democratic organization; we don't threaten each other," the president replies sternly.

"Threaten? Who's threatening who? Whose children are getting dragged off the team bus by the police?" the man snarls.

A woman stands up with her hands clasped in front of her hips, and looks at the board with sympathy:

"We're not after a witch-hunt, we're just trying to protect our children. My daughter was at Kevin's party, and now the police have called her in to get a 'witness statement.' For the love of God, these children have known each other all their lives, and suddenly they're expected to be witnesses against each other? What on earth is going on?"

A man gets to his feet after her.

"We're not trying to accuse anyone. But we all know that . . . what can happen . . . This young woman wanted to join the gang. Maybe she wanted attention. All I mean is: Why would Kevin do something like this? We know him. He's not that sort of guy. Not at all."

Another man remains seated, but speaks up anyway:

"Anyone can see she's just some sort of attention seeker. There's a groupie mentality around these guys—that's perfectly natural. I'm not saying she did it on purpose; it must be something psychological. She's a teenager, for God's sake, and we all know what happens to their hormones. But if she gets drunk and goes into a boy's room, then she's putting him in one hell of a position, isn't she? One hell of a position. It's hardly that bloody easy for the lad to interpret signals like that!"

Maggan Lyt gets to her feet, and blinks sadly at everyone around her:

"I'm a woman myself. So I take the word 'rape' very seriously. Very, very seriously! And that's why I think we need to raise our children to understand that that's not the sort of thing you lie about.

And we all know that she's lying, this young woman. The evidence is overwhelmingly in the boy's favor, and there's not a shred of a reason for him to have done what he's accused of. We don't wish to harm the young woman, we don't wish her family ill, but what sort of signal does it send if we don't put our foot down here? That all girls can cry 'rape!' the minute their affections aren't reciprocated? I'm a woman myself, and that's why I take this very seriously. Because everyone in here knows that this young woman's father is trying to play politics with it. He clearly couldn't bear the fact that there might be bigger stars on this team that he hims . . ."

Peter is standing in the doorway. It takes a few moments for the first person to notice him, then in a flash everyone else turns around. A sea of eyes he has known his whole life. Childhood friends, schoolmates, teenage crushes, colleagues, neighbors, parents of children his children play with. At the back, along one wall, their very presence exuding menace, stand two dozen young men in black jackets. They're not saying anything, but not one of them takes his eyes off Peter. Peter feels their hatred, but he stands there, defiantly straight-backed, as he looks at Maggan Lyt.

"Please, don't let me interrupt," he says.

The room is silent enough for everyone to hear when his heart breaks.

The journalist and photographer will talk to the editor-in-chief when they get back to the newsroom; the journalist will expect the editor-in-chief to send them straight back to the meeting. But instead he will mumble something along the lines of "I don't know if we can really call it 'threatening' . . . People are just nervous . . . we have to understand that . . . Maybe we shouldn't . . . you know . . ." The photographer will clear his throat and suggest: "Look for problems where there aren't any?" The editor-in-chief will nod and say, "Exactly!"

The journalist won't say anything then; she's too young, too concerned about her job, but she will remember the fear in their eyes. And for a long time afterward, she will find it hard not to think of what Kevin Erdahl said to her when she interviewed him after the semifinal. What all sportsmen learn to say when a teammate has done something wrong. The feigned surprise, the stiff body language, the abrupt response. "What? No. I didn't see that incident."

Fatima doesn't knock on her son's door on this occasion, as she always does. When she walks in, Amat is sitting on his bed with a business card in his hands. She perches next to him and declares firmly:

"A boy is allowed to have secrets from his mother. But not if he's this bad at hiding them."

"It's nothing. You don't need . . . Don't worry, Mom," he replies.

"Your father would have . . . ," she begins, but he interrupts her. He never does that.

"Don't tell me what Dad would have done. He isn't here!"

She keeps her hands in her lap. He's breathing hard. He tries to hand her the business card. She doesn't take it.

"It's a job," he manages to say, somewhere between a boy's hopefulness and a young man's anger.

"I've got a job."

"A better job," he says.

His mother raises her eyebrows in surprise.

"Oh? Is it a job where they have an indoor rink so I can see my son practice every day?"

His shoulders sink.

"No."

"Then it isn't a better job for me. I have a job. Don't worry about me."

His eyes flash.

"So who is, Mom? Look around! Who's going to take care of us when your back can't take anymore?"

"I will. Just like I always have," she promises.

He tries to press the business card into her hand but she refuses. He cries:

"You're nothing if you're alone in this world, Mom!"

She doesn't answer. Just sits beside him until he starts to cry. He sobs:

"It's too hard, Mom. You don't understand how much I . . . I can't . . ."

Fatima removes her hands from his. Stands up. Backs away. And says sternly:

"I don't know what you know. But whatever it is, there's clearly someone out there who's terrified that you're going to reveal it. And let me tell you something, my darling boy: I don't need any men. I don't need a man to drive me in a big car to the rink each morning, and I don't need a man to give me a new job that I don't want. I don't need a man to pay my bills, and I don't need a man to tell me what I can think and feel and believe. I only need one man: my son. And you're not alone. You've never been alone. You just need to be better at choosing the company you keep."

She leaves him. Closes the door behind her. Doesn't take the business card.

Maggan Lyt is still on her feet, too proud to back down now. She turns to the board and demands:

"I think we should have an open vote."

The club's president addresses the whole meeting:

"Well, I feel obliged to point out that according to the statutes, it is within the rights of anyone here to demand a secret ballot . . ."

He realizes too late that this is precisely what Maggan is after. She turns to the room and asks:

"I see. Is there anyone in here who isn't prepared to stand by their opinion? Who can't look the rest of us in the eye and say what they think? By all means, stand up and ask to be allowed to vote anonymously!"

No one moves. Peter turns and leaves. He could have stayed to defend himself, but he chooses not to.

Amat puts his headphones in his ears. Walks through his own neighborhood, and the rest of the town. Passes his whole childhood, a whole life. There will always be people who won't understand his decision. Who will call him weak or dishonest or disloyal. They are probably people who live secure lives, who are surrounded by people who share their own opinions and only talk to people who reinforce their own worldview. It's easy for them to judge him—it's always easier to lecture other people about morality when you've never had to answer for anything yourself.

He goes to the rink. Joins his teammates. He may have left his war-torn country before he could talk, but he has never stopped being a refugee. Hockey is the only thing that has ever made him feel like part of a group. Normal. Good at something.

William Lyt slaps him on the back. Amat looks him in the eye.

Ramona is standing in the hallway, waiting for Peter. Leaning on a stick, smelling of whisky. It's the first time in a decade that he's seen her more than five paces outside the Bearskin. She grunts at him.

"They'll feel ashamed, in the end. One day they'll remember that when the word of a boy was set against that of a girl, they believed the boy blindly. And then they'll feel ashamed."

Peter pats her on the shoulder.

"No one's asking . . . no one . . . You don't have to get involved in this just for my family's sake, Ramona," he whispers.

"And you can fuck off if you're going to tell me what I can and can't do, boy."

He nods, kisses her cheek, and leaves. He's reached his car by the time she opens the door to the cafeteria with her stick. One of the men on the board, dressed in a suit, is just loosening his tie and says, possibly as a joke, possibly not:

"How on earth could it have happened anyway? Has anyone asked themselves that? Have you seen the jeans those young women wear these days? Tight as snakeskin! They can hardly take them off themselves, so what chance would a teenage boy have if she didn't want him to? Eh?"

He laughs at his own wit, a few others join in, but the bang when the door flies open silences the whole room as everyone turns around. Ramona is standing there, drunk and furious, pointing at him with her stick:

"Really, little Lennart? That's what you're wondering? Shall we have a bet—your annual salary, perhaps?—that I could get that whole suit off you against your will without a single bugger in here doing a damn thing about it?"

She slams her stick down in drunken rage on the back of a chair, making the perfectly innocent man sitting on it gasp for breath and clutch his chest. Ramona shakes her stick at them all.

"This isn't my town. You're not my town. You should be ashamed of yourselves."

One man stands up and shouts:

"Shut up, Ramona! You don't know anything about this!"

Three men in black jackets step silently out of the shadows by the wall, one of them takes several strides across the room, stops in front of the man, and says:

"If you tell her to shut up again, I'll shut you up. For good."

Amat stands outside the rink, looking his teammates in the eyes. Then he takes a deep breath, turns away from them, and starts walking. His first step is hesitant, the second more confident. He hears Lyt start shouting behind him, but carries on into the rink, not bothering to close the door behind him. He walks past the ice, up the stairs, into the cafeteria, forcing his way between the rows of chairs, stops in front of the board, and looks each and every man and woman in there in the eye. A man named Erdahl first of all, and longest of all.

"My name is Amat. I saw what Kevin did to Maya. I was drunk, I'm in love with her, and I'm telling you that straight so that you lying bastards don't have to say it behind my back when I walk out of here. Kevin Erdahl raped Maya Andersson. I'm going to go to the police tomorrow, and they'll say I'm not a reliable witness. But I'm going to tell you everything now, everything that Kevin did, everything that I saw. And you won't ever forget it. You know that my eyes work better than anyone else's in here. Because that's the first thing you learn on the Beartown Ice Hockey Club, isn't it? 'You can't teach that way of seeing. That's something you're born with.' "

Then he tells them. Every detail. Everything that was in Kevin's room. The posters on the wall, the exact arrangement of trophies on the shelves, the scratches on the floor, the color of the bedclothes, the blood on the boy's hand, the terror on the girl's face, the muffled screams, stifled beneath a heavy palm, the bruises, the violence, the incomprehensible, hideous, unforgiveable nature of it all. He tells them everything. And no one in the room will ever forget it.

When he's finished, he leaves them. He doesn't slam the door, doesn't stomp down the stairs, doesn't shout at anyone on the way out. William launches himself at him the moment he reaches the parking lot:

"What have you done? What have you done you fucking stupid little bitch? WHAT HAVE YOU DONE?"

The hands that push between them are half the size of Lyt's, actually even smaller than Amat's, but they keep the boys apart as if they possessed infinite strength.

"That's enough!" Ann-Katrin roars at William.

Bobo is standing a couple of yards away, watching his mother stare down a young man twice her size. He's never felt more stupid. Never felt prouder.

———

Inside the cafeteria Filip's mother stands up. Waits until the noise has died down. Claps two damp palms together. Looks at the board and says:

"Can anyone demand that we vote anonymously?"

The president nods.

"Secret ballot. Of course. According to the statutes, one person requesting it is enough."

"Then I request it," Filip's mother says, and sits down.

Her best friend is sitting beside her, and tugs at her arm with insulted outrage.

"What are you doing? What are you DOI . . ."

And then Filip's mother says three little words that all best friends have to say to each other occasionally:

"Shut up, Maggan."

Amat backs away without looking at his former teammates, knows what they're thinking anyway. He puts his headphones in, casts a last glance inside the rink, sees the ice shimmering beneath a single fluorescent light. He knows he's put himself on the losing side—he'll never win this. Maybe he'll never get to play again. If anyone had asked him there and then if it was worth it, he would have whispered: "I don't know." Sometimes life doesn't let you choose your battles. Just the company you keep.

He walks back through the town. There's snow on the ground, but the air smells of spring. He's always hated this time of year, because it means that the hockey season is over. He has walked nearly all the way home when he turns into the stairwell next to his, climbs to the third floor, and rings the doorbell.

Zacharias is clutching a video-game handset when he opens the door. They look at each other until the snow melts around Amat's shoes. He's breathing heavily, can feel his pulse in his ears.

"Happy birthday."

Zacharias steps back into the hall so he can come in. Amat hangs his jacket on the same hook where he's hung it every day since he was old enough to reach up there himself. Zacharias is sitting on the bed in his room, playing a video game. Amat sits next to him for half an hour. Then Zacharias gets up, goes over to a shelf, fetches another handset, and puts it in his friend's lap.

They play without speaking. They've never needed words.

Meanwhile, at a meeting at a rink, the members of a club vote on the GM's future. But just as much on their town's future. Their own. Everyone's.

Ramona is sitting in a corner next to a man in a black jacket. He's got a tattoo of a bear on his neck, and is twirling his car keys nervously around his fingers. Ramona pats him on the cheek.

"You didn't have to threaten to shut him up. I could have managed. But thanks."

The man smiles weakly. His knuckles are covered in scars, one of his arms bears the marks of a stab wound, and she's never admired or judged him for that. He and the other men in black jackets grew up at the Bearskin. Ramona has stood by them when everyone else kept their distance, she's defended them even when she hasn't agreed with them, she's had their backs even as she's yelled at them. They love her. But still he says:

"I'm not sure I can get the guys to vote the way you want here."

She nods and scratches his cropped hair.

"I looked Amat in the eye tonight. I trust him. And I'm going to act accordingly. How you choose to act is up to you. It always has been."

The man nods. The tattoo on his neck moves up and down as he swallows.

"I don't know if we can get involved in this. The Pack and the team have to come first."

Ramona gets slowly to her feet, but before she goes to cast her vote she pats him on the knee and asks:

"Whose club is it?"

The man sits and watches her go. Twirls his car keys around his fingers; the Saab logo on them appears and disappears from his palm. Then his eyes wander across the room to a man sitting on a chair in the very front row. He saw him in the Hollow, together with Amat. Kevin Erdahl's father. The man in the black jacket puts his hand in his pocket. He still has the five crumpled thousand-kronor notes there, the ones he picked out of the snow.

He still hasn't decided what he's going to do with them.

44

The love a parent feels for a child is strange. There is a starting point to our love for everyone else, but not this person. This one we have always loved, we loved them before they even existed. No matter how well prepared they are, all moms and dads experience a moment of total shock, when the tidal wave of feelings first washes through them, knocking them off their feet. It's incomprehensible because there's nothing to compare it to. It's like trying to describe sand between your toes or snowflakes on your tongue to someone who's lived their whole life in a dark room. It sends the soul flying.

David rests his hand on his girlfriend's stomach, aware that his whole life is being taken over by love for someone he's never met. His mom always said that every child is like a heart transplant. He understands that now.

His girlfriend's fingers stroke the back of his neck. He's spent all evening talking on the phone, finding out about the meeting, the decisions. He's received an offer he's been dreaming of ever since he started coaching the little league team.

"I don't know what to do."

"You have to trust your heart," his girlfriend says.

"I'm a hockey coach. That's all I want to be. The rest is politics. It's got nothing to do with sports."

His girlfriend kisses his hand.

"So be a hockey coach, then."

Maya rings Ana's doorbell. She says nothing about Kevin on the jogging track, nothing about anything at all. Not long ago the idea of keeping secrets from Ana was unthinkable, and now it's perfectly natural. It's a terrible feeling. They go back to Maya's house. Peter, Kira, and Leo are sitting in the kitchen. They're waiting for their phones to ring, for someone to tell them how everything went at the meeting. But so far all is quiet. So they do the only thing they can do. Maya fetches her guitar, Peter gets his drumsticks, Ana asks if she can sing. She's a terrible singer. She sings so badly that it helps a whole family put up with the wait.

In another part of town, in a rink on the way down to the lake, a meeting of the members of a hockey cub is coming to an end. A vote has come to an end. The results have been counted. Everyone is dealing with the consequences.

A group of men in black jackets are scattered throughout the gathering. Some with their families, others alone. Men and women disappear into the parking lot. Everyone is talking, but no one is saying anything. It's going to be a long night in houses where all the lights are off, but all the people are awake.

The club's president remains seated at the table in the cafeteria long after everyone has left. Tails is standing alone in the darkness out in the stands. This club is their lives. Neither of them knows who it belongs to now.

Amat is sitting on Zacharias's bed when his phone buzzes. A single text. A single word. From Maya.

"Thanks."

Amat replies with a single word. "Sorry."

The thanks is for what he has done. The apology is for how long it took him to summon the courage to do it.

Kevin's parents are the first to leave the meeting. His dad shakes a few hands, exchanges a few brief words. His mom says nothing. They get in separate cars, drive in different directions.

———

Sune goes home. Feeds the puppy. When the phone rings he is both surprised and not remotely surprised. It's the president of a hockey club. Sune stays up after he ends the call, suspects he'll soon be getting a visitor.

Kevin's mom stops her car. Switches the engine off but contemplates switching it straight back on again. She turns the headlights off, but doesn't move. Her body has no energy, she feels feverish, can hardly grip the wheel with her fingers. Her insides have burned to ash, her body is just a shell—that's how she'll remember feeling.

She gets out of the car, walks into the residential area, finds the right row house, and rings the doorbell. It's the last building before the Hollow.

The puppy hears the visitor before the knock on the door. Sune opens up and tries to tell the little creature to go away, but his voice doesn't even come close to hiding who already has the power in their relationship.

"Any difference between hockey players and dogs?" David smiles grimly outside.

"At least hockey players occasionally do what you tell them," Sune mutters.

The two men look at each other. Once upon a time they were mentor and pupil. Once upon a time the love between them was unshakeable. Times change.

"I wanted to come round so you heard this directly from me . . . ," David begins.

"You've got the A-team job," Sune nods.

"The president called?"

"Yep."

"It's nothing personal, Sune. But I'm a hockey coach. This is what we do."

———

Benji's plastered foot isn't a plastered foot anymore, it's a wooden leg now. He's got a black patch over one eye, his room is a pirate ship, and his sister's children are the enemy. They're fencing with hockey sticks, shrieking with laughter as he chases them around, hopping on one leg. They pull the quilt and sheet off the bed and throw them over his head, making him stumble and nearly pull over an entire chest of drawers. Gaby is standing in the doorway, arms folded, doing her special Mom face.

"Shit," one of the kids says.

"It was mostly Uncle Benji's fault!" the other one claims instantly.

"Hey! You don't tell on your friends!" Benji shouts, trying to crawl out from under the bed linens.

Gaby points at her children and says sternly:

"You've got five minutes to tidy up in here. Then you go and wash your hands, and come out and eat dinner. Grandma's nearly ready. And that goes for you too, little brother!"

Benji grunts beneath the covers. The children help him. Gaby goes into the hall so they can't see how hard she's laughing. Laughter that's sorely needed in this town tonight.

Sune draws a deep breath, down to the very depths of his bulky frame. He looks at David.

"Do you really hate Peter so much that you couldn't be in the same club if he stayed?"

David sighs in frustration.

"This has nothing to do with him. I just can't accept what he stands for. This is hockey; we have to be capable of putting the club's best interests ahead of our own."

"And you don't think Peter's done that?"

"I saw him, Sune. I saw him in the parking lot when the police took Kevin off the team bus. Peter drove there and watched because he wanted to see it happen. It was revenge."

"Wouldn't you have done the same in his place?"

David looks up, shakes his head.

"If I was in his place, I'd probably have had a gun with me. That's not what I'm talking about."

"So what are you talking about?" Sune wonders.

"I'm talking about the fact that hockey only works well if it's in a world of its own. If we don't get all sorts of crap from outside mixed up with it. If Peter's family had waited until the day after the final to report Kevin to the police, he'd still have suffered EXACTLY the same judicial consequences. Police, prosecutor, trial, the whole lot, it would all have happened exactly the same, just one day later."

"And Kevin would have been able to play in the final. And maybe the juniors would have won the final," Sune concludes, although evidently without agreeing.

David is adamant:

"That's what justice is, Sune. That's why society has laws. Peter could have waited until after the final, because what Kevin did had nothing to do with hockey, nothing to do with the club, but Peter chose to impose his own punishment. So he damaged the whole team and the whole club. The whole town."

The old man's breath wheezes as it fills his big body. He's old, but his eyes haven't aged.

"Do you remember, David, just after you got onto the A-team, we had a guy who suffered three serious concussions in two seasons? Everyone knew that if he got one more he'd have to stop playing. We came up against a team who had a huge hulk of a guy on defense, and he knew about that, and after the first shift, he purposefully went straight for our guy's head in a hit."

"I remember," David says.

"Do you remember what you did to the other guy?"

"I decked him."

"Yes. Our guy got another concussion, that match was his last. And the referee didn't even give the back a penalty. So you decked the other guy. Because sometimes referees get things wrong, and sometimes there's a difference between breaking the rules, and offending morally, and you believed you had the right to impose your own justice out there on the ice."

"This isn't the same thing," David replies, more confidently than he really feels.

Sune thinks for a long time, pats the puppy, scratches his eyebrow.

"David, do you believe that Kevin raped Maya?"

David takes an eternity to consider his answer. He's been considering it every second since the police picked Kevin up. He's tried to see it from every angle, and he's ended up trying to be rational. Responsible. So he says:

"That's not for me to decide. That's up to a court. I'm a hockey coach."

Sune looks desolate.

"I can respect you, David. But I don't respect that attitude."

"And I can't respect Peter for playing God with this team and this club and the whole town just because this is about his daughter. Let me ask you one thing, Sune: If Kevin had been accused of raping a different girl, if it hadn't been Peter's daughter, do you think Peter would have encouraged that girl's family to report him to the police on the day of the final?"

Sune leans his head against the doorpost.

"Let me ask you something in return, David: What if it wasn't Kevin who was reported to the police? If it had been any other guy? If it had been a guy from the Hollow. Would you still think the same way you do now?"

"I don't know," David replies honestly.

Sune lets those words sink in. Because in the end that's all anyone can ask of another person. That we are prepared to admit that we don't know everything. Sune steps aside and makes space in the hall.

"Would you like coffee?"

————

The doorbell of the Andersson family's house rings. It takes a long time before anyone answers. Kira and Leo are playing cards in the kitchen, and an electric guitar and drum set are echoing from the garage. The bell rings again. Eventually Peter, sweat marks on his shirt and a pair of drumsticks in his hand, opens the door. The club's president is standing outside.

"I've got bad news. And good news."

David and Sune sit opposite each other at the kitchen table. David has never been here before; they've seen each other every day at the rink for almost fifteen years, but this is the first time either of them has been inside the other's home.

"So, you got your A-team job in the end," Sune says magnanimously.

"Just not the one I was expecting," David replies in a subdued voice.

Sune pours coffee. After the members' meeting Sune had certainly been expecting a phone call from a club president, one who had offered David a job as A-team coach—he had just been expecting it to be in Beartown.

"Milk?" Sune asks.

"No, black is good," replies the new coach of the A-team of the Hed Ice Hockey Club.

The president clears his throat. Kira appears in the hall. Leo and Maya are standing farther back; the little brother takes hold of his big sister's hand.

"The members voted. They don't want to fire you," the president says.

His words aren't met with rejoicing. Not even a smile. Peter wipes the sweat from his brow.

"What does that mean?"

The president turns his palms up, and slowly shrugs.

"David's handed in his notice. He's been offered the job of A-team coach in Hed. All the best junior players will go with him. Lyt, Filip, Benji, Bobo . . . they don't play for the team, Peter, they never have. They play for David. They'd follow him anywhere. And without them we can forget all our plans of building up the A-team. Pretty much all the sponsors have called me this evening to cancel their sponsorship deals."

"We can sue them," Kira growls, but the president shakes his head.

"They put all their money in last year on the understanding that the juniors would become a good A-team. We can forget 'good' now—we won't even be able to pay any wages. I don't even know if we'll actually have a team at all next year. The council aren't going to invest, they don't want to put the hockey academy here after . . . the scandal."

Peter nods.

"What about the Erdahl family?"

"Kevin's dad is withdrawing his money, obviously. Switching it to Hed instead. He wants to crush us, naturally. And if Kevin doesn't get convicted in court for . . . everything that's happened, then . . . well, he'll be playing for Hed too. All our best players will follow him."

Peter leans against the wall. Smiles sadly.

"So, good news and bad news, then."

"The good news is that you're still GM. The bad is that I'm not sure we're even going to have a club next season for you to be GM of."

He turns to go, but changes his mind. He looks over his shoulder and says:

"And I owe you an apology."

Peter sighs through his nose and shakes his head slowly.

"You don't have to apologize to me, it's . . ."

"You're not the one I'm apologizing to," the president interrupts.

And he gazes past Peter, down the hall, and looks Maya directly in the eye.

David holds the cup in both hands. Looks down at the table.

"I might sound like a sentimental old woman now, Sune, but I want you to know that I appreciate everything you've done for me. Everything you've taught me."

Sune scratches the puppy. Fixes his gaze on its fur.

"I should have cut you more slack. I was too proud a lot of the time. I didn't want to admit that the game had grown away from me."

David drinks coffee. Looks at the window.

"I'm going to be a dad. I . . . It's silly, really, given the circumstances, but I wanted you to be the first to know."

At first Sune can't get a word out. Then he stands up, opens a cupboard, and returns with a bottle of liquor.

"I think we're going to need stronger coffee."

They drink a toast. David lets out a short laugh, but quickly falls silent.

"I don't know if being a hockey coach makes you a better or a worse dad," he says.

"Well, I think being a dad makes you a better coach," Sune replies.

David drinks, puts his empty cup down.

"I can't stay at a club that mixes up hockey and politics. It was you who taught me that."

Sune fills his cup again.

"I don't have any children, David. But do you want to hear my best advice about being a parent?"

"Yes."

" 'I was wrong.' Good words to know."

David smiles weakly, and takes a gulp of the drink.

"I can understand you being on Peter's side. He was always your best pupil."

"Second-best," Sune corrects him.

They don't look at each other. Their eyes are glistening. Sune exclaims dully: "It's Peter's daughter, David. His daughter. He only wants justice."

David shakes his head.

"No. He doesn't want justice. He wants to win. He wants Kevin's family to feel more pain than his. That's not justice, that's revenge."

Sune fills their cups. They toast with minimal gestures. Drink thoughtfully. Then Sune says:

"Come and see me when your child turns fifteen. Maybe you'll feel differently then."

David gets to his feet. They part with a firm but short embrace. Tomorrow they will head for different rinks, one in Hed and one in Beartown. Next season they will be opponents.

Adri is standing in her mom's kitchen. Katia and Gaby are arguing about setting the table, about which bowls to use, which candles to light. When Benji comes into the kitchen, his mother kisses him on the cheek and tells him she loves him and that he's the light of her life, then she swears at him about his foot again and informs him that he might as well have broken his neck instead, seeing as he clearly doesn't use his head anyway.

The doorbell rings. The woman outside apologizes for disturbing them so late. Her skin looks too big, her skeleton can barely carry her. She has to spend ten minutes getting Benji's mother to agree that she really doesn't need to be invited to dinner, but Benji's mother still taps Adri on the head and hisses, "Get another plate out," then Adri nudges Gaby and whispers, "Get a plate," then Gaby kicks Katia and groans, "Plate!" Katia turns to Benji, but stops midmovement when she sees the expression on his face.

Kevin's mother stands in the doorway and manages to say in a voice that is weak and unlike her own, "Sorry. I'd just like a word with Benjamin."

Kevin is standing in the garden outside the house. Shooting puck after puck after puck. *Bang-bang-bang-bang-bang.* Inside the house his dad is sitting with a newly opened bottle of whisky in front of him. They didn't get everything they wanted this evening, but they haven't lost either. Tomorrow their lawyer will start to prepare all the arguments why a drunk young man who is in love with the young woman is not a credible witness. Then Kevin will start playing for Hed Ice Hockey, taking his team with him, almost all the sponsors, and all their plans for life will be intact. One day very soon everyone around them will simply pretend that this has never happened. Because this family does not lose. Not even when they do. *Bang-bang-bang-bang-bang.*

Benji is sitting on a bench outside his house. Kevin's mom is sitting next to him, leaning her head back and looking at the stars.

"I remember that island you used to row out to in summer, you and Kevin," she says.

Benji doesn't answer, but he's also thought about that. They found it when they were little. Not in the big lake behind the rink, where everyone from the town goes swimming in the summer; they could never have any peace there. They had to walk for hours through the forest to reach another, smaller lake. There was no dock there, no people, and in the middle of it was a small cluster of rocks and trees that from the water looked like no more than an overgrown jumble of stone blocks. The boys dragged a boat through the forest, rowed out, and cleared the interior of the little island until they had a space big enough for a tent. And that was their secret place. The first summer they were only there overnight, the second summer a few days. When they became teenagers, several weeks. Every second that hockey didn't need them, until summer training began. They simply vanished in a puff of smoke and disappeared from town. Swam naked in the lake, dried off in the sun on the rocks, fished for their meals, slept under the starry sky.

Benji looks up at that same sky now. Kevin's mother looks at him intently.

"Do you know, Benjamin, I find it so odd that so many people in this town seem to believe that it was my family who looked after you when your dad passed away. Because it was actually the reverse. Kevin has spent more time in your mother's house than you have in ours. I know you used to mess up the house after we'd been away to make it look like Kevin had slept there, but . . ."

"But you knew?" Benji nods.

She smiles.

"I also know that you kick my rugs on purpose to mess up the tassels."

"Sorry."

She looks at her hands. Takes a deep breath.

"It was your mom who washed your hockey gear and Kevin's when you were young, who made meals for you both, and when older boys picked on you at school, it was . . ."

"It was my sisters who showed up and sorted them out."

"You've got good sisters."

"I've got three lunatics for sisters."

"That's a blessing, Benjamin."

He blinks slowly, presses his broken foot to the ground so that that pain becomes worse than the other. The woman bites her lip.

"It's hard for a mother to admit certain things, Benjamin. I noticed that you didn't meet us at the police station. I noticed that you didn't come round to the house. That you didn't go to the meeting this evening. I . . ."

She very quickly puts her forefinger and thumb to her eyes, swallows hard, whispers. "Ever since you and Kevin were small, every time the two of you caused any trouble, the teachers and other parents always said it was you who started it, and blamed the fact that 'you have no male role model.' And I've never known what to say to that. Because I've never heard anything more stupid in my life."

Benjamin glances at her in surprise. She opens her eyes, reaches out her hand, and touches his cheek softly with it.

"That hockey team . . . that bloody hockey team . . . I know you all love each other. How loyal you all are. Sometimes I don't know if that's a blessing or a curse. I remember when you made catapults when you were nine years old, and Kevin broke the neighbor's window—do you remember? You got the blame. Because when all the other boys ran away, you stayed where you were, because you realized that someone had to take the blame, and that it would be worse for Kevin if he got the blame than it would be for you."

Benji wipes his eyes. She's still holding her hand against his cheek. She pats him and smiles.

"You may not be an angel, Benjamin, I know that much. But, dear God, you haven't lacked a role model. All your best qualities come from the fact that you've been raised in a house full of women."

She moves closer. The boy's whole body is shaking. She hugs him tight and says: "My son has never been able to lie to you, Benjamin, has he? Kevin has been able to lie to everyone in the whole world. To his dad. To me. But never to you."

They sit there, her arms around him, for a single minute of their lives. Then Kevin's mom stands up and gets back in her car.

Benji tries to light a cigarette. His hands are shaking too much to hold the lighter. His tears extinguish the flame.

The dad is still sitting in the kitchen. The whisky bottle is open but untouched. *Bang-bang-bang-bang-bang.* The mom comes home, looks at her husband, stops briefly in the hall, and looks at one of the pictures on the wall. A framed family photograph. It's hanging crookedly, the frame is smashed, and there's glass on the floor. One of the dad's hands is bleeding. The mom says nothing, just sweeps the glass up and disposes of it. Then she goes out into the garden. *Bang-bang-bang-bang-bang.* When Kevin goes to collect the pucks she grabs his arm. Not hard, not in anger, just enough to force him to turn around. She looks him in the eye and he lowers his gaze, her fingers take hold of his chin and force his face up again. So that the son has to look at his mother. Until she knows.

This family doesn't lose. But they will know.

———

The Andersson family are sitting in their kitchen. All five, including Ana. They're playing a childish card game. No one's winning, because they're all trying to let everyone else win. The doorbell rings again. Peter answers it. He stands there in silence, just staring. Kira follows him, but stops when she sees who it is. Last comes Maya.

Kevin's mother stands outside the house, broken, seemingly drowning in her own clothes. Her legs are shaking, struggling until they give way beneath her. They've told her that too much time has passed for the police to use anything as reliable evidence. The girl should have taken photographs, she shouldn't have showered, she should have reported the incident at once. Now it's too late, that's what they said. But the bruises are still visible on the girl's neck and wrists. Kevin's mother can see them. The marks left by strong fingers forcing her. Holding her down. Stopping her from screaming.

She sinks to her knees at the girl's feet, reaches out her hand as if to touch her, but her trembling arms can't reach. Maya stands there empty for a long time, just looking on. She closes her eyelids, stops breathing, her skin is mute, her tear ducts so numb that her body doesn't feel like it's her own. Then, with infinite care, she reaches out her fingers, as if she were picking a lock, and strokes the woman's hair soothingly as she sobs uncontrollably against the girl's legs.

"I'm sorry . . . ," Kevin's mother whispers.

"It isn't your fault," Maya replies.

One of them falls. The other starts to climb back up.

45

Bang-bang-bang.

There are few words that are harder to explain than "loyalty." It's always regarded as a positive characteristic, because a lot of people would say that many of the best things people do for each other occur precisely because of loyalty. The only problem is that many of the very worst things we do to each other occur because of the same thing.

Bang. Bang. Bang.

Amat is standing by the window in Zacharias's bedroom and sees the first of them making their way between the buildings. Hoods over their heads, their faces hidden behind scarves. Zacharias is in the bathroom. Amat could ask him to come out with him. Or he could hide here all night. But he knows that the hooded figures out there are looking for him, he knows that more of them are on their way. They stand up for each other—that's what a team is built on, and their hate now isn't about what they believe Kevin has or hasn't done. It's about Amat going against the team. They're an army, and they need an enemy.

So Amat creeps out into the hall and puts his jacket on. He's not going to let Zacharias get beaten up for his sake, and he can't risk anyone trying to break into his mom's apartment in their hunt for him.

When Zacharias comes back into the room, his best friend is gone. Out of loyalty.

Bang. Bang.

Ann-Katrin is standing at the kitchen window when the young men come through the trees. Lyt at the front, with a further eight or nine

behind him. Some are from the juniors' team—she recognizes them—
and a few are older brothers, even bigger. They're all wearing hoodies
and dark scarves. They're not a team, not a gang, they're a lynch mob.

Bobo goes out into the snow to meet them. Ann-Katrin stands in
the window and watches her son stand with his head bowed while Lyt
lays his hand on his shoulder, explains the strategy, gives him orders.
All his life Bobo has wanted just one thing: to be allowed to belong to
something. His mom watches her boy try to explain something to Lyt,
but Lyt is way beyond reasoning now. He shouts and shoves Bobo,
presses his index finger to his forehead, and even from the window his
mother can read the word "betrayal" on his lips. The young men pull
their hoods over their heads, mask themselves with their scarves, disappear among the trees. Ann-Katrin's son is left standing there alone,
until he changes his mind.

Hog is bent over an engine when Bobo comes into the garage. His
dad half gets up, and father and son glance at each other without either
of them properly looking up. The father bends over the engine again
without speaking. Bobo fetches a hoodie and a scarf.

Bang.

Filip is eating dinner with his parents. They don't say much. Filip is
the best back on the team; one day he will be much more than that.
When he was little and hopelessly behind boys the same age as him
in every measure of physical development, everyone kept waiting for
him to stop playing, but the only thing he never stopped doing was
fighting. When he was the weakest on the team, he learned to compensate by reading the game and always being in the right place at the
right time. Now he's one of the strongest. And one of the most loyal.
He would have been a force to be reckoned with, dressed in a hooded
top and a scarf.

The restaurant in Hed isn't particularly good, but his mother insisted that they come here tonight, right after the meeting, the whole family. They stay until it closes. So when the boys—boys Filip has never been able to say no to if they ask for something—knock on the door of the family's house, Filip, just as he always is in hockey, is in the right place at the right time. Not at home.

Bang.

Amat shivers in the wind, but stands still beneath one of the streetlights on purpose. He wants them to see him from a distance, so that no one else has to get involved. He will never be able to explain how he dares to do this, but perhaps you get tired of being frightened if you've been frightened long enough.

He doesn't know how many there are as they make their way between the buildings, but they look so obviously violent that he knows he won't manage to get a single punch in before they're all over him. His heart is beating in his throat. He doesn't know if they want to scare him, if they want to mark him to make an example out of him, or if perhaps they're seriously planning to make sure he can never play hockey again. One of them is holding something—a baseball bat, perhaps. As they pass the last streetlight before his, a metal pipe glints in another hand. Amat shields himself from the first blow with his lower arm, but the second hits him on the back of the head, then a flash of pain shoots up his spine as the metal pipe hits him across the thigh. He swipes and bites and drags his way through the horde of bodies, but this isn't a fight, it's an assault. He's already bleeding by the time he hits the snow.

Bang.

Bobo has never been good at much except fighting. That's something it's easy to be appreciated for when you grow up in the right surroundings. He isn't just strong and disconcertingly resilient, his reaction time is pretty astonishing considering how sluggish and slow he is otherwise. But he's never been very fit; he's too heavy to run long distances, so he's struggling to keep up with the other masked figures without wearing himself out before they get there. He knows he won't have many seconds to show them who he really is. How loyal he can be, how brave, how selfless.

They slow down when they see Amat. The fifteen-year-old is standing alone, waiting for them.

"He's got balls, I'll give him that, for not running and hiding," Lyt mutters.

When the first blow comes, Amat shields himself with his lower arm, but he doesn't see much after that. Bobo has a couple of seconds in which to step forward from the back and punch Lyt just once in the face as hard as he can, knocking his scarf from his face and sending the huge young man's body crashing into a wall. Bobo elbows another guy—one he's played hockey with since they could barely skate—in the nose, making it explode in a shower of blood.

He only has those few seconds before his teammates realize what he is. A traitor. Amat is lying on the ground, and Bobo fights like a wild animal, headbutting and kneeing and whirling his hands around like hammers. In the end he succumbs to their superior numbers and the collective weight of his attackers. Lyt sits on his chest and rains down blow after blow after blow, bellowing, "You bitch! You bitch! You lying fucking cowardly little traitor bitch!" into the darkness.

Bang.

A car stops twenty yards away between the buildings. Someone who evidently doesn't want to get involved, but who still puts the car's headlights on full beam. For a few moments the whole scene is illuminated. A voice in Lyt's ear shouts: "Someone's coming! Let's go!

Let's go!" And then they're gone. Some are swearing, some limping, but the boots march off into the night and disappear.

Amat lies curled up in the fetal position for a long time, not daring to believe that they've stopped kicking him. Slowly, slowly, he moves his limbs one after the other to check that nothing's broken. He turns his head slightly to one side; it's throbbing with pain, his vision is clouded, but he sees his teammate lying in the snow beside him.

"Bobo?"

The huge boy's face is as battered as his knuckles. At least a couple of their opponents must have been left barely able to get away under their own steam, they must have helped each other leave. When Bobo opens his mouth, a steady trickle of blood oozes from where there should have been a front tooth.

"Are you okay?" Bobo asks.

"Yes . . . ," Amat groans.

Bobo's mouth cracks into a smile.

"Again?"

Amat snorts. It takes an immense effort for him to hiss:

"AGAIN!"

"AGAIN!" Bobo yells.

Smiling, they slump back on the ground, wheezing and shaking.

"Why? Why help me?" Amat whispers.

Bobo spits some red slime on the ground.

"Well . . . I'll never get a place in Hed's A-team anyway. But Beartown might actually be so bad next season that even I stand a chance."

Amat starts to laugh, but he shouldn't have done that, because only then does he realize that one of his ribs is probably broken. He screams, and Bobo might have laughed at him even louder if his jaw hadn't been so painful.

Bang. Bang. Bang.

———

The car a little distance away, a Saab, switches off its headlights. There are two men in black jackets sitting in it. They hesitate for a few moments. It's always hard to know who you can trust in Beartown. But the men in the black jackets have grown up in the Bearskin pub, where loyalty is perhaps prized above all else. And they're violent men, they know how to terrify people, so perhaps they appreciate the courage of someone who knows he's going to get a beating but still doesn't run. So in the end they get out and walk between the streetlights. Amat squints through swollen eyelids as they lean over him.

"Was that you in the car?" he whimpers.

They nod almost imperceptibly. Amat tries to sit up.

"You saved our lives, thanks."

One of the men leans closer and says gruffly:

"Don't thank us, thank Ramona. Hell, we still don't know if we can trust you. But you could have kept your trap shut at that meeting; you had a fuck of a lot to lose saying what you did about Kevin. And Ramona looked into your eyes. She trusts you. And we trust her."

He hands Amat an envelope. As he does so, the other man fixes his eyes on the boy and says, perhaps in jest, perhaps not:

"You'd better make sure you really do end up being as good at hockey as everyone thinks."

When the Saab's engine starts up again and the men disappear into the night, Amat looks down into the envelope. Inside it are five crumpled thousand-kronor notes.

It's hard to know who you can trust in Beartown; the man in the black jacket who's driving the Saab knows that as well as anyone else. So he judges people by what he can see: he saw Kevin's dad go to the Hollow and give Amat enough money to pay his mom's rent that month, and he saw the boy throw it in the snow. He saw the same boy stand up at the meeting in front of the whole town, with everything to lose, without wavering. And he saw the boy tonight, when he knew he was going to be attacked. He didn't run, he stood out here and waited.

The man in the black jacket doesn't know if that's enough to trust someone, but the only person in the world he really trusts is Ramona, and he's only tried to lie to her once. He was a teenager, she asked if he'd found a lost wallet on the pool table, he said, "No," and she called him out on it instantly. When he asked her how she knew, she hit him in the head with a broom handle and roared: "Stupid boy, I own a fucking BAR! Don't you think I've had a bit of experience when it comes to working out if men are lying or not?"

Perhaps one day the man in the black jacket will think about this too: why he only wondered if it was Kevin or Amat who was telling the truth. Why Maya's word wasn't enough.

Bang. Bang. Bang.

In a rehearsal room in Hed, a boy puts down an instrument to open a door that someone has just knocked on. Benji is standing outside, leaning on his crutches, with a pair of skates in his hand. The bass player bursts out laughing. They go to a small outdoor rink behind Hed's indoor rink. Benji has better balance on his crutches than the bass player has on the skates. They kiss each other for the first time on that ice.

Bang.

Two girls are walking through a pitch-black forest. They stop in a clearing and switch their flashlights on. Do their secret handshake. Swear loyalty to each other. Then they each raise a shotgun, and fire shot after shot out across the lake.

———

Bang.

In the rink in Beartown, a father stands at the center circle. Stares down at the bear painted on it. When he was really small, his first day in skating class, he was terrified of that bear.

Sometimes he still is.

Bang-bang-bang.

46

Another morning comes. It always does. Time always moves at the same rate, only feelings have different speeds. Every day can mark a whole lifetime or a single heartbeat, depending on who you spend it with.

Hog is standing in his garage, wiping oil from his hands on a cloth, scratching his beard. Bobo is sitting on a chair with a wrench in his hand, staring out into space with his face covered in scabs and bruises. They're taking him to the dentist tomorrow; hockey has caused gaps before, but this is different. His dad's breathing sounds strained as he pulls up a stool.

"Talking about feelings doesn't come naturally to me," he says, addressing the floor.

"Don't worry," his son murmurs.

"I try to show in other ways that I . . . I love you, and your brother and sister."

"We know, Dad."

Hog clears his throat, his lips barely moving beneath his beard.

"We need to talk more, you and me. After this business with Kevin . . . I should have talked to you. About . . . girls. You're seventeen, practically a grown man, and you're incredibly strong. That brings with it a certain responsibility. You need to . . . behave."

Bobo nods.

"I'd never, Dad . . . to a girl . . . I'd never . . ."

Hog stops him.

"It's not just about not hurting anyone. It's about not keeping your mouth shut too. I've been cowardly. I should have stood tall. And you . . . Christ, boy . . ."

He pats his son gently on his bruises. Doesn't want to say that he's proud, because Ann-Katrin has forbidden him to be proud of the boy for fighting. As if you could forbid pride.

"What Kevin did, Dad, I'd never . . . ," Bobo whispers.

"I believe you."

His son's voice cracks with embarrassment.

"But you don't get it . . . With a girl, I mean, I've never, you know . . ."

His dad rubs his temples awkwardly.

"I'm not good at this, Bobo. But . . . you mean . . ."

"I'm a virgin."

His dad massages his beard and tries to look like he wouldn't rather be hit in the head with a chisel than have this conversation.

"Okay, but you know about, well . . . the birds and the bees and all that crap . . . you know how it all happens?"

"I've seen porn, if that's what you're asking," Bobo says, with big, uncomprehending eyes.

His dad makes a restrained cough.

"I need . . . Okay, I don't even know where to start. It was easier telling you how an engine works."

Bobo clasps the wrench in his lap in his big hands. His shoulders will soon be as broad as his dad's, but his voice still sounds young when he asks:

"Okay, I . . . Does it make you an idiot if you . . . if you want to get married first? I mean, I'm thinking I want it to be special, the first time . . . I want to be in love with someone, I don't want to just . . . fuck. Does that make me an idiot?"

His dad's laughter echoes around the garage so suddenly that Bobo drops the wrench. Laughter isn't a sound this garage is used to.

"No, boy, no, no, no. Christ. Pull yourself together. Is that what you wanted to know? That doesn't make you anything. That's your private life, and it's no one else's damn business."

Bobo nods.

"Can I ask something else, then?"

"Okay."

"How do you know if you've got a nice-looking cock?"

His dad shuts his eyes and rubs his temples.

"I need whisky if I'm going to talk about this."

Ann-Katrin is standing hidden behind one of the doors outside the garage. Hears everything. She's never been more proud, of either of them. The idiots.

Fatima takes the bus through the forest with her son; they are going to Hed. She sits in the next room while he makes his witness statement. She's never been more scared, for both herself and him. The police ask if he was drunk, if it was dark in the room, if it smelled of marijuana, if he has any particular feelings for the young woman in question. He doesn't hesitate on a single detail, doesn't stammer over his answers, his eyes don't flit about.

Kevin is sitting in the same room a couple of hours later. They ask him if he's sticking to his version of the story, if he still claims that the young woman had sexual intercourse with him entirely voluntarily. Kevin looks at his lawyer. Then he glances at his dad. And then he looks the police officer right in the eye and nods. Promises. Swears. Sticks to his story.

All their lives, girls are told that the only thing they need to do is their best. That that will be enough, as long as they give everything they've got. When they themselves become mothers, they promise their daughters that it's true, that if we just do as well as we can, if we're honest and work hard, look after our family and love each other, then everything will be all right. Everything will be fine, there's nothing to be frightened of. Children need the lie to be brave enough to sleep in their beds; parents need it to be able to get up the next morning.

Kira is sitting in her office, and stares at her colleague when she comes in. Her colleague is holding her phone in her hand; she's got a friend in the police station in Hed, and her face is red with sorrow and rage. She can't bring herself to say the words to Kira. She writes them down on a piece of paper, when Kira takes it her colleague is still holding onto it, and when Kira's body hits the floor her colleague is there to catch her. Screams with her. There are two sentences on the piece of paper. Six words. *Preliminary investigation closed. Lack of evidence.*

All our lives we try to protect those we love. It's not enough. We can't. Kira stumbles out to the car. Drives straight out into the forest, as far as she can. The snow muffles the sound between the trees as she slams the door so hard that the metal buckles.

Then she stands there and howls, with an echo that will never fall silent in her heart.

At lunchtime Kevin's mom takes the garbage out. All the houses are silent, all the doors closed. No one invites her in for coffee. The lawyer has sent her an email today, two sentences and six words that say her boy is innocent.

But the street is silent. Because it knows the truth. Just like she does. And she has never felt more alone.

The voice comes gently, the hand is placed on her shoulder with emphatic empathy.

"Come and have some coffee," Maggan Lyt says.

When Kevin's mom is sitting in the kitchen of her neighbor's house, cozy and homey with family photographs hanging slightly askew on the walls without anyone seeming to care, Maggan says to her:

"Kevin's innocent. This sanctimonious town may think it can pass its own laws and mete out its own justice, but Kevin is innocent. The police have said so now, haven't they? You and I know he'd never do what they accused him of. Never! Not our Kevin! This damn town . . . hypocrites and morality police. We're going to take over the club in Hed, your husband and my husband and the other sponsors, the boys on the team, and we'll crush Beartown Ice Hockey. Because when this town tries to oppress us, we stick together. Don't we?"

Kevin's mom nods in agreement. Drinks coffee. Thinks the same thought over and over again: "You're nothing in this world if you're alone."

That afternoon, Benji is on his way to Hed again. He's almost reached the bass player's rehearsal room in Hed when he receives a text. He holds his phone in his hand until the screen is damp with sweat. He asks Katia to turn the car around. She wants to ask why but can see from the way he looks that there's no point. He gets out in the middle of the forest, takes his crutches, and walks straight into it. No one ever sees the text; no one would have understood it anyway. It says simply: "Island?"

The bass player is sitting on a stool in a rehearsal room. He's not playing anything. Just holding a pair of skates in his hands, waiting for hours for someone who never shows up.

It won't be summer for another couple of months, but the water in the lake has started to stir in its winter sleep, and the ice above it is slowly yielding to a few more cracks each day. If you stand on the shore, it's all still a peaceful scene in a hundred shades of white, but here and there are tiny promises of green. A new season will come, followed by a new year, life will go on and people will forget. Sometimes because they can't remember, and sometimes because they don't want to.

Kevin is sitting on a rock looking out at his and Benji's island, the place that used to be a secret, and which as a result was the only place where they never had any secrets from each other. Kevin has lost his club, but he hasn't lost his team. He can see his future. He will spend a year playing for Hed Ice Hockey, then he'll accept an offer from one of the big teams, and then go over to North America. He'll be drafted by the NHL, the professional teams will dismiss the police investigation as "off-ice problems." They'll ask a question or two about it, but they know how it is, of course. There are always girls who want attention; you have to let the courts and the police deal with things like this, they've nothing to do with sports. Kevin will get everything he's ever wanted. There's just one thing left.

Maya is waiting on the steps in front of the house when her mom comes home. Her mom is still clutching the note her colleague gave her, crumpled into a ball, like a loaded grenade. She and the girl rest their foreheads together. Say nothing, because they couldn't have heard anything anyway, the echo of the screams in their hearts is deafening.

Benji walks all the way through the forest, in the snow, on his broken foot. He knows that's exactly what Kevin wants. He wants proof that Benji is still his, that he's still loyal, that everything can go back to the way it was. When Benji emerges and stares at his best friend, they both know that it can. Kevin laughs and hugs him.

The mother holds her hands to the girl's cheeks. They wipe each other's eyes.

"There are still things we can do, we can ask for fresh interviews, I've been in touch with a lawyer who specializes in sexual offenses, we can fly him in, we can . . . ," Kira babbles, but Maya gently hushes her.

"Mom, we have to stop. You have to stop. We can't win this."

Kira's voice is trembling:

"I'm not going to let the bastards win, I'm not . . ."

"We have to live, Mom. Please. Don't let him take my family as well, don't let him take all our lives. I'm never going to be okay, Mom, this is never going to be properly okay again, I'm never going to stop being afraid of the dark, ever again . . . but we have to start trying. I don't want to live in a permanent state of war."

"I don't want you to think that I . . . that we can't . . . that I'm letting them get away . . . I'm a LAWYER, Maya, this is what I DO! It's my job to protect you! It's my job to avenge you, it's my job . . . it's my damn job . . ."

Maya's breathing is ragged, but her hands are still as they touch her mom's temples:

"No one could have a better mom than you. No one."

"We can move, darling. We can . . ."

"No."

"Why not?" her mom cries.

"Because this is my fucking town too," the girl replies.

Maya goes into the bathroom and looks at herself in the mirror. Astonished at how strong she has learned to pretend to be. At the number of secrets she can hold these days. From Ana, from her mom, from everyone. Anguish and terror are roaring through her head, but she becomes calm and cool when she thinks about her secret: "One bullet. I only need one."

Peter comes home and sits down at the kitchen table next to Kira. They don't know if they will ever stop feeling ashamed that they were forced to give up. How can anyone lose like this without dying? How does anyone go to bed at night, how do they get up in the morning?

Maya comes in, stands behind her dad, wraps her arms around his neck. He is fighting back tears. "I let you down. As your dad . . . the manager of the club . . . I let you down, just like every . . ."

His daughter's arms hold him tighter. When she was little they used to tell each other secrets instead of bedtime stories. Her dad might confess in a whisper, "I ate the last cookie," and his daughter might reply, "It was me who hid the remote." It went on for years. Now she leans over and says into his ear:

"Want to know a secret, Dad?"

"Yes, Pumpkin."

"I love hockey too."

Tears roll down his cheeks as he admits:

"Me too, Pumpkin. Me too."

"Will you do something for me, Dad?"

"Anything."

"Build a better club. Stay and make the sport better. For everyone."

He promises. She goes to her room, comes back with two wrapped parcels. Puts them down on the table in front of her parents.

Then she goes around to see Ana. The girls each take a shotgun and head out so far into the snow that no one can hear them anymore. They fire at plastic bottles filled with water, watch the explosions when the shots hit them. They shoot for different reasons. One does it out of aggression. The other does it for practice.

Benji has always felt that he has different versions of himself for different people. He's always known that there are different versions of Kevin too. The Kevin who exists on the ice, the Kevin in school, the Kevin when they're on their own. Above all, there's a Kevin out on the island, and that Kevin is Benji's alone.

They're both sitting on rocks now, looking out at it. Their island. Kevin clears his throat.

"We're going to do all the things in Hed that we wanted to do in Beartown. The A-team, the national side, the NHL . . . we can still have it all! So this town can go to hell!" Kevin smiles with a self-confidence that only Benji's presence can give him.

Benji puts his broken foot down in the snow, presses gently on it, gathers the pain.

"You mean *you* can have everything," he corrects.

"What the fuck do you mean by that?" Kevin exclaims.

"You'll get what you want. You always get what you want."

Kevin's eyes open wide, his lips narrow.

"What are you talking about?"

Benji turns around, until their faces are barely a yard apart. "You've never been able to lie to me. Don't forget that."

Kevin's pupils drown as the rest of his eyes turn black. He raises his forefinger furiously at Benji.

"The cops dropped the investigation. They interviewed everyone, and they DROPPED it. So there was no fucking rape! So don't even try, because you weren't even there."

Benji nods slowly.

"No. And I shouldn't be here either."

As he gets to his feet, the expression on Kevin's face changes in the space of a breath, from hate to terror, from threat to plea.

"Come on, Benji, don't go! I'm sorry, okay? SORRY! FUCKING SORRY! What do you want me to say? That I need you? I need you, okay? I NEED YOU!"

He stands up, arms outstretched. Benji puts more and more weight on his broken foot. Kevin takes a step forward, and he isn't the Kevin everyone in Beartown knows, he's Kevin from the island. Benji's Kevin. His feet are soft in the snow as his fingertips gently touch Benji's jaw.

"Sorry, okay? Sorry . . . It . . . it's going to be all right."

But Benji backs away. Closes his eyes. Feels his cheek grown cold. He whispers:

"I hope you find him, Kev."

Kevin frowns uncomprehendingly; the wind finds its way under his eyelids.

"Who?"

Benji has put his crutches down in the snow. Is hopping slowly over the rocks, up into the forest, away from his best friend on the planet. Away from their island.

"WHO? YOU HOPE I FIND WHO?" Kevin shouts after him.

Benji's reply is so quiet that even the wind seems to turn and carry the words so that they reach all the way to the water.

"The Kevin you're looking for."

In a kitchen in a house sit two parents, each opening a present from their daughter. In Kira's: a coffee cup with a wolf on it. In Peter's: an espresso machine.

47

There are people who say that children don't behave the way adults tell them to, but the way they see adults behave. Perhaps that's true. But children live the way adults tell them to a fair bit as well.

The bass player is woken by a knock. He opens the door with his chest bare. Benji sniggers.

"You'll need more clothes than that if we're going skating."

"I waited for you to come all yesterday evening. You could have called," the bass player whispers, disappointed.

"Sorry," Benji says.

And the bass player forgives him. Even if he tries not to. How can you help it with a boy who looks at you like that?

The Bearskin is its usual self, smelling like a mixture of damp animal and a plate of food someone's hidden behind a radiator. There are men sitting at the tables, nothing but men. Kira knows they've all registered her arrival, but no one is looking at her. She's always been proud of the fact that she doesn't scare easily, but the unpredictability of this group is sending cold shivers down her spine. Seeing them in the rink at A-team matches is bad enough, when they yell horrible things at Peter at the end of an unsuccessful season. Seeing them here, in a cramped room when most of them have been drinking, makes her more nervous than she cares to admit.

Ramona's hand reaches out to her across the bar. The old woman smiles through crooked teeth.

"Kia! What are you doing here? Have you finally had enough of Peter's teetotal nonsense?"

Kira smiles almost imperceptibly.

"No. I just came to say thank you. I heard what you did at the meeting, what you said."

"There's no need," Ramona mutters.

Kira stands at the bar, and insists:

"Yes there is. You stood up when no one else did, and I wanted to look you in the eye when I say it. Even if I know that you all get embarrassed about thanking each other in this town."

Ramona laughs and coughs.

"You've never been much of a one for feeling embarrassed, lass."

"No," Kira smiles.

Ramona pats her cheek.

"This town doesn't always know the difference between right and wrong, I'll admit that. But we know the difference between good and evil."

Kira's nails dig into the wood of the bar. She isn't just here to say thank you, she's here because she needs to know the answer to a question. And she's wary of asking it in here. But Kira has never been much good at being timid either.

"Why did you do it, Ramona? Why did the Pack vote to let Peter keep his job?"

Ramona stares at her. The whole bar falls silent.

"I don't know what you . . . ," Ramona begins, but Kira holds up two exhausted hands:

"Please, spare me the bullshit. Don't tell me there is no Pack. They exist, and they hate Peter."

She doesn't turn around, but she can feel the men staring at the back of her head. So her voice is trembling when she says:

"I'm a pretty smart woman, Ramona, so I know how to count. There's no way that Peter could have won that vote unless the Pack and anyone who has any influence over it voted for him."

Ramona looks at her for a long time without blinking. None of the men stands up. No one so much as moves. In the end Ramona nods slowly.

"Like I said, Kira: People round here don't always know the difference between right and wrong. But we know the difference between good and evil."

Kira's chest rises and falls as she breathes, her carotid artery is throbbing, her nails are leaving marks in the bar. Suddenly her phone rings; she jumps and starts looking for it in her bag. It's an important client; she hesitates as it rings seven times, then rejects the call. She takes deep breaths through her teeth. When she raises her head again there's a beer on the bar.

"Who's that for?" she asks.

"You, you crazy bitch. You really aren't scared of anything, are you, lass?" Ramona sighs.

"You don't have to offer me beer," Kira gasps apologetically.

"It's not from me," Ramona says, and pats her hand.

It takes a few moments for Kira to understand. But she's lived in the forest long enough to pick the beer up without asking any more questions. As she drinks she hears men in black jackets drink a silent toast behind her. People don't often say thank you in Beartown. Nor sorry. But this is their way of showing that some people in this town can actually carry more than one thought in their head at the same time. That you can want to punch a man in the face but still refuse to let anyone hurt his children.

And that you respect a crazy bitch who walks in here without being afraid. No matter who she is.

Out in the street Robbie Holts is approaching. He stops at the door leading down into the Bearskin, smiles to himself. Then he keeps walking without going in. He's got work tomorrow.

David is lying in bed with the two people he loves, laughing as one of them tries to think of names for the other. They all sound like cartoon characters to David, or like someone's great-grandfather. But every time he himself suggests a name, his girlfriend asks, "Why?" and he just shrugs and mutters, "Nice, that's all," whereupon his girlfriend googles the name together with "hockey player" to find out exactly where he got it from.

"I'm terrified," he confesses.

"It's actually completely ridiculous that the world is going to let the two of us be responsible for an entirely new person without having to ask for permission," she laughs.

"What if we're terrible parents?"

"What if we aren't?"

She holds his hand to her stomach, puts her fingers around his wrist, and taps the face of his wristwatch.

"Soon you'll have someone to leave that to."

Jeanette stands for a long time by the fence, just taking it all in.

"God. Your own kennels, just like you used to dream about. When we were kids and you used to go on about it, I never believed it would happen."

Adri straightens up, even if the words are belittling.

"Oh, it hardly breaks even. If they raise the insurance premiums one more time I'll have to give the dogs away and shut up shop. But it's mine."

"It's yours. I'm proud of you. It's so funny . . . sometimes I wish I'd never moved back here, and sometimes I wish I'd never moved away. Do you know what I mean?"

Adri, who has always had a decidedly uncomplicated way of communicating, replies:

"Not really."

Jeanette smiles. She misses that lack of complication. When they stopped playing hockey, Adri went off into the forest and Jeanette went to Hed and found a small boxing club. When Adri bought this old farm, Jeanette moved to a bigger city and started practicing martial arts—every sort she could find. When Adri got her first puppies, Jeanette started having her first matches. For one vanishingly short year she was a professional fighter. Then came the injuries, so she trained to become a teacher to have something to do while her injuries healed, and by the time they had, she was a good teacher but not really as good a fighter anymore. Her instincts had gone. When her dad died and her mom needed more help than her brother could give her, she moved back here. It was only going to be for a couple of months, but now here she is, a teacher at the school and part of the town again. This place has a way of grabbing hold of your insides that's hard to explain. On the one hand, there's all that's bad about it—and that really is a very long list—but there are a few things that are so good that they manage to shine through the crap. The people, most of all. As tough as the forest, as hard as the ice.

"Can I rent one of your outbuildings?" Jeanette asks.

David rings the doorbell at Benji's house. His mother opens up, tired and only just home from work, and tells him she doesn't know where her son is. Possibly with his sister at the Barn in Hed, she suggests. David drives over there. Katia is behind the bar, and hesitates before saying that she doesn't know where he is. He can see that she's lying, but doesn't press the point.

As he's leaving the Barn, one of the bouncers calls after him.

"You're that hockey coach, aren't you? Are you looking for Benji?"

David nods. The bouncer points toward the rink.

"He went that way with his friend. They had skates with them; I reckon the ice is too bad to skate on the lake now, so they're probably on the outdoor rink behind the hall."

David thanks him. It's still dark when he goes around the corner; the boys can't see him but he can see them. Benji and the other one. They're kissing each other.

David is shaking all over. He feels ashamed and disgusted.

"An outbuilding? What for?" Adri wonders.

"I want to set up a marital arts club," Jeanette says.

Adri sniggers.

"This is a hockey town."

Jeanette sighs.

"I know. God knows, everybody knows that. But in light of what's happened . . . I don't think this town needs fewer sports right now. I think it needs more. And I know about martial arts. I can give the kids that."

"Martial arts? Kicking and fighting—is that anything worth having?" Adri wonders.

"It's not about kicking and fighting, it's JUST AS MUCH A REAL SPORT AS . . ."

Jeanette begins to explain angrily until she realizes Adri is kidding.

"Do you miss it that much, martial arts?" Adri asks.

"Only every day," Jeanette smiles.

Adri shakes her head. Coughs hard.

"This is a hockey town." Adri repeats.

"Can I borrow your outbuilding or not?"

"BORROW? A minute ago you were going to rent it!"

The women glare at each other. Grin. You have friends when you're fifteen years old. Sometimes you get them back.

When Benji and Kevin were young, they snuck into the coach's room and went through David's bag. They were only children; they didn't even know what they were looking for, they just wanted to know more about the coach they idolized. When David found them they were sitting there bemused, playing with his watch, until Kevin managed to drop it on the concrete floor and broke the glass. David rushed in and lost his temper in a flash; he hardly ever did that, but this time he shouted at them until the walls of the rink shook:

"That was my DAD'S watch, you little brats!"

The words caught in his throat when he saw the look in the boys' eyes. His guilt about that has never really left him. They never talked about it afterward, but David instigated a ritual, just between him and the boys. Every so often, sometimes only once during an entire season, when one of them had had an exceptional game, something way beyond the usual, when they showed loyalty and courage, he would give the boy his watch, and the boy could wear it until the next game. No one knew about this little contest except Benji and Kevin, but for that single week in any one year when one of them succeeded, he was immortal in the eyes of the other boy. Everything seemed bigger in those seven days, even time itself.

David doesn't remember when it stopped. The boys grew out of it, he forgot about it. He still wears the watch every day, but he doubts either of the boys even remembers it now.

They grew up so fast. Everything changed so quickly. All the best players in the junior team have called David now, and they all want to play for him in Hed. He's going to build a good A-team over there, the A-team he's always wanted to build. They're going to have Kevin, Filip, and Lyt, with a collective of loyal players around them. Strong sponsors, and the backing of the council—they'll be able to build something big. There's only one piece missing. And that boy is standing out there on the ice now, with his lips pressed against another boy's. David feels like he's been kicked in the gut.

His dad's watch glints in the light of a solitary streetlight when he turns his back on them and disappears without being seen. He can't look Benji in the eye. He doesn't know if he'll ever be able to do that again.

All those hours in the locker room that a player and a coach spend together, all the nights travelling to and from tournaments and away games, what are they worth? All the laughter and all the jokes, filthier and filthier the longer the trips were, David has always felt that the team was strengthened by them. Sometimes the jokes were about blondes, sometimes they were about people from Hed, sometimes they were about gays. They all laughed. They looked at each other and they laughed out loud. They were a team, they trusted each other, they had no secrets. Yet even so, one of them did. The last one anyone could have guessed. It's a betrayal.

———

Jeanette hangs a sandbag from the ceiling and spreads a soft mat on the floor of the outbuilding as evening falls. Adri helps her, grunting and reluctant. When they're done, Adri walks through the forest, down into town, to the row houses. It's late, so when Sune opens the door and sees her, he can't help exclaiming:

"Has something happened to Benji?"

Adri shakes her head impatiently, and asks instead:

"What do you have to do to set up a hockey team?"

Confused, Sune scratches his stomach. Clears his throat.

"Well . . . it's not that hard, you just set it up. There's always young lads who want to play hockey."

"What about girls?"

Sune frowns several times. His breath wheezes out of his heavy frame.

"There's a girls' team in Hed."

"We're not from Hed," Adri replies.

He can't help smiling at that, but mutters:

"It's probably not the right time for a girls' team in Beartown. We've got enough problems as it is right now."

Adri folds her arms.

"I've got a friend, Jeanette; she's a teacher at the school. She wants to set up a martial arts club in one of my outbuildings."

Sune's lips seem to approach the strange words tentatively.

"Martial. Arts?"

"Yes, martial arts. She's good. Used to compete professionally. The kids are going to love her."

Sune is scratching his stomach with both hands now. Trying to get his head around what appears to be happening.

"But . . . martial arts? This is hardly a martial arts town. This is a . . ."

Adri has already started to walk away. The puppy follows her. Sune follows the pair of them, swearing and muttering.

———

When David was little, his dad was an invincible superhero. Dads usually are. He wonders if he himself is going to be one to his child. His dad taught him to skate, patiently and gently. He never got into fights. David knew that other dads sometimes did, but never his. His dad read stories and sang lullabies, didn't shout when his son wet himself in the supermarket, didn't shout when he broke a window with a ball. His dad was a big man in daily life, and a giant on the ice, ruthless and invulnerable. "A real man!" the coaches always used to say, admiringly. David would stand by the boards and soak up every compliment, as if they were aimed at him. His dad did everything for a reason, never hesitated, whether in hockey or in his opinions. "You can be whatever you like, as long as you're not gay," he used to laugh. But sometimes, at the kitchen table, he used to get more serious: "Homosexuality is a weapon of mass destruction, David, remember that. It's not natural. If everyone turns gay, mankind will be wiped out in a generation." The years passed, and as an old man he used to watch the news and shout: "It's not a sexual orientation, it's a trend! And they're supposed to be an oppressed minority? They've got their own PARADE! How oppressed does that make them?" When he'd been drinking he used to form a circle with the fingers and thumb of one hand, then insert the index finger of the other hand into them. "This works, David!" Then he would put the tips of his two index fingers together: "But this doesn't!"

Whenever anything, anything at all, was really bad, it was "gay." When something didn't work, it was "gay." It was more than just a concept, it was an adverb, an adjective, a grammatical weapon.

David drives back to Beartown. Sits in the car crying with anger. He's ashamed. He's disgusted. At himself. He's spent his whole life in hockey training a boy, has loved him like a son, been loved in return like a father. There's no more loyal player than Benji. No one whose heart is bigger than his. How many times has David hugged number sixteen after a game and told him, "You're the bravest bastard I know, Benji. The bravest bastard I know."

And after all those hours in the locker room, all those nights on the team bus, all the conversations and all the jokes and the blood, sweat, and tears, the boy didn't dare tell his coach his biggest secret.

That's betrayal. David knows it's a huge betrayal. There's no other way to explain how much a grown man must have failed as a person if such a warrior of a boy could believe that his coach would be less proud of him if he were gay.

David hates himself for not being better than his dad. That's the job of sons.

Adri and Sune go from house to house, and every time someone opens the door and casts a pointed glance up at the sky, as if to point out that it's a bit late to be knocking on decent folks' doors, Sune asks, "Have you got any little girls in the house?" Adri will tell the story as a legend, and say it was like when Pharaoh searched Egypt looking for Moses. Adri's knowledge of the Bible is pretty shaky, it has to be said, but she's good at other things.

She gets told, "But there's a girls' team in Hed, isn't there?" at every door, and she replies the same thing each time. Until she rings one doorbell and the handle is pulled down on the other side by someone who can hardly reach it.

The girl is four years old, and is standing in a hall without lights, in a house full of bruises. Her hands are timid, she stands on tiptoe as if she's always ready to run, and her ears listen out constantly for steps on the stairs. But her eyes are wide open, and stare at Adri without blinking.

Adri's heart has time to break many times as she crouches down to get a better look at the child. Adri has seen war, she's seen suffering, but you never get used to it. You never know what to say to a four-year-old who hurts and thinks that's normal, because life has never shown her anything else.

"Do you know what hockey is?" Adri asks.

The girl nods.

"Can you play?" Adri asks.

The girl shakes her head. Adri's heart gives up and her voice breaks.

"It's the best game in the world. The best in the world. Would you like to learn?"

The girl nods.

Down to his very marrow, David wishes he could drive back to Hed, take the boy in his arms, and tell him that he knows now. But he can't bring himself to unmask someone who clearly doesn't want to talk about it. Big secrets make small men of us, especially when we're the men others have to keep secrets from.

So David drives home, puts his hand on his girlfriend's stomach, and pretends he's crying about the baby. His life will be successful, he will achieve everything he's ever dreamed of—career and success and titles—he'll coach unbeatable teams at legendary clubs in several different countries, but he will never let any player in any of them wear number "16." He will always keep hoping that Benji is going to turn up one day and demand his jersey.

There's a hockey puck on a gravestone in Beartown. The writing is small, so that all the words can fit. *Still the bravest bastard I know.* Beside the puck lies a watch.

48

Maya and Ana are each sitting on a rock. Far enough into the forest for it to take days to find them.

"Did you see the therapist?" Ana asks.

"She says I shouldn't bottle it all up inside me," Maya says.

"Is she good?"

"She's okay. But she talks more than my parents. Someone should tell her that she could do with bottling a bit *more* up inside," Maya replies.

"Has she asked you that 'Where do you see yourself in ten years' time?' question yet? The psychologist I saw after Mom left used to love that one."

Maya shakes her head. "No."

"What would you have said? Where do you see yourself in ten years' time?" Ana asks.

Maya doesn't answer. Ana says nothing more either. They go back to Ana's together, lie down in the same bed, and breathe in time with each other for hours until Ana finally falls asleep. Then Maya creeps out, goes down into the cellar, finds a key, and opens a cupboard. She takes the shotgun and heads straight out into the darkness with an even greater darkness inside her.

Hockey is both complicated and not complicated at all. It can be hard to understand the rules, challenging to live with the culture, as good as impossible to get all the people who love it not to pull so hard in different directions that it breaks. But, when it comes down to it, at its most basic essence, it's simple:

"I just want to play, Mom," Filip says with tears in his eyes.

She knows. They're going to have to decide how he's going to do that now. If he's going to stay with Beartown Ice Hockey or move to

Hed with Kevin, Lyt, and the others. Filip's mom knows the difference between right and wrong, between good and evil, but she's also
a mom. And what's a mom's job?

Tails is sitting at a lunch table, surrounded by his best friends. One of
them points at his tie pin with a chuckle.

"Time to take that off, eh, Tails?"

Tails looks down at the pin. It says "Beartown Ice Hockey" on it.
He looks around at the other men; they've all been very quick to take
theirs off and replace them with pins saying "Hed Ice Hockey." It was
that easy for them. As if it were only a club.

His mom helps Filip pack his bag, not because he isn't old enough
to do it himself, but because she likes doing it. She holds her hand
against his chest and his heart beats like a child's beneath her palm,
even though the sixteen-year-old is now so tall that he has to bend
down a long way to kiss his mom on the cheek.

She remembers every inch. Every battle. She thinks of the summer
training sessions the year when Filip ran until he threw up so much
that he had to be taken to the hospital with acute dehydration. The
next day he showed up at training.

"You don't have to be here," David said.

"Please?" Filip begged.

David held him by the shoulders and said honestly:

"I need to pick the best team this autumn. You might not even get
to play any games."

"Just let me train. I only want to play. Please, I only want to play,"
Filip pleaded.

He got thrashed in every one-on-one situation, lost every drill, but
he kept coming back. At the end of the summer David drove over to
see Filip's mom, sat in her kitchen, and told her about a study that
showed how many elite players were never among the five best in their
youth team, and how it's often the sixth- to twelfth-best juniors who

break through at senior level. They've had to fight harder. They don't buckle when the setbacks come.

"If Filip ever doubts his chances, you don't have to promise him that he'll be the best in the team one day. You just have to convince him that he can battle his way to twelfth place," David said.

There's no way he can know how much that meant for the family, because they have no words to express it. It only changed everything.

Now the mom rests her forehead against the sixteen-year-old's chest. He's going to be one of the best players this town has ever seen. And he just wants to play. Her too.

Tails is standing in the parking lot. The men shake hands with each other, and most of them drive off toward Hed. Two of them stay behind with Tails, smoking, and one of them says:

"Any journalists?"

The other shrugs his shoulders.

"A couple have called, but obviously we're not responding. Anyway, what the hell are they going to do? There's no story. Kevin was cleared. Surely not even journalists can set themselves above the law?"

"Haven't you got a bit of influence with the local paper?"

"The editor-in-chief and I play golf in the summer. I suppose I ought to let him win next time."

They laugh. Stub out their cigarettes, and Tails asks:

"What's going to happen to Beartown Ice Hockey, do you suppose?"

The men look at him quizzically. Not because it's a strange question. But because none of them but Tails cares about the answer.

Maggan Lyt is sitting in her car, waiting. William is sitting in the passenger seat, wearing a tracksuit top with the words "Hed Ice Hockey" on it. Filip steps out into the street with his bag in his hand, and hesitates for what feels like ages. Then he looks at his mom, lets go of her hand, and opens the trunk of the Lyt family's car. Filip gets in the backseat; his mom opens the front door and looks William in the eye.

"You're sitting in my place."

William protests but Maggan pushes him out at once. The boys sit in the back and look at each other. The women in the front do the same. Maggan swallows hard.

"I know I push too hard sometimes, but everything I do . . . it's all for our kids."

Filip's mom nods. She's spent all night trying to persuade both herself and Filip that he ought to stay at Beartown Ice Hockey. But her son just wants to play, just wants the chance to be as good as he can, and what's a mother's job? To give her child the best possible chances. She keeps repeating that to herself, because she knows what it took for her to be really good at skiing. Sometimes she had to train with assholes, and remember that life outside had nothing to do with sports. Filip and William have played together since they were at preschool, and she and Maggan have known each other all their lives. So they drive toward Hed. Because friendship is both complicated and not complicated at all.

Tails gets home. He hears his son's voice; he's twelve years old now and loves hockey, but Tails can remember how the boy hated practicing when he was six. He used to beg and plead not to have to go. Tails took him anyway, explaining time and time again that this is a hockey town. Even when his wife, Elisabeth, mumbled, "But if he doesn't *want* to play, darling, are we really going to force him?" over dinner, Tails kept taking him to training, because he dearly wanted the boy to understand his love for it. Hockey may not have saved Tails's life, but it certainly gave him one. It gave him self-confidence and a sense of belonging. Without it he would just have been a fat kid diagnosed with a "hyperactive personality," but it taught him to focus his energy. It speaks a language he understands in a world he finds comprehensible.

He was worried his son wouldn't want to play hockey, because that would have left him excluded. Tails was terrified at the thought of the boy taking up a sport that Tails didn't know anything about, so he'd end up being the lost dad in the stands who kept getting the rules wrong and couldn't take part in discussions. He didn't want his son to be ashamed of him.

"Give me the charger, then!" his son is yelling at his big sister.

He's almost a teenager. You used to have to drag him to training, and now you can barely get him away, and he begs and pleads about other things now. In the past few days, about being allowed to play hockey in Hed instead. Like all the best players are going to start doing.

"It's not YOUR charger, you stupid asshat, it's MINE!" the boy shouts at his sister as she goes into her room and slams the door.

Tails reaches out his arm to touch him and say something, but the boy hasn't seen his dad yet, and has time to kick the door and yell:

"Give me that charger, you fucking BITCH, you haven't got any guys to talk to on the phone anyway! Everyone knows you WISH you'd been raped but there's no one who WANTS to do it!"

Tails doesn't remember exactly what happened after that. He remembers Elisabeth desperately tugging at his arms from behind, trying to make him let go. His son is dangling, horrified, in the grip of his father's huge hands, and Tails hits him against the wall time and time again, shouting at him. His daughter opens her door, numb with shock. Elisabeth finally manages to wrestle her almost 220-pound husband to the floor, and he lies there hugging his son. They're both crying, one out of fear and the other out of shame.

"You can't become that sort of man. I won't let you . . . I love you, I love you so much . . . you need to be better than me . . . ," Tails repeats, over and over again, in his son's ear, without letting go of him.

Fatima rather hesitantly puts the little car in reverse. She's borrowed it from Bobo's parents; they had to nag her to agree to take it. She saw Bobo's battered face, just like Amat's, but she said nothing. Still says nothing. She just drives her son past Hed, through the forest, all the way to a city that has the kind of store her son is looking for. She asks if he "needs any hockey things" as they pass a sports store. He shakes his head, and says nothing about the fact that he may not even have a team to play on by the autumn. His mom may not have a job then, either. Neither of them points out to the other what they might be able to do with five thousand kronor. She waits outside the store while he goes in. The clerk takes the time to help him get the best value for his money, and eventually he emerges with it, carrying it awkwardly to stop his rib feeling like it's puncturing his lung with each step he takes.

They drive home, turn off a short way before they reach the Hollow, in among the houses in the center of town. Fatima waits in the car as Amat leaves it on the steps.

Maya isn't home. The guitar will be waiting for her when she gets back. "You won't get a better instrument than this for five thousand. She'll still love it in ten years' time!" the store clerk promised.

Tails steps inside the Bearskin. Stands in front of the bar, cap in hand, hair messed up. Ramona puts her hands down on the bar.

"Well?"

Tails clears his throat.

"How many sponsors does Beartown Ice Hockey have at the moment?"

Ramona coughs and pretends to count on her fingers.

"I reckon there's a sum total of one right now."

"Would you like some company?" he asks, his jaw tensing.

Ramona looks at him skeptically. Then turns her back on him and goes to serve another customer. When she comes back she fills two glasses, puts one in front of Tails, and downs the other herself.

"You're a businessman, lad. Go and sponsor Hed instead; that'll be good for your supermarket over there."

"Hed Ice Hockey isn't my club."

She wrinkles her nose.

"I'm not sure you've got the money to rescue your club."

He sucks his lips in, his eyes close, then open again, rather unhappily.

"I'm going to sell the store in Hed. Elisabeth is always complaining that I work too hard anyway."

"You'd do that for a hockey club?"

"I'd do that for a better hockey club."

"So what do you want with me? I don't know what you think I sell here, but it sure as hell isn't gold."

"I want to get you elected to the board."

"Are you drunk, lad?"

"It will take a strong man to rescue the club now. And there's no stronger man in Beartown than you, Ramona."

She laughs hoarsely.

"You always have been a bit thick, you have. Anyone would think you're a goalie."

"Thanks," Tails mutters, genuinely moved.

Because Holger was a goalie. That's a compliment in the Bearskin. Ramona goes and serves another customer. When she comes back she puts a beer in front of Tails, and gets herself a coffee.

When she sees Tails's surprise she mutters:

"I should probably try to sober up if I'm going to sit on the board. And considering how much I've drunk over the past forty years, I might need a couple of months."

Benji and the bass player are lying side by side on their backs in the rehearsal room. Surrounded by instruments along all the walls, watched over by dormant music. Sometimes it's easy to learn to play anything at all. You just have to not play, and then you stop doing that.

"I have to go home soon," the bass player says.

He doesn't mean his apartment in Hed. He means home. Benji doesn't say anything, and the bass player really wishes he would.

"You could . . . come too . . . ," he finds his mouth saying, even though his heart struggles against it.

He doesn't want to hear the answer. Doesn't get one anyway. Benji stands up and starts to put his clothes on. The bass player sits up, lights a cigarette, smiles sadly.

"You could move away from here, you know. There are other lives, other places."

Benji kisses his hair.

"I'm not like you."

When Benji heads out into the last snowfall of the year and the door closes softly behind him, the bass player thinks how true that is. Benji isn't like him, but he's not like the people who live here either. Benji isn't like anyone else at all. How can you not love someone like that?

When night comes to Beartown, Kevin runs alone along the illuminated jogging track. Around and around and around. Until the pain in his muscles is greater than everything else that hurts. Around, around, around. Until his adrenaline grows stronger than the insecurity, so that rage defeats humility. Again, again, again.

He will think he's imagining it at first, that the shadows are playing tricks on his eyes. For a moment he will even think he's just so tired that he's hallucinating. He will slow down, his chest heaving. Wipe the sweat from his face with his sleeve. And only then will he see the girl. The shotgun in her hands. Death in her eyes.

He's heard hunters describe the way animals behave when they fear for their lives. Only now will he understand what that means.

Ana wakes up and looks around the room, murmurs vaguely and sleepily for a few seconds before flying up and hitting her head on the bedside table. She grabs the covers, hoping that Maya is just hidden beneath them, but when she realizes what's happened, terror seizes hold of her like a wild animal's claws. She throws herself down the stairs, thunders into the cellar, screams with her lips tightly closed as if the blood vessels in her head were exploding one by one, when she opens the gun cabinet and sees what's missing.

There's a note in the cabinet. In Maya's neat handwriting.

Happy, Ana. In ten years' time I see myself being happy. You too.

49

In ten years' time, a twenty-five-year-old woman, in a big city far away from here, will walk across a parking lot outside a shopping center. There will be an ice rink right next to it, but she won't even look at it, because it doesn't belong to her life. Before she gets in her car she will cast a glance across the roof at her husband. He will put the bags of shopping in the trunk, and laugh when he catches her eye. He won't look at the rink either; isn't interested. She'll rest her chin on the car roof for a moment, he'll do the same. They will giggle, and she'll think to herself that he's all she wants, everything she's ever wished for, he's perfect for her. She's pregnant. And happy. In ten years' time.

The illuminated jogging track is quiet, but not deserted. Kevin can only see the outline in the distance, he slows down without actually stopping. When Maya steps forward into the light, he doesn't have time to escape. When he sees the shotgun it's too late. She stops three yards away from him, the gun held calmly, her breathing even and relaxed. Her eyes don't leave him for an instant, she doesn't blink, her voice is cold and merciless when it demands that he get down on his knees.

In ten years' time, in a big city far away from here, an illuminated sign will shine out above a rink, bearing a performer's name. There's going to be a concert rather than a hockey game that evening. It won't make any difference to the woman in the parking lot; she'll get in her car and hold her husband's hand across the seat. She won't be under any illusions that love is simple; she will have made a lot of mistakes and felt a lot of pain, and she will know that her husband has too. But when he looks at her, he sees her, deep down inside of her, and even if he isn't perfect, he is for her.

———

Kevin kneels on the snow, his skin stiffening in the wind; his arms tremble as his head sinks to the ground, but Maya presses the barrel of the shotgun to his forehead and whispers:

"Look at me. I want to see your eyes when I kill you."

Tears are streaming from his eyes. He tries to say something, but the sobbing and gasping overpower his lips. Snot and saliva are dripping from his chin. When the cold metal of the shotgun's twin barrels presses against his skin, an acrid smell of ammonia rises up. The stain on his grey jogging pants grows until it covers all of his thighs. He's wet himself in terror.

Maya had been expecting that she would be nervous. Possibly even scared. But she feels nothing. It was a simple plan: she knew Kevin wouldn't be able to sleep tonight, and she hoped he would go out for a run. She was right, she just needed to wait outside his house for long enough, and seeing as she had timed his circuits last time she was standing here, she knew exactly how long it would take him to run around. Where she should hide. When she should step out from the darkness. The shotgun holds two cartridges, but she has always known that the most she would ever need is one. His forehead touching the barrel. After tonight it's all over.

She had been expecting to feel hesitant. To change her mind. To spare him this moment, in spite of everything. She doesn't.

When her forefinger pulls the trigger back, his eyes are closed, hers open.

In ten years' time a man will reverse a car out of a parking lot. When he looks out through the side window he will freeze to ice. A straight-backed woman with a guitar case in her hand will get out of another car. She was given the instrument by a friend when she was fifteen years old; she still refuses to play any other. She will see the man in the car, and she will stop, and for a few terrible seconds they will be back in a small town in a forest far away. Ten years before. When the man was a boy who was on his knees in the snow, begging for his life, and she stood over him with a shotgun and pulled the trigger.

Kevin falls to the ground. He has time to understand that he's dying. His brain is convinced that it's exploding in blood and snot. His heart stops beating. When it starts again, it beats so hard that it bursts his chest. He's screaming with tears, with an infant's senseless hysteria and panic.

Maya is still standing over him. She lowers the shotgun. From her pocket she takes out the single cartridge and drops it in the snow in front of him. She crouches down and forces him to look her in the eye as she says:

"Now you'll be scared of the dark, too, Kevin. For the rest of your life."

In ten years' time the parking lot will be full of other people. Kevin's wife will be pregnant. Maya will be standing a few yards away, with every possibility in the world of ending his life. She could walk right over and say what he is, humiliate and annihilate him in front of the person he loves most.

She will have all the power in that moment, but she will let him go. She will not forgive him, she will not pardon him, but she will spare him. And he will always know that.

And she will always know that he still, ten years later, sleeps with the light on.

When he drives away, sweaty and shaking, his wife will ask who the woman was. And Kevin will tell the truth. All of it.

———

In ten years' time Maya will walk toward the rink. The security guards will hold back eager hands and try to quiet the voices calling out to her, but she will stop patiently and sign everything that's handed to her, have photographs taken with everyone who asks. On the sign above them the words "Sold out!" will be flashing alongside the name of the performer who is appearing that night.

Hers.

50

Ana runs straight out into the night without knowing where she's going. Her eyes flit about in panic until she sees the lights of the jogging track and hears the scream. When she reaches the edge of the forest she sees it all. Kevin and her best friend. He's on his knees, crying hysterically. Maya turns and leaves him, passing between the trees before stopping dead when she catches sight of Ana. The fifteen-year-old girls look into each others' eyes. Then they hug, without words, and go home.

Early the next morning, Ana will go and pick up the cartridge from the jogging track. She will put it back in its place with the rest of her dad's ammunition. If anyone ever asks her where she was that night, she will say, "At home." If anyone ever asks her what her best friend was doing, she will reply: "Sorry, I didn't see that incident."

The door of the rink opens. A boy on crutches comes in. Peter is on his way through the corridor outside the locker room, heading in the other direction, but stops in surprise.

"Benjamin . . ."

He doesn't know what to say after that. He's never known things like that. So all that comes out is:

"How's your foot?"

Benji looks past him, toward the rink. Like everyone who loves that last inch where the floor turns to ice, he can feel the wing-beats from over here. His eyes swing back to Peter when he replies:

"It'll be healed in time for the first A-team game. If Sune thinks I'm ready."

Peter's eyebrows knit together. He clears his throat uncomfortably.

"Benji . . . we aren't even going to be able to pay any wages to the A-team. Christ, we might not even have a club by the autumn."

Benji puts his weight down on his foot. The good one this time, not the broken one.

"I just want to play."

Peter laughs.

"Okay, but, God, Benji, with your talent and your passion, you could really *be* something. I mean, seriously. You could be playing at an elite level in a couple of years. Hed Hockey are going to have a fantastic team, financial resources, you'll have much better opportunities to develop there."

Benji gives a nonchalant shrug. His answer is as short as it is uncompromising:

"But I'm from Beartown."

When skating classes start in the rink that year, four teenagers have been asked to attend as instructors. They stand in the center circle, in the team's colors: green, white, and brown; like the forest, ice, and earth. This place built a club that was like itself. Tough and unyielding—in love as in everything else.

The boys look down at the bear painted beneath them. When they were little they were scared of it, and sometimes they still are. Amat, Zacharias, Bobo, and Benjamin: two have just turned sixteen, two will soon be turning eighteen. In ten years' time two of them will be playing professionally. One will be a dad. One will be dead.

Benji's phone rings. He doesn't answer. It rings again, he takes it out of his back pocket and looks at the number. Takes a deep, cutting breath, and switches it off.

At a bus stop stands a bass player with a suitcase. He calls the same number, for the last time. Then he gets on the bus and leaves town. He will never come back here, but in ten years' time he will suddenly see Benjamin's face on television, and will instantly remember everything again. Fingertips and glances. Glasses on a battered bar top, smoke in a silent forest. The way snow feels on your skin when it falls in March, and a boy with sad eyes and a wild heart teaches you to skate.

When the children tumble over the edge out onto the ice, passing that last inch and losing their foothold, the boys at the center circle laugh and help the little things get up again. Try to teach them that there are other ways to stop than just drifting headfirst into the boards.

None of them sees the first skate of the child who's the last one out. She's four years old, a scrawny little kid in gloves that are too big for her, with bruises everyone sees but nobody asks about. Her helmet slips down across her eyes, but the look in them is clear enough.

Adri and Sune come after her, ready to hold the girl up, until they realize that there's no need. The four boys at the center circle will build a new A-team next season, but that doesn't matter, because in ten years' time it won't be their names that make the people of this town stand taller.

And they'll all lie and say they were here and saw it happen. The first skate of the girl who will become the most talented player this club has ever seen. They'll all say they knew it even then.

Because people recognize the bear around here.

Cherry trees always smell of cherry trees.

They do that in hockey towns.

ACKNOWLEDGMENTS

First of all, thank you to all the people who helped me with the most difficult parts of this story, but who for various reasons asked not to be mentioned here by name. I owe you a huge amount.

A particularly deep bow is also directed toward all the hockey players, managers, referees, and parents who have let me attend games and training sessions and ask strange questions.

Special thanks to my friend and fellow author Niklas Natt och Dag, my publisher Sofia Brattselius Thunfors, my editor Vanja Vinter, and my agent Tor Johansson. Apart from my family the four of you have been the most important people in the completion of this book. Thank you for sticking up for me right to the end.

I would also like to express my immense gratitude to the following individuals, without whose help this would have been nothing more than an idea and a pile of paper: Tobias Stark, historian and ice-hockey researcher at the Institute for Sports Science at Linnaeus University. Isabel Boltenstern and Jonathan Lindquist, inexhaustible sources of knowledge and entertaining bastards who were tough but fair critics, even when it hurt an author's fragile ego. Erika Holst, John Lind, Johan Forsberg, Andreas Haara, Ulf Engman, and Fredrik Glader, hockey experts who were incredibly generous with their time when my ideas were hopelessly vague. Anders Dalenius, for informative conversations about dogs and guns. Sofia B. Karlsson, for wide-ranging chat and wise answers about sport and life. Robert Pettersson, for a lonnng and patient email exchange. Attila Terek, for specialist knowledge of chemistry. Isac and Rasmus at Monkeysports in Södertälje, for letting me wander about the store for a whole day, and teaching me about hockey equipment. Lina "Lynx" Eklund and Pancrase Gym, for letting me come on fact-finding visits and hear you talk about your love of sport. Johan Zillén, for never being shy of giving your opinion. Also: all the legal experts in a wide range of areas who helped out along the way with details and terminology, as well as everyone else who in various ways read and thought and suggested when I sent you parts of the manuscript. There are too many of you to list here, but I hope you know that I know.

I'm grateful to the hardworking staff of my American publisher, Atria Books, particularly Atria's publisher Judith Curr, my editor Peter Borland, my publicist Ariele Fredman, as well as Suzanne Donahue, Kimberly Goldstein, Michael Selleck, Sonja Singleton, Albert Tang, Jim Thiel, Hillary Tisman, and Daniella Wexler. And thanks to Simon & Schuster Canada publisher Kevin Hanson and editor Brendan May.

But, most of all: my children. Thank you for waiting while I wrote this. NOW we can play *Minecraft*.